DOGS OF WAR

Book Six in the Defending The Future series

EDITED BY:

MIKE McPHAIL

eSpec Books
Stratford, NJ

PUBLISHED BY
eSpec Books LLC
Danielle McPhail, Publisher
PO Box 493,
Stratford, New Jersey 08084
www.especbooks.com

ISBN (trade): 978-1-942990-33-8
ISBN (ebook): 978-1-942990-34-5

(Previously published by Dark Quest Books, ISBN: 978-1-937051-05-1, 2013)

Series Website: www.defendingthefuture.com

Design: Mike and Danielle McPhail
Cover Art: "Scouts" ©2013 by Mike McPhail
Mike McPhail, McP Digital Graphics
www.mcp-concepts.com
www.milscifi.com

Copy Editing: Danielle McPhail
www.sidhenadaire.com

✦ AUTOGRAPH DUTY ROSTER ✦

Mike McPhail	Edward J. McFadden III
Brenda Cooper	Tony Ruggiero
James Chambers	Bud Sparhawk
Christopher M. Hiles	Janine K. Spendlove
Eric V. Hardenbrook	Patrick Thomas
Peter Prellwitz	Robert E. Waters
Jeff Young	Vonnie Winslow Crist
Judi Fleming	C.J. Henderson
David Sherman	Danielle Ackley-McPhail

Contents

This book is dedicated to **our canine comrades-in-arms**:

those who have fought, and still fight today along side the men and women of our Armed Forces.

FOR THE LOVE OF METAL DOGS
Brenda Cooper

THE SKY THREATENED RAIN. I PULLED MY COAT TIGHT AGAINST A COOL WIND as I watched as the dog handler head toward me up the small hill. He was a pretty-boy, body-builder style, maybe ten years younger than me. His golden blond hair contrasted with slightly oriental eyes. The dog trotting just behind him was a Belgian Malinois, a dark fawn color with a darker snout and ears, and a small white star pattern on his chest. "Welcome to base camp," I called out when they got close.

The specialist stopped about five yards from me. The dog sat right at his feet, watching me with no more than mild suspicion. It still made me nervous. We had never been a dog family, and I found them unpredictable and a tiny bit frightening. Dogs always knew that, too. I think the soldier noticed me stiffen, since his face grew a slightly mocking grin. "I heard you were camp mom."

"Try again." He was gorgeous to look at, but in my experience good looks and brains were often available in inverse proportions to each other. I watched him struggle through possible responses to my challenge.

"Specialist Lawson."

At least he could read a name tag. "Emilie. And you are?"

"I'm Pebble." He pointed at the dog, "And this is Sacha."

I would have believed the names more if they were reversed. "Why Pebble? That's a name for small things." Which he wasn't.

"I knocked out an enemy dog with a rock."

"And they didn't call you David?"

"That's my real name. Didn't make a very good nickname." He stood in front of me, silent, looking ill at ease. When I didn't pick up the conversation, he pointed to Buster. "Tell me about him. We've never worked with robodogs."

He didn't sound like he wanted to, either. Not that I particularly wanted to work with this pair. In fact, I'd heard the flesh handlers like Pebble looked down on our partners and us. They didn't like being upstaged, and lately, outnumbered.

But Buster was the closest thing I had seen to brains with no beating heart. I'd take him at my side over any human I'd worked with yet. "Buster can do almost everything Sacha or you or I can do."

Pebble looked dubious.

"I'll show you. Willing to put Sacha to a test?"

"After I introduce him to you." He signaled the dog, who came up close to me and sat. "Lean down and greet him. Pat his flank, not his head."

All military dogs are soldiers, and I wasn't about to show him disrespect even though I didn't like flesh as much as metal. The way he held himself told me he wasn't much happier than I was, but he held still while I patted his shoulder and upper back, his coarse fur tickling my arm. Pebble said "Friend" to the dog, who twitched his nose quite casually.

"Ready?"

"A race?"

I shrugged. "We can start there."

"Where?"

"How about to the building with the showers and back?"

Pebble grabbed the dog's leather harness, pulled out a small pen-like instrument, and shone a red dot on the back of the shower building. "Touch Return," he told the dog.

I simply told Buster, "Go to the showers and come back as fast as you can. Don't hurt the dog."

"Okay," Buster said.

I nodded. "Go!" I said.

Both animals sped away from us, Buster a streak of black and Sacha a streak of brown.

Pebble looked thoughtful. "I wish Sacha could talk."

"He states facts and confirms orders. It's not a conversation."

"I bet he can tell you if he's hurt."

I nodded, hearing a painful truth in his voice.

He stared at the dogs, already almost half-way. Both fast. "When are we going in?" he asked.

"Rumor has it the day after tomorrow. Not like it's my choice. Or yours." We were both specialists. I could have had a higher rank, but if I allowed that I'd lose the ability to handle dogs.

He would have had a mission briefing and know as much as me. This was a NorAM eco-peace mission into the wilds of British Columbia. A nest of property-rights protestors had decided to create a city in spite of the fact that the whole county had been turned into a nature preserve for black bears twenty years ago. "I hear they pissed off the Canadians by importing serious weaponry across the border."

"Not to mention that they've flattened a few miles of forest. We run spy drones over the place every day. They're growing. Two bands of Rightsers joined up already, and there's more rumored. The plan is to get in there before it's too big to be a skirmish. Can't have a full-on war inside Canada's borders."

Buster was ahead, but not quite as far as I expected. They'd neared the shower building, neither animal looking ready to slow. We watched as the dogs both stopped—barely—and turned. Buster slowed to manage the turn, taking it wide. Sacha flowed through the turn from here it looked like he was going one way and then he was going the other. Liquid vs. metal. Even though Buster was still ahead and pulling away, Sacha was faster than I expected.

"Is he enhanced?" I'd heard stories about GMO dogs.

Pebble shook his head. "Just through years of breeding. His ancestry goes back to 2018 in the canine breeding program—he came from a line they bred for SEAL teams." Pride swelled his voice even though Buster was skidding to a stop at my feet, and Sacha was at least five lengths behind.

"Is Sacha trained to detect?"

"Explosives and people."

"Can he beat Buster? Shall we try that next?"

"I'll bet on him."

Sacha won on human scent, and Buster took him on nitroglycerine, TNT, and two common training taggants. "That's enough for now," I said. Buster had proven himself, and besides, I could smell the grill. "Dinner?"

"After I feed Sacha."

Buster drank sunlight. Even in the grey northwest there was plenty for him, and more stored in his batteries. He could operate in pitch dark for a week.

The dog got his dinner, but Pebble and I had just filled our plates with soy burgers and salad when the loudspeakers in the mess tent went off. "All hands to the amphitheater."

Pebble started to set his plate down, but I leaned over and whispered, "A soldier never wastes calories."

We ate standing up while Captain Jules Thorne gave us our orders. He started with the attack teams—twelve Special Forces pairs with one dog each. "Send the dogs in first. We have spare parts for them but none for you." He always said that, and I always pretended to laugh even though I hate the order. He looked at me. "Lawson. You're leading Specialist Baxter and his dog, and taking Estrogen with you. Northern perimeter watch, starting at 19:00 hours."

I bit back a bitter reaction. We'd be out of the main attack, probably because of the green team with the real dog, maybe also because I was a woman. Captain Thorne told me it was because I was mouthy, but I didn't think so.

Pebble didn't notice my mood, but instead he grinned at me. "Now we can test the dogs in the field. See who wins then."

So he really was stupid.

"The field isn't a test," I told him as we waited in a small clearing for the other two members of our team.

"It's the best test ever."

"Being sidetracked might get us killed. How many field ops have you and Sacha done?"

He looked proud of himself. "This is our third operation together. But Sacha's been deployed for three whole tours."

Goddess save us all. I pursed my lips and stamped my feet against the growing chill. Buster and I had been together for two years, and I gave my dog a long appreciative glance. At the moment, he wore one of the smallest milbot dog bodies. When he sat in shadow he looked like flesh and blood. His limbs and head were black, his tail and body a burnished charcoal grey with silver toenails.

Estrogen lumbered up and slapped me a high-five with his huge meaty hand. "Emilie. We will be taking Buster and kicking some ass."

I grinned and leapt up to plant a kiss on his blocky, rugged cheek. Inappropriate in the military, but there were no officers around, and Estrogen was as gay as they made them and so proud of it he'd picked up the nickname and made it sing for him. Besides, he was at least ten years younger than me. Which didn't stop me from enjoying the rough feel of his skin and the slight hug he grabbed me into for the briefest moment. Besides, any risk that came with the kiss was worth it; Pebble looked stunned. I grinned. "Pebble—meet Estrogen."

"Es...Estrogen?" he managed to stammer.

"Yep," the big man said. "Did you meet Buster yet? Best dog ever."

"Essie...he's a handler. Got his own dog." I pointed at the edge of the little field, where Sacha and Buster sat together.

Estrogen squinted. "That's a real one." He grinned ear to ear and headed off.

Since I could speak through Buster's speakers, I used them to say, "Fuck you."

Estrogen just waved.

The captain had named me leader, so I gathered them up for a short pre-trip lecture. "We've spotted sentries out here three times in the last two days. New sightings from the sats will be beamed to our glasses. But don't trust them—the sats miss a lot in these trees. The drones are better, but the main attack team will get those. I'll send you Buster's view of things from time to time." I looked hard at Pebble. "Are you ready?"

"Yes, ma'am."

Ma'am my ass. I put Buster in front and let Sacha stay with Pebble for now. Wet cedars surrounded us, cutting off some of the light and some of the rain. The rich loamy dirt smelled like forest and our footsteps were nearly silent as we walked over the rotting carcasses of last year's leaves.

I traded out which dog was on point every half hour. This was Buster's third turn, and neither of them had alerted for anything. I alternated between paying close attention to the darkening, dripping damp we were plowing through and watching the main attack team close in on the compound via my Virtual computerized glasses. They had a longer name, but I could never remember it. They were the most direct way for Buster and me to interact, and the whole camp used them for comms and cameras as well. Dusk started slipping pools of darkness under the trees, but Buster had excellent night vision we could all use if we wanted to see through his eyes. I didn't overlay it yet since it made me slightly nauseous.

We walked until the colors all greyed. Even clouded over, the night sky gave some light to the clear parts of the trail, but in most places the trees were thick enough to give the night an eerie, swaying blackness.

Buster stopped dead in front of me and sat down. His silent signal made me put my hand back flat to signal the others to stop.

They were quiet, even Sacha.

I blinked at my glasses. At first nothing looked different, but then Buster's view came alive in a small square on my right lens. I blinked twice to make it bigger. Just the path, sloping slightly uphill, and the long shadows of trees. Words scrolled along the bottom of the picture. "Two traps. People behind traps."

A red dot blinked on my right lens. A warning from Estrogen.

More unfriendlies?

An unmanned aerial vehicle popped up to my side, hovered. The size of my head, and close. It whirred softly, like a hummingbird.

If I got a good look, I was probably dead.

None of our intel said they had UAV's. Maybe the nasties had jail-broken some 3D printers.

It targeted Estrogen with some kind of beam weapon.

Estrogen turned toward it and a flash of light from the drone illuminated his wide eyes and stole some of my night vision. He raised his gun, but crumpled before he used it.

"Get," I told Buster.

My dog leapt at the machine, six feet of angry milbot and a lot heavier than the insta-drone. He bore it to the ground and grabbed it with his teeth.

Estrogen didn't move.

A woman screamed. Deductive reasoning suggested she had to be an enemy. I was the only woman on our little team.

"We're under attack," I said to my glasses, and through them, to the captain. "Estrogen is down. Unknown number of enemies. We got a drone."

Buster bit down so hard on the drone it crunched.

I looked for Pebble just in time to see him head off the path between two trees. Damn green soldier. Probably running after his flesh dog.

I stayed in a low crouch and tried to assess the situation.

Buster let out three warning sounds in quick succession, little yips with a high tone that flashed red onto my lenses. I ducked and rolled right. Pain exploded in my foot.

"Attack," I commanded Buster through clenched teeth.

My legs curled into my belly of their own accord and I clutched my right foot. At least it was still there, although my fingers found a hole in my leather boot near the toes.

Buster poured into the woods. He had the smarts to choose the best tactics given the information he had. Looked like he was following Pebble. Good thing—the fire in my foot made it hard to think.

I glanced over at Estrogen. I wasn't close enough to tell if he was breathing. I didn't get closer; any enemy left watching would expect that.

Rain poured onto the canopy of cedar above me and dripped down in thin streams.

The screaming stopped.

I listened to my own breathing, listened for Estrogen to move or call out.

Rain fell. Cedars rustled and swayed in a light wind.

A bird sang.

Buster poked his blessed black nose out from between two trees and gave me an audible follow signal.

He wouldn't give an audible signal if there was anything really bad nearby.

I barely managed not to cry out as I stood even though I kept the weight off of my damaged foot, which throbbed as if it had its own beating heart.

"Come," I hissed at Buster. This body was so small there was no elegant way to ride him. I put my hurt foot sideways across his neck and tucked the other one up his back flank for balance. It was something he and I practiced. We managed. If I was lucky, he wouldn't scrape me off on any trees.

A hundred yards down the path, Sacha stood over a dead woman dressed in jeans and a tan shirt with two guns on her waist and a machete that had clearly fallen from her hand when the dog had taken her down.

Sacha was messier with his kills than Buster.

Pebble stood in front of a man he had shot. My glasses had dimmed to green and three hot spots of activity were leaving us. "Pebble," I called. "We need to check on Estrogen."

He nodded, but stood still and pulled a camouflage-colored ball from his pocket, commencing a short game of fetch.

"Do you have to do that now?"

He pointed at the dead men. "He needs his reward." He threw the ball for the dog three times, ruffling his fur and—to my utter surprise—almost crying.

"Is that the first time he's saved your life?" I asked him.

He nodded.

I patted Buster on the head, but then stopped, feeling foolish.

"We're ready now."

I nodded.

Estrogen breathed shallowly. Thank God. But shaking him produced no effect. He was too big to ride Sacha, too big to carry, too heavy to drag. We tucked his glasses into his pocket and covered him with my space blanket and Pebble's camo tarp.

Pebble pointed to my foot. "Maybe you should stay and watch him?"

"We both stay, for now. Our people know where we are."

We found a big cedar we could sit under and still see Estrogen. It sucked not to be able to do anything. But there wasn't a medical quick-fix or handy serum for being stunned out like Estrogen.

I didn't want to pull my boot off, but blood leaked slowly though the hole. I stared at it for a while but then I needed to look away. "Where are you from?" I asked.

"California. North of Shasta, little town called Weed."

"I've been there. I've got an "I Love Weed" shirt somewhere at home. If mom hasn't thrown it away."

He laughed. "You?"

"Town named Concrete, in Washington."

"So we're both from towns with weird-ass names," he said. "How long have you been NorAm?"

"Fifteen."

"You don't look old enough for that."

I spit laughter. "Flattery doesn't work out here." Lights flashed to draw my attention to words flowing across my glasses. "They're moving in now."

"Guess it will be a while before anyone has time for us."

"Yeah."

"What made you show up out here?" he asked.

"Meaning since I'm a woman?"

He grimaced. "Meaning at all."

I blinked a command to patrol our perimeter at Buster while thinking about what to tell him. "My family liked the services."

"Anybody else on active?"

Buster took off. Sacha stayed, clearly only paying attention to his master. I hesitated, then said, "My dad was in for twenty. He's a vegetable. Took a bad one in the Texas Rebellion. Pretty nasty."

"I bet he's proud of you."

"He doesn't know my name any more. He doesn't remember his own name. He's drooling in a VA hospital in Charleston. Before it happened, he told me never to join up."

Sacha thumped his tail hard, twice. Pebble put his finger to his lips.

I didn't hear anything but the rain, which had started again. My glasses didn't identify any threats near us. Attack stats scrolled along the bottom. Our main force had engaged the enemy hand to hand, and two firefights had just started around the perimeter of the compound.

I pinged Buster; he sent back an all-clear.

"Sacha smells something," Pebble whispered, barely over the decibel level of an out-breath. "A person."

I whispered, "Scare," which meant just that, but allowed an attack if Buster determined he was in danger.

Pebble glanced at me, and when I shook my head he gave Sacha a wait command. The Malinois lay down, fully alert, fully attentive. In spite of that, perhaps by the cock of an ear or the slight droop of his muzzle, Sacha managed to communicate his feelings about being left out of whatever Buster had been sent to do.

Tough. We didn't have spare parts for him.

Buster's screaming scare bark startled all of us to attention.

A crashing through cedars, a thump, and then more footsteps convinced us Buster had scared the intruder away.

"So we're two for one," Pebble said. "But Sacha has a kill."

Dumb green recruit. "We're not competing with you out here."

He shrugged. "Can't stop me from keeping score. Sacha saved me from the soldier, Buster saved you from the drone, and now he chased off a single undesirable. I'm ranking them about even since Sacha had to take on a human."

The drone Buster had killed was at least as dangerous as the human, but I managed not to say anything.

My foot felt huge in my boot. I undid the laces. Some of the pressure came off but pain sang up the back of my calf. "We'd best just wait in quiet." I said.

He nodded, although he looked a little concerned about me fussing with my foot. Almost worried. Not what I needed.

The clouds had thickened; the night was even darker. Watching the battle at the compound inside of my glasses kept me from going crazy with pain.

The data was hard to read. But then, it's truly impossible to fit a battle between thirty or so soldiers on our side and about twice that many rebels inside the frame of a pair of glasses. The clues were words and color, and red and green blended a bit before the colors faded more to red.

Loss. Unimaginable. I tapped my glasses a few times as if that would change the lives back to green and turn the distant men and women back on.

There were six left. I didn't ask my glasses to tell me who. I'd learn soon enough.

Sacha nosed up next to Pebble, as if he felt what Pebble must be feeling.

Buster had no reaction, of course. All tactics, no feelings. He sat and watched out into the gloomy dark, patient.

Pebble said, "Maybe nobody is coming for us."

"Maybe not." I sat there for a moment, staring into the trees and into the flashes of the battle both at once. "Can you make a travois?"

"A what?"

"A stretcher that you can pull along the ground. Indians made them. You need two long fat sticks and then we'll use the blankets." That would leave us only Sacha free, which I didn't much like. I messaged Jules that we'd get back to camp on our own. No answer. I pinged camp, and got a simple, "Good luck."

We started back down the trail with Sacha leading, Pebble pulling Estrogen awkwardly in the middle and me balanced badly on Buster in the rear. I must have looked as ridiculous as a full-sized person riding a miniature horse. But Buster was made to pack a hundred and fifty pounds, and I was twenty under that, so he could do it.

Pebble struggled so hard he fell twice.

Ten minutes in, Estrogen woke up, wide-eyed and disoriented. "It's okay," I lied to him. "We're on our way back to camp and you'll be as good as rain about the time we get there." If we were lucky. Or maybe he'd still be a huge, disoriented soldier with a big heart. I managed to lean over and touch him on the arm once, but it almost over-balanced me right into the dirt.

"Hey, mama, it'll be OK. We got your dog with us. He's always been good luck."

We heard the explosion at the same time my glasses blossomed red.

"Shit," Estrogen said. "Don't tell me."

I swallowed. His glasses were tucked in his pocket, since he'd been out. They're like gold; lose them and you pay in a few ways. So he didn't know what I knew. The whole compound had gone up bright enough that no one was communicating on our channels any more. I knew the lot of them, and a few of them well. The hole in my middle hurt as much as my damned foot.

Pebble stopped and turned around so he was facing me while he was still holding up Estrogen. He'd lost all color, and his eyes were big and rimmed with white.

"Face forward," I told him. "Maybe some enemies got away."

He pursed his lips and turned.

"Ever seen it go bad before?" I asked him.

"In training."

When everyone with red paintball slime on them woke up the next morning as if they'd never been taken down. He was probably having a hard time. "We can't stop," I told his back after he started walking again. "We'll rest in camp. There's dog food and bandages there."

After a half hour of slogging, Estrogen announced, "I'd rather stumble home on stunned legs than be dragged over every rock and root in the forest."

We stopped and let him up. He stood unsteadily, blinking and looking like he might just lie down and sleep right there. Then he pulled himself together. "That's better." I had him stay in front of me so I could see how he was. He had to work hard to keep his limbs going, but at least he went. After a while I made us all stop and eat a bit of energy bar. We'd been out for hours and two of us were injured. Except for the dogs, we didn't look or feel exactly like a high-capability team. There were only three miles between us and the camp—an hour on a straight trail with no problems, but probably two or three hours in the dark and the mud.

Sacha gave a warning bark just as we hit a steady pace again. There were no pings on my glasses to indicate a human. My Buster's-eye view showed heat. Animal heat.

I slid off of Buster into a one-legged stand, using a sapling for balance.

Sacha barked again, sharply, and lay down on his belly, staring ahead of us. Whatever it was, Buster didn't react to it.

One dog thought it was dangerous and one didn't.

Then a piece of the night moved.

And breathed.

Pebble growled a command that stuck Sacha in place and pulled his gun.

"Don't look at it."

"What?"

"No eye contact."

"That's crazy," Pebble whispered. But he was looking at the bear's chest and not its face. Good enough.

"Bears will walk away," I whispered back as casually as I could over my racing blood. "You don't have to shoot. You can just make noise and be big." If he shot, it would tell everyone for miles around that we were here. I bent down and picked up a rock and lobbed it behind the bear and to the side.

Sacha whined as the bear took two steps toward us.

"It's okay," I whispered. "Estrogen. Be big."

Estrogen waved his long arms above his head and whistled.

Sacha stood in spite of Pebble's command, his hackles up. He barked and lunged, but stopped a few feet short of the bear.

The bear hesitated. I tensed.

It looked around at us all, then it shook like a wet cat and turned and lumbered off as if we didn't matter.

Buster had never been programmed for bear. If Sacha hadn't alerted us, we might have been close enough to really scare it, and even black bears are dangerous if they feel cornered.

The rest of the trip back was merely wet and cold and hard. The remaining camp staff included a medic, so my foot got wrapped and braced. The doctor kept her mouth thin and her eyes down except for the occasional glance at the door. "Maybe some of them will come back," I whispered.

"Maybe," she said, her voice laced with forced cheerfulness.

I called Buster to me and we hobbled out to find Pebble. "How are you?" I asked.

"I was feeling really bad not to be part of the attack."

"Me, too." If we had been, we'd have saved them all or we'd be dead.

"I wish I knew how they are," he said.

"Don't you?"

He kept looking down. "Yeah, I guess."

"You and Sacha did good," I told him.

"Thanks," he whispered.

"I think you won," I said.

He looked over at me, his eyes dark in his dark face. "How do you figure that?" he asked.

"The bear. If it was up to us, we wouldn't have seen it until we were on top of it."

"The one drone could have killed us all."

"It could have," I said. And then I told him, "Handy to have both kinds of dogs. Maybe we'll get assigned together again some day."

"I'd like that." I'm sure if it had been light enough I would have seen him smile.

FATHER OF WAR
James Chambers

Kanigher heard the distant dog howl for the fourth straight night.

Its lonely voice filled his mind with a restlessness that kept him awake hours after the other prisoners fell asleep. In the gloom of the bunkhouse, his heart raced, and his head throbbed. Sweat coated him. It soaked through his coarse uniform and into his cot's thin mattress. He had been on the brink of dozing off when the howling stopped. Now the quiet gathered around him, an almost tangible presence held at arm's length only by the sleep sounds of the other prisoners.

Kanigher waited. No more howling came. Its absence troubled him.

Since the first night he'd heard the dog crying in the dark, its howls had lasted as long as the moon hung in the sky. The lunar glow still fell through the barred, slit windows high on the bunk room's walls, but the animal remained silent.

Maybe something killed it, he thought.

Kanigher sat up, slung his feet to the rough floor, and shivered.

In the bunk above him, Menendez rolled over and mumbled a name.

His dead daughter's, Kanigher remembered.

He kept her name like a mantra.

Everyone in the camp relied on something from the past to carry them through the days.

Kanigher lived on the memories of what he'd accomplished before his capture, the hope that his work had at least saved some of his fellow soldiers' lives. For all he knew, though, the brass had cut his program the day after he went MIA.

He rubbed his eyes, then yanked the blanket off his bunk and draped it over his shoulders, resigning himself to a sleepless night before another day of hard labor in the Pit. He knew it was pointless to care about the dog or why it had stopped howling. The dog roamed free in the ruins outside the walls. Kanigher most likely would never set foot outside them again. If the animal ever wandered too near the prison camp, the guards would simply kill it for sport.

Yet the howl echoed in his mind. He couldn't let it go.

Since he'd first heard it, he'd sensed something familiar in the bestial voice. Something lonely and searching. Something purposeful. A question only Kanigher could answer, though the only answers that occurred to him were impossible ones.

He ran a finger over the old scars along the side of his head and around his eyes.

The program, his work, his mission—all that existed only in his past.

As much pride as he still took in it, only survival concerned him now, and he'd begun to question the value of even that. Death, at least, would free him from the back-breaking hours in the Pit and his captors' cruel whims. He supposed, though, if he were ready to die, the howling dog wouldn't have so roused his curiosity.

He walked to the end of his three-tiered bunk and, careful not to disturb his sleeping bunkmates, climbed it like a ladder, raising his face to peek out one of the windows. The night stretched into blackness diminished only by the camp lights. He discerned the faint shadows of the tall buildings in the lightless town, rising above the prison walls. In the early days of his imprisonment, he'd seen signs of life out there. The flickers of flashlights or campfires. Evidence of survivors. All gone now. Escaped, perhaps. Or dead from starvation, disease, or exposure. Or killed by soldiers. The enemy still patrolled the empty streets, but a long time had passed since he'd heard sounds of combat from outside the wall or seen air patrols fly over them. The town seemed so quiet he figured the entire region stood behind enemy lines now.

He descended the bed frame and returned to his bunk.

Outside the bunkhouse's single exit, something scratched.

Kanigher froze.

His eyes darted to the locked door.

The scratching noise repeated itself.

Low. Persistent.

Skritch, skritch, skritch.

A faint huff of breath came. Then a muffled grunt.

Kanigher glanced at the other prisoners. Exhausted from fourteen-hour shifts in the Pit, none of them stirred.

SKRITCH, SKRITCH, SKRITCH.

Kanigher crept to the door. He stepped to the right, crouched with his back against the wall, and listened. The guards sometimes carried out random night raids, rousting prisoners and beating them. Kanigher had experienced his share of them, though, and unlike this, those attacks happened fast, the guards bursting through the door, shouting, flashing bright lights, waving guns and batons.

The scratching paused. Something clinked.

A small beep and a hiss sounded. A line of light appeared in the door, ran several inches up from the ground, two-thirds of the way across, and then back to the ground, tracing a crude half-oval. The glow flared for a second before the thick section of steel door dropped inward, sliced by a strip of quick burning acid-flash tape. The piece thumped the floor, trailing wisps of smoke.

Kanigher recoiled, shedding his blanket, bracing himself.

His pulse thundered in his skull.

A shape emerged through the crude opening.

Slender white paws appeared.

A compact, whiskered face with tall ears came after them.

The animal wriggled on all fours into the bunkhouse then stared at Kanigher, panting, its tongue hanging out.

Traumatic dementia, Kanigher thought. *First you imagine dogs howling. Then you hallucinate dogs crawling under doors. Textbook breakdown.*

He had seen other prisoners snap, talking to invisible people, running from demons only they understood. Inevitably, the guards took them to the infirmary. None ever returned.

Kanigher blinked, wishing the little dog away.

Instead, it pressed its whiskered muzzle against his hand and licked his palm. Warm and wet. Its tongue soft. And the smell of the dog—Kanigher couldn't deny the distinct reality of its scent. Or its body heat. Sensations so familiar and wonderful yet so long denied him. They set his heart racing. He stifled a gasp and tried to make sense of the little, black-and-white animal sitting by him, licking his hand. A Boston Terrier. Athletic, large for its breed. Not a dog he'd have chosen for his work but an intelligent, willful, and loyal breed, and with genetic enhancement, capable enough for the right missions. A harness rigged with miniaturized equipment hugged its body, and a cybercowl covered a quarter of its face, interlaced with goggles that shielded its protruding eyes. Kanigher read the dog tag dangling from its collar: Bug Eye.

The dog licked Kanigher's hand three more times then sat in an attention pose and stared at him, its mouth hanging open in a dog smile.

Kanigher stared back at it.

The dog lifted a paw and tapped his hand.

Still skeptical, Kanigher studied the familiar gear strapped to the dog's body. It included a small nozzle with cartridges for spitting out strips of flash-acid tape, which had been used to cut the hole in the door, as well as several small pouches along the dog's back, arranged in a configuration Kanigher knew so well he didn't hesitate popping one open and pulling out a tiny square cookie. He gave it to the dog, which ate it, then circled around and presented Kanigher with a tool strapped to its side. A low-level laser torch, powerful enough to cut the lock on the door.

Kanigher reached for it, then stopped.

The dog's presence made no sense, especially not equipped with the rig he wore.

A rig and gear *Kanigher* had designed years ago.

Although the equipment had been streamlined and refined, it remained recognizably his.

He had to be imagining it, dreaming, sleepwalking, or...

The saliva drying on his hand felt so real.

And the dog's scent.

And its warmth.

The howling...

Not this dog's. But seeing his rig, the familiarity of the howling dog's voice haunted Kanigher even more. He refused to let the thought forming in his mind take shape, unwilling to risk entertaining something so improbable. He scratched the Boston between his ears, and the dog lowered its head, enjoying the attention for a moment. Then it snapped back to position and tapped Kanigher's hand with its paw again.

Kanigher took the laser torch from its clip.

The dog retreated to the door and waited for Kanigher.

Kanigher didn't move. The dog wriggled out through the opening, then poked its front paws and head back in and gave an exasperated huff.

Kanigher glanced at his fellow prisoners, none of whom stirred.

Positioning his body to conceal the light, he activated the torch and cut the lock from the door, catching the handle as it fell, and then setting it silently on the floor.

The door swung open, and Kanigher stepped outside onto the edge of a familiar dirt path he'd never before set foot upon at night. The camp felt like a graveyard, the squat silhouettes of the other bunkhouses like grave markers. Kanigher searched for guards and spied them on the far side of the yard on the wall and in their towers, rifles poking over their shoulders. For years he'd gone nowhere, done nothing without them watching him, ordering him, threatening him. The tiny freedom of being outside without permission almost paralyzed him.

Bug Eye took off to the left, then waited for Kanigher, who stood still, overwhelmed by the vastness of the night. Running back, the dog jumped up and hit Kanigher's thigh with its front paws, jolting him. It settled on all fours, huffed, then darted off again.

Gripping the laser torch for use as a weapon, Kanigher followed.

Bug Eye led him along a winding path that skirted the camp's lights, guiding him, step by step, closer to the eastern wall. Along the way they passed the wrecks of the camp's standard-issue hover-eyes, taken out before they could sound an alarm. As they neared the wall, Kanigher spied a faintly glowing hole in the steel barrier. It looked wide enough for him to fit through if he squeezed his shoulders together. No simple laser torch had sliced through the foot-thick wall, though, which meant someone with heavy equipment and stealth tech had sent the Boston in for him.

A sweeping spotlight crossed the path ahead of them. Bug Eye stopped, and Kanigher hunkered down and waited for the light to pass before continuing. He considered going back for the others in his bunkhouse, but it would only heighten his risk of capture and endanger them since he had no idea what awaited him outside the wall. He still wasn't sure any of this was real, but he promised himself if it was he'd send back help if he could.

As they resumed their approach, the light swung back and flared on them twenty yards from the hole. Kanigher lost sight of the Boston in the blinding brightness.

Harsh voices shouted in Chinese. An alarm screeched.

Instinctively, Kanigher dropped to a crouch.

A gunshot cracked, sounding like thunder. Another round hissed through the air in front of him. He fired the laser torch blind and heard someone scream in pain. When his eyes adjusted, he saw guards scrambling atop the walls, aiming rifles at him, and others on the ground running in his direction. A searing, fiery brightness came then with a raged roar and concussion that knocked Kanigher to the ground and jolted the laser torch from his hand. Gunfire followed, dim in his ringing ears. Kanigher scrambled to his feet, disoriented, clueless as to where to run.

Teeth dug into his hand, biting firmly, but not hard enough to break his skin.

Warm breath. Hot saliva running onto his wrist.

A dog's mouth.

Too large for the Boston.

It tugged on Kanigher until he moved with it, and then it let go of his hand and picked up speed, forcing Kanigher to jog. He stumbled on the rough ground, but kept moving after the dog. A brown-and-black Belgian Malinois, it wore a different version of Kanigher's cybercowl, fitted above its left ear and eye. Its harness held pouches like those on the Boston Terrier's, but the largest bore a red cross in a white circle.

Another explosion quaked the night.

Kanigher crouched and covered his head with his arms.

Muffled screams and shouts filled his aching ears as the roar faded.

Some in Chinese, some in English.

The other prisoners, Kanigher thought. The explosions must have panicked them awake, and he'd left his bunkhouse door open. He hoped none of them were hurt.

A fourth explosion erupted much closer than the others. Shrapnel sliced Kanigher's forehead, and the blast pushed him forward, driving him through the hole in the wall behind the running Belgian. Blood in his eyes, he fled the chaos at the camp and trailed his guide down a darkened street littered with burned-out cars and debris from the bombed buildings. His head throbbed. He wiped blood from his eyes, trying to clear his sight. Kanigher struggled to keep up with the trotting Belgian. Bug Eye ran beside it, the two dogs stopping at regular intervals to sense the night and pick a safe path through the maze of streets.

Kanigher recognized the pattern.

Run five to ten yards. Stop. Scent, listen, look. Then another five to ten yards.

Stop and go.

A system he'd invented and perfected in years of training soldier dogs.

He intended it for safe, fast movement over unknown terrain.

Although he'd field-tested it he'd never had an opportunity to see it in live action.

He kept within one yard of the Belgian. They turned the corner down a new street, and Kanigher glanced back at the fire rising from the camp. A pillar of smoke drifted above the wall. The voices and gunfire faded. Patrols would soon be prowling the city. Someone had blasted the camp to cover his escape, but in the din and flash of combat, Kanigher hadn't seen who. He hoped—whoever they were—they were well hidden and had an escape route.

The dogs led Kanigher along a desolate side street cluttered with trash, broken bricks, and cracked cement. The Boston scurried down the block then sat, facing the intersection, watching. The Belgian circled back to Kanigher and lowered to a down position. Kanigher knelt down and scratched the dog between the ears.

Kanigher read its tags: Nightingale.

"Good girl," he said.

The Belgian wagged its tail.

Kanigher opened the First Aid pouch on the dog's back, took out an antiseptic wipe and a tube of liquid skin. He cleaned and dressed his wound to stop the blood flowing into his eyes. In another pouch, he found a stash of cookies and gave the Belgian two. The dog gobbled them, then snapped back onto its feet, curled away from Kanigher, and ran down the street, Bug Eye beside it. Kanigher hurried after them.

They raced through the empty town. Sharp rubble dug into Kanigher's feet, shredding his flimsy prison sandals, but he ignored the pain and pushed himself to keep up. The dogs sniffed out their trail, winding a path east toward the edge of town. They passed the looming shape of a ballistic personnel carrier, five stories tall and embedded in the earth, one of the secret weapons that had enabled the enemy invasion. Then they rounded a corner and came to a plaza outside an office building. A headless statue on a cracked pedestal loomed over them. The building's demolished upper floors threw down jagged lunar shadows.

The sound of distant engines grumbled, echoing off the old buildings.

Soldiers starting pursuit.

Kanigher resisted the panic brewing in his gut.

They had put a fair distance between them and the prison camp, but jeeps, tanks, and hoverbirds would overtake them if they remained in the open. Kanigher scanned the area for hiding places. The office building appeared far too damaged and unstable, and piles of rubble clogged the entrances to all the other structures in sight.

The dogs stood side by side, ears pricked up.

Waiting.

Seconds ticked away.

The motor sounds grew and spread out from the prison camp.

The rhythm of hoverbird blades picked up and cut the night.

Kanigher's heart pounded in his chest. He knelt by the dogs, trusting them, knowing they saw a different darkness than he did and heard a greater range of night sounds. A single, sharp bark came, and then the dogs took off running.

"Wait for me!" Kanigher cried.

He rushed after them, struggling to keep his balance on the litter-strewn street. The dogs raced around the damaged office building, along a side street, and then down an alley. Kanigher chased them, ignoring his tightening fear as the alley sloped down into a darkness that swallowed the dogs and left him blind. He slowed, picking his way carefully through debris. Ahead of him the dogs sniffed and panted. Their nails scratched concrete and jostled rubble.

Kanigher's foot struck a wall. He stopped.

The noise of hoverbird engines grew louder.

"Where are you?" he whispered.

He clicked his tongue twice, a standard signal he'd used with his dogs. A low blue light appeared. It painted an aura around the silhouettes of Bug Eye and Nightingale and revealed a third dog, a Doberman Pinscher, also rigged with a harness and cybercowl of Kanigher's design. The light glowed from its collar. The three dogs surrounded Kanigher and ushered him through a narrow opening at the end of the alley into a tunnel. They walked for several minutes. The motor sounds died away behind them. Kanigher caught his breath. Soon the yellow-white glow of a field lantern appeared up ahead, pouring out of an opening. When they reached it, the Doberman sat beside the door like a sentry. The Boston and the Belgian entered the room. Kanigher inched his way to the opening and peeked inside.

An American soldier sat across the room, her back against the wall, head slumped onto her chest. Blood stained her uniform. She seemed very still, but her torso rose and fell with her breath. A fourth dog, a Chocolate Lab, lay beside her, its head on her leg. Blood spotted its fur. Its cybercowl covered nearly a third of its head, encompassing one ear and both its eyes, and it too wore a harness like the other dogs. Bug Eye and Nightingale sat on either side of the soldier. Kanigher approached the woman. All three dogs tracked him, ready to attack if he made a move to harm her. Slowly, he took the woman's hand and pressed two fingers against her wrist, feeling her weak pulse.

The soldier kicked her leg, shuddered, and then snapped up her head. "Who's there?" she said.

The Lab lifted its head, bared its teeth, and growled at Kanigher.

Kanigher rocked back on his heels. The woman removed her helmet and tucked it onto her lap. A partial cybercowl covered her left temple, her ear, and encircled half of her left eye. In the poor light of the field lantern, she looked ghostly, like she'd lost a lot of blood. Her eyes locked on Kanigher's.

She stroked the Lab's neck and said, "Easy, girl."

The Lab stopped growling.

Kanigher read the woman's nameplate and rank insignia. "Are you badly hurt, Lieutenant Haney?"

Haney squinted, eyeing Kanigher's face. She reached into a pocket on her sleeve, pulled out a mobile intelligence data unit, and tapped on the screen. The glow lit her eyes. An image resolved onscreen, and she held it up to Kanigher, comparing his face to the face of a man in the picture. Though he hadn't seen it in years, Kanigher knew the photo: outside his old kennel and training facility, a red bandanna in his hand, he knelt beside a German Shepherd, Sarge. A good dog. The first Kanigher had put through his cybernetics program. Involuntarily, he touched the old scars in the side of his head where his cybercowl had been mounted when he was Sarge's handler. Enemy soldiers had ripped it from him when they took him prisoner. In the picture, he didn't yet have the cowl. He looked fifty pounds heavier, his hair clean of the gray that shot through it now, his face smooth and unmarred by scars and bruises—and he was smiling.

"Captain Kanigher?" Haney asked. "Is that really you?"

Kanigher read the doubt in her eyes and, in an odd way, he shared it.

He must have seemed to her like a ghost risen from the grave. He certainly felt like one. She knew his name, knew who he'd been, but he couldn't say for sure he was still that same man in the picture anymore. He opened his mouth to answer, but no words came.

Haney pulled herself up higher against the wall. "Wow. I can't believe we really found you." She coughed lightly after speaking.

"How bad is it?" Kanigher asked.

Haney mustered a false grin. "Could be a lot worse, could be a lot better."

"Let me see."

Haney nodded then rolled her stained uniform shirt up to her left armpit, exposing the bloody wound in her side. She had field-dressed it, cleaned it, then sealed it with liquid skin, but several nasty slivers of metal still poked out from her flesh, letting blood dribble out around them, slowly bleeding her to death. Kanigher recognized the projectiles. Needles from a hover mine. Each a foot long and embedded deep in Haney's side. At least she'd left them in. If she'd removed them, barbs on the ends would've ripped out her insides. He guessed she had a fifty-fifty chance of survival without immediate medical care.

"What's the prognosis, doc?" Haney asked.

"Like you said. Could be better."

"Story of my friggin' life."

Kanigher leaned back on his heels as Haney lowered her shirt. "You need a doctor. Soon. To stop the bleeding."

"Roger that. Soon as the rest of the squad returns, we can bug out. We get fifteen klicks out of town, and we can call for air evac. They won't come any closer. Too dangerous, especially now we've stirred up the hornet's nest out there."

"Fifteen klicks. Can you walk that far?"

"Got no choice," Haney said. "Move it or lose it."

Kanigher nodded. A quiet moment passed, and he became very aware of the dogs still watching him, protective of Haney, but signaling something more with their stare. Something like—affection? Admiration? He recalled the plaintive howling of the unknown dog, how it had seemed meant for him.

"Lieutenant," Kanigher asked. "How did you wind up here?"

"Ran into trouble about seven klicks east of town. An old battlefield, full of leftover live ordnance. The dogs did great. Led us across most of it safe and sound, but the mine that got me was sitting in the crook of a tree branch. Its hover unit had died god knows how long ago, and it was stuck. No sound, no scent for the dogs to pick up on, but as soon as I blipped its proximity sensor—*wham!* Knocked me and Sallygirl on our asses and gave us a good sting. My second, Sergeant Andru, wasn't so lucky. Seven needles in his neck and head. Didn't make it out of the field."

"I'm sorry," Kanigher said.

"Thanks. He was a good man."

Haney stroked the back of the Lab's neck then gestured for Kanigher to check the dog's side. Five needles, twins of those embedded in Haney, protruded from between Sallygirl's ribs.

"Sallygirl got it worse than me," Haney said. Then her voice turned shaky and clipped. "She's the only reason I'm still alive. She jumped in front of me, took the worst of what came our way."

"Sallygirl's a good girl," Kanigher said. At that, Sallygirl raised her head a few inches, met Kanigher's eyes for a moment, then settled down again on Haney's leg. "But what I meant was why are you here in the first place? This town. Behind enemy lines."

Haney scrunched her face. "Damn, Cap, isn't it obvious? We came for you."

Kanigher shook his head. "No, no. Bullshit. I'm not worth you and Sallygirl sitting here with those needles in your sides or your Sergeant Andru's life. Not after all this time. There are a hundred other soldiers in that camp worth more than I am."

"Not to my squad," Haney said.

"Your squad?"

"Guess I should introduce you." Haney gestured to the Boston. "You've already met the little guy, Bug Eye. His size comes in handy, and he's got more determination than most soldiers I know. He can get in and out of anywhere if you give him the right scents. And Nightingale you met. She's our scout. Carries our med gear too. Outside the door there is Marshmallow Soldier. As fierce as he looks, but he goes soft the second you give him anything sweet. There's not an explosive he can't sniff out, no matter how well hidden. Sallygirl is our tracker. The rest ought to be here soon. I feel them nearby."

Kanigher touched his forehead indicating where Haney wore her cowl.

"Yep," Haney said. "Plugged in and ready to play. I guess you'd know all about that."

"It's been a while. I imagine it's different now."

"The tech, yeah, a little. We get and send clearer sensory and emotional impressions than your original equipment, but it's still only impressions. Thing is, dogs are dogs. They're smart, and you treat 'em right, friends for life."

Kanigher nodded. "I worried all this went away with me."

"Almost did. A year after you were captured, the brass tried to shut it down. One of my squad convinced General Kubert your program was worth funding. They hired new geniuses to continue your work, and it took off. They're adapting your cybernetics work for human/machine interfaces now. Making good progress too. Rumors about top-secret programs and new kinds of weapons. Hasn't ended the war yet, but it lets us hit a whole lot harder."

"How... how bad is it?"

"Like me. Could be a whole lot worse, could be a whole lot better," Haney said. "The Coalition occupies four states. Used to be six. We're in one of the occupied ones."

"They dropped you behind enemy lines to rescue me?"

"My squad only works behind enemy lines. Guerilla warfare. Hit-and-run. Us and a few other squads likes us spread throughout the occupied territory. We drive the Coalition nuts, fouling up their supply lines, screwing their communications, spoiling their food. You name it we gremlin it. I've been deployed almost a year straight now, and they still haven't quite figured out what the hell keeps hitting them."

"Are we winning?"

"That call's way above my pay grade," Haney said. "Every day seems the same to me. Cloudy, with a chance of explosions and gunfire. Coalition is dug in deep from Providence to Atlantic City and over to Pittsburgh, but we stopped them advancing past Pennsylvania, even pushed them back a good way. Two years now we've had troops on the ground in China and Russia to busy them on their own turf. Mexico's on fire and the border is a no-man's land, but they never did get a foothold in Texas. We kept them out of the Northwest too. Our allies are propping us up best they can, but they've got their hands full with their own fights. At least no one's gone nuclear yet so that's considered a plus. But it's going to be a long war."

The news stunned Kanigher. "We'd been fighting five years when they captured me. How long have I...?"

"You don't know?"

Kanigher shook his head.

"Guess it all blends together, the beatings, the hard labor, the lousy food—kind of like being in the infantry," Haney said. "Hard to keep track when you're living like that."

"Hey," Kanigher whispered. "How long?"

"Eight years." Haney looked away and rubbed Sallygirl's head while Kanigher absorbed her answer.

"Guess I should've known," he said.

Bug Eye and Nightingale jolted to all fours, eyes and ears alert. Sallygirl lifted her head, and from the corridor, Marshmallow Solider growled. Seconds later, a tremor ran through the ground. Kanigher put a hand down to brace himself until the rumble ended.

"Tanks," Kanigher said. "Looking for us."

"No doubt about it," Haney said. "Probably backed up by hoverbirds and foot patrols."

"If we stay here too long, they'll find us," he said. "The rest of your squad may not be able to get here."

Haney shook her head. "Don't worry. Those Coalition bastards can't always go where my squad can go. That's what makes us so effective."

In the corridor, Marshmallow Soldier filled the doorway. His blue light flashed three times, darkened, then flashed three more. The click-clack of nails on cement and the scrape of metal echoed down the tunnel. The Doberman backed into the room. Two shapes followed him and moved into the light, a pair of German Shepherds. One, young and lithe, wore a standard harness rig and cybercowl, which wrapped the right side of its head. The second stood taller than the other dogs. It took Kanigher several seconds to accept what he saw, but he knew the moment the dog moved into the light that it was the one who'd howled. Impossible as it seemed, he knew its face and its stance. He knew its scent, and he remembered the sound of its voice.

The Shepherd made eye contact.

It was Sarge.

Kanigher wasted no time doubting it. The red bandanna from the photo, now faded and pocked with holes, encircled its neck. This was his dog, the first of the cyberdogs he'd created and trained, older and scarred, gray in the fur around his muzzle, a chunk missing from one of its ears, and yet still possessed of the same warm, intelligent eyes he remembered. He offered Sarge his hand. The dog sniffed it, then licked it, and then Kanigher knelt down and let the dog lash his face with its tongue and press its muzzle against his neck. Kanigher stroked it and scratched its side. He felt as much steel under his fingers as he did hair and muscle. He backed off for a better look. Cybernetics and prosthetics comprised close to a third of Sarge's body, including his rear legs and part of his torso, no doubt increasing his strength and speed far beyond what it had once been. His cybercowl covered the left half of his face. His rig, larger and more complex than all the others and integrated into his body cybernetics, bore a launcher for high-yield mini-mortars—bombs the size of cherries—and a compact projected-energy gun. The weapons used in the breakout. He glanced at the other German, which wore only a standard cybercowl and saw it armed with a similar rig, though mounted only with an energy gun.

"Sarge has been looking for you a long time," Haney said.

"I can't believe he's still alive," Kanigher said.

"Around the time the brass tried to shutter your program, Sarge was deployed with a platoon in Oregon doing explosives detection. He caught wind of an underground encampment, enemy tunnels, an ambush waiting to happen, and he saved hundreds of lives, including General Kubert's nephew. Even got wounded in the firefight. After that the lab boys put new gear to the test on him first, and he made everything they threw at him work. They say it was like he was trying to make you proud. I had my doubts when I got assigned to be his handler, but he wiped them out fast. He's been looking for you all along. Caught your scent a year ago, and he hasn't let it go. He made sure the rest of the squad knew it too. Like he was worried you might be forgotten if something happened to him. He knows he isn't getting any younger and this is probably his last tour. Now or never. Him and all the others, they're like your children. You and Sarge set the course for them, for all of us. You gave us a lifeline."

"I heard him howling," Kanigher told her. "I didn't want to believe it was him."

"Yeah, he was damn stubborn about that. I couldn't keep him in with me while I planned the break. He smelled you in there. They all did."

Kanigher rubbed welling tears from his eyes. Sarge circled him and sat at his side, ready position, his head pitched toward Kanigher's, awaiting orders. The other dogs fell in around Kanigher, all but Sallygirl, who stayed with Haney.

"It's your squad, now, Cap," Haney said. "I guess, in a way, it always has been."

Kanigher raised an eyebrow. "What about the others?"

"This is everyone. It was me and Andru and the dogs."

Kanigher laid his hand atop Sarge's head. "All right, then. Let's move out."

He helped Haney onto her feet. Weak, but steady, she pulled a couple of buzz tabs, one red and one blue, from one of Nightingale's pouches. She ate the red and fed Sallygirl the blue.

"A little boost to keep us vertical," she said.

Sallygirl stood with a whimper and walked out the door.

"Sallygirl's a smart one. No sense in wasting time," Haney said.

They moved out, Kanigher and Sarge right behind Sallygirl, the others behind them in a loose ring around Haney. Silence and night greeted them at the end of the alley. Bright Eyes, the other Shepherd, took point, and they moved through town using Kanigher's stop-and-go routine. They walked east through abandoned streets and dense shadows. Soon the buildings came farther apart, and treetops marked the open horizon outside town. A trash fire burned a block or two south of them, and the wind carried its heat and smoke across their path, filled with the odor of burning rubber and wood. The dogs hesitated as the cloud flooded their senses. Kanigher spied the fire glow on buildings in other parts of the city and wondered if the enemy knew about the dogs and had lit them on purpose. Regardless, they had another five klicks to reach their evac point. Kanigher sought an alternate route, but debris choked the nearest streets, leaving them only two options: double back or forge ahead. Kanigher urged the squad onward. They covered a few more yards, and then the dogs stiffened. Their ears pricked up. They scanned the night in every direction, enough warning for Kanigher to drop to a crouch, pulling Haney with him, shuffling them both into the meager cover of a pile of rubble.

The air whined, and then the ground shook and fire erased the night.

Broken rocks, concrete, and glass rained on the ground.

When the echo of the explosion died, Kanigher heard soldiers yelling.

He peered through a gap in the rubble. Ahead of their position sat a tank parked on a cross street, four soldiers around it, all gazing in the direction of his squad, weapons ready. One scrambled for a grenade launcher propped against the tank treads. Another buckled the strap under his helmet. Lit cigarettes glowed on the ground. If not for the soot and the heat from the trash fire, the dogs would've detected the cigarettes, the scents of tank oil and human sweat. Kanigher chided himself for not turning back, but there was nothing he could do about it now.

Haney rested her rifle in a crook in the rubble, then handed her sidearm to Kanigher, who took it even as his eyes scanned for the dogs. He saw only Sallygirl hunkered down behind a neighboring rubble pile, head on her paws, eyes glued to Haney.

The soldiers opened fire.

Shots chewed up the remnants of the street and pinged off the rubble. Haney returned fire, scattering the soldiers, all but the one holding the grenade launcher, who stood steady and aimed on their position, preparing to wipe them out with one shot—but he never fired.

Landing like a demon falling from the sky, Sarge hit him from the shadows, clenching his teeth on the soldier's neck even as he tore him sideways to the ground. The grenade launcher fell and rolled away. Bright Eyes and Marshmallow Solider took down two other soldiers, coming at them from out of their line of sight, hitting them hard and fast, bringing them down, and lunging past the hands they raised in defense to rip at their necks and faces. Kanigher and Haney eased out from the rubble and fired on the fourth soldier, ripping bullets across his chest and dropping him. On the ground, the other soldiers all lay still, and the dogs withdrew from their corpses. A soldier in the tank snapped the hatch shut. The engine rumbled, and the turret swiveled, bringing the gun around on Kanigher and Haney.

The sound of hoverbirds filled the air.

A flurry of barking rose from the dogs, and then the animals scattered.

Sarge, Bug Eye, and Bright Eyes raced toward the tank and leapt onto its body.

Marshmallow Soldier and Nightingale bolted for Kanigher and Haney. Nightingale took Haney's wrist between her jaws and dragged her away. Marshmallow Soldier stood by Sallygirl, locked eyes with Kanigher, and barked three times. Kanigher took the hint. Careful not to drive the needles in her side any deeper, he slung Sallygirl across his shoulders in a firemen's carry. She whimpered in pain, but settled against him. Behind him, a small explosion erupted. He turned to see the tank turret broken and fouled by a shot from Sarge's mortar. Now the dogs worked the hatch with their energy weapons.

"Move out!" Kanigher shouted at the dogs.

They couldn't hear him. He caught up to Haney.

"Order them to fall back and come with us," he said. "Through your link. Do it now!"

Haney nodded. Kanigher watched the dogs. Only Sarge lifted his head long enough to meet Kanigher's eyes. He wagged his tail, barked, and then resumed working at the hatch.

Kanigher started back, but Marshmallow Soldier grabbed his hand, urging him forward. Lights from three hoverbirds painted the buildings now, closing on the tank's position. The dog's energy beams flared and the hatch exploded free of its mounts.

Bug Eyes and Bright Eyes scrambled off the tank.

The hoverbirds dropped low, spotlights painting the vehicle. Like a living shadow, Sarge skipped the edge of the lights and vanished into the tank. Kanigher hesitated, waiting for the dog to reemerge, resisting Marshmallow dragging him on to a rubble-strewn back street that led away from town. A huge explosion rocked the night, spewing from the tank, catching the low-flying hoverbirds in its blast. Three more followed as the hoverships ignited.

Fire painted the sky.

Sarge's howls echoed in Kanigher's mind.

Haney faltered for a moment, knees weak, her expression blank, and Kanigher knew what she'd felt through her cybercowl, the last impressions from one of her dogs.

He couldn't bring himself to ask which one.

They trudged on to the evac point, keeping to shadows, the dogs picking a route over ground no tank could travel. Twice they heard enemy soldiers nearby, but Nightingale led the squad safely around them both times. Bug Eyes rejoined them one klick out, and when they reached the rendezvous, Bright Eyes sat waiting there for them, a bloody gash in his side.

Kanigher knew Sarge wouldn't be coming. The knowledge gutted him and filled him with pride at the same time. After all those years, their reunion had been far too short.

They held their position, hiding in the dark for an hour before their ride set down in the clearing. Kanigher hesitated, unwilling to leave his fallen dog behind, like so many others had been down through the history of soldier dogs. Then he thought of all that Sarge had given his comrades, of all that Sarge had given him, and all that he might do now with his freedom. He had no choice but to honor Sarge's sacrifice. Haney placed her hand on his shoulder. He let her lead him into the hoverbird. As it lifted into the dark, Kanigher's memories of Sarge howling blotted out the sound of its blades.

THE SHEPHERDS
Christopher M. Hiles

PITTSBURGH HAD BEEN BURNING FOR SIX MONTHS. THE ATTACK CAME swiftly. Humanity never had any chance to defend against it. The entire planet was destroyed from orbit, every country, on every continent burned at once. Somehow, the aliens blew up anything emitting an artificial electronic signal. Jim had seen it himself. He'd been camping with friends when it began. Two of them grabbed their cell phones, attempting call home, only to be engulfed in flames right in front of him.

Recently, the Underground had received intelligence that a human work detail was operating in Crafton, a borough just west of downtown Pittsburgh. The source wasn't always reliable; but, his cell leader thought it was worth investigating; maybe they could rescue some more fighters and, better yet, take out a few of the bad guys. He sent Jim and his dog, Schmidt, down to provide overwatch for a snatch and grab. The other members of his team had spent the past few hours in the ruins of the houses lining the route the work group was reported to take. He and Schmidt had spent a few more hours working their way into a sniping position.

Jim shifted his elbow slightly to get a better view of the area. He and Schmidt had been lying in a ditch most of the day, waiting for their target. They finally saw movement, but no humans yet. He held his position, watching the aliens through his scope.

They were squat, bulbous creatures with four legs and could grow as many arms as they needed. They didn't seem to have a recognizable head.

Aside from the few in front of him now, he'd only seen a couple of recently dead ones up close. Soon after they died, they slowly oozed into a grey fluid that smelled like burnt Fritos. Within a day, they were nothing more than an extraterrestrial puddle. A few former biologists seemed fascinated with them. All he cared was that they dropped when he hit them. With no discernable head, center mass was best.

Despite their awkward shape, they moved fast. They could close on a victim a couple hundred yards away in a few seconds. Their ability to leap huge distances gave them their name: Bounders. Running was a bad idea, barring having something to move behind. They couldn't change direction in mid-jump, which made them cherry sniper targets.

Jim caught a flash of light in a window of a single story ranch house below. It flashed twice more. Schmidt tightened his forty pounds of muscles and let out a low growl.

"Yeah, they're coming, boy. Easy," Jim said.

He was Jim's secret weapon. The Bounders were lethal in combat; but, they were terrified of dogs. Just as well, dogs didn't like the aliens much, either. They would enter a frenzy when they spotted a Bounder, attacking with a berserker's fury. Only Schmidt's police K9 training kept him under Jim's command and in control.

Jim focused in on a street corner below as a group of prisoners with a Bounder escort came into view. He counted the aliens. "Four," he muttered. "There were only supposed to be two." He counted ten humans. "At least they got that right."

The work group continued down the road. Jim watched as they approached the ruins of a yellow house with a large sycamore in the front yard. A small swing still hung off one of the tree branches, swaying in the breeze. He adjusted his scope a half mil and aimed at the lead Bounder standing to the side of the group. Jim took in a deep breath, slowly blew it out, and pulled the trigger. The alien dropped. As he cycled the bolt, two of the last three charged in his direction. The third one began to move but the work group descended on it using whatever weapon was at hand.

Two resistance members came out of the houses and made a beeline toward the group, shouting at them to clear out of the way. Enough people in the group moved to clear line-of-sight One of the resistance soldiers dispatched the Bounder with a few shots from his rifle. His partner hustled the group toward an alley.

The two Bounders making their way at Jim advanced in a zigzag, changing direction after landing, each leap clearing over ten yards a stride. Schmidt snarled and stood. "No, wait!" Jim said. Schmidt erupted out of the ditch and had reached full speed before Jim could stand.

"Dammit!" he said.

He moved into a kneeling position, settled his right elbow on his right knee, and fired. The round caught one of the Bounders in a hip, blowing off one leg and part of another. It let out a screech as it tumbled across the sidewalk. Schmidt closed the remaining distance to the second Bounder and met it in midair. The alien squealed and flipped the Australian shepherd off, sending him sprawling into a grassy yard.

Jim dropped his rifle and pulled out a .45 caliber handgun. He squeezed off two rounds, winging the Bounder, before Schmidt pounced again. The dog brought the oozing alien to ground, ripping a hunk of flesh off its trunk. It frantically grew appendages to push Schmidt away. He ripped at them too, sending grey goop oozing to the asphalt.

Jim sprinted toward the combatants. "Schmidt! Off!" he shouted when he was within fifty feet. Schmidt's head shot up. Jim took the opportunity and pulled the trigger. The alien went limp.

He heard a whistle and looked up. A tall man in camouflage waved at him and gave him a thumbs-up before following the rest of the stragglers as they moved behind the yellow house.

"Schmidt, come," Jim said. The dog loped up to him, tail wagging. The "haunch" of an alien leg hung from his mouth. "Don't look so damned satisfied. It could have been your leg in one of their… whatevers." Schmidt tilted his head and spit out the leg. "Come on."

It didn't take long for the Bounders to send in a team to check scout the area. Jim felt the ground rumble as two spherical shuttles emerged over the burning city. Schmidt whimpered at the high-pitched squeal of the shuttles' engines, a pitch higher than Jim could hear. One hovered while the other landed and collected all the remains of the Bounder guards and those of only one human. Jim didn't recognize her. He noted everything he saw, waited for the ships to leave, and took the long route home.

He didn't arrive back at camp until well after dusk. An old man everyone called Doc tended a small fire near the camp's perimeter. A piece of corrugated metal was rigged above it in an attempt to disperse the smoke. He greeted Jim with a smile that was missing more than a couple of teeth, "Welcome back, Saved some supper for you." He handed Jim a stick with a hunk of roasted deer skewered on it.

"Thanks, Doc."

"Gonna have to share a bit with your pup. Folks you saved were damn near starved."

Jim flicked a bite of deer to Schmidt who plucked it out of the air and Doc gave him one of the larger bones. Schmidt curled up by the fire and began gnawing on one end, content.

"Matt's lookin' for ya," Doc said, pointing a well-calloused thumb toward another fire where the cell's leader stood surrounded by a knot of people Jim didn't recognize.

Matt was a short, balding man with grey eyes and a scalp full of scars. A retired Navy Chief Petty Officer, he had been on a fishing trip with his son when the attack occurred. His wife died in the opening salvos, along with his daughter-in-law and grandchildren. He had opened up to Jim about it once. He didn't cry or break down. He just laid out what he found in a monotone.

He didn't fight like a man out for revenge. He fought like a man waging a war the same as any other commander. Sometimes, at night, Jim heard Matt toss and turn, mumbling. It wasn't unique among members of the resistance. A lot of people did it and nobody said anything the next morning. Dreams were their own kind of therapy and it was an unwritten rule that those on guard duty kept the secrets revealed as if they were the therapists.

"Good work, Jim," Matt said, looking up from a map.

"Didn't rescue them all, Chief," Jim said.

"She died fighting the bastards," said a young woman standing next to Matt.

"I guess that's something," Jim said.

"Schmidt okay?" Matt asked.

"Yeah, he's rather proud of himself."

Matt grunted and handed Jim the map, "You up for going out again right away?"

"Need to pull some ammo, but I should be okay."

"Good. This is Mary. She's one of the people we pulled out of Whispering Woods near the airport a few days ago. The Bounders picked her up three days ago," he turned to her. "Ma'am."

"I was scouting out a path for my group. We were trying to get a bunch of kids out into the mountains," she paused and took a deep breath. "My group ran into a few patrols and…," she took another paused. "I am the last adult left. The older kids were told to hide in the case that we were separated. They should still be out there."

"Last known location is marked on your map. It's about 10 klicks from here. Mary grew up here and knows the area. I need the two of you to get out there, find the kids, and get them to the rendezvous point. Quicker the better," Matt said.

"How long is the rendezvous good for?" Jim asked.

"They move them every five days. This one has about 36 hours left," Mary said. "And it's about five miles from where I left them."

"Eight klicks on top of the hike to get to their last known location; better get going," Jim said.

"Good hunting," Matt said as he shook Jim's hand.

Jim resupplied and waited while Mary was outfitted with new clothes and gear. When she returned, she looked less diminutive and more like a hunter. He must have given away his surprise.

"What?" she said as she slung a shotgun over her shoulder. "I'm a country girl."

"Yes, ma'am," he said with a smile. "Ready to go?"

She nodded. Mary was a woman, in her late twenties. Her skin may have once been porcelain; now, it was a patchwork of sunburn, dirt, and abrasions, all topped off with a tangle of shoulder-length red curls. She pulled most of it back in a short, loose ponytail. Schmidt immediately took to her. He trotted along next to her as they left the camp, constantly nuzzling his snout into her hand.

Mary broke the silence after they had moved away from the camp, "Thank you for saving us."

"No problem," Jim said. "We don't get opportunities like that very often."

"You've saved other groups?"

"Mostly in ones and twos and almost always before they are caught. Usually, when we attack, they just kill the prisoners."

Mary looked down, "I see." They walked awhile before she spoke again, "So, Matt said you were in the military."

Jim nodded, "Still am."

"Still? The military still exists?"

He shrugged, "I'm still here. There are a few others so I'd say it exists in some way."

"You were in the Navy with Matt?"

"Oh, no. Army. And he retired a few years before I signed up."

"So, you're a solider?"

"Yup."

"A member of Delta or something?"

"No."

"Ranger?"

"Not as such."

"Infantry? Aviation? Artillery? What?"

"I fixed vehicles. Nothing fancy. Just a grease monkey."

"But you were trained, right?"

"To fight? Yeah, everyone has to go through basic training."

"Well, you're a hell of a shot."

"I like to hunt. Been doing it since I was a little kid."

He had grown up near Lexington, Kentucky. His entire family were hunters. His sister held the family record for the largest deer. He wondered where she was or if she was even okay. She didn't live in the most populated area and told him she would be out hunting when the aliens struck. He'd like to think she was out there bagging the grey bastards just like he was.

Mary scratched behind Schmidt's ear, "Was he yours before the attack?"

"A friend's. He's a retired police dog."

"What happened to your friend?"

"He survived the attack. We were at a hunting lodge when they came. He died when we tried to go back to his house. I had to drag Schmidt away."

"I'm sorry," she said.

"Me, too."

They made good time as they moved through the woods. Jim was surprised she didn't want to take a break, especially when only a few hours ago she was a slave in a work party. He ached and, at times, had difficulty keeping up with her. His long legs were used to hiking but she almost jogged. He pressed on in spite of the pain.

They arrived close to the children's last known location. The wooded area was dense and the little light from the moon that filtered through only gave him about five feet of visibility.

"They should be right here," she said, consulting the map.

"Maybe they moved—" a scream rang out in the night air.

He couldn't tell which direction it came from. Schmidt had no doubt. His snout pointed toward the north, foot raised, hair standing on end.

"My God," whispered Mary. She lowered her shoulders and disappeared into the brush.

"Shit," Jim said and followed with Schmidt trailing behind him.

The duo burst out of the brush and into a clearing. Mary took off in a full sprint, moving toward a group of children surrounded by several Bounders. The children were hemmed in, with two being carried back to the main group on the top of their captors.

"Help her, boy!" he yelled and Schmidt tore off after Mary.

Jim dropped to a knee, unslung his rifle, aimed, and took a shot at an alien moving toward Mary. Jim saw it tumble to the ground and slide away before losing it in the tall grass. He scanned the area while cycling the bolt. Three aliens broke away from the kids and came toward him. He fired, reloaded, and fired again. The second shot buried itself in a Bounder, causing it to go down in a spray of grey goo.

Two still charged him, hard. He slung the rifle and pulled a grenade out of a satchel on his belt. He waited until the Bounders were within a couple of jumps and then pulled the pin, dropped the spoon and grenade to the ground, and dove over a nearby log. He felt the thud as the Bounders landed where he had been. The grenade went off in a spray of mud and shrapnel. The aliens' howls drowned out the echoes of Schmidt's snarls and the kids' screams.

Jim grabbed his rifle, unclipped the holster on his .45, and jumped to his feet. He counted two more aliens, both attacking Mary, who fended one off with her shotgun. Schmidt leapt out of the grass and onto the second one. Jim brought his rifle up and fought to control his breathing. Schmidt tore at the Bounder's flesh causing it to squeal and wildly spin around. Jim couldn't get a clear shot so he shifted to focus on Mary.

She was fully engaged with a Bounder, dodging strikes from its manipulators. She fired a shotgun blast that missed high. The alien moved in and knocked her down. She grunted when she hit the ground, the shotgun flying out of her grip. She rolled away, gripping her side. With her on the ground, Jim finally had a clear shot. He steadily exhaled and then blasted the alien's trunk. He cycled the bolt and thumbed the safety.

Schmidt's snarls abruptly ended. Jim slung his rifle and pulled his .45 as he ran toward his dog. He had to jump over the alien body to prevent himself from tripping. Schmidt's snout poked out from under its side. Jim pushed the alien over with his boot, allowing Schmidt to scramble free. He jumped up, tail furiously waving, and licked Jim's face.

"You're welcome!" he said, "Mary? You alright?"

"Yes," she said as she stood up. "The kids?"

Jim scanned the area before spotting the group clumped around something they were beating with sticks. They rushed up to the children and saw the remains of an alien that was oozing out of several open wounds.

"It's okay. You can stop now," Mary said, gently.

One of the boys turned around and screamed, "Mary!"

The kids dropped their sticks and charged toward her, all talking at once. "I'm okay," she said, tears running down her cheeks as she tried to draw all of them into a group hug. "How about all of you?"

The children talked over each other explaining how they lived just like grownups. One of the older children was able to shush the group and said, "We hid just like you told us, Ms. Mary, but they spotted us."

Jim holstered his weapon after scanning the clearing. He pulled the map from his pocket and examined it. The moon lit the sky brightly this far out of the city, but the trees grew thick on the borders of the field and he couldn't see far into the woods.

"Mary," he said. "We have to go."

She stood up, holding one of the children, a little girl no older than five. "Everyone, this is Mr. Jim. He's going to help us. We need to move fast and keep very quiet, understood?"

The kids nodded and the little girl hugged Mary's neck closer.

"What is the dog's name?" asked a blond boy, one of the children who had been beating on the Bounder.

"Schmidt," Mary said. "He's going to help us, too. Now, everyone, follow me." She glanced at the map Jim was holding and then started off west. "This way."

The group was deep into the woods when Jim heard the low humming of the alien orbs. The children looked toward the sound and a few began to cry. But, they kept moving. Mary handed the five-year-old to one of the older kids and took up the point position. Schmidt kept close to Jim, who covered the rear, but broke off from time to time to ride herd on any stragglers, gently nudging them back in line with his head.

They walked for over an hour before some of the younger children began to slow. Mary called a halt for a short rest. Jim pulled a canteen from his pack, poured some water in a divot on a rock for Schmidt, and handed the canteen to a child.

Mary came back to Jim. She looked green and had worked up a heavy sweat.

"You alright?" Jim asked and patted the space next to him.

"I'll be fine," she said as she lowered herself down.

Schmidt stopped drinking to sniff at Mary's stomach. He backed off and started whining. "According to him you're not."

"K-9 truth detector," she said and lifted her shirt. A bruise covered her right flank. It seemed swollen, as well. "One of them got a hit in."

Jim inspected it, "Could have hurt a kidney or your intestines."

"You a doctor, too?"

"My sister's a nurse and I used to quiz her when she was in school," he said. "Does it hurt?"

"You could say that," she said and winced as he touched it.

"I got a few hydrocodone pills and a bit of morphine."

"*And* a pharmacist!" she said, delicately lowering the shirt back over the wound.

"Nope…just a Boy Scout. This looks pretty bad. We should try to get you numbed up so we can make it to the rendezvous faster."

"I'll pass, thanks."

He pulled a prepped syringe out of his bag and uncapped it, "I insist."

She sighed and gave him a pleading look, "I need to keep my head."

"You need to be able to keep moving."

She looked away and nodded. He rolled up her sleeve and made quick work of it. She sat back and relaxed her muscles.

"How," she paused and tried to shake the growing cobwebs out of her head. "How far are we?"

Jim recapped the needle and dropped it in his bag. He pulled the map out of his pocket and unfolded it, "Just a couple klicks."

She nodded, "Mostly flat ground. We should make good time." She grunted as she stood, refusing help from Jim.

"Do you want me to take point?" he asked.

"No, this is practically my backyard. You're sweet for offering, though," she turned to the children. "Time to go."

They complained and took some prodding. Mary enlisted the older kids to help get them moving. Jim gave Schmidt a scratch and then told him to go to Mary. He cocked his head at Jim. "Go on, I'm following," he said. Schmidt gave a bark and trotted off after Mary.

Though the lighting was poor and the children tired, they made good time. The forest abruptly ended at a two-lane road. Mary crouched down at its edge, Schmidt at her heel, and scanned the area. Jim joined them.

"They are supposed to be a hundred or so yards that way," she pointed. "I don't see them."

"Maybe they moved?"

"They wouldn't leave the area until after the deadline."

"They may not have had a choice," he brought his rifle up and peered through the scope. "I don't see any movement. I'll scout it out."

Mary put her hand on his arm, stopping him. It felt cold on his skin. "No," she said. "They won't know you. I'll go."

She headed off before he could object. He motioned for Schmidt to follow her. The dog whined and ran to catch up. Jim raised his rifle and scanned the area ahead of her, then turned back toward the children.

"Stay here and stay low," he said.

He returned his gaze to the scope. She neared what looked like an intersection. Schmidt trailed an arm's length behind her. She stopped and appeared to call out. Jim still couldn't see any movement. She said something else. Hello, maybe? Schmidt stood up, stock still, his muscles coiled and ready to pounce.

"Shit," Jim said.

He scanned the area and caught something moving and a flash. A Bounder sprang out of the forest. The flash was a blast from Mary's shotgun. The Bounder fell on her, knocking her to the ground. Schmidt took off across the road toward the tree line.

"*Shit*," Jim repeated and turned to the kids. "Get back in the woods and stay there!"

He jumped onto the side of the road and sprinted toward the intersection. As he drew closer, Mary's head and shouldered emerged from under the alien and she fired another blast at the tree line before collapsing. Jim heard Schmidt snarl, followed by an alien squeal. He slid to a halt next to Mary.

"Two more," she whispered. "Past the road."

Jim scrambled up the ditch to the road just in time to see a Bounder fling Schmidt through the air. He landed on his side and slid to a halt behind a tree. Jim swung his rifle to his shoulder and fired. The round hit home, spinning the alien around in a spray of grey fluid. The second one jumped toward Schmidt. Jim charged across the road, fumbling with the rifle's bolt.

As he ran down the embankment, something caught his foot, sending him to the ground hard. His rifle went flying. When he opened his eyes, he found himself face to face with the body of a human, its head split open. He felt like he was sitting on something and a quick glance confirmed it was another corpse which, in turn, was draped over a third.

The sound of an alien's scream snapped his head toward the trees. The source was in the air coming toward him. He tried to roll but his pack was caught on whoever he was laying on. He ripped a knife out of its scabbard and held it up, bracing for the hit. A blur of brown shot out from his left, meeting the Bounder in midair. Schmidt and the four-foot alien hit the ground next to Jim in a ball of angry teeth and fur. Schmidt tore at the alien's body, ripping off chunks. It howled in a rage, frantically attempting to grow manipulators to right itself. Jim dropped the knife, pulled out his pistol, and took aim. The alien's screams ended with a bang.

Jim scanned the area and saw no other apparent targets. He rolled on his back and took a few deep breaths. After a moment, he untangled himself from the corpse and got to his knees. The remains were fresh. Blood still seeped from the large wounds. They wore Army uniforms. Two of them looked young, one was older. Jim carefully pulled a map that was sticking out of the older one's pocket and unfolded it. The crossroads was marked with a red circle and a time of 0730, the rendezvous deadline.

"Damn," he said as he stood. "Schmidt?"

Schmidt poked his head over the side of the road and gave a whine.

"Thanks for the save, boy." Jim climbed the embankment. "Mary," he called out. "The guys you were going to meet up with got jumped. They didn't make it, but I got their map and I think I can navigate us to one of their forward operating bases." When she didn't respond he crossed the road to where she lay. She wasn't breathing and the color had completely drained from her face. Her eyes stared vacantly in the direction of where she had left the kids.

He slid down the ditch to her side and pulled her out from under the Bounder corpse. The area around her abdomen was soaked with blood. He sighed and ran a hand over her face, gently closing her eyelids. As he stood, he saw movement in the trees. Two of the older children slowly emerged, sticks in their hands, their eyes fixed on Mary.

One of them looked up. "Who is going to protect us, now?" he said.

Jim looked at Schmidt, who gave a short whine, and then to the boy, "We will," Jim said. "Now let's get you out of here."

DATA DOGS

Eric V. Hardenbrook

JOHN CHECKED HIS LIPSTICK IN THE MIRROR ONE LAST TIME. HE TILTED HIS PILL box hat at a jaunty angle, smoothed his skirt and stepped out the door. He shifted his arm and brought his extra-large purse around to extract his key to lock the apartment door. His dog, tucked inside, had the key in her mouth waiting.

"Well thank you very much, Mrs. Nesbit," John scratched behind her ear, then took the key and locked up the apartment. "Would you like to run today, sweetie?" John took each step down to the sidewalk with care. "It certainly wouldn't do to turn an ankle would it, dear?" John held Mrs. Nesbit out at arm's length. "It would be worse to ruin these heels, they're my favorites and the last pair that match this outfit. Staying in fashion is never easy, but even in this size it's important, my lovely."

John swept down the sidewalk head held high, surveying the area. His apartment was in a very respectable part of town. The importance to him wasn't just seeing and being seen, it was the proximity to his target.

"Okay, Mrs. Nesbit, time to get in some exercise!" John made little pouty faces as he pulled Mrs. Nesbit from the bag. "We've got your special leash today, dearie." Then he started with old-school baby talk, "Time to test our new leash. Look at the fancy clip all silver and leather. Who's the dangerous girl?" John squatted down with knees together and to the side while he petted and scratched his partner. Mrs. Nesbit, for her part, loved the attention.

John looked over Mrs. Nesbit from head to toe, all ten inches of her. Her outer fur was a gorgeous, sandy blonde color, slightly curled. Scratching a little deeper he could feel the stiff bristles of her undercoat. Her ears pointed up and her cute little nose was black as a button. John gave her an extra little squeeze as he set her down. He was very careful to avoid pushing the studded bow on his partner's head off center. Mrs. Nesbit did click a little on the concrete of the sidewalk, but he wasn't worried about his partner's nails. They were genetically modified and hardened to allow greater digging capacity. He held her up on her hind legs with one hand and looked into her eyes while he clicked the break-away leash to her chest harness. The eyes looking back were deeper, more intelligent that most folks would believe. Mrs. Nesbit gave a little whine and showed her teeth.

"Soon, sweetie, soon." John focused his right eye on her teeth. He wanted desperately to reassure Nesbit. Checking the signal overlay on his retina display he saw she was up and running. Her teeth had been specially designed with inboard data capabilities. Essentially she could chomp on a hard line and suck up the data there. All she needed to do was get to them.

"Let's see if you can get into the garden today? Do you want to do that?" John went back to pouty face and baby talk. "Who's the meanest little hound? Is that you? Oh, you little sweetie!" John stood again and started to stroll. "Let's go have some fun, dearie!" Mrs. Nesbit yipped a little bark and scrabbled along the sidewalk out the end of the leash run.

John's gaze swept the area around the discreet little shack. It sat just far enough off the sidewalk as not to be too noticeable, but prominent enough to let others know to stay clear of the high, black iron picket fence. It was an ostentatious use of metal, clearly meant to impress during these hard times. There was his favorite guard. The guard staff depended on a computerized algorithm to randomize their shifts. Sadly—for them at least—it was an older program and one he'd recognized. He'd figured out their schedule easily. This government control center staying away from the cutting edge of technology was the reason he'd landed this assignment in the first place. Many places these days would be less vulnerable to a direct attempt to siphon off their most valued information. This place being just a little behind helped him out. He stole a glance at the guard and chuckled a little to himself. The guard hadn't seen him yet and was bent over checking something as they approached.

"Dahling! I'm so happy to see you in your little hovel this morning! What a splendid view to be greeted with." John gave a little twitter of a laugh.

"Ah, good morning, uh, miss. How is the little one today?" The guard turned in place and offered a small treat in the palm of his hand. Mrs.

Nesbit barked and popped up onto her hind legs with tail going a mile a minute.

"Oh, Mrs. Nesbit has been so feisty today. She's clearly happy to see you, too."

As soon as the words left John's mouth his partner took her cue and dashed toward the fence, barking like mad. John spun slightly with the pull of the leash and bumped into the guard. The leash yanked as the dog made for a gap in the fence, giving way just at the right moment.

"Mrs. Nesbit! You aren't yourself! Come be a dear and don't upset your friend with the cookies!" John yelled, staying clear of anything that resembled a command. He glanced at the guard as he hesitated at the fence. The guard shook his head only once in the negative and John backed away from the fence still calling, "Dearie, don't make such a scene! What will the neighbors think?"

Nesbit tore under a decorative shrub and started barking and digging like a fiend. Two of the other guards (not nearly as pliable as the one in the shack) ran from the back door of the secured building and headed for the hedgerow to secure the little miscreant. As they got close, John clenched his jaw, twisted his lip ever so slightly, and whistled a high pitch tone.

"Now look what you've done, Mrs. Nesbit! You've gone and gotten our friends all flustered—and you made me whistle like I'm some kind of spectacle. You get back in your bag this moment!" John thrust his arm forward. Mrs. Nesbit rushed out from under the shrubs opposite the guards and back through the pickets.

As the guards wandered back to their posts eyeing him warily John held up the end of the broken leash. "I am so sorry. This designer goes right to the bottom of the useful list. His work looks tough and leather, but it turns out it's not very strong... and we are strong aren't we, sweetie? Yes, we are!"

John apologized again as he saw the guards from the building shaking their heads and mumbling to each other. He threw a last wink to the pliable one and headed back toward the apartment.

John looked at the door to the apartment and sensed something was wrong. He didn't put on his voice, but whispered, "Nice work this morning, Nesbit, but something doesn't seem right here. We haven't been gone that long, but it could be anything. Be ready."

Nesbit growled and hopped from the bag to the concrete step, tense and ready.

John keyed the lock and swung the door in. Striding into the foyer with confidence, he swept the building with his augmented eye. Nesbit growled and stalked around the corner into the living room. There were life signals here. Definitely somebody in the kitchen.

John sashayed down the little corridor and burst around the corner with a shout, "Donato! Just what do you think you're doing trying to sneak up on me like this! Come here, you big sweetie!" John had closed the distance to the man standing beside the kitchen table before the reaction shown in his face could reach the rest of his body. "Give me hugs, you sweet thing!" John's voice rose up quite loud until he embraced the other, then he whispered into the man's ear, "You start acting like you're part of this right now or you're a dead man."

"Well, how could I not stop by to see an old friend since I was in town..." Donato faltered at the end.

"This is so wonderful! I'm going to set the screens for the afternoon sun—you know how hot it gets these days—then we'll really have the chance to sit and chat!" John made for the control panel and darkened the windows. He stretched his leg out in a very un-ladylike manner, hooked his toes on the door, and kicked it shut. Along with the standard home polarization/heat protection package, he activated his own special bit of anti-surveillance tech. He didn't turn back to his uninvited guest until he confirmed all the screens were in place. Making sure nobody else could eavesdrop was vital. Once this was done, he could stop acting and get the answers he needed. The console beeped and Nesbit barked once, growled and scampered out of the living room and across to the dining room.

When John swung around he shocked the other man again with the ferocity of his scowl and the new-found depth of voice, "Who the hell do you think you are? What's the big idea of skulking in here like this? Are you trying to screw everything up?"

"Who the hell is Donato? My name is..."

John burst into 'Donato's' thought, "I don't give a rat's ass who you are! I know you're part of Resource Command or you couldn't have gotten in here. Donato is now your cover name. You'll stick to it and you'll like it!"

Donato's answer was terse, "You're right about me being from Resource Command. The higher ups are tired of you dragging your feet and acting like a..." Donato faltered again, "like a..." he waved his hand up and down at John.

"Shut up, asshole! You could have wrecked the whole thing!"

"That's the point!" Donato regained some traction. "I'm here to bust a few things up and force out the info we need!"

"Exactly how are you going to do that, you fool?" John's arms tensed and his fists balled. If this got physical it would end ugly. The Resource Command he knew had rigorous standards.

Just then a slightly muffled yip drew both men's attention. Mrs. Nesbit stood in the archway to the living room with an oddly colored rope-like item hanging from her mouth. The muffled yip came again and John got a better look at the short end to one side of Nesbit's mouth. It was a snake. Mrs. Nesbit had snatched it up just behind the head, thus stopping any chance the snake had of doing any damage. Not that Nesbit would be hurt should the snake have actually scored a hit.

"What the hell is that?" John shot.

"Tell it to put the snake down!" Donato started to back away, head swiveling as if looking for cover.

"Mrs. Nesbit is not an IT!" John roared as he spun back toward Donato.

Donato actually jumped he was so startled at this reaction. His swivel changed from looking for cover to looking back and forth between John and Nesbit. His lower jaw swung ever so slightly as it dangled there in astonishment.

"My partner will put that down just as soon as you finish explaining yourself, dammit!"

"You don't get it! It's a plastic snake!" Donato backed into the refrigerator, shocked that something was blocking his retreat. "IF Nesbit there is what I think, then there's a chance the embedded signal will set it off!"

"Oh, don't be a moron! How the hell did you get this job anyway? Did they brief you at all?" John threw a disgusted look at Donato. "And I'm not going to tell you again. Mrs. Nesbit is my partner, not an 'it'. Say 'it' one more time, you're going to catch the beating of a lifetime. Got it, *Donny*?" Nesbit growled around her mouthful. John turned away from the other agent to see what his partner had caught.

Donato stared again at the duo of man and dog. "You're bat-shit insane, aren't you?"

"Shut up and tell me what you're supposed to be doing." John had bent down to examine the snake. Nesbit dropped it and sat proudly. John absently scratched behind her one ear. Experience had taught John all the right spots. He and Nesbit were inseparable.

"I'm here to speed the operation along," Donato said. "Some folks don't like the way this operation has been handled by the canine corps and they've decided it's time for me to get in there and crack it open."

"You mean that literally don't you?" John examined the snake in his hands. It looked real enough if you didn't examine it closely. Looking at it now, he was less certain about his haste in waving off the other man's concerns. This wasn't a *plastic* snake as he'd thought he'd heard at first. It was *plastique*. This guy must have been pushed in from the drone section. "How many of these do you have?"

"I've got a whole bag full and then some," Donato sounded a little proud. "You've got to have the highest remote operator rating available to make these babies go."

"My God. You're trying to win the armchair cross aren't you?"

"The Distinguished Warfare Medal is nothing to scoff at," Donato seemed a little put out.

"How did they ever put you in the field? You still think this is a vid-game." John stood and tossed the nearly headless snake back at him. "You have no idea what we're up against on this. What are you going to do once things blow up?"

"I'm supposed to take my data extractor in and pull as much as I can get before I have to bug out. What are you supposed to be doing, *Suzy Homemaker?*"

Donato failed to duck as the straight left jab caught his right cheek bone. John swiveled and brought his right arm around in a deadly arc, but pulled up as he heard Mrs. Nesbit bark. As Donato staggered back cradling his face John said, "You're right, Nesbit. Too much paperwork to deal with if something happens to *dear old Donny.*"

"Paperwork! You just wait, asshole," Donnato backed away holding the side of his face with his free hand. "When I get back to the real world I'm going to let them all know what you're up to, freakshow!" Donato stomped up the stairs. "You're out of time and soon enough you'll be out of the service all together!"

John stooped and Nesbit leapt into his arms. "Don't worry, Nesbit, we'll get past this just like we've gotten past everything else," John carried his partner in one arm while pulling his wig off with the other hand. "That idiot poser won't stop us and won't keep us apart," John's glance up the steps toward the bedrooms upstairs was one of concern as much as malice. Sometimes his anger issues got the better of him. Hitting the other agent might not have been the best idea.

John hadn't heard so much as a peep from his freshly minted room-mate the rest of the day. He'd gone through his regular routine. He'd eaten, then gone and checked the style pages for reference material. Once the easy part was done, he double checked the security system, then headed into the sealed off basement to work out. He spent a great deal of time playacting at being over the top and helpless when he was out and about, but he took his workouts very seriously. He'd always hit the maximum physical score for his unit. He couldn't power lift like some of the brutes he'd worked with in the past, but he was whipcord tough and could run for days. He also took great care in maximizing Nesbit's workouts as well. It wouldn't do to let her get soft. He would do anything for Nesbit.

Nesbit was the leaping off point for the wandering thoughts of John's mind while he was working out. Since the anger had drained away the abrupt 'conversation' he'd had with this other agent swirled in his head. The long struggle for recognition as part of the elite Resource Command had taught him hard lessons in anger control. It had never been easy to get others to believe in his miniature partner. His was the perfect dog to modify for missions like this, but traditionalists couldn't see any breed other than Shepherd or Doberman as a canine soldier. He'd spent a lot of time defending his own *eccentricities* in the past as well. He and Nesbit had actually been a perfect match when the specialized post opened up. Both outcasts, they had bonded at once. In the end it was just a question of getting others on board with the idea.

Clearly, somebody that wasn't 'on board' with the covert operation had sent this other agent. It was a disheartening sign that politics was directly affecting his work, or a dangerous sign that they were becoming impatient. Being a field operator was more than blowing things up and snatching what you wanted from the wreckage. John had hopes of actually getting away undetected when this mission was finished.

Sweat dripping, head now clear John turned off Nesbit's modified tread mill so she could finish up just as he did. John would have to try to work with this new agent and incorporate the mechanized snake bombs into his plan... somehow. He'd need to try to reintroduce himself to the new agent, maybe even ask what his plan was. John decided that a shower and a little relaxation would further his thoughts in the right direction.

Just as John finished with his routine and settled in with a drink and a reader for the evening the door to Donato's room opened.

"Look who's decided to rejoin the world, Nesbit." John didn't even glance toward the stairs. Mrs. Nesbit gave an odd growl that tapered off to a bit of a whine. That gave John pause. So much time together had allowed him and Nesbit to communicate without words. He shifted his reader screen to mirror and tilted it toward the stairs. Donato was dressed in black over black, holding a large gym bag on his shoulder. Nesbit whined ever so slightly and John turned the screen back to what he was reading before the mirror caught Donato's eye. Let him wonder how he knew.

"Going to the gym?"

"No, freak. I'm pushing my timetable up and finishing this op tonight." Donato checked his pockets one more time and picked up a key fob from the table in the foyer.

John set his reader in his lap and turned, "You'll fail." His voice was as flat as he could make it. "You have no idea who's on shift right now or where to get what you need." John hesitated for a moment. He needed to move past the freak comment. The mission mattered. Keeping Nesbit mattered. "Beyond that you stand out. People in this area are all connected in some way and they care who's wandering in their neighborhood. Local law will have you picked up before you get halfway there."

"I won't fail. You have no idea what you're talking about." Donato grabbed the door handle, ignoring all the security protocols, and stormed out into the blazing heat of the evening.

Nesbit whined. "Dammit. We're going to have to change our plans." John said as he hoisted himself up out of the chair and walked toward his room. "It's a shame... we're probably going to lose the fabulous outfits hanging in the closet. Get your special harness. I'll start getting ready."

It took longer than he wanted, but John held onto hope as he got into his best operations outfit. A long, light flowing skirt made of a mixed material, both stretchable and durable, but still fashionable. Black went with everything after all. A light grey puffy blouse that had long sheer sleeves was a fine addition. He slid his feet into sensible, low heel shoes that also happened to have extra durable soles and a lightweight metal frame hidden behind the black leather. A wide, zebra-striped hat topped the outfit, keeping the late evening sun off his face. He'd learned the fashion rules and one simply can't have the makeup run due to sweating in the late-day heat.

Mrs. Nesbit rode in her usual seat. She had on her best black harness, complete with dull, metallic-grey micro-fibers woven into the mesh and a zebra-striped bow to match John's hat.

John took a last look around the place he'd been calling home as he absently patted Nesbit. He blinked, and realizing that as long as he and Mrs. Nesbit were together home was anyplace they were, he strode to the control panel by the front door. Punching in a final code, he and Nesbit hustled out into the evening.

Together they strolled down the street as if on an evening walk. Most folks avoided the late-day heat, but not everyone. John waved when acknowledged by others from the neighborhood, but didn't stop for conversation. Mrs. Nesbit clicked along, tugging now and then against the new leash.

"Please, Mrs. Nesbit, you know we need to have the leash for everyone else not for us." John shifted his grip to the other hand. "If it were up to me we wouldn't even be out here tonight. That Donato is so very irritating."

Mrs. Nesbit yipped. "No, dear, we're going around from the other side. The fat, lazy guard is on duty right now. Franco or Frank or something like that..." Nesbit growled. John went on, "Yes, I know, dear. He doesn't smell good to me either." As they walked John kept his eyes and ears open while trying to think where dumb ass Donato would set up.

Nesbit barked again, pulling off to one side. John glanced and hesitated, almost missing his next step. "He wouldn't be that stupid, would he?" he glanced down at his partner. Nesbit tugged at the leash and angled over toward a small local cafe. John ran a scan without thinking. He had learned over time to trust his partner totally. The name of the place was *"The Supplier"* and was due to close in about ten minutes. There was only one person in the customer space, everyone else from the area knew it was only polite to give the staff the last minutes of the day to close up and tighten down security before dark. John glanced away and realized he had a direct line-of-sight to the government building's back side, away from the entry and the guards across the small garden they maintained.

"He really can't be that stupid...." John crouched down and brought the small dog in close. "He's going to make a mess of everything, sweetie. We're going to have to get you in there and pull everything we can." John's hands rubbed behind both of Nesbit's ears and surreptitiously set the subcutaneous transmitter to the on position. His hopes of getting away unscathed from this mission were dwindling rapidly. "You dig and chew, sweetie, just like training. I'm going to try to get Donny out of here. Meet me for treats, sweetie." With that John unclasped the leash and set Mrs. Nesbit off running. Turning back to the shop he resettled his hat and swayed up to the front door. Glancing back briefly he noted the patrol car a few blocks distant slowly rolling his direction. He soldiered on, but between the new guy and letting Nesbit run on her own, he was afraid the jig was up. In one corner of his eye he picked up his partner's signal.

As he entered the shop, a single, computerized tone sounded. It wasn't strictly needed, but some people liked the charm. John wound his voice up, "Donato! There you are, darling. You know you can't be out this late! Pick up that silly old reader of yours and let's get back to the house."

Donato didn't react. As John saw the small man behind the counter slip into the back room and heard a safety latch close with a loud clack. Looking back, John saw retina lights flashing in Donato's eyes. He had to be running a huge amount of controls to have that show up. Bad for staying undercover, but worse for his eyes in the long run. He wondered if this guy had any idea that he'd volunteered to give up his sight in the name of Resource Command. Most folks only gave up the one eye. This guy was burning them both down with no back-up plan. John just didn't understand guys like Donato. What else did he have? At least with Mrs. Nesbit as his partner John knew he'd never be alone. Donato called him a freak?

"Put your hands where we can see them!" a computer-amplified voice thundered at the front of the shop. The glass didn't rattle. No shop went without bulletproof front windows anymore. Thinking fast, John did the only thing he could come up with. He shrieked like a little girl and ran out the door with both hands high in the air waving back and forth.

Thankfully the local enforcers hadn't thought it was a big threat and they only sent a standard triad. Less than a three-man team didn't have much chance of success these days. Fortunately John knew their standard procedures. He dashed directly into the sight-line of the driver as he knelt behind the lightly armored car door and kept waving his arms to distract the restraint officer crouched at the rear quarter of the vehicle.

"Get down now!" the officer still in the vehicle gave an amplified shout.

Just as John considered trying for the gun in his bag a roar sounded from ahead of him and a wall of pressure knocked him to the ground. The pressure was followed immediately by heat and debris. He rolled once, sticking his hand into his bag to take advantage of the first confused moment after the concussion from the bombing.

Thankfully this triad didn't seem to have a lot of urban experience. The officer at the back of the car brought his weapon back toward the ready position but shook his head to clear it. The officer behind the door had slipped with the force of the blast, leaving a clear line into his open door. That was the opening John needed. He whipped his slim line Evans Stinger into a two-hand grip from his position on the ground and fired off two quick shots. The on-board computer in the triad's car popped and sizzled as the officer running it slumped forward.

The driver recovered and snapped a shot in John's direction. Chips of concrete zipped past John's ear. He shifted his aim and fired a volley at the driver. Two of the triad down, and John rolled left away from the remaining officer's position. John didn't think he would be in time, but when he heard the shot it didn't come at him as he expected.

"Fool," flashed across his mind as he struggled to one knee, his skirt getting caught up and hindering his maneuver. The third officer had shot at Donato. There was a spider-web crack and a divot directly in front of Donato's head. John sighted carefully and took the last officer down.

"What are you doing?" John shouted back at Donato.

"What do you mean *me*? I'm going to go and get the data we need!" Donato blinked rapidly as he half-jogged out of the shop.

"How do you expect to get in there? You've set off every alarm in the city!" John picked up his hat and stood, skirt scrunched around his knees.

"I'm going to go in through the hole I made in the fence! That's how I'm getting in!" Donato made to brush past John.

John froze. He rolled his eyes, but couldn't find Nesbit's signal. There was nothing, no static, not a flicker.

"I don't care if you want to help or not, I'm going!" Donato had taken John's inaction as defiance. "The guards should be tied up with recovery efforts anyway..."

John dropped the hat and slapped his hand onto Donato's collar bone, twisting up a handful of shirt. Using his opponent's unbalanced stance John twisted at the hip and half-threw, half-dragged Donato up against the front panel of the triad's vehicle.

"I've lost Nesbit's signal. IF something has happened to my partner because of this, there won't be any place on this planet for you to hide." John's right eye sensor blipped. He spun and fired directly into the head of the driver he'd failed to finish off before. Releasing Donato, he snatched up his hat, tossed the still-warm Stinger into his bag, and started trotting toward the government building he'd taken so much time building his cover story for, not caring if Donato followed. More sirens screamed in the distance.

It was a short jog, but John was still glad he'd put his favorite ops shoes on. He could see the jagged points of the fence looking like broken teeth and a pile of rubble strewn in a huge radius around the back of the building. Still no signal.

He hiked his skirt up further and hopped into the remains of the back garden through the gap in the fence. Reaching his hand into his bag he brought the warm Stinger back into view. "Nesbit," he whispered. Gravel crunched behind him. Looking back, he saw that Donato had indeed followed. There was a flash in his retinal sensor, still on since he'd scanned the shop. He dropped flat to the ground. One of the guards popped into view from behind a broken piece of concrete wall and shots echoed out.

Donato cried out in pain and went down. John squirmed behind a piece of debris as the next shot ricocheted past him.

"I'm hit. Ah! You've got the help me!" Donato whined in a high pitch.

John's sensor picked up a second guardsman headed their way, but he had no angle. John wasn't going to be able to keep behind his cover and stop both the guards from finishing off Donato. He didn't hesitate.

Breaking cover he fired a shot in the direction of the closest guard and spun to take aim at the next. As his vision zeroed in on the second he realized he was too late. The guard's gun barrel pointed right at him.

Just as John thought he was done for something shot out of a pile of debris and collided with the shooter's groin. It was Mrs. Nesbit. The shooter made a horrendous squeal and failed to fire at all. Nesbit clawed at the guard's leg while tearing at his groin with her teeth. Her digging claws worked faster on leg than they did on dirt.

Another shot rang out as the closest guard fired back at Nesbit, attempting to stop the attack. John's rage returned and his aim steadied. One shot, and the first guard went down. His second shot was mercy for the guard with the savaged legs and groin.

Mrs. Nesbit turned and darted in and out of the rubble, racing back and forth, up and over on a path that defied logic, using her smaller stature to go under and through places John would never have thought were a clear route. He smirked at the idea of trying to squeeze a shepherd into that mess.

"Help me. I still need to get the data." Donato pulled himself to his feet and struggled toward John.

John turned and stooped as a filthy, bloodied Mrs. Nesbit hopped into his arms. He held her close for just a moment, then started looking her over to see if she was hurt. He noted the wound on the back of her neck that had apparently taken out her transmitter implant. All her other parts were in order, if a little messy. He peeled back a section of her ops harness and checked it. The dull red mini LED flashed twice in quick succession. She'd gotten the data and gotten out in time.

"You need to help me!" Donato all but whined as he staggered past John.

John plopped Nesbit back into her bag seat and grabbed shirt again, yanking Donato toward the hole in the opposite side of the fence. They might have time to make it to the extraction point if they could avoid any other trouble. Not likely as sirens wailed in the background.

"The job here is done, despite all your stupidity," John spat. "My partner finished the job."

"But, what do you mean?" Donato looked genuinely confused. "It couldn't have done..." Donato apparently lost his thought as the dog's face lurched out of the bag, fangs bared in a blood-spattered visage, growling the whole time.

"Do not mess with my partner ever again." John smiled as he jogged along. "Mrs. Nesbit is one mean hunting bitch."

EGO TRIP

Peter Prellwitz

Earth date: Wednesday, October 11, 2389

"As the shuttle I had taken from Earth passed clear of the Moon, I saw her for the first time, hanging in space, still and quiet, yet also threatening. It was the heavy cruiser *Knowler's Bane,* and with the recent destruction of the feared Martian cruiser *John Adams* finally accomplished, this ship—called *Bane* by its crew—was perhaps the most powerful in the system."

Thia Naylor reread her paragraph. Too over the top? *No,* she thought, unconsciously shaking her head. It was just bold enough to grab attention. And the netzine *Terran Revealed* was read by those who wanted to see what lay beneath the surface of the obvious. They wanted to be shown the real workings of their public servants, their celebrities, and their military. Thia had little use for the first two, instead focusing her investigative reporting skills on the Interplanetary Transit Authority. As Earth's protector, the ITA had battled against Mars and her people these last sixteen years, suffering many setbacks. Now in the fourth war, ITA had achieved all but total victory. *Knowler's Bane* was going to Mars on a final attack run, hoping to break the will of the few thousands that remained on the red planet and end the wars. Wonderful news, but there were some who wondered whether this was less about ending the war and more about revenge for the hundreds of millions killed on Earth during the conflict. And many who wondered were *Terran Revealed* netters.

"Ms. Naylor?" the pilot called out over the static-laden intercom. The *Bane's* starboard fusion engines had been badly damaged on the last tour and disrupted short-range communications. "We're on final approach to the *Knowler's Bane* and I'm required to inform you that full monitoring will commence in less than thirty seconds. Please secure for landing and boarding clearance."

The comm popped and then shut off; a sure tip-off that monitoring had already begun. Thia debated typing some cover copy—letting herself be monitored as she wrote positive material on the ship—but didn't want to raise suspicions for attempting a well-known ploy. And with the lead she'd been given, Thia didn't want to risk gaining extra scrutiny, which would already be high on a war assignment. Instead, she exited her sliver puterverse access and settled into her seat. The only passenger on the smallish shuttle, she had the best seat; her baggage the second best. She ized her Press Credid card to her blouse, the card and blouse forming a positive and negative field, bonding to each other.

Her stomach shifted and rebelled slightly as the gravity altered unexpectedly for a brief moment. "Captured escort," came the explanation over the comm. "Secured docking on Pad 1 of civilian hanger in three minutes. Ship's time is 1731 Greenwich Mean Time."

Five minutes later, Thia exited the shuttle onto the small, tightly secured hanger of *Knowler's Bane*. She had the hanger to herself. There were pads for three shuttles and one was occupied. Nearly identical to the one she'd just disembarked from, the shuttle on Pad 3 was closed up and dark. No hanger crew were evident and her pilot remained in their shuttle. Looking ten meters up to the control bay observation port, the aligned titanium of the window had been shifted from transparent to opaque. Beneath the window was a door, also opaque; the only apparent egress into the ship from the hanger, though she knew there would have to be others.

Not one to wait for things to happen to her, Thia walked toward the one door. She snapped her fingers and her suitcase moved behind her and followed.

Less than ten meters from the door, it suddenly became transparent, showing her an escort of two. They stepped through, an unlikely pair for crew members. The taller one was a fairly handsome woman, perhaps in her forties, with short, blonde hair drifting to gray that curled just past her ears. She wore a plain ITA uniform and a cool, distant smile. She looked to be in excellent condition—not surprising on a combat ship—but the most striking feature were her amber eyes, deep inside which were flashes of color as her programmed mind interfaced with the ship's puterverse at speeds far beyond human ability. Thia inhaled sharply, somewhat offended. The woman was a ripe.

The second member of the greeting party was a dachshund. Short, black, with tan paws and snout, he was large—maybe massing 15 kilos—but seemed trim. She looked at him and he at her a moment before Thia shook her head and looked back at the woman who had stopped directly in front of her.

"Welcome aboard the ITA combat vessel *Knowler's Bane.* You are Corinthia Naylor, war correspondent for the netzine *Terran Revealed*, Denver, Colorado," she stated with a flat voice but still smiling. "Your retinal patterns match to within a tolerance of .02 percent of the recorded image. I am the ship's ripe, Daisy." She waved a hand at the dachshund. "This is the ship's mascot, Ego. We are to escort you to your quarters. Follow me, please."

"Wait a minute, Daisy," Thia said, her irritation creeping into her tone. "Why are you my escort? Doesn't Captain Woodward know the insult he is giving me by sending a ripe and a... a dog? And an illegal breed at that."

Daisy turned back toward her, still smiling. "The captain does send his apologies for the breach in etiquette in appointing me to greet you, but it cannot be avoided. All other crew are engaged in prelaunch activities. We will be underway within twenty minutes, now that you're aboard. As for Ego, the dachshund breed is illegal on Earth, but while this is a Terran ship, it is under ITA military jurisdiction, which makes no statement concerning the breed. Now, if you will follow me, I'll answer any further questions as we go." She turned toward the door and passed through, followed closely by Ego, thus forcing Thia to follow, her suitcase eager to take up the rear of the odd procession.

She stepped up her pace and came beside Daisy. Thia tapped her right ear, which activated her subdermal cording bot.

"How is it that you are available if the ship is in prelaunch status?" Thia asked. "As the ship's ripe, your duties must be many and varied."

Daisy turned her face toward Thia. Though the woman had once been human, her persona was now gone, that aspect of her mind partitioned off from her consciousness and reality, forever lost; there was no known way to return.

And a human mind could be riped many times, each different from the other. A prostitute; a worker in a high risk occupation; a control system at a factory; the options were nearly limitless. And in each riping came a personality, programmed to be obedient or efficient; sexual or mechanical;

calm or forceful; content or driven; again, the options were limitless. Thia wondered how many of these ripings this mind had already been through; how many bodies or machines it had occupied over the decades or even centuries; an ephemeral transferal of the nebulous mind—and some said soul—to wherever it was required, a new persona fitting the needs of whomever had ownership.

Daisy smiled, just as she was programmed to do.

"They are, Ms. Naylor. But I am attending to them as we speak. I am currently operating at nineteen percent capacity."

"And how much of that is being used by our conversation?"

"Less than one-tenth of one percent. If you have no further questions, I am required to ask if you understand and agree to the *Articles of Civilian Conduct* aboard a military ship in combat." Thia nodded. "Very good. Also, that you understand you are under military law while aboard the *Knowler's Bane,* and are subject to the procedures and penalties as detailed in the ITA *Code of Military Conduct.*" A second nod. "Very good. Finally, that you understand that as we are in a state of war with the humans on Mars, and that once we are underway this ship will be considered in a state of combat, that such procedures and penalties increase in swiftness and harshness, as recorded in Sections 21, 23, and 86 of the ITA *Code of Military Conduct.*" A final nod. "Very good. Please step onto the eledisc."

They'd arrived at the eledisc tube. As they stepped on, there came a flash beneath their feet as a disc of planed solid energy appeared. It was more than large enough to accommodate both humans, the dog, and the suitcase. "Deck 5," Daisy stated. It began lifting them. She turned to Thia. "Your quarters are on Deck 5. We are on Deck 11. You have escorted access to Decks 3 through 17. You may not access Decks 1 or 2 unless given explicit permission by Captain Woodward. Decks 18 through 24 are forbidden to you."

"Military systems and weaponry?" Thia asked. Daisy nodded. That much information was universally known, just as it was known by all that Decks 3 through 17 were support systems, living quarters, hangers, auxiliary and backup systems, storage and other such uninteresting ship functions.

They arrived at Deck 5 and went to their right only five meters before stopping at a shimmering door of planed energy on the left. Daisy waved her hand over it and the shimmer faded, revealing the entrance to a small bedroom.

"These are private quarters 526 and are yours for the duration of your assignment."

"Thank you. When can I expect my escort?"

Daisy pointed to Ego, who was already entering the room to inspect it. Thia stared at the dachshund for a moment when realization hit. She looked up sharply at Daisy.

"You're kidding. The *dog* is my ship's escort? You can't be serious."

"I am always serious, Ms. Naylor, but I'm assuming your incredulity is directed toward the situation and Captain Woodward, who ordered it. Since this is your first mission aboard the *Knowler's Bane,* I conclude you are unaware of ship procedure. Yes, Ego is your escort. He has been trained to go to any approved location you clearly state to him. You will then follow him. He will ignore any location outside your access rights."

"So he stays with me the entire time?"

"That is correct, Ms. Naylor."

"What if I'm allergic to dogs? Or just don't like them? Or am too insulted by this treatment to accept it?"

"In all three scenarios, my response is the same: I will escort you to the civilian shuttle hanger and you may depart at any time in the next thirty-eight minutes, which is your shuttle's maximum safe travelling distance. Afterward, if you do not agree to ship procedure—or cannot—you will be detained in your quarters for the duration and Ego will be reassigned as ship mascot."

Thia knew there would be no point in arguing with a ship's ripe. Daisy had no more control over responses and thought patterns than a computer, which she was little more than. Though she was angry and insulted by Captain Woodward's treatment, Thia had a grudging respect for how well he'd corralled her. For now.

Rather than acknowledge to Daisy how well she'd been handled, however, Thia simply walked into her quarters and activated the energy door behind her. She pretended the rude snub would somehow reach the ripe and stab at her ego. But Thia had enough experience with ship's ripes on her numerous war assignments to know Daisy had no ego to stab.

Neither did the other Ego. He was snuffling around the room, eager and happy to explore the new surroundings. He stuck his nose on and under everything, then, when Thia unlocked and opened her bag, he jumped up on the bed to sniff her belongings.

"Hey," Thia snapped. "I'll let you sleep anywhere on the floor that you want, but the bed's mine. So off!" She made a half-hearted swipe at Ego's backside. He jumped a little to one side, dodging the light reprimand, and looked at her with forgiving eyes. Sensing a little give in Thia's attitude, Ego then buried his head into the blanket and looked slyly at her from the side.

"Good technique," Thia conceded, unable to resist smiling. "I can see why your relatives are all over the galaxy. Your cuteness level is off the scales. All right, you can stay."

She unpacked, then slid her bag under the bed, unlocked. At some point she knew it would be searched, and always enjoyed making it harder for them. This time, however, she did have something to keep hidden, so she left it unlocked. An odd sort of strategy, but one that had worked often for her.

Thia straightened, then looked over at her new companion. "Time to get to work. Okay, Ego, take me to the nearest crew's mess."

Ego gave a sneeze, then jumped down off the bed. He trotted over to the door and waited, wagging his tail while staring at it.

"Sorry. Guess the door won't open without me. Okay, I'm coming."

Thia turned off the door and they left. Ego took off to his left at a brisk trot, forcing Thia to hurriedly close and seal her room and chase after him to catch up.

The crew's mess was on Deck 5, so they didn't need an eledisc. Thia didn't really care; she was just testing Ego. To maintain a sense of normalcy, though, she went ahead and interviewed the three crewmen there, doing vacuum pieces she'd never put in *Revealed,* but could pick up some creds selling to some feel-good netzine. She did discover that the trip to Mars would be about seventy hours, due to ongoing repairs to the damaged starboard engines. She was glad to hear that unexpected news; the lead she'd been given was convincing but also vague. It would take time to follow it without being caught.

Leaving the mess with Ego in tow, Thia looked both ways along the corridor. The *Bane* had an overall length of three hundred and twenty-eight meters, with all but fifty-two meters of it being habitable, and a beam of ninety-seven meters and twenty-four decks. There were any number of place she could ask to be taken to; none of them interesting. The reality of having an escort she couldn't complement, establish a rapport with, bribe, bully, guilt, or otherwise manipulate was sinking in. Woodward, whom she'd never met, was obviously an accomplished captain or he wouldn't have this command. But this handling of Thia was brilliant, much to her disgust.

They wandered the various decks she was allowed for the next two hours, achieving little. Thia would try to work an angle to a story but would only get replies from the crew and minor officers that were straight from the ITA PR department. She'd smile and thank her source of vapid information, then give Ego the next destination that she wanted to be led to. It became obvious there was nothing for her other than the helpful tones of a well-trained crew that had nothing to tell her.

Or almost nothing. It was back in the mess on Deck 5, interviewing AB Fischer, that the first snippet of a clue came out that the *Knowler's Bane* did indeed have a story to tell.

"So how long have you served on the *Bane*, Gregory?" she asked. They were seated across from each other at the end of a mess table. Fischer was just finishing his dinner. Ego was off, using his cuteness to scam scraps from the many crew members who were having a late dinner.

"Four years now, Ms. Naylor," he replied.

"And what are your duties?"

"I'm a Mechanics & Systems Assistant, ma'am. I do general upkeep, upgrade and repair of internal systems."

With some effort, Thia refrained from moaning. This made the fourth crew member in thirty minutes to describe their duties with those exact words. She tried a slightly different tact. Anything to get something useable.

"There seem to be a good number of you with those duties. I'm sure the *Bane* is in excellent condition. Were you involved in damage control after your fight with the *John Adams*?"

"Everybody was, Ms. Naylor," he replied frankly. "I want those Martians dead just like anybody else, but... damn... they put up a fight. Yeah, I was on damage control after that. Even the Captain was. Took us two weeks to get the *Bane* home from Mars."

Still nothing new. This was all common knowledge. The three-day running combat, the loss of a dozen ITA combat ships, and the ending of the fatally wounded *John Adams* as she dove into Mars itself to make certain that her one-of-a-kind technologies would not be copied and used against the Martian people. The tidbit about the captain pitching in to do damage control was mildly interesting. Time to wind up the interview.

"So did you get any other stations to work during damage control?"

"A few, yeah. But since I'm lead MA for Eledisc 4, they wanted me to stay focused on getting..."

There came a small yip from Ego, who'd returned and was sitting under them. Fischer started a bit and looked down at Ego. He then looked back at Thia.

"Excuse me, Ms. Naylor. I need to return to my duties." He stood and left abruptly, dropping his tray off on the way out. He never looked back.

Thia and Ego returned to her quarters, Ego leading and following as various things caught his attention. Once inside, she secured her door and pulled out her suitcase and ized it open.

It had been searched, and they had missed what she'd hidden. She opened the fabric along the spine which had the assembly for powering and controlling the case's movement, rudimentary judgment, personality, and recognition matrix. She pressed a small area near the case's small power cell and a blue indicator flashed twice. It now also powered the illegal puterverse access portal on her Press Credid card, completely inert and undetectable until that moment. It could only send burst transmissions—a hundred nanoseconds at a time—but it was untraceable and unmonitored, even by ITA. She resealed the luggage and locked it this time typing an alphanumeric code, then slipped it under the bed. The power transfer was good up to a kilometer, so Thia had the run of the ship. And she knew exactly where she wanted to go.

"Let's make one more trip, okay, Ego?" she asked the dachshund, who'd been stretched out on the bed, watching her with admiring eyes. "Take me to Eledisc 4."

Ego quickly came to his feet, then jumped lightly to the deck and ran to the door, overjoyed at the chance to help his companion. Thia opened the door and Ego scampered to the right and down the corridor. Again, Thia could not resist a smile and laugh. She'd versed about the breed, as had just about everyone. Dachshunds were the galaxy's mystery. Though no truly sentient life had yet been found in over two centuries of exploration, life abounded on Earth-type planets. But for all the billions of animal, bird, fish, insect, and plant species that had been found and catalogued, nothing was precisely like anything else from planet to planet. Except dachshunds. They were the crazy constant, appearing on all planets for no good reason, all with the same genetic makeup, and identical to the dachshunds that had once been on Earth before being outlawed as a xenospecies in the late 23rd century. Nobody knew why, but given their ease and grace in space travel, it was half-humorously, half-incredulously speculated that perhaps wiener dogs had once ruled the cosmos.

Ego slid to a stop in front of an eledisc tube that was designated '4' and got on. He turned back at Thia and gave a yip of victory. She stepped on.

"Deck 3, please." The energy plane glimmered and they moved quickly up two decks. Thia tapped her credid. It was now scanning. She had less than a minute before it would be detected.

"Deck 17, please."

The eledisc descended fourteen decks without incident. It reached Deck 17 and dinged. Thia tapped her credid again, powering it down, and stepped off the eledisc. She didn't need to do anything on this deck, which was mainly hydroponics and casimir drive power collectors. In fact, she very much wanted to get back to her quarters and see if the scan found what she suspected. But while taking rides up and down an eledisc might be fun for a dog, it was sure to raise suspicion if a reporter did it. So she and Ego walked around Deck 17 for twenty minutes and interviewed the two crew members who could spare the time. Finally, she had Ego escort her to Eledisc 5, where they ascended the twelve decks to Deck 5 and their quarters.

It was close to midnight when Thia typed out the final sentence on her sure-to-be-ITA-approved transcript and hit Commit/Send. She always typed when on board. Not only did it give an added sense of accomplishment to her as opposed to normal direct access to the puterverse, it was also more difficult to be tracked or spied upon. And it set a pattern for when she really did need to type out the true journalism she did and was respected for from fellow war correspondents.

The sliver puterverse access sent an open copy to the ship's comm control office and an encrypted copy to the *Revealed* office. Once CCO had analyzed and approved her submission, the encrypted copy could be unlocked by her editor. Thia didn't care. Her netzine wouldn't publish this article, except possibly to mislead ITA. But by submitting an article, they did know that Thia was on to something, and they would power up their anonymous puterverse location to accept her actual report, which would show up within two days. And it would be quite the report.

Thia looked over at her Press Credid card, which projected a phased holographic image above it that could only be seen by her through a holocontact lens on her right eye. The image showed the *Knowler Bane's* secret. She didn't have twenty-four decks; she had twenty-five.

Twelve up. Thirteen down. There was an extra deck between 14 and 15, and it was accessible from Eledisc 4. Whatever went on there, it was not only being kept secret from most ship personnel, it was almost certainly being kept secret from Earth government and the population. It held secrets that would probably be shocking to the general public. And embarrassing. What was there, Thia had no idea. But she was going to find out within the next day. As much as she wanted to go tonight, she knew she'd be under extra surveillance during the first twenty-four hours on board. Better to continue cementing her passive role as a patriotic reporter and do another round of interviews tomorrow, then investigate Deck 14.5 tomorrow night.

She shut down her systems and stood up from the small work area. She'd changed into her sleeping clothes two hours earlier before starting the report, and was ready for bed. Ego had long since claimed the foot end of her mattress and was curled up and making a soft snore. He woke up when she got under the covers and stretched, giving a yawn. He wagged his tail half-heartedly, then crawled under the covers and back down to her feet and began licking them. It was a bit of a surprise for Thia, though she'd heard dachshunds were like that. And it did feel wonderful, so she allowed it. She called for the lights and the room went dark save for a small glow from her Press Credid card on the work area.

Like many who'd spent years at war, Thia had learned to sleep when opportunity allowed and had drifted off in less than five minutes, despite the anticipation of what tomorrow would bring.

She woke abruptly. The room was set to brighten as the ship's day shift began, but it was still dark. She lay still in her bed, staring up at the ceiling, trying to recall what had awoken her. Either that or for the sound to repeat itself.

It was the latter. There was a soft pulling sound. Thia felt chilled. Someone was in her room and under her bed. But no grown person could really fit beneath the low bed. In growing fear, she heard tapping on the case's alphanumeric pad. The tapping was smooth and rapid, like a child's nimble fingers playing a favorite game. Except they didn't sound like fingers. They sounded like… like…

Childhood nightmares of monsters and things not-quite-seen but which exuded evil swept over Thia, turning her chills into sweats. She'd been reporting on the wars for eight years now. She'd been on ships under attack a half-dozen times. Had been embedded with dropship shock troops as they'd landed on Mars and begun their slaughter. Had even been captured briefly by the Martians during the Ceres peace negotiations of the Third War. She'd been alarmed, frightened, and scared many times. But never had she experienced the immobilizing horror that now left her helpless.

She shifted her foot to see if she could rouse Ego. Dachshunds were known for the tenaciousness and recklessness in fights. Perhaps he'd help.

Ego's warm body twitched, so she nudged him again. He had to be in a deep sleep to not wake up from her prodding. The sound under the bed paused for a moment, as if listening. Thia lay still and after a moment, the tapping continued as the intruder continued to work the lock pad.

She was about to nudge Ego a third time when the suitcase gave the four-note access tune and unlocked. The tune also unlocked Thia's body from its frozen terror and put her back in the present. She felt anger rising up and a return of control. This invasion of privacy could not be tolerated, even under these circumstances!

"Lights full on," she called. The rustling under the bed continued as her luggage was searched. "Lights on!" she repeated. But the room stayed dark.

There came a movement from Ego now. In the dim light of the credid card, she could make out the bump in the blankets shift and grow as Ego got to his feet. He worked his way under the blankets and toward the edge of the bed to her left. He paused with just his snout hanging out, listening to the sounds coming from under the bed.

"Get him, Ego!" she whispered. Ego turned his head to look at her.

Deep inside his eyes, there was an amber glimmer. With deliberate ease, Ego rose up to his hind feet on the bed and faced Thia. He took a half-dozen steps toward her until he was against the left side of her midriff, staring down at her with anger and... and contempt.

Thia heard a small snort on the right side of the bed and turned her head to see another dachshund, standing on its hind legs with its snout on the bed not ten centimeters from her face, staring at her with suspicion and hatred. It gave a short snort and a lip curled slightly, revealing its teeth. The horror crashed over her as she realized what was happening on Deck 14.5 and why ITA didn't want it discovered.

They were riping animals.

Riping technology had been in use in growing forms and purposes for just over three centuries. Almost from its inception, however, the riping of an animal had been outlawed. Not because of the moral implications of placing a human mind into an animal's brain, but because the instincts inherent to a species played havoc with the programmed human mind, twisting it in ways that were both extreme and highly unstable. And dachshunds were inherently vicious predators; their instincts drove them to hunt without fear and kill without mercy.

Ego lowered himself and planted his front two paws on her chest. She looked back at him, unable to breathe. Not from his weight but because of his presence. Her body trembled uncontrollably. He stared at her for a moment, then looked briefly at the other dachshund. Although no words or sounds were exchanged, she was certain they were communicating, for the dog turned and walked on it hind legs to the desk. Thia lifted her head slightly to look, but Ego put a front paw on her forehead and pushed it down. He turned his head toward the activities of the other dog. There came the sound of the chair being moved closer, followed by scuffling noises as it climbed onto the chair. Ego nodded his head once and the room went pitch black as the other dog deactivated Thia's Press Credid card. There came the sound of the dog jumping down and landing as a human might. She heard clicking noises from back claws as the dog walked across the floor and worked the door controls with its front paws to allow entry.

Thia's heart pounded uncontrollably, the only movement her body could make beside the short, raspy breaths of terror her lungs could manage. In the few seconds after the room plunged into darkness, her eyes adjusted enough that she saw the dim amber deep in Ego's eyes as he turned his head back and looked down to her. He placed his head beside her left ear and she felt his controlled breathing, saw the dog's left eye close to hers. His snout touched her ear and she felt his lips curl back against her cheek, teeth pressed up against her, and she heard a growl of cold, programmed evil that overwhelmed her mind and shut it down into deep, clutching horrors of primal nightmares.

Thia struggled to escape from her quagmire of darkness. Her thoughts spun and mutated, showing Ego and his glowing eyes as they changed to the fiery eyes of a burning demon, which made her retch and convulse. Sobbing, she thrashed on the bed and pulled at the sheets. But there were no sheets, and it wasn't her bed. A blinding light penetrated her closed eyes and she shouted and raised herself up on her hands. Blinking rapidly, she realized she was lying on the deck of a large, unfamiliar room. There three men stood over her. One held a UV transkin injector.

"Sir?" one of the men called out. "She's conscious."

There was a licking sensation on her hand. She looked down to see...

Ego looked up at her and wagged his tail slightly.

Screaming, she jumped to her feet and tried to back away. Two of the men—uniformed guards—took her by the upper arms, less to restrain her and more to keep her from falling over, because her balance was far off.

She shook her head to clear the cobwebs, but couldn't. Perhaps that was for the best: they somewhat muted the terror of seeing Ego. Thia looked down at her hand. Had she been drugged? Not knowing made it worse. She also realized she was still in her night clothes. She'd never felt so exposed or helpless. A blurry figure stepped up. Thia blinked rapidly and turned her head from the light shining on her.

"Ms. Naylor? It's a pleasure to finally meet you. I'm Captain Woodward."

"Cap...Captain Woodword..." she stammered out. Where were her wits? What was wrong with her? She turned her head back to him "Where am I? What have you done... done... to me? Did... did... you... drug me?"

"Done? Not a lot. Just an anti-shock serum to keep you steadier of emotion. I apologize for the side effects you're feeling. You were in deep shock when my men entered your quarters, so when an initial dose didn't revive you after twenty minutes, I ordered a second. You'll be calmer, but more... compliant for a few hours. Not to be concerned; you'll be fine. That is, so long as Ego doesn't lick you again."

Thia jerked her head to Ego, who was sitting on the floor, admiring her. She touched her hand where he'd licked it, then looked at Woodward, who smiled.

"Ego has been altered so his saliva delivers a topical psychosomatic drug to humans. He's the one who's been drugging you."

"As for where you are... this is Red Deck; the one you found during your eledisc trips awhile ago. Please... have a look around; it's not that big."

The room was only the size of a crew's mess, though that was the only comparison. Its main function seemed to be that of a medical lab or sick bay. Occupying the center and left of the room were four bays set up in two pairs; one bay in each pair having identical riping equipment, monitors and instruments. The other two bays had a different set of identical equipment, though she didn't recognize it.

The right side of the room had a communications setup, with holos puterverse monitors covering the bulkhead. There were a half dozen uniformed men monitoring them, with another half dozen men—probably officers—behind them at command stations. All the men were wearing ITA uniforms, but with an additional patch on their right sleeve with a blue 'N' on it.

On the far wall was a closed door. The captain noticed her looking at it.

"That leads to the crew quarters and mess. There are thirty-two officers and crew total, and they never leave this deck." He looked at Thia and shook his head. "Which now applies to you as well. You'll be confined to Red Deck for the duration of the wars, and probably some time afterward, I'm afraid. Still, better than being spaced, which is what your netzine has been informed. I believe, Ms. Naylor, that you're not going to be welcome on Earth again. You may wish to consider permanent emigration when released."

"I don't un...understand," Thia said in a slow speech. Collecting her thoughts was difficult. "This isn't a sanctioned op... op... operation, isit? Is... it?"

"Oh, it's sanctioned," Woodward replied. "Just not by ITA. This is a hidden branch that's been operating since before the first war. We do the things nobody wants to know about."

"W...we?"

"I've been an agent for fourteen years," he said simply.

"Captain?" an officer from the comm side called. "We have a green on Location A43. Permission to execute?"

"A moment, Lieutenant. Come, Ms. Naylor. The news reporter in you will want to see this." He nodded to the two men holding her and they half-assisted, half-dragged her to the comm panel where the lieutenant waited.

"You've experienced the riping side of the operation first hand. We've been successfully riping dogs for a decade now. Dachshunds are among the best subjects, though bulldogs, beagles and—oddly enough—dalmatians are also excellent candidates. We've been able to keep continuous surveillance on most of the significant political figures on Earth for years. But for Martians, we only used dachshunds. Their military caught on fairly early and actually used our tactics against us, purposely feeding us false information that led to the destruction of dozens of our ships. But now that the wars are all but over, the remnants are unaware of our advancements and tactics, so we're able to reintroduce our canine agents, though retasked, now that the objectives have changed." He turned to the lieutenant. "Display and prime."

The holo brightened and sharpened, showing a low view of a cavern floor. The view lifted up and Thia saw a bank of atmospheric converters; the kind used by Martians to generate a breathable atmosphere in sealed locations. There were twenty or thirty people—men, women, and children—in the cavern, doing various activities.

"A Martian refuge," Woodward said. "They're buried deep underground in a hundred locations. Most are impossible to bombard from space and are defended with such determination that we'd lose a hundred troops from direct assault and still not reach them. So, we introduce a riped dachshund in an area that they send scouting parties to, and sometimes they bring them back."

"And you... you... f-f-find out their weak points to... to... attack," Thia stammered.

"Weak points?" Woodward replied, then shook his head. "No need, Ms. Naylor. We already know their weak point. It's the air builders. Take them out and the Martians die. Well, the ones that survive do."

"Primed, sir," The lieutenant said crisply. A blue indicator blinked slowly on his comm panel.

"Sur...vive what?" Thia asked. On the monitor, the view had shifted to a young girl as the dachshund ran to her arms. The captain tapped the blue indicator. The camera flashed to a solid white and blinked out.

"Man's best friend," Woodward replied.

COVERT STRIKE

Jeff Young

THE HARDEST PART WAS SWALLOWING THE MOLECULAR SUIT. ESTEBAN HESI-TATED as he stared down at the cylinder of gray fluid. It didn't matter that there were elements in place in his c-core that would cut off the gag reflex, the autonomic reflex of breathing, and his digestion. All the programming in the world couldn't stop him from hating this part. As well as the part where it all came boiling out his mouth, covered him whole and lay on his eyes like crude oil until his c-core linked up to integrate all of his senses. After that, he felt like a god.

Five members of the infiltration team were already embedded on the asteroid settlement Terra Infirma out in the Ganymede float points. He was the last to arrive. He shouldered his carryall, spared a look at his reflection in the nearby window to ensure that none of that gray slop adhered to his beard stubble. He hated carrying in the msuit this way but knew it would pass inspection. Then Esteban left his crew slot to make his way to the access hatch. Hooking his feet in the toe loops and keeping a grasp on the sidebars, he lurched along with the other passengers. The crew hauler was redolent with sweat and the semi-rotten odor of overworked algae cyclers. His ID fleck listed him as a mining specialist and his key files indicated he was here to deal with some equipment issues—issues that were the result of tampering by Carlos and Isobel. He handed over his fleck to the disinterested security merc who never even acknowledged him, tapping the small computer to his scanner. The merc swept him with the scanner and, once he was satisfied, he lobbed the fleck at Esteban, who caught it before it struck him in the face.

Esteban took one step forward before the other's hand caught his shoulder.

"What the hell's behind your backpack?"

He didn't hesitate, because hesitation was guilt. After all, the merc wasn't after the truly incriminating merchandise in the backpack. All the same, Esteban wasn't going to just give up the main reason he was here. He slid a finger across his fleck and a large number flashed up in green, blinking to indicate a potential credit transfer. Shrugging his shoulder he slid the pack off revealing the cylinder previously nestled against his back. "Go ahead, scan it." He tapped the signature seal. "It's Dom Perignon, hermetically sealed. My friend's getting married. Got him something special."

The merc glared at Esteban for a moment, but his dark eyes remained focused on the fleck in between Esteban's fingers.

"Fine," the guard said pulling out his own fleck and tapping it against Esteban's, "But if that comes back on me...."

"I know, I'll be taking the long walk to the Great Red Spot. Don't worry, I expected to pay an import fee."

"Just doin' my job," replied the merc and gestured Esteban along.

Esteban stepped off onto the reddish surface of the port, bouncing in the low spin. He drew his shoulders up in a sigh of relief and coughed as he sucked in thin air laced with something that smelled like burnt gunpowder. A second scan wouldn't have identified the still form of the hawk in her transit case, but if he could avoid it, why take the chance. *Damn, mercs. Welcome to the Out Rim,* he thought, *where they couldn't even afford anything close to professionals.*

Red dust stuck to everything, dimming the lights, the flash signage, and the clock that read 0600. It even clung to the all of the Out Rim propaganda plastered to the walls. 'Out Rim Free' was the most favored message. They were free all right; free to starve without the support of the Inner System.

Out here, little pockets of rebellion made a lot of noise. Their bid for freedom from the influence of the united worlds of Earth, Mars, and the Moon was doomed to be short-lived. The Out Rim forgot very easily that there was strength in unity and that it took everyone working together to keep the masses of the Inner System fed, clothed, and sheltered.

Esteban's square jaw betrayed no reaction as he shuffled along. He might be here in the Gany Float points with Jupiter filling a substantial portion of the sky but his oath was to protect the Inner System.

His ire was interrupted by a pair of arms that slid around his waist from behind. The short blonde stubble of Isobel's hair brushed the side of his neck as she whispered, "Good morning, Easy. What the hell took so long?"

Sliding her around to his left, he threw an arm over her shoulders and gave her a clipped smile. Tall and lanky, Isobel had a typical Martian physique. She probably felt right at home in the one-fourth gee of Terra Infirma's spin, whereas he was still adjusting. Esteban had gone on a few missions with Isobel before. She was prickly at times and had a reputation for sarcastic wit. However, her familiarity with information architecture was formidable. She was even rumored to have a wetdrive implanted with enough storage to transport an AI.

Isobel snorted once and took the opportunity to throw him a jab in the ribs. When he pushed her away, she caught his wrist and pulled him down one of the corridor ways that branched out from the port. He felt her fingers slide on his wrist and recognized the grip that could let her throw him or pull his arm down to snap it over a knee. Some things didn't change. He let himself be led to the nearest slider cylinder. Just as it started to move, the merc from the port jumped onboard.

"Sure it's not you getting married?" the guard joked leaning against the railing.

Isobel started forward and ran into Esteban's bulk as he stepped in front of her.

The merc snapped a drug capsule open under his nose and inhaled deeply. "I changed my mind. Perhaps we can share out a little of that champagne." He looked Isobel up and down, "And maybe a few other things." His grin was as slick as his hair, yellowed teeth glistening in the passing lights from the stations that flew by. "I'm off duty, so we have all the time in the world."

Looking forward, Esteban saw a break in the pattern of lights. They were coming to an extended area of darkness. He could feel Isobel's hands busy behind him, and he prepared to move.

"Just what I was hoping to hear," said Isobel.

Esteban did the opposite of what the merc was expecting. He twisted forward, arm interlocked with Isobel launching her with his momentum at the guard, who still lounged against the railing. Her knee caught him in the throat and he gave a surprised sigh, sliding to the floor as Isobel rode him down. She sheathed her knife in the merc's flesh right under his ear. When her adversary hit the grating, she reached down and wrenched his head around snapping his neck to be sure. Quickly and efficiently, they pulled the body behind them into the shadows of the rear of the cylinder car, cleaning away any stray blood.

Isobel looked up at Esteban, "Good thing we're almost there, Easy. Get him up and pull up that flack hood. We'll just drag him along between us and it'll look like he's had too much." She pulled out a black, flexible collar and slid it around the merc's neck. "That'll scramble the signal from any tracker in his cranial core. A piece of recycle like this, it'll be a good, long time before anyone notices. They'll just be happy he isn't around."

Esteban reached down and dragged the dead weight up to his shoulder. *Dumb bastard,* he thought looking at the slack, surprised expression on their victim's face. Esteban pushed the merc's eyelids closed. Their lieutenant, Carlos, wasn't going to like it. Like most of the officers in the Inner System Corps, Carlos didn't like much of anything. This wasn't going to help.

Isobel pulled them off at a seedy looking level where half the ceiling lights were out or flickering on the verge of extinction. Passing through the doorway after her, Esteban found himself in a rat hole of an apartment. The omnipresent red dust clung to everything and boot tracks crossed the floor. Trash was piled on and beside the one couch. He slung their burden onto it, dislodging a cloud of dust. Esteban looked strangely at Isobel when she stepped up onto the man's back and pulled aside a cushion to reveal a static cleaner. She ran it over her shoes and then pulled aside the wall hanging above the couch, stepping through the dark gap it concealed. "Do your shoes before you come through," she said handing him the cleaner. "And hurry up, Carlos is waiting."

In the next room, Esteban found himself blinking, his eyes having become accustomed to the inconsistent light. Carlos gave him a quick once over, his jaw tight. Then the lieutenant strode forward to clasp Esteban's hand, pulling him further into a compartment that was the exact opposite of the entry room. Military-grade clip lights revealed an "L" shaped room with cots and aircel mattresses along the walls. Various pieces of equipment covered a heavy field chest. Among them was a long, clear tabular fleck whose surface showed an image of a rotating cut away of Terra Infirma's interior. After snapping the entry panel back into place, Isobel came to rest on one of the cots, reaching for the fleck. Carlos gestured Esteban to the remaining cot as he dropped his short frame down onto the one behind him.

"You're just in time, Sergeant. We're prepared to move tonight." Carlos' voice had a rasp to it that came from too many missions that ended in atmospheric venting. His hair was longer than Isobel's and an even steel grey.

"We'd have gone without you anyway," interjected Isobel, who lay back, lifting the tablet over her head to stare up at the shifting lines on its surface.

Carlos gave her a sharp look, which she pointedly ignored. "Good thing we're not staying long since you brought a casualty with you," he said shaking his head.

"Like that room next door wasn't a casualty already, sir," Isobel replied and then she spun around to launch the fleck at Esteban.

He caught the device easily, his eyes never leaving hers. The map of Terra Infirma was a lopsided ellipsoid deformed by an ancient impact that left a massive crater on its system North end. Highlighted were four two-klick long cylinders than ran North to South along its six-kilometer long central axis, starting at the South end.

Carlos pointed at the longest of the shafts. "That's our target. They're old mine shafts, long abandoned, but there's been a lot of activity there in the last month, as well as excessive high-bandwidth transmissions both in and out. We'll start here." He indicated a join between a regular shaft and the larger cylinder. "You can see with an environment like this where Strike could be very useful."

Esteban glanced at his carryall on the floor. On top was the ovoid case where his companion, the heavily augmented Harris's Hawk, Strike, lay in cryogenic slumber. Strike could easily fly through the area scanning with her sensory adaptations. Since she was still mostly a biological and small in size, she was unlikely to trip any alarms looking for incursions. "What are we expecting, sir?" he asked.

"Odds are, bio weapons," replied Isobel her lips twitching.

Esteban felt that twitch on the inside. Their msuits would protect them but not Strike. What was he getting her into? There were always risks in every operation. Always the chance they might not come back. But he couldn't ask Strike to choose, instead she would do what she always did—trust him.

"Bio weapons that will be designed to affect humans," Carlos' voice cut across Esteban's thoughts.

Esteban blinked and looked away. Was he that obvious? "Yes, sir."

That will have to be good enough for now, Esteban thought, even though he already wished this mission were over. Their escape from Terra Infirma would depend on the remainder of their team. Only Carlos had contact with the other three members who would back up the infiltration team and secure their exit.

Carlos tipped his head in the direction of the other end of the compartment. "The head's down that way. Thought you might like a shower, after being on the transport that long."

Nodding his thanks, Esteban grabbed his carryall and walked toward the small room.

"You use all of the hot water and—" started Isobel.

"And you'll have to join me if you want some," finished Esteban.

"In your dreams, Easy."

Standing there with the water coursing over his head, Esteban thought of home. He guessed it was the hint of salt in the water that brought that memory to mind. Salt was always in the air on the fan deltas where he grew up, except at their centers. The splayed out arcs of rock pulled down from the Andes Mountains and dumped into the sea were covered with manmade soil and irrigated by desalinated water. In a place where land was at a premium, the only solution was to create more. Even though they were artificial, the fan deltas attracted a mix of settlers, including his displaced American parents. Strike had been born there and he looked forward to taking her back after the mission. Something felt so right watching her fly above the fields of the delta with the mountains visible in the background. Instead he was serving Earth more than 600 million kilometers from home. Shaking his head, Esteban got back to the task of washing away the inevitable red dust.

That night, Esteban pulled on his tool vest, which did a good job of concealing the additional hardware that he carried in the pockets lining the interior. He'd fallen asleep after the shower and dreamt of flying. His ultra light was so high up in the sky the joins between the fields below were no longer visible. Still Strike urged him on, and he continued to rise. Just when he thought he could feel the oxygen begin to thin, she'd dove past him, a brown blur lancing downward to Earth. He'd woken up. Lying there, he finally realizing the alarm in his peripheral vision blinked madly to stir him for their mission.

Strike's case was stowed in his backpack and the readout in the corner of his vision counted down the time until she could be decanted. He shoved the tabular fleck into the pack, along with some ration bars. It didn't go all the way down due to the extra compartment on the bottom where he'd hidden four metal cylinders of dangerous payload. The black nano contents would be used to destroy whatever they found today. Both the backpack and the vest he wore under it helped conceal the presence of the illegal flechette gun he strapped to the middle of his lower back.

Carlos gestured Isobel and Esteban ahead of him. Since they'd entered together it made sense that the two of them would travel together. The lieutenant would follow a discrete distance behind them to avoid association. Tools swung from around Isobel's hips and filled pockets on her thighs and calves. He'd watched, surprised, as she folded her linear-accelerator or lin-acc rifle up impossibly small and slid it into her backpack. The last thing he'd seen of the apartment was Carlos setting up a small incendiary bomb that would scour the area free of traces of their DNA and deal with their unexpected guest in the next-door compartment.

In passing, Isobel smacked the body of the merc on the shoulder, "Nobody's missed him yet." She tapped her head, indicating she was listening to the local comm chatter. "Hell I don't blame them." Then she was out the door. Esteban followed, kicking up the red dust. Its gunpowder odor made his nose twitch.

The mining slider had a nasty judder to it that made Esteban's teeth ache. Two other workers shared the ride. The red dust covering them lifted into the air with each shake. The bigger of the two slept. Esteban was happier when the other miner shook the big one awake and they stepped off into an ill-lit shaft. Isobel and Esteban rode it for another two exits before Isobel hit the emergency stop. Esteban held the pin light for her while she went to work on the interface. After she made a few adjustments, Isobel could now set their true destination.

When they arrived the rough mineshaft was full of sharp angles from the illumination of the pin light. Esteban tacked it to his shoulder and stepping forward, pulled Isobel after him. She tapped the fleck in her hand and the slider shot away out of sight.

"There," she said, leaning over the edge to look into the darkness. "That should confuse things. So, you ready to hunt down the latest nasties the Out Rim's brewed up, Easy?"

Esteban snorted once and then started down the shaft.

They traveled about a half a klick through the winding channel until a sudden reflection brought him to a halt. An airlock extended from the rough-hewn wall of the corridor. He unslung his pack while Isobel pressed past him. She pulled out her fleck and started to work on the access panel. Esteban unsealed Strike's case. The green indicator flashing in the corner of his eye signaled she was ready for decanting. He started the process while she opened the airlock. As the biofibre caul melted away from Strike's form,

Esteban looked toward his partner. "Hey, tech head, what's taking so long?"

"Maybe you want to play with quantum-encrypted interfaces while I hold your little feathered friend?"

He shook his head and played the pin light over Strike's form. The cryosleep was unsettling and he hated doing it to her. It made her look like she'd been stuffed by a taxidermist.

Behind him, the airlock chuffed as the large door slid to one side. "Coming, Easy?" asked Isobel as she stepped up. "Or are you going to sit there like usual with your bird in your hand?"

Esteban bit back a reply as he cradled Strike in his right arm and grabbed the ring on the top of the pack, hauling it into the confined space. Isobel slapped her palm on the actuate panel and the door slammed shut. They walked up the ramp to the exit, where Isobel reviewed the panel there.

"Best get your msuit on. From here on in we're on the clock." With that, she yanked the seal of her work coveralls down.

As Esteban turned away, he heard tools hit the floor as she shrugged out of the rest. He placed Strike on top of his pack and then started working out of his clothing. He found it amusing that they hadn't given each other what privacy they could afford due to their nudity, but rather to avoid seeing each other evacuate the msuit from their stomachs. He gave the quiescent mass the signal before he spent any more time thinking about it. In his mind, Esteban knew it only took seconds, but it still felt like he was vomiting out an octopus that then did its best to strangle every inch of him. Damn, he hated as the sensation of the suit covering his face. There was no appreciable transition when the msuit linked with his implants; he just stopped breathing as the msuit infused oxygen directly into his blood. Even though it was only several microns thick, its sensorium gave him the ability to scan through the complete spectrum of incoming radiation and since it was direct input, it put his regular heads-up display to shame. The msuit also mediated his response to the low gee. Hell, the thing was so self-sufficient it could walk him to a med unit if he was injured during wartime.

Isobel stood off to his left, a shapely black shadow of herself reaching for her work coverall. Even though he couldn't see her eyes, the impression of her pointed stare at him and a cocking of her head to one side made him reach for his own clothing as she slid a leg into the coverall. *Check your comline and keep your mind on your work,* reminded Isobel as she shot him a nasty look, then took her closed right fist and stuck it to the middle of her forehead, making the hand sign for "idiot."

When he was kitted up, Esteban reached into the pack for the ration bars. Giving the msuit the command to roll back from his head, he tossed Isobel one of the bars. It may have been purely psychological in nature, but evacuating the msuit always made the wearer hungry. Chewing on the bar, he slid on the pack and picked up Strike. Isobel looked in his direction and then activated the panel on the airlock.

When the other side slid back, the smell of growing things surprised Esteban. Strike squirmed in his arms, talons sinking into the heavy fabric of his work coverall. He moved her to the heavier material that shielded his wrist and forearm. She rasped at him for a moment, hooked beak open, while she lifted each foot up and down until she settled, blinking in the surprisingly bright light.

Looks like someone's got a green thumb. Guess we should find out why, said Isobel, her form limned in the light falling through the open doorway.

She snaked an optic wire out of the doorway and relayed the image to Esteban. There wasn't a discernable horizon in the half-kilometer wide cylindrical corridor. The curvature was obvious to either side and green plants covered everything. Jutting up from the surface were plinth-like pylons. The pylons wound in a spiraling pattern into the distance in either direction gradually becoming indistinct. Vines grew around them and plants sprouted from their surfaces, even small trees in the spaces between them. The light source, like a white-hot thread, plunged down the center, held up by supports attached to the ground and the ceiling. Blisters covered its surface. They shone with radiance, lit from the fusion reaction at the thread's core.

That's one hell of a lot of plants, was all he could manage at first. Strike fussed on his wrist. She could sense the open space and he knew she was anxious to explore. Esteban signaled the msuit to cover his head once more to confirm his link to Strike. While she was only 52 centimeters tall, her body was dense with micromachinery. Her bones were replaced or augmented with carbon nanoweb and the data store in her lower back could hold massive amounts of information. Like his msuit, Strike's senses were expanded to most of the electromagnetic spectrum. Throughout his service, she was his only constant companion. Since the day he'd found her shoved from her mother's nest in the family's rookery to the day that Earth had called him to serve. What had started as a project to save her and let him experience some of the joy she felt in flight had changed when he'd joined Earth's defense force, but it still kept them together. However, like now, each time he launched her into the sky, he never stopped fearing she might not return.

He glanced at Isobel, watching her unfold her lin-acc and sling its strap over her shoulder. Then he surrendered his eyes to Strike's input. There was no real way to describe what he saw in human terms. Even input from a remote-guided micro-drone wasn't the same. Strike was so fast and sure in her flight. While the input came in a wide spectrum, Strike wasn't overwhelmed. Millions of years of evolution made her flight instincts rock solid as she dipped and rose through the obstacles of the panels. With a whirling arc she swooped around the central light source.

Data came pouring in to Esteban. His implants tabulated figures estimating the output of the fusion source, the illumination, and the temperature gradient until he shunted the information aside to be stored in his own data store. There was wind in the cylinder so there had to be some sort of air circulation. The whistling, the long scrolling columns of data, the infrared and electromagnetic overlays became too much and Esteban pushed all of it to the sides of his peripheral view. For the moment, he just wanted to be with her as she flew.

He never wanted to admit how much he missed this. He'd felt like he'd been trapped in a damn metal box the whole way here, while she had it even worse. At last, now she was finally free.

Checking the distance, Esteban found that she'd flown half the way to the North end of the cylinder. That was when he felt the hand come down on his shoulder. Minimizing her input, he looked up to find Carlos had joined them.

Why all the plants? the other man wondered.

If they have enough then they can stop cracking O_2 from water, sir, Isobel said as she looked back over her shoulder.

But this is more than they'd even need for that. It's almost too much for even self sufficiency.

Esteban interrupted, *Sir, Strike's found the security monitors. They are along the central trunk of the lighting system.*

Logical, replied Carlos. *Any sign of the data spike transmissions we detected before?*

Esteban closely watched the map of the interior grow as Strike flew farther North up the cylinder. The only data movement he could discern was along the trunk.

Given the bandwidth flow, is the data traveling up or down the trunk-line? Carlos asked.

Down, replied Esteban as Strike passed the halfway point and through the haze of mist falling from the tops of the pillars in the area, watering the plants below. *I suppose you want me to turn her around.* At Carlos's affirmative Esteban pulled up the map of the interior generated by Strike's flight and messaged her an image indicating the direction in which to proceed. She pulled a tight arc, rushing by the hanging vines, making them swing with her passage. He heard the others' indrawn breaths at the suddenness of the maneuver and chuckled himself. A few moments later Strike flew overhead, looping twice above him before proceeding South. It was always strange to see himself from her viewpoint. It was also heart-warming that she's spared a moment to check in on him. Her red shoulder feathers stood out against the omnipresent green. Then Strike was away, flying faster than before.

In the left of his perception, Esteban saw Isobel building a model of the cylinder's interior. Noninformational lattices of power ran up and down the walls of the cylinder and up each pylon. Smaller lines of a darker hue ran up each pylon as well to monitor the plants health.

So where the hell is everybody? wondered Isobel.

Strike's picking up movement, but they are all agricultural bots, Esteban replied, looking over the information again for larger heat sources. *Maybe this is a secret from most of the colony.*

Carlos broke in, *Isobel, do you have enough information to camouflage us from the overhead monitors?*

Yes, I'll have a patch for our msuits in a moment that will give the transmission characteristics of farming mechs. she replied as she removed the excess tools from her coverall.

There's food growing out there, Esteban commented as he reviewed a close pass of one of the pylons. *But the strange part is that only about a third of it looks harvested. The rest of the plants have gone to seed or the fruit is rotting.*

This makes no sense, stated Carlos, as he leaned against the doorway and peered out into the greenery.

Only because— started Isobel.

We're not looking at it right, finished Esteban. *It's a seed farm. Sure they're generating O_2 and food, but the one thing they depend on Earth for is seed stock. But why would they need this much?*

Isobel had the answer to that question, *If you were creating generation ships....* Her voice trailed off as the enormity of her suggestion hit her.

Carlos ran a hand through his thinning hair. Sweat shone on his forehead. *All right, it's an interesting theory. How about some proof? We'll need that before we go back.*

Esteban turned back to scan the images coming from Strike. When he had enough composited together, he found something interesting.

Sir, there's a path we can follow down the corridor. He hadn't noticed it at first because it spiraled around the cylinder walls and he'd been looking for straight lines. There was also an offset to the way the pylons rose from the floor, so it would be possible to make their way between the loops of the spiral, creating a minimal amount of damage to the plants. If they were lucky they might even avoid leaving an identifiable path to their destination.

Fine. We'll move out. Esteban show us the path. Link the information to Isobel. She can keep feeding us the map as it grows from Strike's feed. Full suits.

Isobel took point, Carlos the center, and Esteban brought up the rear. Even though the pylons broke up the landscape and the arch of ceiling hung like green cloud cover, Esteban was happy to be walking through fields again no matter how strange they were. The msuit overlay marked out the path as they trudged along. Esteban stopped and stared for a moment. Strawberries. How long had it been since he'd even seen a strawberry?

He looked to the right where Strike's footage continued to run. She could see the end of the shaft now. A reddish dome rose above the green where the trunk of the lighting system came to an end. All of the electro-magnetic traffic funneled down to that point. Now she started to register the data spikes that Carlos mentioned. They weren't traveling down the trunk line though. Instead the pulses came from lines running down the outside of the dome. It was an odd structure, more of a lattice than a solid building, and the plants and vines had been cleared away from its sides. Strike flew a close pass and Esteban saw something hanging inside the dome, suspended from the framework. He urged her onward, targeting the interior of the building. She hesitated for a second and then gave in, swooping down between the metal frame and passing close by a strange, organic-looking ball of wiring with an asymmetrical black mass at its center. The intensity of the information flow spiked off of the scale.

For a second, Esteban felt Strike falter. Her wings beat out of time and the view whirled around. Then every input in the msuit flashed white with overload. Esteban fought to close his eyes but couldn't because they weren't even open. Sound roared in his ears and pressure pummeled him all over as his senses were stunned. He crashed forward into a pylon, clawing at the hood of the msuit in an effort to pull it off. Everything hurt. Then, just as suddenly, every last bit of input shut off. He was in absolute blackness. The firewall. The firewall on the msuit must have shut everything down. On one knee, hand leaned against what he assumed was a pylon; he fought the urge to hyperventilate—because he couldn't and it wouldn't make his situation any better. The worst part, despite the sensory deprivation, was that last second of input from Strike. He'd seen her vitals spike, felt her panicked attempt to stop, and then nothing, nothing at all from her because when the msuit overloaded, it had felt like the entire universe had screamed at him in anger. Now he couldn't tell if she was still alive. Hell, he couldn't even be sure *he* was still alive.

He made a fist and struck the pylon. That was all the proof he had for the time being. Esteban fired off a command to the msuit to roll back the hood but the command was ignored. The fail-safes must have deemed the corridor environment too hostile after the recent incident. He stretched out his hands and found his way back to his feet. After a few fumbling attempts, Esteban ran into Carlos. Then the lieutenant's hand came to rest on his shoulder, his command override making the hood of Esteban's suit roll back leaving him blinking in the green light and humid air.

"Where's Isobel, sir?" Esteban asked looking around.

"I have a bad feeling she's gone to the same place that Strike didn't come back from." Carlos pointed to a path cut through the greenery. Then he picked up her abandoned lin-acc rifle. "We need to get her back."

"Yes. Get her back," Esteban replied, although he wasn't particularly thinking of Isobel. He hesitated a moment. "A Faraday cage," he said, "the dome's a Faraday cage, it's designed to keep out signals—wait that's not it. The cage is keeping something *in*. They're not just farming plants here, sir, they're farming artificial intelligences as well, all in the same spot."

He sighed. Twists. AIs that were not given the overriding command to preserve human life. Neither the In Rim or the Out Rim was supposed to be using artificial intelligences in their military forays at all, let alone twists. The Ceres Agreement forbid their use, but that hadn't stopped incidents before. For now, Esteban shrugged off the implications as he ran through the undergrowth after Carlos.

For a moment Esteban caught sight of Isobel ahead of them. She walked a straight path toward the cage, swerving only as necessary to avoid the pylons. The cage was just visible now and Esteban's chest tightened as he thought he saw a small dark gray form with prominent red shoulder patches perched among the copper-colored bars. The twist, it must have reached out through Strike's feed. In the seconds that it took Esteban's msuit to react and throw up the firewall, it had determined what it needed. It needed Isobel and her wetdrive. The AI had commandeered her msuit. Unfortunately, hijacking the suit also captured the soldier. The suits had tremendous flexibility and were designed for independent mobility to help injured soldiers incapable of fighting or even walking on their own. The security on the suit's low-level processing nets were no match for an AI.

Carlos had come to the same conclusion. He'd dropped to one knee and shouldered the lin-acc. Its muzzle tracked toward the distant cage and Esteban was certain the lieutenant was not aiming at the AI. There was a brief whine as the coils spun up the ammunition. Carlos was targeting Strike, the link in the chain that allowed the twist outside access to Isobel. Esteban took a breath and the lieutenant interrupted him before he could speak. "It's not a choice between your bird and her, son. Not a choice at all."

Isobel was 400 yards away and moving onward. "Sir, just let me try. She's got instinct triggers built in that I can use to shy her away from the cage. Just," he stopped and took a ragged breath, "just let me try."

Carlos never took his eye from the scope, "Then try. You've got 30 seconds."

Esteban fought his way around the msuit's firewall until it gave him a comm link to Strike. Then he started putting together the necessary commands. In the meantime, he spoke to her. "Hey girl, it's Easy. You recognize my voice don't you? Now I want you to listen because I need you here with me. I want you to come to me."

"Damn," Carlos said through gritted teeth, "she's turned so she's looking our way. Whatever you're going to do, make it fast."

"Strike, I want you to come to me," said Esteban as he readied the trigger. He fired off the command and the brown form of Strike disappeared from his view. "Come to me, Strike. Come to me," he shouted, praying that his voice would carry down the cylinder. He couldn't see her. She was gone. Isobel had also dropped from sight. Carlos lowered the lin-acc and rose to his feet. Esteban loped through the green after Carlos.

Esteban considered the implications as he ran. If the Out Rim were planning on creating generation ships, then they would need pilots. Pilots who could look after vast, complex ships and, more importantly, make choices that would be for the greater good. It would take a twist to make a choice where most of the crew survived and some did not. A standard

AI would never choose if it had to harm a human.

But why had the AI reacted like it did? Then it came to him, they'd caged it within sight of the outside world and it wanted out. Just like Strike always longed to be free when he put her in the roost at home for too long, the twist wanted to be free. No wonder the twist reacted the way it had. It saw Isobel as a means to that end.

Isobel lay just ahead sprawled in the foliage. Esteban threw back his head, scanning the space overhead in search of Strike. When he did finally see her, he was surprised that she still circled the cage at the end of the corridor. Was she still under the twist's thrall? Worry knotted his gut until he noticed that Strike's targeting centered on him. She knew right where he was. If the AI were in control, it would have targeted all of them. It was a slim piece of evidence to make a case with, but Esteban was certain she was now free from coercion. As Carlos knelt by Isobel and used his overrides to rollback the msuit from her head, Esteban kept thinking about Strike's behavior. He'd once surprised a wild Harris's Hawk as it sat outside of Strike's roost, staring in at her. For a while it had hung around on occasion coming to rest on the cage itself. Was it possible that Strike shared a similar empathy with the twist?

Isobel gave a ragged breath, distracting Esteban from his thoughts. He turned to her as her eyes flickered open.

"Well this sure as hell isn't heaven, since Easy's here." With that she shook her head and, brushing off the lieutenant's concerns, struggled to her feet. She blinked owlishly and yawned, "I've had a nice nap. I assume that was a twist that just hijacked me. Let's incinerate that bastard."

Carlos looked up at Esteban and raised an eyebrow. Evidently he had his doubts, too. Esteban stepped into the conversational breach. "What if we could take it back with us? Would that be more of a coup than just destroying it?"

"Damn thing tried to kill—"

Carlos cut her off with a sharp look.

Then another possibility occurred to Isobel and she couldn't keep quiet. "There is no way you are putting that thing in me. I am not carrying something that just turned me into a meat puppet. That piece of recycle can hang there until eternity rots."

"Specialist." Carlos's tone brooked no argument.

"I agree with Isobel." Esteban's answer had the lieutenant swinging around to look him in the face. "Isobel's wetdrive is a known quantity. It's scannable and if we are stopped on our exit she would not be able to hide its contents."

"But a cryosleep-frozen bird hidden in a cylinder that's supposed to be champagne would? Strike doesn't have the capacity to carry a twist."

Isobel remained quiet for a moment and Esteban imagined her thinking furiously, her clever mind running at top speed. "But we don't need the whole twist, just the kernel. There have to be things that AI doesn't need to survive: especially if we are turning it off for its transit. If we trim it down to the essence of its awareness then it just might fit."

"Do you think we can do this without its cooperation?" asked Carlos skeptically. Esteban could tell that he was intrigued by the idea. Bringing back intelligence about the Out Rim's plans to create generation ships, as well as one of their twist pilots, would be quite an accomplishment.

"I think we might be able to secure that," Esteban said, "after all what is the first duty of any prisoner?"

"To escape," answered Isobel, "So you think that they never realized that growing the twist inside of a cage where it could see out but never be free would make it unhappy?"

"Here's my suggestion. Show it Strike's footage. Start with where she is now circling the cage. Then give it the footage of the cylinder, but how Strike sees it. To me nothing exemplifies freedom like a hawk in flight. Let it see its world for the first time. Finally, give it a very brief overview of the solar system. That should be enough enticement. Strike is still circling the Faraday cage. She can land again and transmit our offer. Isobel should be able to up the response times on the msuits so that we are not overwhelmed again. What have we got to lose?" Esteban looked from Isobel to Carlos as they considered his proposition.

Carlos pointedly looked at Esteban's backpack. "We'll be burning that structure to the ground, including the twist, if it doesn't like our offer. I'll contact the extraction team and ask them to begin preparations for our withdrawal." The lieutenant stepped away from his team, opening a private comm channel.

Isobel looked hard at Esteban, her arms crossed over her chest. "Easy, just why are you so sure that thing wants out enough to trust us?"

"Because, I get the same feeling from Strike when I put her in the roost. I know I'm protecting her, but at the same time I want her to be free. The weird part is that it's not that I'm sure it wants out, rather that I'm sure that Strike is convinced it wants out."

"And you trust her. Well, Easy, I've said it before and I'll say it again. You're one strange bird."

The destroyer that picked up their small transport ship pulled away from Jupiter's well and started in-system. Esteban handed over Strike's case to the deck officer and reached down for his pack.

"You brought me champagne? You shouldn't have," he smirked, showing off the container to the other men in the bay.

"Careful with that. There's two brains bigger than yours in that canister," yelled Isobel from the other side of the bay.

The officer looked startled for a moment and decided to hand the cylinder back to Esteban since he'd now shouldered his pack. "We can toast a quiet trip back with something else later on, sir."

The other man smiled at Esteban. "Well, we've already had enough excitement. The destroyer caught a flight of Out Rim ships practicing in near Jupiter. We came through and broke them up. Should put the fear of the ISC in those rebels for awhile."

As Esteban thought about the seed bank, the twist, and the plans to use the asteroid as a generation ship, he wondered if the Out Rim could be cowed by something as simple as a military attack. "Yeah, I'm sure that'll teach them." He hoped he sounded convincing. All he wanted, though, at the moment was some rack time. Time where he could review Strike's flight footage and dream of flying with her once again.

WAR DOGS
Judi Fleming

WHATEVER YOU DO, DON'T CROSS THE LINE PAINTED ON THE FLOOR IN front of the heavy bars, Sergeant Perro," the medtech warned me for the sixth time.

"Got it," I said with a casualness I did not feel. Sweat snaked down my spine despite the chill in the cargo bay of this brand new interstellar battleship. I was no longer distracted by Corporal Jodan's sweet curves, nearly hidden under the crisp white medical uniform.

The horse-sized black beast in front of me growled low and deep in his chest. I felt it in my ear bones more than I actually heard it. He licked his lips and bared his teeth in anticipation, a quick, deliberate move as he tried to make eye contact with me.

I stayed my distance as directed but reached up to rub where the implant itched under my skin behind my left ear. Doubt crawled inside me. Exactly why had I volunteered for this special duty? Ten years of boring drills and muscle-straining workouts could end in a swift, bloody death with my next forward movement.

Come closer. Must smell you, the war dog commanded directly into my mind. The feel of it was foreign yet somehow comforting at the same time. My uniform stuck to the sweat on my chest and sides as I struggled against the urge to step forward.

The medtech elbowed me and snapped, "Pay attention to me, soldier. These dogs are too expensive to risk damaging them. He could break a tooth dragging your body through the bars."

She wasn't joking. This corporal had great pride for her genetically modified beasts, bragging about their development as she inserted the chip against my skull.

She raised a hand gracefully, hovering perfectly over the thick orange line on the floor. The war dog's tail raised a bit higher and wagged ever so slightly.

"Hello, my friend," she said. He huffed a breath and stuffed his muzzle between the bars, straining to reach her hand. His tongue lolled out, comfortable with her. His body language told all who looked on that this was his friend, part of his pack. But he was also clearly waiting for his chance with me. His stiff shoulders and direct, challenging eye contact screamed his readiness for my face-off.

But I'd done my homework about dog behavior and read every file I found on our battle cruiser's computer. I knew not to make the direct eye contact until I had established a position to allow it. I knew to curl my shoulders in a "non-threatening manner." Yet knowing didn't help slow my pounding heart. I had been too confident. Too cocky. This animal could tear me limb from limb. A real, live, snarling war dog. Vids didn't do them justice.

"Why aren't you riding him into battle?" I couldn't resist the question while I stalled for a bit of time to key down my nerves.

"I ride his beta female, Mayhem." Her smile had the faraway look of a rider communing with a war dog out of sight, but still close enough to hear. "This is my last tour onboard before my orders put me back as a combat medic where I belong. I'm part of your team if you make this match, Sergeant Perro."

I cleared my throat and asked, "What's his name?"

"Phobos," she replied. "The war god Ares' son and the personification of fear. He's the biggest we've ever bred. And the meanest too."

She actually smiled at that. She was a bit more over the edge than I first suspected.

The cage rattled as he lunged forward without warning. The medtech hadn't reacted to him, but turned to face me.

"This might not be your match. You may have to wait for the next batch to mature. He's been a difficult one to match with a rider. He's the alpha male of the war dog platoon. But your psych eval says you two match, so step up and follow the training."

I toed the line next to her instantly and invited him up with the shift of my body language to canine.

Mine, Phobos roared inside my skull as he lunged against the bars again. His nose smeared cold and wet against the back of my hand as he tried to drive his head through the bars toward me.

I don't know why I didn't flinch, but I held fast despite the medtech's iron grip on my shoulder as she tried to haul me backward.

Phobos sniffed hard, leaving tracks of dog snot along the curve of my fingers and up over my knuckles.

"So what will it be, boy? Can we be friends, Phobos?" The name felt odd on my tongue as I finally met his eyes. He was a handsome brute and I felt tiny next to him, though I was a broadly muscled six foot four. I knelt next to the bars in one fluid motion, keeping my hand steady against his nose.

I saw laughter in his eyes then and he drew back, tongue lolling as he sat down. I reached through the thick bars to scratch him along the bottom of his jaw line and down his neck. Phobos was magnificent and he was mine and I was his. Pack. This was my new combat partner and I couldn't wait to hear what he had to say about it.

I could feel my legs go rubbery and sweat bead on my brow in relief. I had accepted a pretty damned big bonus to take this assignment. And it was my only chance to see Earth, to take the battle right back to our home world and win back our planet first hand.

The medtech smiled and said, "It took years to crack the DNA combinations to get both intelligence and this size. Some were big and dumb, some were small and vicious. Others were roll-over pet-me kind of animals," she said watching me keenly as I stepped back to face her. "You know this is our last hope to take back Earth now that the G'NuN have mucked with the atmosphere."

"Yeah, I figured those bonuses for this were too good to be true. So shall we let him out and get the pack together with the troops and see what I've got to work with?"

If she'd had a tail, I swear she'd have wagged it.

"Why the hell is he so pissed off at me, Jordy?" I whispered to Medtech Jordan as Lieutenant Beckman stormed down the cargo bay to toward crew quarters, leaving us to adjust our riding gear. Our introduction hadn't gone well. He was an aristocrat's son, I was generic spacer spawn.

Jordy laughed softly and stroked Mayhem's rough chocolate brown fur, pausing in her efforts to adjust the riding harness. "He rides a bitch," she said as if it explained all.

I waited.

She stopped and looked at me directly. "The alpha bitch, mate to your male."

"So?" I asked. "Sergeants lead the troops into battle." It seemed logical to me that he rode Char. She was magnificently matched to my Phobos, broad and heavily muscled, yet a sleeker version of my boy. I dug my nails into the thick black fur of his shoulder blades, evoking a rear leg thumping groan of pleasure from him.

Fix harness, he commanded and I did.

"Ever wonder why the L.T. has the scar across his chin? Well, Phobos tried to tell him to shut up and back off in more than one way. So he's pissed that you got 'his' dog and that he's the only officer in the battalion riding a bitch. And he's an arrogant aristocratic ass besides. No disrespect intended, Sergeant."

Five platoons of twenty riders in our company and I had to have the only one hung up on gender. Idiot. My platoon was a solid twenty riders with fifteen bitches and only five intact males. The other four were all Phobos would tolerate.

There was no spaying and neutering these beasties. If they were to breed, let them do it and the more puppies the better. We'd been directed to ride them until they died or denned up and whelped a litter. We'd be supplying our own replacement mounts if the battle took that long.

There were ten men and ten women riding in our platoon and every single one of them cared for their war dogs with a passion and devotion that made me proud. Even the L.T., from what Jordy had said.

I was the last to be matched with my beast on the battleship and the final person to round out our battalion. Jordy was rushing me through my first and last week of introductions and exercises before we pushed light speed for the jump back to Earth. Up until today, the lieutenant had been in strategy meetings up on the command deck. He'd come down today to tell us to pack and to meet me.

It was hard to believe I was going. All those hopes and dreams as a kid on my generation ship as our race escaped from the wars and watched colony after colony fall behind us to the attacks of the G'NuN.

When they landed on Earth herself, that was more than most could tolerate and the fleet fighters began calling for volunteers to reclaim our home. Saying if we didn't, we wouldn't have a home. And they had been right.

Earth fell to the G'NuN when I was sixteen. Old enough to enlist and hop a recruiting ship back to Command Central. Earth had been my dream back then, a place I had never seen and could never truly hope to see if I stayed on my lumbering generation ship toward its final destination many lifetimes away in space.

Now my guts twisted into knots thinking that when I woke up, we'd be diving down through the G'NuN thickened, jungle-like atmosphere of Earth and hitting the ground astride our war dogs to take it all back. Plasma and nuclear weapons weren't allowed. This was home. So the peoples of Earth had fought long and hard and planned and schemed and developed a weapon of war that wouldn't destroy our own planet while winning its salvation. The reptilian bodies of the G'NuN in the soupy atmosphere made them invisible to our tech. They were fierce fighters and deadly in their swiftness. Because of this we humans just didn't have what it took to defeat them once they infested a planet.

But somewhere in the past, on a distant colony, someone's pet dog had discovered an advanced G'NuN scout and had torn it to pieces. And the colonists had gathered all their dogs and taken on the G'NuN who tried to land and breed and steam the place up with their strange atmosphere-bending technologies to make a warm and cozy swarming place like all the others.

Phobos raised his hackles, sensing my thoughts and seeing the images flash past my mind's eye. He hated the G'NuN on some molecular level. A deep, seething, all-consuming desire to tear and crunch washed over me.

"Soon, my friend, soon. One more big sleep and we're there." I checked the harness one more time and put him in his light-jump kennel before tucking myself in my own tube next to his. Then jump-prep mist knocked me out before I had time to settle.

Next thing I knew, the clang of tubes opening and the excited, whole-body wagging anticipation slammed through me.

UP, up, up! Phobos commanded and I bashed my forehead on the tube frame as I slid out.

"Bo, my boy, you've got to remember I'm human and can't move that fast," I said as I hauled his kennel open and checked his equipment. I slammed on my helmet, keying up the info screens that scrolled through checks, computer links and orders.

I barked "Fall in," and strode to our platoon's designated spot in the cargo bay.

My link with Phobos was like another overlay in my vision, his point-of-view flavored with scent, and sounds beyond my range of hearing.

Ready, ready, ready, he barked as he checked his pack while I checked their humans. He welcomed Char, nuzzling her muzzle and mouthing over her jaws as the L.T. strode up.

"We're in first," he said. We already knew it from the orders scrolling across the face plate. This guy was a jerk. The faint trace of fear scent coming from him made both Phobos and Char show teeth at him. I could see the struggle on his face as the conversation about stepping up rippled between the L.T. and his very confident mount.

Kill. Phobos stated more as a fact than as a question.

I deliberately misunderstood and answered, "We'll be on the ground and after those damned G'NuN shortly, Bo."

The landing gear whined in the atmosphere as we dumped speed and thumped to the ground.

Earth.

"Mount up!" we sergeants thundered as our perfect formations became a rodeo of dogs and soldiers fighting a blood lust we all felt.

My balance astride Phobos's monstrous frame was perfect from months of determined simulators trying to snap me off. Our minds tuned into one fine lance as we reached out together to taste the air and listen beyond the noise of the double-sealed doors whimpering open against the pressure of an atmosphere thick and soupy and white after the cold vacuum of space.

Metal pinged and muscles quivered as we waited for the orders to advance. The damned L.T. was drawing it out, basking in the attention of a whole battalion waiting on his command.

Char didn't wait, she bayed out a high pitch keen and our platoon surged forward, my Bo overrunning her in two strides.

Home. Mine. Kill. The words tumbled over and over as he searched for the scent, becoming a mantra that barked commandingly back for the rest to follow. All of them.

The war dogs spilled out of the cruiser, riders wrenching their minds back to the orders on their vids. Pulling them into their assigned wedges, toward locations, reading the terrain ahead and relaying the stats back to their mounts.

In less than a minute, my pack was swallowed in the fog and I could no longer hear those behind us. The joy of the hunt, of stretching legs with no restrictions, of scenting the quarry and knowing that his alpha status gave him the best, the strongest pack surged through me.

I fought his command to plunge forward and engage. "Around," I ordered, showing him the lay of the land and the advantage of the approach as his senses matched with the GPS readings on my faceplate. Again our minds and bodies merged as he accepted rather than fought against me.

There were no more words, the ideas and input blurred into action. Wild and primitive, we knew simultaneously what each other offered and accepted the pairing. The thunder of our hearts seemed louder than the paws that flashed over barely seen ground as we came up on a group of G'NuN walking toward all the noise the landing cruiser had made.

The clash of teeth on bone and the spike of impacting bodies felt ghostly as adrenaline and kill instinct combined inside a mist white world. Throats were torn out and heads were blasted off and then it was over. A couple dozen G'NuN lay dead around us as our pack nosed through to make sure the job was well and thoroughly done.

More. Mine. He yipped once in a recall and we formed back up. Phobos didn't want to share in the kills with those packs who would soon follow us.

Strike. I agreed as I measured our condition and we charged. The Lieutenant screeched at us, ordering us back, but I ignored him.

We raced up a ridgeline and Char's rider challenged us, breaking us out of our huge strides. The L.T. was ranting at us, visor up as he tried to make himself heard over the howling welling up from the packs separating out in the valley behind us.

In a flash, he dropped away from Char's smoking back as a corpse, and we dashed down the other side toward the enemy firing on us. We were quick, but not quick enough. Yelps of pain echoed around us as we surged over the G'NuN camp, overwhelming them at close range with teeth and blasters. The barrel of a laser locked onto me and Char leapt riderless through the air between it and us. Half her body blinked out as she short pulse consumed her.

Phobos was on the reptile before its claw pulled the trigger again. Pain lanced through us both as we were slammed to the ground. Pain for his lost mate and pack members as they snarled and slashed and fought. Pain and loss and longing as they died.

My throat closed around a howl caught on the verge of escaping my lips. *Regroup,* I commanded through Phobos and they did.

A quick circle around the bodies, noses touching noses and genitals as the dead and wounded were acknowledge and we raced off into the dripping forests.

We hunkered down a good distance from the carnage and dismounted, each rider who was left checking their war dog and those who were rider-less.

Jordy did the triage and called in the status for our remaining group. Ten fully functional, three wounded but mobile, seven wounded or not returned, or missing or dead.

I sent the wounded back to the cruiser, scanning the vids and readouts showing the progress of the rest of the battalion. Most fared worse than our platoon.

We had to trust each other. I relayed back to allow the dogs the lead on timing attacks. That asinine lieutenant had broken our momentum, and had given away our position. We'd have been on the group like ghosts from the mist, just like the first attack if he hadn't made that stupid maneuver.

Phobos pitched back his head and howled, loud and long and low. Answering howls filled the world and those were answered by wave upon wave of canines in the distance.

Phobos cataloged the answering howls for me. War dogs, wild dogs, wolves, and foxes. All answered and his mind blossomed into a map of distances, strength and locations of their calls. A chill raised the hair on the back of my neck and my flesh goose pimpled. His ruff was already up as he turned his head and listened a moment longer, huffing once to taste the air.

He howled again, Chaos answered and the cascade of voices silenced all other noise in the forest. Moments ticked by, concepts flashed through his mind, only to slip across mine. I grasped at them, trying to hook a tooth on their meanings and importance.

Reports. Dammit if they weren't reporting back to him. Locations of scent. Distances from packs, number of enemy, strengths of remaining units.

He pondered it all, his gold-flecked eyes meeting mine and I looked away, acknowledging his right as alpha. He mouthed my hand and wrist then nosed my crotch hard as he accepted my new place in the pack command structure.

Instantly I relayed back, "Listen to the damned dogs and let them do these next charges." The chatter on the screen and in my ears was infuriating. Trying to get them to understand in words that couldn't properly convey this much meaning from so many senses stupid humans didn't have would be impossible.

I settled for, "No, dammit, I don't give a shit who thinks who's in charge and you don't need to know my name, just mount up and get ready."

Phobos stood next to me, tossing his head back for a long string of commands and urging me to mount once again. I checked my weapons and motioned for the others to do the same.

My soldiers looked a little too confused and scared through their determination, but I could do nothing for that now. We had to move before the G'NuN regrouped or had time to plan and scheme. And this was just the first continent we had to clear out.

We were off in a rush, me lending my knowledge of terrain and strategy to him through our mental link and running the explanation through the wide open mic as we moved and danced around an elaborate battle plan streaming from his mind.

Day after day, week after week, month after month, we marched on. We'd climb into the cruiser as we cleared out areas. Tending the wounded, rotating out for sleep, mating and whelping of pups who grew to beasts without riders in a scant few months. We humans becoming fewer and fewer as time unraveled in an endless series of engagements and slyly crafted triumphs.

We found the landing ships of the G'NuN and annihilated them. We found the breeding colonies and feasted on the eggs and new born hatchlings when supplies became low.

We hunted the wild hunts of boar and deer and elk and bear who fled from us in terror while we reveled in the overwhelming joy of the kill and the warm, rich blood. Our packs filled the nights with their howls and dreams and the glorious sight of stars and moon coming through the thinning fog more clearly with each passing year. Other war dog battalions were slowly clearing them from other strongholds throughout the galaxy. The human race had survived yet another menace to its survival.

Jordy had just had our fourth child when the battle cruiser commander approached us with the message. As the rider of the strongest alpha, I had been in charge for nearly a decade, though his pups lead the active battle groups now. My beard and hair were no longer regulation like his, but the Commander snapped a salute just the same.

"Commander," he said as I smartly saluted him back, acknowledging him as my equal in this. He paused, groping for words.

"Sir?" I asked, noting the smell of unease around him. "What seems to be the problem?"

"The closer colonies want to start sending people back. They ask how much longer before we're sure we've finished mopping up and when we can deploy to other planets."

I stared at him, incredulous. Leave? How could he ask us that?

Phobos got to his feet, stiff with age and hard use, but still powerful enough that no one challenged his authority. He strolled over and sat next to me, eye to eye with the smaller man.

Home. OUR home, he said and I repeated his words instantaneously, his mouthpiece for our twinned desires.

"We're not leaving our home, Commander. We're staying right here where we belong. Humans lost this planet and made it for us to defend. They are no longer welcome here."

He stared at us, incredulous. "But..."

I watched the man's eyes grow wide as Phobos growled that low, deep growl that sent a shiver across his bones.

"No," I stated flatly, "Relay back that Earth is saved and preserved and trespassers here will not be tolerated." I smiled, showing teeth as I sized him up before saying, "You and your crew are welcome to leave any time you want, Commander. Just set the com satellite autobeacons with our message on your way out of the solar system."

I turned back to my mate and nuzzled our new pup without watching him leave. The overlayed view from my alpha's eyes of his tail-tucking retreat would have made my tongue loll out in laughter too.

SO (NOT) LIKE DOGS
David Sherman

HE HANDLER ROSE SLIGHTLY FROM HIS HIP-BENT STALKING POSTURE AND sniffed, seeking the scent that had brought his charges to point. His head twitched side to side, frequently pausing for an instant to peer through the spindly foliage of the scrub forest. The fact that he smelled nothing other than the greenery of the flora and the dust of the rich earth, or saw nothing other than thin trunks, spiky leaves, and dense undergrowth meant nothing—he knew that although his eyes were sharper than those of his charges, his nose was nowhere near as sensitive. It would soon be night, when scent told more than vision could. He would rely on the beasts. He lowered himself back to his normal hunting posture, his back parallel to the ground, his tail feathers jutting straight back in counterbalance to his head on the end of its long neck.

Intelligence knew that the main line of the alien game was a quarter day's march ahead of where the Handler now was, and that the game had placed a guardian line of outposts well in advance of their main line. His mission, his pack's mission, was to destroy one of the outposts, to create a hole through which a large force could charge to assault the game's main line. He squealed a happy squeal, his wasn't the only patrol sent to wipe out an outpost in this area. The hole they would make in the guardian line would be huge.

The ninety members of his pack, half the Handler's height though otherwise looking very like him, hissed softly as they looked up at him expectantly, bouncing up and down in their excitement for action. He returned their looks, and his mouth opened in a tooth-exposing grin. He patted the air, telling them to be patient...that their time would come soon enough. Then they could slash and rend and eat to their hearts' content. He would gleefully join them in the eating. But first he needed to discover exactly where the furless and scaleless prey was, and how many were there. He wasn't concerned about how they were armed—he knew his charges moved too fast for the aliens to track and aim at them.

The Sixth Marine Regiment had made planetfall on Semi-Autonomous World Troy on D Plus 4. The following day its second battalion had its first engagement with the ferocious aliens who had evidently wiped out the entire population of the planet. Second battalion's Echo Company suffered the least heavily of the battalion's companies in that engagement, which was why Echo was tasked with putting out a platoon-size observation post five kilometers ahead of the battalion's line. Captain Eli Fryer, Echo's commanding officer, only had to transfer four Marines from other platoons to bring first platoon up to full strength. Second Lieutenant John Leims, first platoon commander, wasn't fully happy with getting four Marines he didn't know under these circumstances.

"I know them, sir," Staff Sergeant Mitchell Paige, the platoon sergeant, told Leims. "And so do most members of the platoon. These're all good Marines. They'll fit in with no problem." Paige had been with Echo, 2/6 for more than two years, where Leims had only joined the company a couple of weeks before the deployment.

"If you say so," Leims said. He didn't sound convinced.

A squad of Combat Engineers and one of sappers went with first platoon. The Engineers' heavy equipment took most of a day to construct defensive works and living bunkers on both the forward and reverse slopes of a four-hundred-meter-high ridgeline that overlooked a road junction in a forest of middling-height, spindly trees; they camouflaged the works as they went. The sappers took a little less time to seed the approaches to the ridge with sensors; visual, audio, motion, scent.

Before they left, the engineers and sappers gave the infantry Marines all the shotgun shells they had. Two men in each fire team carried an M7 shotgun instead of the standard-issue M-82 rifle. Most of the Marines had done little more than orient on the M7—learned how to load and aim, but not well enough to gain any proficiency. Corporal Truesdale took one of his fire team's shotguns as he'd done more firing with it.

As soon as the sappers were out of the way, Leims and Paige registered artillery and rockets, and directed a practice run of AV16C Kestrels.

"No sweat, Lieutenant," Paige told him. "You've got a whole platoon of Marines to keep you company."

"Yeah," Leims answered. In his mind he saw the speedy, herky-jerky rushes of the alien soldiers and their smaller attack. . .dogs, for want of a better word. A platoon of Marines didn't seem like enough company.

Second Lieutenant Leims had never felt so lonely.

The Handler crouched down, facing his pack Alpha, and leaned in, shoulder to shoulder. He stroked the Alpha, from the feathery top of its head, down its long neck, and its longer back, all the way to its twitching tail. He murmured nonsense words into the Alpha's ear hole, calming it. Satisfied that the Alpha was no longer too excited to listen to commands, he instructed it to stay in this place, and to keep the rest of the pack there, until he returned.

The Alpha hissed its understanding, and gave the side of the Handler's muzzle a long lick with its raspy tongue.

The Handler gave the Alpha a last, long stroke, then stood and headed in the direction where he knew the aliens must be putting their outposts. He would locate and observe the nearest outpost, then make his plan and fetch his pack. He looked forward to the panic the aliens would experience before they died.

"Look alive, second squad," Sergeant Alexander Foley said into his helmet comm's squad circuit during the day's brief dusk. "We're all alive and I want us to stay that way. Anyone who gets himself killed will have to answer to me."

Lance Corporal Harry Fisher snorted. "What's he going to do, follow us to heaven to kick our asses?"

Fisher's fire team leader, Corporal Don Truesdale, leaned over inside the bunker his fire team was in and smacked the back of Fisher's helmet. "No, dummy. He'll follow you to *hell* to kick your ass. Now pay attention to that visual pickup."

Fisher curled his lip, but bent his attention to the visual sensor receiver that was the fire team's responsibility.

"Everybody else, watch sharp," Truesdale ordered his other men. "Memorize the shadows."

"Right, memorize," PFC Oscar Upham murmured softly enough that Truesdale could ignore it.

A moonless night. Black on black. Experienced infantrymen watched the shadows deepen and merge as dusk turned to night, memorized their shapes so that if they later saw a shadow that hadn't been there before, they knew it might be an approaching enemy. But the downward slope that was second squad's front held only knee-high scrub, no trees or boulders or anything else that would protrude above the scrub. And the forest beyond the roads below the ridge was too uniform to show anything. But maybe that uniformity was the point of memorizing the shadows; any anomaly would clearly show up.

First squad was on second's left and third was on the reverse slope, held in reserve. One of the two scatterer gun teams attached to the platoon was between the two front squads, the other was with third. One fire team per bunker, Foley with the scatterer team in the middle. Fifty meters between bunkers. Seven bunkers covering a front three hundred meters wide. The command group was with the reserve on the opposite slope.

The Handler found a spot from where he could observe the ridgeline without being seen himself by a foe with vision as poor as the aliens' was known to be. Moving slowly so as to not disturb any of the foliage around him, he withdrew a magnifier from one of the pouches on his chest strap. That and a few other straps were his sole garments. The magnifier showed him the line of bunkers the aliens had constructed. He didn't know how many of them occupied a bunker, but seeing their size and knowing the size of the aliens—close to his own when he stood erect—he estimated that only three or four of them were in each structure. Fewer than thirty alien soldiers. Maybe many fewer. He tucked his muzzle under an arm to muffle his chuckle. His pack would make quick work of them. The packs to his flanks would do likewise with the stretches of ridge they were to clear. Then the main attack force would charge through, to attack and destroy the alien army.

"Hey Corporal Truesdale, take a look at this," Lance Corporal Fisher said as dusk deepened. He leaned out of the way so his fire team leader could look at the visual sensor display.

"What am I looking at?" Truesdale asked, ducking his head into the display's hood.

"Maybe something, maybe nothing. I'm not sure. That's why I want you to take a look."

"Are you focused on a spot?"

"Yeah."

Truesdale peered at the display, wishing he had a heat or infrared sensor to compliment the visual display. But the engineers and sappers hadn't brought any heat or infra sensors. Dammit.

"What do you think?" Fisher asked after a moment of stillness from his team leader.

"Wait for it," Truesdale murmured. Then, abruptly, "Got it!" He withdrew from the hood. "There's a Duster out there." "Duster," short for "feather-duster" so called because of the feather-like structures that trailed from the aliens' arms and jutted from the base of their torsos. "I think he's a scout, anyway he just pulled back." He looked at where he knew Fisher was and nodded. "Looking good, Marine. Even knowing there was something to see, I had a hard time spotting him. Take over." He withdrew to the bunker's entrance and picked up the comm to the squad leader.

"What do you have for me, Don," Sergeant Foley asked. Truesdale briefly told him what he and Fisher had seen.

"Thanks, I'll pass it up. Let me know if you see anything else."

"Roger that, honcho," Truesdale answered.

Having seen what he needed to see, the Handler stealthily withdrew, returning to his pack. That was when he noticed something that looked wrong. He surreptitiously examined it, without pausing in his movement. Yes, it appeared to be some sort of visual pickup. No matter. Even if the aliens had seen him, which they might well not have, the dashing and darting of his pack was too fast for the aliens to kill more than a few of his beasts. Yes, let the visual pickup let them know he was there, let their fear increase. Their foreknowledge wouldn't change the outcome once he attacked.

The pack was still where he'd left it, all members accounted for. Even though one was too badly injured to participate in the coming fight. and another was partly lamed. The Handler stroked the Alpha and murmured into its ear hole, praising it for keeping the pack together and in place. That only two of the beasts were injured was good; the Alpha hadn't had to kill any of them to keep them in line.

The Handler sent the agreed-upon message, informing his commander that he'd scouted the alien defenses and he and his pack were ready to advance to the assault line.

He settled back to wait for the command to strike.

All along the outpost line in front of the Sixth Marines, reports came in of sightings of individual alien scouts. Something was up, but nobody knew what. Whoever this enemy on Troy was, the Marines—any humans for that matter—hadn't had enough contact with them to have any understanding of their tactics. The word went down from Regiment; "Prepare to repel boarders."

"'Repel boarders,' I guess that's as good a way of putting it as anything else," Corporal Truesdale said when Sergeant Fryer passed the instruction to him over the squad comm.

Truesdale heard the shrug in Fryer's voice when the squad leader said, "Just think of your bunker as a ship's rigging and you'll be fine."

"Right." Truesdale got off the comm and told his men, "We're in simulated ship's rigging. You better not be simulated sharpshooters when the bad guys come." One of the duties of the original US Marines, centuries earlier, was sharpshooters in ships' rigging, shooting down on the officers and crew on the decks of enemy vessels.

"We gonna be able to see 'em coming?" PFC Campbell asked.

"We can hope. Cop some Zs, Campbell. Everybody else, look sharp. Got anything on the display, Fisher?"

"Negative," Fisher answered. Minutes later, "Belay my last, I've got a *lot* of movement."

The Handler lowered his torso between his legs, his thighs and lower legs formed triangles along his sides, his feet angled toward the ground, his toes relaxed with his entire weight well distributed on them. He resisted the urge to tuck his head under his arm—it wouldn't do to be asleep when the order to attack came.

He didn't have to wait long for the order to advance to the assault line. With a few, sharp commands he got his pack into movement formation and began the short march to the assault line. The Alpha trotted here, there, and around the pack, keeping the beasts in proper formation. The Handler smiled; this was the best Alpha he'd ever worked with, its intelligence was well above that of its mates. It was almost like having another Handler with him.

When they reached the assault line, the Handler went from beast to beast, stroking each and murmuring to them. The beasts gazed up at him adoringly, hopping from clawed foot to clawed foot in their excitement at the anticipated charge into mayhem and bloody food.

"Get ready!" Sergeant Foley ordered over the squad comm.

"Get ready!" the fire team leaders needlessly echoed. "Infras," most of them added.

Corporal Truesdale looked at his men through his infrared goggles and was gratified to see that PFC Upham had his shotgun in hand, and looked like he knew how to use it. "Keep your eyes on your display," he told Fisher.

"It looks like they're starting to move forward," Fisher reported.

"How many are there?"

"It's hard to tell without infra. Best guess, more than twenty right in front of us. Could be a whole lot more, though."

Truesdale repeated Fisher's report to Foley.

"Put him on the squad comm," Foley ordered. "I want everybody to get his reports without delay."

"Aye-aye, Sergeant." Truesdale reached over to Fisher's comm unit and, working mostly by feel, switched his transmissions from fire team to squad comm. The he peered out through the embrasure, straining to see the alien enemy.

The Handler got his pack on line facing the alien positions that he knew were on the ridgeline, even though he couldn't see them in the night's darkness. Not being able to see them from this distance wouldn't be a handicap; his charges could smell them well enough at this range. A little closer, and he'd be able to smell them as well. The smell of the aliens would be enough to guide the Handler and his pack almost as well as vision would.

Second Lieutenant Leims, in his command post, watched the platoon's display feeds. He'd already called for a standby illumination mission from the regiment's attached artillery battery.

"All hands, listen up," he said into the full platoon comm. "Nobody fire until the illume pops. Then hit 'em with everything you've got." He glanced at his platoon sergeant, then back at the displays. "Do they even know we're in front of them?" he asked.

"Is that a rhetorical question?" Staff Sergeant Paige asked.

"I guess it is," Leims said after a moment. Nobody knew when the aliens might attack, how close they would approach before they attacked.

"I hate this waiting," Leims muttered.

"No more than the Marines up front," Paige said softly.

Leims swallowed. "You're right."

The Handler looked side to side and allowed himself a smile. His pack was maintaining good order, keeping their line straight. He wondered how close they would get to the prey before he could release them to the attack. He wondered how long he and his Alpha could keep the pack in good order.

The orderliness of the line was starting to break when the command finally came. The Handler shrilled out a hunting caw, and his pack broke formation, charging forward, jinking and jiving, dashing here, darting there, making themselves impossible for a larger predator to focus on for the kill.

"They're too damn close" Second Lieutenant Leims said when the aliens were almost to the road at the foot of the ridge. "If they begin their charge now, the illum won't get here until they're on us." He turned to his communications man. "Call that light mission *now!*"

Seconds later, flares began popping open above the ridge's side and the beginning of the scrub forest on the other side of the road junction, bathing the area in a cold, eerie, blue-tinged light.

The Handler squawked outrage. He hadn't anticipated illumination—at least not this soon, his pack had barely begun clambering up the side of the ridge. Then he saw the alien fire coming, and missing almost every member of his jinking and jiving, dashing and darting pack, and crowed out a cry of victory.

He joined the manic scramble toward the alien positions. Now this way, now that, now in a third direction. A beat this way, two beats that way, a beat and a half in another. Mixing up directions and intervals between. Never going in any one direction long enough for anyone to adjust aim sufficient to make a lucky hit on him

He cawed out another jubilant cry; there weren't as many of the aliens in the bunkers as he'd thought, and they didn't have any truly rapid-fire weapons, weapons that from sheer volume could create casualties in his pack. This line would be very easy to burst through.

"Scatterers and shot guns, hold your fire," Second Lieutenant Leims ordered on his all hands comm. He could clearly see the aliens on his displays now. They were running fast, but their zigzagging slowed their advance up the ridge—they were running two or three meters for every meter they climbed. The shotguns were relatively short-range weapons; they wouldn't be effective much farther than halfway down the slope. The scatterers were also shorter-range than normal machine guns.

"Mitch," Leims said, "get the other gun team in place, toward the right flank." *At least they aren't shooting at us*, he thought.

"Aye aye, sir," Staff Sergeant Paige said, and ducked out of the command post, already talking to Corporal Robert O'Malley, giving him orders.

In less than a minute, Paige was shifting second squad's first fire team into the other squad bunkers to make room for the scatter gun team in its bunker.

The aliens were now halfway up the side of the ridge.

Close enough, Leims thought. "Everyone, open fire!" he shouted into his comm.

More fire suddenly erupted along the alien line. It took the Handler a couple of heart beats to realize that the fire wasn't the same discrete slugs that had been all the fire coming from the aliens, the slugs that almost always missed.

There was a ripping fire from the center, one that threw out too many slugs too fast to be always dodged. And a similar ripping came from the left side. These tore through the pack, and many of the beasts were flung backward, gouting blood and chunks of flesh and bone from the impacts.

Most of the aliens' fire missed the beasts of the pack, but some sprays of pellets were wide enough for some them to hit a beast before it could dash and dart out of the way.

The Handler shrilled out in fury at the loss of so many in his pack. He and the Alpha urged the pack on.

Corporal Truesdale was proud of the fact that he was a Marine Rifle Expert. That meant he was a better shot than nine out of ten of all human marksmen. But, damn, these creatures were hard to hit! The pellets from the shotgun's shells spread out, but not wide enough to always hit a dodging target before it jinked out of the way.

The aliens zigzagged so fast Truesdale couldn't take aim and fire before his target was off in a different direction. After a few wasted shots, he decided to simply fire without aiming, directing his shotgun blasts into wherever the mass seemed densest. He was satisfied to see an occasional alien drop. A few more fell, shot by bullets from Marines' rifles. Others from slugs thrown by the whirring barrels of the two scatterers, putting out more than two thousand tiny pellets per minute in a widening spray.

But there were so many of them, and they were rapidly clambering up the side of the ridge. There was no chance the Marines could kill all of them before the charging enemy reached them, and the bunkers all had open entrances in their rear.

If only Truesdale could shoot the one that was twice the size of the others; he knew it must be the leader. But it moved just as fast as the smaller ones, and was equally hard to hit.

The surviving pack members—most of the original ninety were still alive and in fighting form—ran straighter, with fewer changes of direction, as they closed on the line of defensive positions. That gave the prey more time to aim, but the Handler cackled with pleasure when he saw that the longer time the prey had to aim wasn't enough to make much of a difference—he though he lost no more than two additional beasts because of it.

He crowed with increased pleasure when he saw the foremost of the pack reach the bunkers and run between them. Soon, very soon, all of the prey would be dead, and the feasting would begin.

"Fisher, Upham," Corporal Truesdale shouted, "turn around, stop them from coming through the hatch!"

An instant later, both Fisher and Upham fired at three of the small aliens trying to jam their way into the bunker at the same time. One was blown backward by the force of a shotgun blast from Upham, a second crumpled when three rapid shots from Fisher slammed into it. Freed of its mates, the third pounced at Fisher, extending the claws on its feet and snapping with the teeth in its long muzzle.

Fisher didn't have time to scream before his throat was shredded. Scarlet blood spurted from his carotid arteries. Intestines boiled out of deep gashes in his abdomen. He thudded to the floor of the bunker.

Truesdale heard Fisher's corpse hit the floor, and spun in time to see the third alien shudder from a blast from Upham's shotgun. He spared Fisher a quick look; it was obvious the lance corporal was dead. He had to deal with the living.

"Campbell, turn around and help Upham keep them out!" Truesdale shouted. Without waiting to see if Campbell obeyed, he turned back to the embrasure and fired four quick shots at two aliens that were trying to squeeze through it. Both fell back, their feathers tattered and flesh shredded. He fired three more times and saw two more aliens die and two others run screaming down the hill.

The Handler cawed, appalled at the undisciplined way his beasts milled about, some trying to squeeze through embrasures clearly too small for them to fit in, others jamming themselves at the rear entrances to the defensive positions. He saw them being killed in far greater numbers than they were killing the foe. For the first time he wished he had some soldiers with him instead of only the pack. Soldiers would have rifles, and could shoot the alien defenders without having to enter the positions.

But he didn't. And his rifle and knife were the only weapons his force had. It was up to him to turn the tide.

He dashed to the side and around to the rear of the nearest bunker.

Where did the big Duster go? Truesdale demanded of himself. He knew he hadn't shot it and was sure no one else had, either. *He must have made it between the bunkers, and was behind the positions.*

Few of the aliens were still on the side of the ridge below the defensive line. Truesdale fired three more times and saw one of them go down, crumpled. Another reached his bunker and tried to climb through the embrasure. Truesdale reversed his grip on his shotgun and slammed its butt down hard on the alien's thrusting, snapping muzzle. He heard bones shatter, and the alien jerked backward, weakly cawing in pain. Truesdale shot it, then looked for more. He didn't see any, so he turned his attention to the bunker's entrance.

The Handler stepped around the corner of the defensive position and watched pained as two more of his beasts died in its entrance. They didn't fall all the way down, there were too many bodies already laying there, stacking up. He stepped forward and stuck his rifle though the entrance, moving its muzzle around so his fire would go to every corner as he pulled the trigger as rapidly as he could.

But before he got off more than a few shots, someone grabbed his rifle and jerked it out of his hands. He staggered.

Truesdale flung the alien's weapon into a corner of the bunker and sucked air between his teeth at the pain in his hand from grasping the hot barrel. But he had no time to worry about it; the aliens were still attacking even though there were far fewer of them.

"Give me a hand clearing this," he ordered, and grabbed the neck of the alien on top of the pile. A quick yank pulled the thing inside. Upham and Campbell lent themselves to the job, and in fifteen seconds enough bodies were cleared out of the way for Truesdale to scramble over them to see outside.

He saw dead and dying aliens scattered on the ground near the entrances of the bunkers. Others were screeching and scrabbling at the entrances, trying to get at the Marines inside them.

And Truesdale saw the big one, standing bent at its hips, torso parallel to the ground, tail-feather-like structure jutting out behind, head on its long neck twisted toward him. A saw-bladed knife was in the alien's hand. It opened its maw wide at sight of the Marine, exposing glistening, rending teeth. The alien shrieked and charged, bending its arm back to the side to swing its knife in a disemboweling slice.

Truesdale dove to the side, under the swinging blade. He rolled and sprang to his feet, facing the alien which had already recovered and was charging again. It was close and coming too fast, Truesdale didn't have time to bring his weapon to bear and fire. He fell back to avoid the alien's knife. This time the alien was prepared for tbe movement, and twisted its stroke to swoop downward rather than across.

The Marine cried out at the sudden pain in his right wrist. He rolled and swung out with his good arm, catching the alien's foot. He yanked, and it crashed to the ground.

Ignoring the pain in his right wrist, Truesdale pounced onto the alien's back and grabbed its neck just below its head. He leaned all his weight onto his left hand and jumped up, to crash back down, landing his knees on the alien's back. He felt bones break.

Then Upham and Campbell were at his side. Campbell shot the alien in the side of its head with his rifle, and ordered Campbell, "Guard us!"

"Its dead, Honcho," Upham shouted at Truesdale, who was shaking the alien's neck. "And you're going to be dead if you don't let go of that and let me take care of you."

Dazed, and weakening from loss of blood, Truesdale let himself be pulled off the big alien. He watched dumbly as Upham tied a tourniquet around his right wrist. "Where's my hand?" he mumbled. "I don't see my hand."

"Corpsman up!" Upham called out.

The rest of the platoon was topping the ridge, and the last of the alien attackers were falling to their bullets.

"They were like a pack of rabid dogs," Truesdale said when the Corpsman asked what happened to him.

Echo, 2/6 only lost one man killed in the battle with the "dogs" of war. Only one Marine other than Corporal Donald Truesdale was badly wounded in the action. The planned assault against Second battalion, Sixth Marines never happened.

Corporal Truesdale returned to full duty three months later, with a newly regenerated hand at the end of his right wrist.

FRIENDLY FIRE
Edward J. McFadden III

PFC Wes Quarter watched Tiger disappear into the tall grass. The cloned Shepherd/Springer Spaniel hybrid was equipped with an M30 headset, which wrapped around its head, and was held in place via a series of straps. The head gear provided full visual, sound, and control of two lasers to the animal's handler. Wes tuned in his remote vision, and the retractable eyescreen hinged to his combat helmet relayed the landscape Tiger saw.

Wes had been Tiger's handler since his DNA had been mixed in a petri dish when they arrived on H2 and though the dog was nothing more than military property, a tool, he had come to have feelings for the animal. If not feelings of love, certainly of admiration, loyalty, and respect. Tiger had been trained utilizing the cruelest of methods, and he was conditioned to attack anything that walked on two legs, with the exception of Wes, the only living thing the animal would trust. Tiger's main function was night guard duty, and Wes always felt ashamed when he left to monitor things from a safe distance, while Tiger patrolled their assigned perimeter, like now.

Wes stayed alert. Though the night seemed quiet, that didn't preclude the possibility of danger. This was H2, a water moon orbiting Extara 13. It would have been the perfect place for a base—plenty of potable water, oxygen-rich, a veritable Eden. Except for the locals... His jaw tightening at the thought of the vicious Kantari, Wes turned his attention back his remote display.

The ground rose slightly before Tiger, the paths between the immense stalks of grass well worn and the ground pounded into hardpan, likely by passing animals or the Kantari. The canine paused, sniffed the air, and Wes knelt, staring into the thick grass as he waited for his partner to move on.

Wes heard a shuffling sound, and he rose, expecting Tiger to move toward the noise. Instead, the dog sniffed the air again, and looked side to side, revealing nothing unusual.

The area grew quiet, until Wes heard only the pounding of his heart and the scraping of the giant Gula plants, which the soldiers of Space Fleet, Planetary Recon Battalion Alpha 19 called grass because of the uncanny resemblance to the turf found on their home planet of Earth.

Wes was starting to worry when he saw movement in the grass. He toggled to his eyescreen, and saw Tiger moving—fast.

The nasty scent of spoiled milk made Wes freeze, as he tried to blend into his surroundings. Two Kantari, sweat covering their gray elongated bodies, burst through the grass and tackled Wes. One grabbed his feet, and the other his arms, as they splayed him on the ground. Wes struggled, jerking his legs and arms as hard as he could, trying to free himself, but the Kantari pinned him in place. Wes's mind raced. How had he let this happen?

He knew the Kantari were a vicious race, but he also knew they had primitive brains, and hadn't discovered a level of technology that would allow them to fully blossom as the violent beasts they were. Wes jerked against their hold, but the monsters were three meters tall. One of them clicked and hissed a message to the other in their strange language, which the soldiers called BS. The other drew a knife. The Kantari were known for gutting those they got their hands on and eating the entrails.

Wes increased his attempts to break free, and managed to wretch one hand from his attacker's grip. The Kantari who was holding it struck him in the head and forced him back to the ground. As Wes looked up at the creature, his mind superimposed his wife's features over the ugly bastard's face. The memory was a kick in the gut, a reminder of why he needed to fight. He wouldn't let the Kantari rob Hanora and the kids of a future with him in it. He would not die at the hands of an alien that couldn't even make a fire without help. He *would* see his family again, he told himself firmly. Bucking and thrashing gained him another punch to the head. Wes refused to give up, but his gut clenched as the Kantari pinning his legs knelt across them and started yanking away his body armor.

A disorienting rush of movement in Wes's retractable eyescreen served as his only warning. Tiger burst through the foliage, eviscerating the Kantari tearing at Wes's armor. Orange blood spurted from the alien, splattering Wes and leaving an ugly mass of skin and muscle on his chest. Ignoring the stench and gore, Wes tried once more to free himself. In a blur of black and white, Tiger went for the other one's throat before the first Kantari had hit the ground.

The second beast swatted the canine aside like a bug. Wes rolled away, tearing his arm out of the Katari's grip and rising to a crouch. The remaining Kantari snarled and yelped as Tiger locked his jaws on the monster's leg, shaking it so violently the alien fell, and landed in a tangled heap where Wes had been moments before. With a smooth motion revealing many years of service, Wes drew his combat knife, flipped it in his hand, and plunged the twelve-inch, notched blade into the Kantari's chest just below its neck, where Wes knew the alien's eight-phase heart was located. More blood and screeching, but in moments the alien lay lifeless.

Wes straightened and looked down at Tiger, who sat at attention next to his handler, every muscle taut and ready to spring. "Easy, boy," said Wes, stroking the animal. "Saved my ass again. What's that? Three times?" Tiger leaned in and planted a strong lick on Wes's face—a rare display of affection from an animal that saw most living things as the enemy.

Wes moved his hand behind the dog's ear, scratching vigorously in reward. Tiger had certainly lived up to his name tonight. And not just because of the genetic mutation that had given him black stripes on a white coat, despite his Springer Spaniel DNA.

Tiger straightened back to attention, the animal's eyes darting about, scanning the tall grass around them. So much for a quiet night. Wes hadn't expected they would end up in a face-to-face conflict when he'd volunteered for the patrol. The kill bounty would be nice, though. It might even be enough to cover an extra two months of stasis for Hanora and the kids.

"What's happening out there," came a voice over Wes's comm channel, interrupting his thoughts.

"The Kantari seem to be getting more aggressive, if that's possible," Wes answered. "But we handled them. Two combatants terminated." Wes looked sidelong at Tiger.

"Congratulations, soldier."

"No. Not me. My partner."

Wes sat hunched on his bar stool, alone in a corner though people packed the canteen, his mind running through the events of the prior night.

Tiger had saved his life again, and what had he done to reward the animal? Brought him back to his cage for a day of sleep, interrupted by occasional training by torture. Then he picked him up and dropped him off for guard duty, where Tiger had been assigned to protect a section of the safe zone containment blockade from Kantari incursions. Wes looked around the room, guilt seeping from him like sewage. He was supposed to be monitoring Tiger from a safe distance, but the events of the last few cycles had thrown him for a loop, and he needed some time to think.

Voices floated across the bar, and Wes heard two old spacers pissing and moaning to the bartender.

"Base HQ don't know their asses from a hole in the ground! The transport ship for Kray's guys is overdue 926 cycles. They forgot about us!" yelled a tall man who hadn't shaved or ironed his uniform in months. Inspections rarely occurred, and this led some of the Space Fleet vets to let themselves go some.

"It could just be a relativistic snafu. We're out over a 100 ly, Lou. Even for the brains at HQ, hitting the coordinates perfect requires no changes in the structure of space in the flight path. One little hiccup could account for several cycles of time delay." That was Sergeant Tate, one of Space Fleet's scientists.

"Yeah. Tell that to the guys who are supposed to go home. Some of these guys have families waiting in stasis. What about them? Who will pay their storage fees?" The two men paused, and Wes pondered his own situation. He was 119 light years out with three Earth years left on his duty cycle, and his wife Hanora and their two children waited for him on Earth, matching his transport stasis cycles in order to minimize time dilation age differences. When he completed his commitment he would have enough money to stake a claim on a new world where people didn't live on top of each other. Problem was, everyone knew Space Fleet HQ lengthened soldiers' deployments and blamed relativistic time deviations, and there was some truth to that. When Space Fleet took responsibility for deviations, family stasis was renewed and paid for by Space Fleet. Wes scratched his head. But on an out-world, things got complicated.

"Well, that better not happen, or they'll have a revolt. The civvies back on home rock already think they pay too much money to have us out here," said one of the spacers.

"Yup," said another spacer. "When was the last time we even got a status report from the front?" Advance warships had been deployed to Galactic Center, where an unknown force ate the very fabric of space. Early reports showed images of giant robotic machines crunching through the universe like a rock grinders whittled away stone. Some speculated that the threat was a nano swarm gone wild. Some said that in the end, all there would be was nano feeding on itself in vacuum.

However, early reports had been encouraging, and there were several counter attack plans under way. Plus, the threat was still several hundred light years from Earth, and moving very slowly. But with several alien races expanding across the galaxy, human nature finally took hold. Earth was one of the most prosperous planets in the known Milky Way, and war was its business.

"Why don't we head back up and waste all these Kantari?" rasped an old spacer Wes recognized. It was Lieutenant Gibb.

"Because we aren't murderers, Lieutenant!" The XO's voice was unmistakable. The place froze for an instant before everyone jumped to attention.

"We don't waste everything we find, you jarhead. These Kantari are nasty. Just the kind of nasty we need on our side."

"Sir, their—"

"Shut your face, Lieutenant!" Everyone stood at attention, and the XO walked among them, looking his men up and down. Luckily for Wes, he'd been sitting in the back, and there were several soldiers standing in front of him, shielding him from the stare of XO Damon Seszer, who might remember the evening's duty roster. "When the scientists get here, when the nano is done building the base, they'll figure out how to communicate with them. Explain shit. Make a deal. How stupid are you, Lieutenant?"

Lieutenant Gibb's mouth fell open a crack, then snapped shut. The XO drew himself up, twisting his body like a coiling snake, getting ready to rip Gibb, when the alarm klaxon sounded, and everyone went running.

Wes pulled on his helmet as he ran from the canteen. He toggled up Tiger's M30 only to learn he was out of range. "Shit," yelled Wes, and he turned and ran toward the section of barricade Tiger patrolled. If HQ found out he wasn't monitoring his canine, he'd be shipped off planet to mine ore, or to perform some other grunt task until his deployment was over, if it ever ended. Somehow, there always seemed to be extensive time deviations when it came to transporting soldiers who had been dishonorably discharged.

Maybe the attack wasn't in Tiger's patrol area, thought Wes. The crowd of soldiers increased, which meant Wes' hope meant what it usually did—shit. There was laser fire. Wes drew his Aspec 19, a handheld weapon that shot laser bursts at the rate of one per second.

The sounds of laser fire increased ahead. Most of the soldiers around Wes took up defensive positions. The Kantari attacked the encampment every few days. They weren't very bright, but they were a persistent bunch. The aliens usually attacked along the perimeter wall at night. Their night vision was far superior to that of humans, even with the various tech enhancements humans utilized. They'd lost three soldiers during the last raid, but over 100 Kantari had been cut down.

This night wasn't going much different for the Kantari. Wes was close enough to the action now that he could see several canines attacking Kantari on the walkway that ran around the top of the barrier. The Kantari had excellent climbing ability. Their sticky skin seemed to adhere to every smooth surface, which was why the canines stood alone as the first line of defense along the top of the wall.

Wes knelt and toggled in on Tiger. This time he got a connection. It was fuzzy, and gave out every few moments, but the image was clear enough for Wes to see Tiger fighting several Kantari on the gangway above. "Sit. Up angle. Sight." Tiger followed the commands, and Wes fired, the two lasers on the M30 chirping to life and taking out the Kantari in front of Tiger. Gray pieces of Kantari soaked in orange blood splattered the gangway, and Tiger lurched forward, bolting toward a stream of Kantari that swarmed over the wall like a wave of gray ooze.

Then Wes was up and moving, weaving in and out of soldiers waiting to fire at anything gray. The barricade wall that encircled the encampment and made up the safe zone was made of pieces of steel welded together and rounded, making the wall an almost impossible climb for a human. The Kantari saw it as just another slick rock in their jungle, except this one had snakes living under it. What the Kantari failed to recognize was that, when enough of them were on the wall, it would be electrified, and they'd get toasted. Despite their numerous prior attacks, they never seemed to learn this simple, painful lesson.

When Wes reached the front, he stopped and ducked behind several soldiers crouched in firing position, waiting for the Kantari to start jumping from the barricade. Tuning in Tiger, Wes saw he was in range of the Kantari as they streamed over the wall. Tiger's M30 shrilled, and many Kantari fell, but others scrambled over their dead comrades, hurling themselves off the wall toward the soldiers below.

Wes heard static on his comm channel, and then, "Thirty seconds to blockade defense activation."

"Tiger, to me!" shouted Wes. Tiger heard the command via his M30, skidded to a stop, turned, and headed back the way he had come.

He wasn't going to make it.

To his right, Wes saw a stack of storage containers. He ran toward them, holstered his weapon, and leapt upward, grabbing the top of the first container. He pulled himself up and ran across the steel box, hollow metal sounds accompanying each step. As fast as he was able, he climbed two more, and soon was bent double with pain. Tiger was close now, ten meters above on the gangway.

"Five seconds to blockade defense activation," said the calm voice at HQ over the comm channel.

Wes rose, and yelled, "Jump to me!"

Tiger stopped short, and looked down at Wes with pleading eyes.

"To me!" yelled Wes into his mic, and Tiger jumped.

Tiger slammed into Wes, and they fell to the deck. Tiger licked Wes' face, and then got off his handler.

ZZZZzzzzzzzzz, sounded the sizzle of electric through metal, followed by shrieks of pain. Charred Kantari fell from the wall, their smoldering corpses still twitching with life. Laser fire erupted all around them, and Kantari fell like rain, burying Wes and Tiger beneath a bloody mountain of charred flesh.

Wes and his canine waited, orange blood dripping on them, the smell of burnt meat so nauseating Wes gagged. As the minutes passed, the laser fire lessened. Within minutes they clawed their way from beneath their dead enemies. "Close one there," said Wes, and Tiger sat at attention, watching his handler, waiting for orders.

As they climbed down from the storage containers, a soldier came into view. Tiger jerked forward, growling, coiling as he prepared to strike. "Sit. Stay," yelled Wes, as he reached into his pocket and drew out a leash. Tiger looked up at him with confused eyes, and Wes felt the pit of his stomach go cold. Sometimes when he looked at Tiger, he didn't see the fighting killer he was, he saw just a dog. A dog that could never play catch, or sleep peacefully at Wes' feet while he read.

Wes knelt, and held out his hand. "I'm sorry, boy. But shit is what it is. Come on," said Wes, as he snapped the lead line around Tiger's neck, and led him back to his cage.

After a few days of not being called out by his lieutenant, or any other higher up, about not monitoring his canine, Wes began to relax. Things had been quiet, the Kantari choosing to lick their wounds and retreat into their lairs to regroup. A total of 61 duty cycles had come and gone on H2—more than three weeks back on Earth—before he visited Tiger off hours.

Wes had decided that he was becoming too close to the animal. He had risked his life to save Tiger, and though at first he had felt like he owed the animal, his soldier's brain eventually convinced him that he was being irrational. Would he risk his life to save his laser pistol? Or his knife? Wes lit a thin cigar and stopped to gaze out on the sea to the east. The stogie was made from a local plant called Tevertin, and though he didn't inhale the smoke, he enjoyed the pleasant aroma and the taste on his lips.

He walked atop a parapet wall, which gently sloped down to the kennels on the interior of the blockade. This made putting the canines on guard duty much easier. Looking out on the sea, Wes remembered Earth, and swimming in its salty oceans with Hanora when they were young and free. He could never swim in the seas of H2, however, unless he wanted to be eaten by a Kantari, or worse. When he reached the kennels, Wes stubbed out his cigar and put it in his fatigue pocket. The things cost ten ration points, and he'd smoke it to the nub.

As Wes pushed through the large swinging doors that separated the medical and surgical wings of the canine MASH unit, he heard a squeal that made him stop short. He hid behind a stack of empty cages, and slowly eased his head around them so he could see down the length of the kennel. The kennels reeked of piss and death, and barking and cries of pain filled the space. Wes tilted his neck back sharply, cracking it, trying to ease the sudden wave of stress that washed over him.

Tiger's cage was halfway down the aisle. Its door stood open. Tiger was being trained. As Wes made his way down the long line of cages, he heard Tiger growling over the whining and barking of the other canines. He reached a gap, and peered around the corner, staying out of sight.

Tiger stood in the center of a large green circle, chained in place via a thick black collar that went around his neck and head, replacing his M30. Two soldiers poked the canine with large sticks, prancing around just outside the circle. The soldiers hooted and laughed as they danced in an odd rhythm, driving the long bamboo-like poles into the animal's midsection.

Tiger bit and fought against the poles, growling and foaming at the mouth in his rage.

Wes slinked back behind the protection of the cages, his mind spinning. This wasn't what the animal deserved. He cringed, pain lancing his neck, as he remembered the reason he was still Private First Class Quarter, and not Corporal or Sergeant. He had disobeyed orders once, and that mark on his record prevented him from advancing, and thus earning more credits for his family. Wes rarely talked about the incident, though it wasn't something he hid.

They had been hit with a piece of space debris while en route to H2. Wes had been out of stasis on a duty cycle when it happened. The captain had ordered Wes to seal a compartment that would have saved a section of the vessel, but cost the lives of nineteen men. Wes had chosen to destroy an expensive medical bot to keep the hatch from sealing, while the men escaped. His actions had earned him a sharp reprimand, and he had almost been dishonorably discharged. But even the brass knew that sometimes you had to break the rules.

Wes looked around the corner again and saw that Tiger had given up, and was lying prone in the center of the circle, while the two soldiers watched him. Wes felt the urge to draw his weapon and pop the two bastards, but then he remembered they were just doing their jobs, as terrible and unfair as those jobs were.

Wes slipped back the way he had come, too bothered by what he'd witnessed to visit with Tiger now.

When Wes got back to the barracks, he received word that he was to report to Major Tenet's office, and that he was to double-time it. He thought of Hanora and his children as he jogged across base, cursing himself for having that beer instead of monitoring Tiger. Now he'd be busted out of Space Fleet for sure, and most likely stranded on H2 for the rest of his life. Odds were, he'd never see his family again.

Major Tenet's office was right next to the XO's office suite, which was convenient because both places' primary purpose was to deliver bad news. Tenet handled personnel matters for the XO, and was known for his heartless demeanor. When Wes arrived, he was told to sit. He waited for twenty minutes before they ushered him into the major's office. Wes stood at attention until Tenet spoke.

"At ease. Have a seat, soldier," said Tenet, who sat hunched behind a large holoscreen monitor. Wes sat, and tried not to fidget. His heart pounded, and tension seeped from his pores, his fear giving off the intoxicating stench of desperation.

"You know why you're here?" asked Tenet.

Wes loved these questions. The "I already know, I just want to hear you say it" tone. But Wes had a family, responsibilities, and he was prepared to make any sacrifice if it meant seeing them again. He had ventured out into space, risked his life countless times, so Hanora and their children could have a better life. "No, sir," said Wes.

Tenet leaned back in his chair and eyed Wes, but as he did so, a smile crept across his face. Wes' heart thumped. Tenet didn't look like a guy who was about to crush a family to dust. "Damn HQ," the major spat, and rocked forward in his chair, and leaned across his desk. "As I'm sure you've heard, there's been some trouble back home, and more funding is being shifted to the Torigen war and the Zeffer effort. That means no more ships out this way for a while."

Tenet rocked back, signaling that Wes should be able to figure it out from there. When a few moments passed, and Wes didn't speak, Tenet said, "Four of our destroyers, along with two W class transport vessels, are going to move on to more base locations. You'll head up a new canine team on the Kaspine Destroyer captained by Admiral Gross. If things work out, you might get a bar or two, and get that mark off your head."

Wes smiled, and then frowned. When he looked at Tenet, he saw sadness on the old spacer's face. "No animals permitted on the Kaspine. Your canine will be euthanized, and you will grow a new team of specimens once you arrive at your final destination. If you would like to be with the canine, or terminate the animal yourself, be at his kennel tomorrow at 0800. The Kaspine leaves orbit in six cycles. Questions?"

Wes sat there for a moment, not fully believing what he had heard. Even though he had known from the beginning that when he got shipped out, Tiger would have to be retired—because no one else could control him—he still felt like crap. Tiger was different. Wes said, "No, sir."

"Dismissed."

Wes left the office in a daze, wandering aimlessly until he reached the canteen, where he blew 100 ration points on a large whiskey that he drank in one long pull. When he was done gagging, he rested against a wall, and reflected on the idea that his new mission brought him closer to Galactic Center, and further away from the only three people he cared about.

When he managed to get back to the barracks, he collapsed on his rack, unable and unwilling to close his eyes for fear of what he might find there.

Wes arrived at the kennel early, and was able to spend a few minutes alone with Tiger before the robot doc arrived. Unlike the old days, Tiger would be euthanized via lethal injection, and Wes would hold Tiger, and comfort him as the life left his eyes. Wes thought the animal could sense what was about to happen, his eyes filled with sadness and disappointment—at least that's what it looked like to Wes, because deep down he knew what he and Space Fleet were doing was wrong.

The large med-bot floated across the kennel toward Wes, coming to a stop next to Tiger. The dog sat at attention when the bot arrived, and Wes stroked the top of the animal's head.

"PFC Quarter, restrain your canine," said the bot in a simulated male voice.

Wes knelt, and put his left arm around Tiger, his right hand resting on his sidearm. He was shaking, his entire body racked with grief. Flashbacks of the breach in space, and of the nineteen men scrambling through the wedged-open containment hatch filled his mind as he looked down at Tiger. He caressed the animal gently, thought of his family, and then kissed the top of his head.

The bot's syringe arm came forward, and pricked Tiger in the chest. The animal stood steady, trusting his handler until his very last breath.

A tear slipped down Wes's face as Tiger collapsed into his arms, trembling. "Sorry, brother," he said, rocking back and forth. When Tiger's eyes closed, and his muscles went slack, Wes screamed, but there was no one there to hear him except the medical bot, which stood by, waiting for Wes to release the dead canine so it could dispose of the corpse. There was no ceremony. No honors. Nothing but the harsh reality that, to Space Fleet, they were all nothing but tools.

Wes watched the view screen in front of the cabin, as he strapped into his seat. The screen displayed H2 in all its blue-green brilliance. He wouldn't miss that hellhole, not until he got to next one, which was bound to be worse. He had been assigned to the first duty cycle, and didn't have to go into stasis yet, so he got to watch H2 disappear into the blackness.

His headphones came to life with a burst of static. "One moment. Something's a bit off on our flight plan. Awaiting orders." The earjack sizzled with static as it blinked out, and Wes thought of Tiger. About how his cloning had been a bit off.

The transport ship's plasma rocket rumbled to life, and Wes leaned back and closed his eyes. Tiger waited for him behind his closed lids, the memories bringing a haunted pleasure that made him smile. Reaching into his pocket, Wes fingered the slick containment capsule that held the preserved sample of Tiger's blood he had secretly extracted before the canine was euthanized. Damn the rules. And damn HQ. Wes looked forward to seeing his friend again, seeing the look of trust in his eyes. Wes shuddered as the plasma rockets engaged and he was driven back into his seat.

And if that trust never came, it didn't. PFC Wes Quarter would do it all again anyway. Because that was his job.

THE FORGOTTEN
Tony Ruggiero

Prologue

THE U.S. SOLDIER AND HIS DOG RAN THROUGH AN OPENING IN THE FENCE. Through shortened breath he labored, "We only have one chance to escape, boy—but we got to move!" The words sought purchase in the soldier's mind as justification for his actions.

"Stop or we will shoot!" the pursuers shouted. "You are in violation of the Military Dog Extermination Order!"

The soldier kept running and did not turn around. The words *Extermination Order* repeated over and over in his head. The directive was brief and concise: Destroy all military working dogs so that they could not spread the disease. No exceptions—not even if the dog had saved countless lives.

Extermination Order... Extermination Order...

Between his labored breathing and the repeating phrase in his head, the soldier did not realize that his dog had stopped.

The shepherd, a remarkable animal of strength and agility, stood in the field watching its handler go in one direction as the pursuers approached from the other. There was no doubt in the animal's mind as to what needed to be done. He knew his orders.

P R O T E C T.

The shepherd ran away from its handler and toward the pursuers. Shots rang out, and then the night fell silent.

Years Later on Agricultural Planet CP-22

"This is some scary shit, I tell you, Doc. They were just sticking out of the Godforsaken ground on this Godforsaken world! Light years from Earth—I never signed up for this kind of shit! They wanted an agricultural and grazing specialist not a...who knows what—speaking of which, what the hell do you think did this?"

Doc Casey ignored the agitated man as he examined the remains carefully. The remains were definitely of a steer, of that there was no doubt, but his attention was drawn to one of the larger bones with the bite marks. He measured the indentations from every possible angle, including the depth that they had penetrated into the bone.

"Where did you find this, Tom?" asked Doc. He spoke without taking his eyes away from his work as he fed information into his tablet. A former field medic, he was now what the settlers referred to as a Doc hopper—jumping from colony to colony to offer his medical services as needed—and to the highest bidder in the colony management office. It was a demanding job, but also an efficient way to retire very quickly if you weren't killed on some backwater planet in the process. Yet, others also did it for the constantly changing environments and people—no connections. It was a great way to remain detached.

"Over by the North zone—at the base of the mountains," Tom Delaney answered quickly. He was your run-of-the-mill settler; anxious to get somewhere else and then scared to be there.

"How long ago?" asked Doc.

"Three-four days ago. It was partially buried, but the rains and dust storms cleared it off just enough to be visible. I was setting up the auto plows to prep a new field for planting feed corn. These damn dust storm seem to come up out of—"

"And you haven't seen anything like this before?" Doc asked, cutting him off.

"No. Why?"

"What about other missing livestock?"

"Damn, Doc—you do realize where the hell you are?"

Doc looked up with a look of no comprehension on his face. "What are you talking about?"

"This place is so desolate and marginally occupied that a cow could wander off and never be noticed for...well, until we went looking for it, I guess. Right now, there are about a hundred human beings here. The cows and other livestock outnumber humans by a hundred to one."

"What about the embedded tracking devices?" asked Doc. "Can't you determine the status of the animals that way?"

"Well," Tom began hesitantly, "we can launch some probes to start checking but honestly, they seldom work here."

"Why not?"

"Interference of some sort," said Tom.

"Have you reported it?" asked Doc.

"Sure did, and asked for new ones that can cut through the interference. I don't expect we'll ever get them, though."

"Why not?"

"Because we are primarily an animal colony. We aren't exactly at the top of the list for requirements—especially expensive ones. First priority goes to human colonization planets; besides, there is not supposed to be any predators here."

Doc knew Tom was right. Colonizing was an expensive commodity with a long payback curve. The cheaper you kept it, the faster your return came back, and the happier the investors were to keep on investing. Most colonies were for people, but this one had been engineered for livestock; the entire planet was designed to be nothing more than a big grazing area—in the middle of nowhere. Having met all the basic requirements of -air-soil-water...etc, and having been determined that there was no complex or predatory type life on the planet; it was therefore suitable for use.

"Yeah," Doc said looking over at Tom. "I forgot about that," he said but then added, "Maybe you should send some people out to check for missing livestock." He gazed back at the bone. If there is not supposed to be any other predatory life forms on the planet—then where did the bite marks come from? He hoped that his tablet computer could offer more information about the owner of the teeth marks. He couldn't identify the pattern, yet something about them bothered him—as if he should know what they were. There were forty-two teeth: twenty on top and twenty-two on the bottom. Something about that number was vaguely familiar. He thought back to med school remembering that they had looked at other species' anatomy for comparison as well as used for practice...perhaps this had been one of them.

"How long has the colony been here?" asked Doc, wishing that he had read the orientation package more closely.

"About nine months."

"And the military cleared it when?"

something as simple as a mix up of designations? Yeah—right. Someone misplaced a planet? No—it's something else...but what? And then you add the canine issue and what do you have? One big potential clusterfuck ready to explode into something.

❖

At sunrise the next day, Doc and Tom met at the central headquarters with gear and provisions for a few days. The usual morning mist lay thick and impenetrable. They began to stow the gear into the vehicle.

"Did you learn anything new?" asked Tom.

Doc smiled and chuckled. "No, nothing *really* new." He momentarily thought about sharing his conversation with Sam, but decided to wait. Then, feeling a bit of the same paranoia he had when talking to Sam, he added, "You haven't told anyone have you?"

"No, why?"

"Well, think about it, Tom, the last time canines walked the Earth, they were thought to be carrying an infectious disease. Can you image the reaction if someone was not prepared to see one? We would have mass hysteria with the few colonists that we have."

"Yeah-I guess so," he agreed.

"Well, let's get going," Doc said. "Let's head out to where you found the bones. You drive."

CP-22 is very much like Earth, Doc thought as he looked out over the wide expanse of land. The biggest difference was that there were no trees, and the sky was not as blue. Doc missed trees. It had been quite a while since he had been home but he remembered the mountains, oceans, and trees...

"This is it," Tom's voice broke through Doc's daydream. "This is the North zone, and we are at the base of the mountain range, which signifies the end of the grazing area in this section. As you can see, we have utilized every square inch right up to where that damn brush is—some tough shit, I tell you."

"Where were the bones?" asked Doc. He looked away from the cleared area and toward the mountain. Although there was a lack of trees, there was a variety of waist-high shrubbery all along the unclear area.

"Over here. I went to take a leak and found them," said Tom as he walked off. In a few seconds, he stopped and pointed toward the ground. "Right here."

Doc examined the area where the bones had been found. He saw nothing unusual although he wasn't really sure what unusual meant at this point. He then began to circle the area, making bigger and bigger revolutions as he expanded his search. He didn't know exactly what he was looking for, but searching the area felt like the right thing to do.

In a few minutes, he found himself ensconced in the brush, which made his movement very difficult. He was about to give up when he saw what appeared to be some kind of path along the rock wall that formed the base of the mountain. It was not visible from a distance, and unless someone knew it was there, they would probably not find it.

"Tom," he called, "over here."

"How the hell did you get over there?" Tom asked as he made his way toward Doc. "This stuff gets so thick you can't get through it."

"Do the livestock get over here?" asked Doc.

"No. They can't get through it and the animals don't like it to eat."

Doc scanned the area and then his eyes came to focus on a spot on the ground. "Tom, what do you make of this," he said pointing to a spot on the ground.

Tom walked over and stood next to Doc.

"It looks like...paw prints."

"A lot of paw prints," added Doc as he pointed to various spots on the ground. He knelt down to examine them more closely. In some areas the tracks covered the entire ground.

"Are they canine?" asked Tom.

"I'm not sure," said Doc as he slowly rose from his crouched position. Then in a more cautious tone he added, "But I think the odds are pretty good that they are."

"Why is that?"

"Well...because there is a pack of them staring at us from the ledge up there." As both men looked up, they were greeted by deep growls and bared teeth.

More snarls came from behind them. The two men slowly turned and faced the animals. They were solidly built dogs—Doc estimated their weight from one hundred to one hundred and fifty pounds, dark colors with short and long hair, heavily muscled, and they stood about waist high. From what he remembered from the tablet information, he surmised that they were mainly Shepherds and Labradors.

"Well, this leaves no doubt," said Doc tentatively.

"Yeah," agreed Tom his voice shaky at its core. "What do you think we should do?"

"Nothing—at least for the moment. Let's see what they have in mind."

The dogs slowly positioned themselves around Tom and Doc and began to come closer to them, which would eventually force the two men to move. Doc somehow sensed that the look in these animal's eyes was not one of anger but rather of fear or mistrust...he wasn't sure how to describe it but he felt that uncertainty played a part here somehow.

"Okay," began Doc, "seems like they want to herd us along to follow the trail."

"Call for help?" Tom offered. "I have my comm device."

"Reach for it slowly—see what they do," said Doc.

Tom slowly moved his hand toward the device. As his hand touched it, a growl emanated from the shepherd closest to Tom. "That would be a 'probably not a good idea' growl," said Tom.

"Yeah," agreed Doc, "let's keep going and see where they are taking us."

As they walked, Doc and the animals looked at each other curiously, which made Doc feel odd in a way like running into an old friend that you hadn't seen in a long time and you were both lost in thoughts of the past and unsure where to begin.

After two hours, they arrived at the base of a series of caves that were hidden under a huge stone overhang so they weren't visible from above. Doc guessed that there had to be at least a hundred openings. An all-black shepherd moved to the front of the pack. He was the largest dog Doc had seen so far, heavily muscled, and his coat was deep and thick. The animal's eyes were brown like the majority of the others, but that was where the similarity ended. Doc had seen that look before in the military—the thousand-yard stare it was called—the eyes were those of someone that had seen too much in their life. All the other dogs watched this one closely, which led Doc to believe that he was probably the alpha or leader. The dog looked at Doc and then raised its head and howled. The sound sent shivers down Doc's back. A few seconds later, the sight that followed made his breath catch in his throat. Dogs came out of every cave. There had to be at least fifty or sixty of them.

"Oh my God," said Tom. "How can this be?"

"That, my friend is a good question," said Doc.

The eyes of the dogs riveted on the two men. As earlier, there seemed to be a feeling that something should be familiar between the two. For seconds, nothing happened, and then the shepherd that had howled looked at Doc. He didn't growl this time, but made a chuff sound as he moved his head to the right. Doc looked in the direction and saw a cave.

"You want us to go there?" he pointed in the direction of the cave.

Another chuff emanated from the dog.

"I'll take that as a yes. Let's go and have a look, Tom."

They walked to the cave and went inside. The dogs did not follow but remained at the entrance.

"That's rather foreboding," said Tom looking back at the stationary dogs.

"Yes it is," agreed Doc as he walked around the area. "Either this is our jail cell or something else," he said as he moved into the more dimly lit areas toward the rear of the cave. "Over here, Tom. Please tell me you have some kind of light?"

"I do," said Tom proudly as he removed a device from his pocket and turned it on. The beam pointed into the darkness of the cave. Suddenly, a stark white light illuminated a series of cots with dead bodies on them. Tom dropped the light.

"Damn," he said. "Sorry." Tom quickly retrieved the light and shined it back in the direction, the beam unsteady due to his shaking hand. There were about a half dozen cots, each had a body...or more precisely, the remains of a body on it, more closely a skeleton.

"Okay, scared the shit out of me too," said Doc. He took the light from Tom and moved forward to examine the remains. "Been dead for a quite a while—maybe fifty or sixty years."

"Who are they?" asked Tom.

Doc examined the tattered clothing that covered the remains until he found pieces with writing on them. He read aloud: "United States Army."

"That can't be right," said Tom as he reached out to see the cloth.

Doc went to another cot and picked up clothing and read, "United States Navy," and another, "United States Air Force," and lastly "United States Marine Corps."

Doc sat on the ground. All the pieces seem to fall into place. After a few seconds he said, "*They* sent them here."

"Who sent them here?" asked Tom.

"At some point during the hysteria on Earth, the military sent the dogs they had here to save them from being put to death. Then they hid that information—that's why there is no record of CP-22. It really does not exist because they don't want it to—they don't want the dogs discovered."

"What are you taking about—what record?" asked Tom.

Doc relayed the conversation he had with his military contact.

"But who are these dead people?" asked Tom.

"I guess they were their handlers," said Doc. "The men and women who trained and cared for the dogs—they couldn't let them go on their own so they sacrificed their own lives to see them to safety."

At that moment Doc felt the warmth of hair and skin on the underside of his hand. He looked down and saw the black shepherd's head there. He fought the instinct of fear to remove his hand and allowed it to slowly and lightly stroke the head of the animal. The feeling that Doc had earlier—the sense of familiarity of something returned, but this time he thought he understood it—love, trust, and companionship. The shepherd looked up at him and through watery eyes seemed to acknowledge Doc's own thoughts before the dog moved off and went out of the cave.

"But how did they survive all this time?" asked Tom.

"There must be something around that can explain some of this," he said as he shone the light around. They found a desk and upon it sat an old style log book with handwriting in it. Doc opened the first page to the words: *Faithful-Fearless-Forever*. He began to turn pages, scanning the contents, much of which had deteriorated. Some of the information he glimpsed:

—there were six humans and twenty five dogs in the original party

—the dogs were all war heroes

—had a probe jammer in place to block reading any life form signals in this area

—they were able to synthesize a food source from the local indigenous shrubbery and stockpiled years of it knowing that their deaths were imminent and combined with the fact that no humans had arrived

—were concerned about the dogs' survival.

Doc closed the book. "There is a lot more but it's hard to read. We should have someone salvage it. Let's get some air," he said.

As they exited the cave, a dozen dogs, a mixture of Shepherds and Labradors, sat in the sun patiently waiting for them. Beyond them, hundreds watched their every move. In that vast crowd of dogs, the men could see mixes of the two main breeds, unlike the main group nearest to them who were clearly purebreds. Doc's thoughts quickly responded to what he saw: *they were standing in formation*. The fear and apprehension seemed to have passed—it was as if they felt something that put them at ease. Doc wondered of his moment with the shepherd in the cave.

"What's this about?" asked Tom referring to the obvious change in demeanor.

"My guess is that they are rediscovering what their ancestors—the original twenty-five dogs, passed down to them," said Doc, "their need for companionship, as well as the need to serve and to please." The black shepherd came up to Doc and sat down in front of him.

"After all that time-why didn't they just go feral?"

"Maybe something to do with their training, or the side effects from the bug. I'm not sure, it might take a while to figure out," said Doc. "Makes you wonder what other side effects there might be."

Tom's communication device buzzed. He started to reach for it and then stopped. "You think it's okay?"

"Yeah—I think we are passed that point," said Doc as he smiled and reached down to pet the shepherd. "Good boy," Doc murmured.

Tom answered the device and began conversing. "What? Say again," he said just as the sound of a large detonation reached them causing them to cover their ears.

"What the hell is that?" asked Doc.

"The call was from the colony," Tom began, his voice wavering. "They said...they said they were under attack by unknown forces. They've got dead...lots of dead...many wounded."

"Unknown forces?" asked Doc.

"No identification on the craft," said Tom. "They just blew up the main colony area where the majority of colonists live and work."

Doc and Tom crawled their way to the edge of the outcropping to look into the colony area. There was not much left to the encampment. Most of the buildings had been leveled. Smoke still billowed in spots making it hard to see. However, as Doc used the binoculars he came across survivors. They were outside in a fenced area—there had to be at least fifty or so. Guards patrolled the perimeter of the fence wearing some type of environmental suit. There were no discernible marking on the suits, which made any kind of identification impossible; however, it did confirm that the attackers possessed a humanoid shape. They also carried rifle-like weapons.

Back when Doc was in the service, there had been a lot of scuttle butt about other alien races but none had ever been encountered...until now. *CP-22 is becoming the home of many firsts—the dogs and now the alien invaders. Was this a coincidence or was there a connection?*

"I don't know about you," Tom's voice cut through Doc's thoughts, "but right now, I rather be back with the dogs."

"Yeah, me too," agreed Doc. He brought the binoculars back up to his eyes and scanned the area again.

"What are you thinking?"

"Well," Doc began, "I only see a couple guards. I'm guessing that the rest are off looking for more colonists. I'm thinking that if we can take them out we can get the colonists and high tail it back to where the dogs are before anyone gets back. It's a pretty good spot to hide out while we figure out what to do next."

"Wait for help?"

"Probably," agreed Doc. He turned his attention back to the vehicle they had parked out of sight. "Is there anything that might function as a weapon in there?"

"Well, there are some cattle prods," offered Tom. "They deliver a nice little jolt. It's good for convincing a cow to go along with your suggestion."

"Might be enough to distract them or disable their suits electronics. It will have to do. Let's go, it will be light in an hour or so."

"Move and you're dead," said the voice.

Doc stopped in his tracks. "Shit," he cursed.

"Turn around and drop the...whatever the hell that is!" the voice demanded.

It suddenly dawned on Doc. *English? The guard spoke* English?

Just as Doc turned, the guard gave an agonized scream. There stood Tom with his cattle prod still embedded in the man's back. Whiffs of white smoke came from the power pack of the environmental suit.

"That's good enough," said Doc motioning for Tom to remove the prod. As soon as Tom did so, the man fell unconscious to the ground.

"Now I'm curious," said Doc, "let's have a look at our English-speaking invader."

They removed the helmet to discover an ordinary human being.

"What the hell is going on?" asked Tom. "Who the hell are these guys?"

"That is a good question," said Doc. "But I am going to put my money—"

"No one cares about *your* money, Doc Casey, but rather the money that can be made *from what you have found*."

Tom and Doc turned in the direction of the voice. Lights glared into existence, initially blinding them. As their eyes adjusted they saw half a dozen men with rifles pointed at them. "I told you it would work," one of them said to the rest of the group. "He would try and rescue the colonists. It's the military thing that fucks up their self preservation way of thinking."

"Who the hell are you?" asked Doc.

"Names are not really important in our line of work," the man said as he removed his helmet. But if it makes you happy you can call me...let's see, how about Bruce—yeah sure."

The other men laughed at the man's comment as they removed their helmets as well.

"What do you want?" Doc asked.

"Do you really need to ask that question?" Bruce said. "We have been listening to what is going on." He pointed toward a tablet that one of the men carried—it was just like Doc's. "And we have been listening to what *you have been doing*, Doc—canines. So tell me, how many are there?"

"What do you care?"

"Oh, Doc—I do so care and you can't be that fucking stupid. Do you know what they are worth? They're fucking extinct! Just one of them will bring millions."

"You've come for the dogs?" asked Doc incredulously. "Killed these innocent people because of the dogs?"

"This has to remain a secret," said the man adamantly. "If word ever got out the government would go snake shit. We have to make sure that nothing interferes with our plan."

"What about them?" asked Tom as he pointed to the prisoners.

"Well—they are going to have to take a little... holiday, or there will be some unfortunate accident—I haven't decided which yet. I am bringing in an entirely new crew of discreet people I can trust."

"You're a sick bastard," said Doc.

"Well, be that as it may, Doc, why don't we cut to the heart of the matter? Where are they?"

Doc said nothing.

"Oh come now, I have a dozen men searching the immediate area—based upon where your tablet went. Do you think we won't find them?"

Still Doc said nothing.

"Fine, you want to be stubborn—well there's a cost." the man said and turned and fired his weapon at Tom. The bullet struck him in his shoulder driving him to the ground. "He has another shoulder, legs, hands...etc. This game can go on for quite a while."

"Screw you," Tom spat.

"Oh well if this is how you wish to play," Bruce said as he turned the gun in Doc's direction. "What's it going to be, Doc, a leg or an arm?" He cocked the weapon and aimed at Doc's head.

At that moment the lights went out. Doc heard the sound of a generator cutting off in the distance.

"Damn it!" Bruce cried. "What the hell's going on? You two," he pointed to his men, "go and see what the hell is happening."

As the generator came to a complete stop, a momentary silence fell over the group. In that moment, Doc heard the sound of the dogs. Lots of them running and growling. Men began to scream. Shots sounded. Someone knocked Doc over as they fell into him, driven by the four-legged attackers. He quickly rolled free from the jumble of bodies. In the dim light, he watched as the dogs, anywhere from two to four of them, attacked each man and drove them to their knees. The gunfire continued and Doc watched as many of the dogs went down. But there were too many of them and eventually all of the men ended up on the ground, each guarded by several dogs.

Doc went over to where Tom lay. He examined the wound. "Went through," Doc said. He removed a cloth from his pocket and placed it over the wound in front and then stuffed some other cloth down the back of his clothing. "Keep pressure on it."

"Look," Tom said indicating behind him.

Doc turned and saw the black shepherd walking toward him, limping.

Without hesitation, Doc moved to meet the dog and checked the leg. After a quick examination he said, "It's only a flesh wound." With no other cloth to use as a bandage he searched the area for something to use. He saw the intruder, Bruce, lying on his back, his arm, which had held the weapon earlier, soaked with blood. In one of the man's pockets Doc saw a neckerchief of some sort. He snatched it and wrapped the dog's leg. "There you go, boy," he said. He then cradled the dog's head in his hands and stroked its ears. "Good boy—and thank you."

"What about the others?" Tom called to Doc. "The one's he sent looking for the dogs?"

"My guess is that they were met with a similar welcome," said Doc. He turned to the dog, "Am I right, boy?"

The dog chuffed in response, which Doc accepted as confirmation. He turned toward where the colonist prisoners had been kept. The pens were empty, the prisoners having scattered for cover when the shooting began.

"You can come out," Doc called. "The men that attacked you have been captured but we can use your help with them. Come out but do not be alarmed by the *dogs*. Yes I did say dogs—they will not harm you nor are they infectious in any way, shape, or form. They..." Doc's voice broke a little at the memory of the gunshots. "Some of them sacrificed their lives for ours."

Slowly the colonists emerged. Some appeared in shock and others devastated by what had happened. Everyone stared in amazement at the dogs. Smiles came to their faces as they approached. Many of the dogs met them and Doc couldn't help but think of a reunion of man and dog; a contrast of bewilderment and innate recognition embedded in both species. But the happy thoughts of the reunion were lost as he surveyed the area. At least a dozen dogs lay still on the ground. Anger surged from deep in his gut. He regarded their attackers—most had only minor injuries, yet if these dogs had wanted to they could have literally torn the attackers to pieces. A part of Doc wished that they had done just that.

He walked slowly over to where the leader of the attacking group lay on the ground. Doc placed his face within inches of the man and said, "So as to your earlier question, Bruce, *here are the dogs*. What do you think now, you son of a bitch? I guess you'll have to put your plans of getting rich on hold."

"Someone will get them..." Bruce said.

"Someone already did," said Doc, "about a hundred years ago some bastard just like you. He turned to a couple of the colonists and said, "Get him out of here before I feed him to the dogs."

The first light of the day was breaking and with it the arrival of the early morning mist that was commonplace on CP-22. Doc busied himself ensuring that all the invaders had been taken into custody by the colonists and properly restrained. Once the prisoners and the colonists had been settled into an area of shelter, Doc noticed that the dogs had slipped away. He looked into the oncoming mist and saw shadows of the animals slowly moving deeper into the fog and disappearing. For a moment, he thought he saw the black shepherd standing tall as it silently acknowledged each dog as it passed him. And then there was something else...Doc thought he saw the handlers with them. *Like ghosts.* He turned from the haze and looked around the area; the bodies of the dead dogs were gone as well. Then for some reason the words on the first page in the journal came to his mind, Faithful-Fearless-Forever.

"They're gone?" said Tom.

"Appears so," said Doc not taking his eyes off of the mist as if waiting for something to happen.

"It's hard to believe," began Tom. "Many of the colonists are wondering if the dogs were real. I think a few of them are in shock."

"Do they understand what they did?" pleaded Doc. "They saved us—*they saved all of us*. They didn't have to."

"I know," said Tom reassuringly placing his hand on Doc's shoulder.

"It seems like it never stops some days."

"What?"

"The way mankind always fucks something up. Whether its fear or greed, we're quick to judge and condemn. And who suffers—the innocent ones; those who just wanted to be our friends and companions."

Silence settled between the two men for several moments. Finally Doc spoke. "What that ass Bruce said: 'Someone will get them.' If they monitored my tablet, someone else may know as well."

"What do you think we should do?" asked Tom.

"The right thing for a change," Doc said.

The morning mist was thicker than usual, but as the air warmed and it dissipated, the outline of the figures became clear. The Soldiers, Sailors, Airmen, and Marines stood at parade rest in their crisp dress uniforms and shining boots. They lined the path from the military transport to the center of the remains of the colony where Doc's friend, Colonel Sam Kurtz, stood with him.

"I hope you're right about this," Sam said to Doc. They stood off to the side of the soldiers looking in the direction of the mist, waiting. "If not, I will have a lot of explaining to do.

"They'll come," Doc said simply.

At first there was a shadowy movement in the mist and then the black shepherd appeared at the edge. Doc walked to the fringe of the mist to meet the dog. When he was next to the dog, Doc dropped to his knees and petted him. The dog chuffed and nuzzled his hand with its head. For several moments the two just sat there as if the rest of the world no longer existed. It was their defining moment of man and dog. Then Doc looked toward the men and women in uniform and then back at the shepherd.

"This is for you, fella," Doc began, "you and those that came before you—the ones that never gave up on us—*the Forgotten*. We're asking you to take a chance. Trust us again and come home."

The dog looked at the men and then up at Doc. There was an anxious disposition of the dog that Doc could not tell if it was from apprehension or excitement. After several moments, the dog turned toward the mist and chuffed several times. Slowly a line of animals emerged.

"I'll be God damned," Sam said.

Side by side they came, Shepherd, Labrador, and some mixed breed. As they came up to where Doc and the black shepherd stood, the dogs exchanged glances; some form of acknowledgement and then they moved on toward the transport.

"Atten-*hut!*" cried Sam. The men and women moved from parade rest to the position of attention. As the first pair of dogs reached Sam, he raised his right arm and saluted. Although military discipline dictated that their eyes look straight ahead of them, many of the honor guard could not help but to stare at the marvel before them. A few faces even became tear-streaked. Sam held his salute until the last dog passed him.

Doc and the black shepherd came up next to Sam. Doc saw the look in Sam's eyes—he was overwhelmed as were many of the honor guard. He turned away from Doc for a moment—toward the quickly dissipating mist as he wiped at his eyes. Sam looked in that direction for a few seconds and then said, "What's that?" as he pointed toward the mist.

Doc looked in the direction that Sam indicated. In the last part of the dissipating haze he saw the image of a man and next to him a dog. The man saluted and then he and the dog turned and vanished.

There was an awkward moment of silence when someone should have said something, but neither man did. Finally Sam said, "I'm not sure what I just saw."

Doc hesitated for several seconds before speaking. "A farewell...a long overdue acknowledgement and perhaps a new beginning," he said.

TRUE FRIENDS
Bud Sparhawk

COMMAND TOLD US TO MOVE FORWARD INTO THE VALLEY BUT THE CAPTAIN WAS not so sure we should do that. "Doesn't smell right," he said as he tested the breeze coming up the steep slopes leading down to the twisting river that had been nibbling away at the valley's bottom for centuries. "I think we should avoid going down there."

I tried to see what worried him but my limited human senses weren't up to the task. All I could see down below was the tree cover and untidy piles the flooding river had deposited along its banks. There had to be heavy rains pouring down the hillsides to move that much that effluvia. Aside from what looked like completely natural cover, there were no reflections from shiny surfaces or metallic glints that hinted at alien presence. Except for a cleared area farther along, the valley looked as if it hadn't been disturbed in years.

The settlers must have bypassed this valley after taking a look and figured it too risky to furrow fields and plant crops in the flood plain. They could have planned to do that later, after they had the leisure to invest effort in marginal lands. I should say, *should have come* later because the damn Shardie invasion had wiped out all the settlers' dreams and efforts.

Back in the early days of the war humanity had modest success driving off the aliens, but once they learned how to integrate human minds into their glistening machines they turned the tide against us and began defeating our best efforts. By the time our third colony was lost the Council agreed that euthanasia was a far better choice than allowing the Shardies to appropriate more human souls. We pulled back again and again, ever conscious that we could not continue to lose colonies, lose resources, and worst of all, lose too many souls. We knew that unless we fought back humanity would be lost.

Thanks to bitter experience we managed to evacuate nearly eighty percent of the colonists long before the aliens attacked, lost ten percent in a vain attempt at defense, and surrendered the rest to the exigencies of war when it became obvious there was no other choice.

There was no such thing as surrender where the Shardies were involved.

EVE swooped over the edge of the cliff, racing downslope to catch an updraft and soar just above the treetops as she raced down the valley. "No sign of activity," she reported on our combat net as she swung back and forth, riding the air currents to stay aloft with minimal energy effort, while mapping the entire bottom. "Couple of heat sources. Small animals, I suspect. No metal. No reflections. No flares."

Her last burst was encouraging. Glass or metal would mean we'd uncovered another Shardie remnant. We'd already cleared a dozen pockets that had remained after we destroyed their orbiting craft and bombarded their emplacements. The signature of Shardie presence was the intense heat, the "flare" that EVE had mentioned.

I watched EVE lift high, turn, and make a high-speed scan of the far slope, just to ensure that there was nothing there. The Shardies tended to prefer flat ground, but you could never be certain.

She banked again and swept the near side a second time. "All clear," she said just as she caught an upwelling fountain of air, soared high over our heads and angled back to base. "Good hunting," she called as she disappeared from sight.

"No sign of signal," BUZZARD12 reported from his position on the lip. I couldn't see the squat tractor's sensor array from my position, but knew he'd double-checked EVE's report with his own sensors that covered everything from infrared to high UV. His eleventh instance had been lost in our first encounter after landing, consumed in that hellish torrent of silver the Shardies unleashed whenever we drew close.

The modern assault force marines were far different from those primitive Cybermarines who'd been thrown into battle in the early phases of the Shardie War. Those were men who'd given up their memories and much of their humanity to turn themselves into machines almost capable of doing battle with the Shards. There were enormous losses of fully human and Cybermarines before COMMAND decided that spawning the minds of the Cybers was a much more efficient method of producing warriors than reserving a trooper's consciousness to a single instance.

Once humanity got past the squeamishness of producing multiple copies of individual marines, the step to install them into advanced fighting platforms was logical and straightforward. Today instanced marines inhabit powerful and deadly machines capable of fighting Shards in every environment. Our assault force was highly mechanized; resembling an ancient armored battalion with its array of tanks, artillery, and machines that had no historic precedents; manglers, torsors, and battlehatts.

RAPTOR6 was configured as a battlehatt, carrying four AR96b launchers, a belt of K92 repeaters, and two heavy KBAR-6 assault cannons. His size and configuration made maneuvering awkward, but the sheer power of his weapons more than made up for it.

RAPTOR6 had lost his left gun emplacement when he rammed it down the throat of a charging Shardie carrier. He chose a refit instead of letting the Captain call up another instance. Like most of his mates, he had developed an attachment to his latest episode and thought having that memory too valuable to lose. "I want to remember how I blew that monster off the map," he bragged, "Three rounds right down its fucking throat. Man doesn't get to do that many times in his life. No thank you, I want this memory to become part of my permanent memories."

That would have to wait until we rejoined the fleet. Our ground assault force carried no capability of spawning a new instance for RAPTOR. That required far more resources than we could spare. We could call down a replacement RAPTOR from storage, but RAPTOR7 would be from the copy made six months before, when we had set out from base and have no recollection of his superb shot. *Better,* he thought, *to risk the loss of this instance in combat, than to lose it voluntarily.*

There were multiple copies of RAPTOR across the stars—as many as were needed by COMMAND. Each of those copies originated from a single marine who elected to continue to serve as part of a fighting machine and had his mind spawned into multiple copies.

As these copies spread across the universe each RAPTOR instance acquired unique memories from their experiences. When they managed to survive long enough to spawn new copies from their then-current instance their subsequent instances would branch from there, forming their own unique memories.

You could look upon RAPTOR's heritage as a skein of threads, each unique to its predecessors, and each as individual as any natural human. Were multiple RAPTORs to meet, they would be strangers, as unlike as distant relatives, sharing only their most distant memories and their original ancestor's personality.

What every RAPTOR or any of the others wanted was to preserve their unique consciousness and to extend that as far into the future as possible. Would any other human want otherwise? True, a RAPTOR duplicate would live on, as would the children of any parent, but that was small comfort to *this* instance of RAPTOR.

"I say we check it anyway," WILSON advised the Captain. He was our tactician and could draw on fifteen data streams at once. "The topographic maps from the settlers indicate a few caves at the base of the cliffs four klicks ahead. Good hiding places that might shield a Shardie flare."

"Didn't EVE check them with her side-looking radar?" the Captain demanded.

"Only to confirm their existence," WILSON replied. "She couldn't see more than a few meters inside."

The Captain sniffed again. "I don't like the smell of this place, but we'll check them out. Where's a useful route to the valley floor?"

While RAPTOR6 trundled to a spot where he could provide covering fire, three manglers and I rappelled down the cliff in fifty-meter bounds. I was wary of the manglers swinging to either side. Their enthusiasm outweighed their caution and having four two-ton marines being less than careful about lane control made me and the other Trues nervous.

"Watch out, you meat pups, don't get squashed," BUZZARD12 joked as his massive foot landed next to my leg. I wasn't sure if the move had been deliberate or not—the instanced like to play little jokes on we pitifully vulnerable true humans.

Although I shared the general configuration and appearance of most true humans, my frame probably resembled my ancestors' no more than did my other, more mechanical companions. Even among true humans physical enhancements were the norm. Most of us meat marines bulked up our musculature, improved our senses, and supplemented our twitch nerves and red muscles to obtain more rapid reactions. Alas, the brains of true and enhanced humans were little advanced from their heritage.

But COMMAND was working on that.

The vast number of civilians—colonists in particular—were still trapped on the evolutionary treadmill that some wretched little tarsier had started a couple million years ago, breeding imperfect copies of themselves as modified by circumstance, environment, and mutations. But the majority were not the only branches of humanity. Other versions were adapted to extreme environments, had adopted enhanced capabilities, or otherwise supplemented their natural attributes with mechanical devices, much as WILSON had done.

But we meat marines were sometimes useful. "Squash me and you'll gum up your joints," I responded. "Hard to scrape my crap off your sole with those cumbersome hands of yours, BUZZARD."

BUZZARD12's hands were the size of forklift tongues and capable of peeling armor plate off a battle cruiser. I'd seen his previous instance rip an attacking Shardie mobile apart, just before a silver flood consumed both. That act had saved my ass and for that I was still in his debt, even if this instance of him couldn't remember. We were good friends.

We got to the first set of caves quickly and confirmed that RAPTOR6 was targeting our location, just in case a glitter of Shardies suddenly erupted. I was more nervous than my companions, having made my recording long before departure and having no hope of my frail human form being restored, Instead and if my mind survived, I would be configured into some advanced form and remember nothing of this. The others were only months out of date and could easily shrug off the loss. Not so for me.

I entered the cave slowly, behind Givens, a short, heavily muscled marine who liked to arm wrestle with BUZZARD12, not that she ever won, but the exercise did her good. "Smells," she grunted as we squeezed into ever narrowing passage.

"More than that," I replied. My nose wasn't as good as the Captain's, but even I could catch the slightly sweet smell of decay and dissolution.

"Oh shit," Givens said and stopped so abruptly that I goosed her with the tip of my HO-83. I always held the muzzle low, ready to rake fire on the rise.

I looked past and, in the area illuminated by our headlamps, was a set of pens containing the remains of a dozen dead animals—large animals judging from the size of the bones. "Cattle," Givens snarled.

I checked the water bowls and auto feeders. All of them were empty. From the positions of the dead animals it looked more likely they had died of starvation. No signs of trauma anywhere.

"Who could have put them here and why?"

"Maybe some settlers put them here for safety and didn't make it back. Who knows? Damn shame, what happened here."

We reported what we found and, as we were moving down the valley toward the former farmhouse we found a crude set of pens. Three had been smashed open, their occupants missing. From the scatter of debris it was obvious that they had broken free rather than been rescued. There were remains in the other pens. Dogs.

We examined one of the least decayed corpses. All the remains were about the same size, more or less and probably of a single breed; not that I'm an expert on the species *canus lupis familiaris* by any means.

"Not a lot of decay," Givens said.

"Different bacteria. Different biochemistry."

She prodded one corpse with her toe. When it fell apart I spotted what looked like a bit of twisted fishing line.

"Looks like it got tangled with something before it died," Givens said. "Must have spun around and around to escape and then died."

"Yeah, looks that way," I answered, although it was hard to understand how it could have cut through skin and muscle. Poor thing.

We reported what we found to the Captain, who was checking the site of the farmhouse. Apparently some farmer had decided to risk farming this valley after all. Like all other human constructions that had been on this planet, nothing remained. No metal or plastic within the mound that resulted from a Shardie deconstruction. It was typical of the way the Shardies reduced buildings to nothing more than piles of fine sand.

After a brief pause the squad spread wide as we moved to examine the rest of the valley. The Captain put our manglers on the flanks, let Phillip, the torpor take the lead, and told us ordinary humans to stay in the van, tagging along behind the others like pups following their mother. On the ridge above us RAPTOR6 tracked us, keeping watch against any explosion of hostiles and ensuring that we were continually within his range. I wasn't reassured. The armament RAPTOR6 could throw at this range had too large a kill radius for my comfort.

Dark fell quickly in the valley the instant the minuscule dot of this system's pathetic sun disappeared behind the ridgeline. With no moon, the darkness was absolute, at least for we humans. Some of the others had enhanced vision and the Captain... Well, the Captain never had a problem, it seemed.

Givens and I bedded down in a small copse of stunted trees while the others powered down far apart to minimize losses in the event of an attack. WILSON stood guard atop a pile of storm-washed boulders the size of houses. Spring floods must be damn violent, I thought, to move those rocks around. Even BUZZARD12 would be hard put to shift one of those.

Something woke me from a sound sleep. I lay still, trying to determine if it was a dream, a sound, a rustle of movement, or a shift of wind?

I had just dismissed the incident as nerves when another small noise caught my attention. It was on my left and close. Carefully I slipped my hand onto the stock of the HO while twisting my body slightly. The fabric of my suit made a slight sound. Whatever it was skittered away.

I flipped on my torch and saw that something had chewed on the discarded ration pack I'd tossed aside.

"Everything all right?" WILSON said.

"Did you see anything?" I asked. He couldn't have missed it.

"Small animal. Night creature. Nothing threatening," he answered, which was no answer at all. I doubted that it was "nothing" since most local wildlife would be wary of us, if not frightened to death. True humans, as well as the others, probably smelled inedible to them.

I checked around but found no sign of what it might have been.

"COMMAND says we're to stand and wait for orders," the Captain announced after his morning briefing and sent four manglers ridge-wise to help bring RAPTOR6 down a less precipitous incline. The incline was out where the valley emptied into the broad tidal "plain" that stretched six hundred kilometers to the edge of the placid sea. On other worlds this would have been called a tidal plain, but lacking a moon, tides were something this world would never see. What waves danced across the waters were the result of wind-drifts and thermal flows.

The Captain took WILSON to investigate the remains in the caves, while the rest of us decided to relax a bit and, since this valley was completely safe, find a little solitude. BUZZARD12 and his mates simply powered down for the interim since remaining awake consumed too much energy. I decided to go for a run to stretch my legs.

I had gone two klicks from camp when I sensed something tracking me. I activated the HO I always carried with me. Just because we considered the valley safe didn't mean I could be stupid enough to go unarmed.

I scanned the area, looking for anything out of the ordinary and spotted a patch of white between two boulders. There should be no white in this terrain. I circled while keeping the spot of white in sight, trying to find a place where I could get a better view without drawing closer than necessary.

It was a dog, a Goddamned scrawny, emaciated, filthy mutt, trying its damndest to hide.

I crouched down and whistled. "Here, girl," I said uncaring if the gender were correct or not. "Come on, boy." I snapped my fingers and whistled again. "Come on, come on."

The dog didn't move.

I pulled out the ration pack I'd brought with me, pinched off a hunk of the meaty block, and tossed to toward its hiding place.

The dog didn't move, although I thought I saw a slight tail wag. I retreated a dozen steps and stayed low. Perhaps it was frightened of me. It didn't move.

I walked further away; watching as I retreated a hundred steps, two hundred, and three hundred. That's when I saw a flash of white emerge from the rocks and swoop toward the morsel I'd left. It was a good start.

Throughout the afternoon I pinched off more chunks and left them behind, venturing ever less far before turning to watch the starving dog gulp down my offerings. As it grew used to me, and no doubt motivated by hunger, the dog appeared less wary, less frightened. Soon, I hoped, it might be close enough to touch.

Then it was over. The dog disappeared into the brush without a whimper. I looked around to see what must have startled it. Moments later I heard the distant sounds of BUZZARD12 powering up. Damn. Loud noises must frighten her.

That night I asked WILSON to alert me should he detect any sign of animal movements. I left a morsel near where the ration pack had been as an offering of comfort. This was the way my distant ancestors had tamed the wolves and turned them into companions, helpers, and pets.

The morsel was gone in the morning light.

"Saw a dog, yesterday," Givens said as we did our morning patrol of the camp's periphery. "Mangy, brown thing. Wild. Almost shot it."

"That accounted for two of the escapees," I replied. "Nice to know something survived those filthy aliens."

"Wonder how they survived. Can't be that much they can eat out here."

I recalled the dog's emaciated look. "Not much nutrition from the wildlife." It would have to eat a lot of game just to survive. No wonder it wolfed down those rations.

When our patrol was over I retraced my steps and didn't have to wait long before I glimpsed a familiar form lurking near. Closer, but still wary.

I sat with my back against a rock and tossed out morsels to entice my shy friend closer. It took a while for it to work up enough courage, but eventually it was eating portions within my reach.

Definitely a female. Part collie, I guessed. Couldn't be more than two years old. Cute thing. "Coleen," I said, naming her without further thought.

By afternoon I had Coleen eating from my fingers and licking at the grease. By the time I needed to head back, she let me pick burrs from her fur. She followed me to camp.

Givens was sitting with her back against BUZZARD12's leg with a brown version of Coleen beside her. It looked about the same age.

Givens glanced at me as we settled beside her. The dogs sniffed one another and then settled as well. "Think we'll get in trouble?"

"Captain might object," I suggested.

Givens scowled. "Screw him." Which matched my own feelings. "We Earth types need to look after one another." She ruffled his dog's fur.

Just the same, we were careful to stay well away from the Captain and WILSON when they returned. The dogs must have sensed our unease because they faded into the underbrush. Smart dogs.

The next day Givens and I swept the perimeter again. The morning patrol was stupid, but SOP was to do a morning sweep so sweep we did. The dogs joined us at the furthest point from the camp. As usual, we had nothing to report and decided to have some fun with the dogs.

It took only two tosses before the dogs learned to play catch and then it was as if we could never throw the sticks fast or far enough. My arm tired before either dog was exhausted. We lay down to rest in the shade, our dogs beside us, and breathed contentment. This was a welcome break from the constant stress of combat, of sniffing out those damned aliens and eradicating them.

"Watch this," Givens said as she tossed a stick into the air and, at the top of its arc, fired the HO. Both dogs disappeared, frightened by the sudden roar of the weapon. "Whoops," she said.

The dogs rejoined us the next day as if nothing untoward had happened and, by the third night the dogs were completely at ease with us. They lay beside us while Givens and I worked on our equipment, ate our rations, and just talked about nothing much. At night Coleen snuggled against me, resting her head in the crook of my arm, her gentle breathing in counterpoint to my own. It was a bit of unexpected comfort, a relief from the death and destruction that was our usual lives.

"Where are they?" The Captain's booming voice startled me from a sound sleep. Givens was struggling to her feet, weapon already in her hands as I reached for my own.

"This is not a drill, damn it! Put your weapons down and answer me—where are those animals you two have been hiding?"

"We haven't been hiding…" I began, but the Captain cut me off.

"Don't lie to me. WILSON filled me in on the animals that have been sneaking into camp. Where are they?"

"They're just some starving dogs we found," Givens explained. "We fed them and they sort of adopted us."

"Dogs? How in the name of seven hells did you find dogs on this planet?"

I stuttered out my own tale and how I had enticed it near, taught it to chase sticks, and how they accompanied us on our daily patrol. "They're pretty tame to Givens and me," I added. "But pretty shy about the others."

"Shy? More like wary of detection, I'd say!" The Captain sounded furious. "What were you two idiots thinking?" he demanded. "Was it too hard for you to do some simple math? The Shardies overran this planet four years ago, wiped out the settlers in less than a year and held this place until we arrived. Do the math. How could the dogs have survived the attack? How would they have eaten enough to survive this long?"

"They're pretty smart," Givens volunteered.

"Of course they are, you fool!" the Captain roared. "They were probably made that way. Christ, didn't you notice the Shardie implants in those remains? Didn't you think about what those intact pens implied?" He fixed us with a cold stare. "Didn't you fucking think why the Shardies hadn't deconstructed them as well as the farm house? These animals are more of their damn weapons."

"But what could they do?" I asked. "I mean, they're just dogs. It's not like they have guns or anything. Where's the harm?"

"If these dogs never had contact with humans then why are they so friendly? Did you think about that?"

"Instincts?" I ventured. Sure, I never had a dog before so why should I feel so sympathetic to this one? Why couldn't it work that way for Coleen as well?

The Captain didn't like that excuse. "Maybe they're so friendly just so you would take them to the ship, let them find out more about us, where we might be vulnerable and then, when the time is right, get that information back to their fleet."

"Isn't that somewhat far-fetched, sir? I mean, they're just dogs...."

"I don't care. We are not taking them with us," the Captain replied. "And we can't take the chance of leaving them behind to report on whatever they've already learned." I knew where this was going and didn't like it one bit. "You know what you have to do," he continued. "Unless you'd like one of the manglers to...."

"NO!" Givens shouted a millisecond before I could voice my own objection. "No. I, that is we will take care of it."

I agreed, although the words were bitter ashes in my mouth.

The next morning we prepared for our usual patrol of the perimeter, although both of us knew it would be anything but usual.

Givens was silent as she cleaned her HO-83, carefully fitting the weapon's components together and checking twice that they were seated properly before proceeding. The checks were unnecessary since there was only one way the HO's components could fit together.

"I've been thinking," she said at last. "Could the Captain be wrong? Maybe some dogs survived long enough to have pups. Maybe there are a lot more dogs out there, living off the land."

I considered. The idea made sense, but why didn't we see more than these two? "Can't take them with us, even if that were true. Captain's made that pretty clear."

Givens slapped a component home with too much force. "Doesn't feel right. My dog's done nothing wrong."

"Except being friendly, which might be a trick."

"Shit!"

We both knew that we were delaying what we had to do. I slapped a fresh magazine into the breech and clicked the safety home. "Let's get this over with," I said softly, trying to lend a bit of dignity to our task.

Givens nodded but remained silent as she joined me.

We walked slowly, taking extra care to examine any possible hiding places that might conceal a remnant Shardie, sometimes doubling back to check a second time, just to be certain, you know.

The dogs joined us at the usual spot, bounding up with tongues lolling and tails wagging, every muscle of their bodies quivering in welcome.

"Do we do it now?" I asked as I scratched behind Coleen's ears and was rewarded with a tail way and slurpy lick.

"I'll take care of my own dog," Givens said bitterly. I could hear that tension in her voice. "Come on, boy." The two of them headed off to the west, disappearing between the trees. I sympathized. It wouldn't be easy, this necessary bit of business.

"I'll see you back at camp," I yelled and headed toward the caves. We'd almost arrived when I heard the ratcheting sound of Givens' HO-83 in the distance. That took longer than I expected, but then, wasn't I doing the same thing, delaying the inevitable, debating the right thing to do, ever mindful of the Captain's concerns, and wondering if death by my hand was more merciful than letting Coleen slowly starve on this planet's paltry nourishment and finally die alone and unloved.

Coleen had bolted at the sound of gunfire but eventually returned to where I waited outside the cave mouth. I fed bits of ration to Coleen and watched the way the wan sunlight reflected off the valley's blue-green foliage. If I squinted my eyes I could imagine sitting back on Earth, resting after a day's hike with my faithful companion.

In a few years humans would return and turn the forest into farms, tilled fields, and stockyards full of animals. In time villages, towns, and cities would arise and take away this pristine beauty that the Shardies wanted to deny us.

Coleen would never see any of that—her life would never be that long. I picked up a stick and tossed it downhill. As she ran to fetch it I clicked off the safety on my HO and loosed a full clip. The terrible sound echoed from the hillside.

Givens turned her face away from me when I got back to camp but not before I saw the redness of her eyes. "I heard," I said and slapped her shoulder.

"Me, too," she bit back and then straightened. "Captain says the lifts will be here soon so we should pack out and join the others."

I had failed to notice that all the mechs were making their way toward the plain and, in the distance, saw the growing black dots that could only be our transport. "Yeah, time to leave this all behind," I replied as I fell into step behind her.

Just before we reached the transports I risked a glance back toward the caves, trying to see the bit of white that was my Coleen.

THE MARINE BREED
Janine K. Spendlove

> "Old breed? New breed?
> There's not a damn bit of difference
> so long as it's the Marine breed."
> —Lieutenant General Lewis B. "Chesty" Puller, USMC

"Run, run, run!" I bark at my partner. Sometimes Bud isn't as fast as me or as aware of the danger of our situation. Like now, as a dozen of the six-legged monsters come at us from over the black, rocky ridge straight ahead. I could smell them, even from here, half a click away. Like skunk covered in deer piss then rolled in cow pies for good measure. A part of me is almost envious; except for I know the canidaes (or *cans* as we call them) only bring death.

Despite our plasma rifles and body armor there's no way we would survive the encounter without reinforcements. We're scouts, and I guess we found what we were looking for. As Bud and I retreat (though my fellow Marines would say we were just "attacking in a different direction") I glance over my shoulder to make sure the *cans* aren't gaining.

Merciless, they kill — then eat — everyone they catch.

This why, to me, the cans are monsters. And maybe that's extreme, considering that they look like a six-legged version of me, but they're nothing like me. Nor can I call them aliens, for if anyone on New Texas is alien, it's me and my fellow devil-dogs. Oh, and the young colony of Roddenberry we're protecting.

We leap across a narrow crack in the black stone, and the *cans* get closer. Their smell, almost overpowering to my senses, is thicker, and from all sides now. I howl out loudly to the perimeter guards that we're inbound, and that we've got *cans* on our tail. I know they'll be ready. I know my Marines will look out for me and Bud. Marines fight for Marines. Always have, always will.

People think Marines are dumb, especially my kind, the grunts. That we don't understand or think about these sorts of things — but they forget, you learn a whole lot by just listening and observing. You don't gotta say much to do our job, but you do gotta know how listen and how to act.

We slide down into the sandy cave opening that serves as the entrance to our patrol's temporary base of operations. The Marines, humans and dogs alike, explode out of the mouth of the hole with fierce battle cries and howls. After a few moments the plasma rifles and teeth have done their work. The monsters are nothing but bits of carrion, scattered and smoking, left for the birds and lizards of the desert to feast on.

I blow out my breath in a sigh, fluttering the fringe of black hair that dangles before my eyes.

And then I see it. A dog, a white lab mix, Private Daly, whining and nudging his human, Corporal Syzmanski. The *cans* got her. Daly licks her face, but Ski doesn't move. Daly looks at me, a black smear of blood across his muzzle, and I don't think I've ever seen anything more heartbreaking in my life.

Bud walks over to comfort the grieving Daly, while other Marines pick up our fallen. No Marine left behind.

I lower my head, ashamed. Ashamed because I am so glad that it was Ski and not Bud. That it's Daly, and not me, who is alone now.

Turning, I jump down behind a rocky embankment. I can't watch anymore.

I miss the Earth. Running through the fields, with Charlie, my partner of three years, hunting birds and playing. But then I got drafted, just like everyone else, to fight for this hell-hole of a planet. Times have definitely changed, and we have gotten desperate. Charlie died in a hunting accident, and I'd only just weaned our youngest when the "recruiter" came by our farm to draft me.

I smell Bud before I see him, and he jumps down next to me. Covered in black streaks of blood and dirt all over him, the smell of death is thick in the air. Bud scratches behind his ear before finally settling down nearby.

He doesn't say anything. He doesn't have to. We both know how lucky we are.

Daly is still curled up by Ski's body. I can hear a faint, low whine coming from him and he mourns his fallen Marine.

The hair on my neck raises and I look for *cans*, but there are none. Just bodies.

Bud and I split some field rations, like we do every night, and watch the first moon rise as the sun sets over the darkening sky. I laugh to myself as Bud impatiently tears open the gray package of processed foodstuffs with his teeth, but I can't blame him. I've been known to do the same thing myself.

A stiff, frigid wind blows across the flatlands, making me thankful once more for my thick coat. I can feel Bud shiver against me, so I snuggle closer hoping our shared body heat will help him settle down and get some sleep while I keep an eye out for the *cans*. I know they'll come back — they always do.

We've been told by the xeno-biologists that the *cans* are somewhat in-telligent — almost as smart as me — and have rudimentary communication skills. But I can't talk to them and neither can Bud. Though I never expected him to be able to. The thought of Bud trying to talk to the *cans* actually makes me smile a bit.

As the twinkling stars fill up the sky and the second moon rises, I wonder if I should feel guilty for killing creatures so much like me, but I don't. Not even a little bit. Supposedly we're fighting to prevent more colony massacres like what happened in New Austin (the aftermath of that was horrifying. Poor Bud had nightmares for weeks). But like I said before, we're not fighting for colonists, we're fighting to keep each other alive. Marines take care of Marines; it's been that way since we were born in Tun Tavern all those centuries ago back on Earth.

And it's because of that camaraderie that despite all the hardship and austere conditions, I love my job.

Bud shifts, nestling in closer to me, and I smile once again as I look down at my favorite devil-dog. He is my best friend and best companion ever. We share everything: food, water, nasty conditions, keep each other warm, and somehow, when I'm with him, I don't feel as homesick. Sure, he smells bad and sometimes has fleas, but still, I feel bad for all the other Marines who don't have a battle buddy like mine.

Just then I smell it. Too late, I realize one of the *cans* is still alive, and a dark, hairy shape fills my vision. I leap at the monster, baring my teeth and going for his throat. I hear Bud wake and surge to his feet. The high-pitched whine of his plasma rifle cuts through the chilly night air, and I smile. My smile turns into a grimace of pain when I feel a tug and a fire sear through my gut as the *can* slashes two sets of claws through my thick belly fur. Then a plasma blast rips the *can's* head off and I collapse to the ground.

"Chesty, no!" I hear Bud scream, as he vaults over the embankment and lands by my side. Other Marines run over, but then hang back, giving us our space. I blink and notice the world is darker, and it's much harder to breath. The desert ground is wet and sticky under me, and all I can absurdly think is that my fur will be dirty and matted, and that Bud will make me take a bath.

Bud pulls me into his arms, and for the first time I see my favorite devil-dog cry.

"No, girl, no. I'm sorry, I'm so sorry." His voice cracks and he squeezes his eyes shut.

I try to lean up to lick his tears away. I don't want him to be sad. But I find I can't move. All I can do is lie in his arms and wait.

He pulls me tighter and I close my eyes. I don't hurt as much anymore.

I think of Earth. I think of my old farm, and my puppies playing in the fields, chasing birds.

I hear Bud's heartbeat and I smile. He is safe.

I am happy.

STRAY SHOT
A tale of The 142nd Starborne

Patrick Thomas

WHAT GOOD IS A SENSOR IF THERE ARE SO MANY WAYS TO TRICK one?" Corporal Louise Harpole asked. It wasn't the first time the defuser had started this conversation and likely wouldn't be the last. It just helped take her mind off the danger involved in her job.

Sergeant Dartanian Cooper grinned as he petted a large golden dog. "People may be able to fool sensors, but nothing fools old Blue here. Right, boy?"

The dog barked and nodded his head.

"Despite all my time with Blue, I still can't believe how intelligent the Host Canine Corps is," Corporal Harpole said.

"Shows what a century of selective breeding and genetic engineering can accomplish."

"I don't see how you're taking all this so easily. Planetary Governor Cross is a sick bastard."

Cooper shrugged. "Slick too. He's not the only mouse to play when the cats flew back to Earth." Cross had tried to turn himself into a dictator after his Host military contingent pulled out. Many of the other folks on Kilimanjaro tried to stop him, so Cross responded by taking the planet's children hostage during the school day. "The rebels sent out a distress call and the 142nd Starborne came to the rescue."

"You mean the three of us came. Most of the 142nd is still waiting somewhere safe," Harpole said, the corners of her eyes crinkling up.

"We are the first wave of the rescue since we are most qualified to find out which bunkers Cross hid the kids in, not to mention find and dismantle the explosives. A real shame that all the *Behemoth's* sensors can't measure up to the nose of one good dog."

Blue made a sound that was more laugh than bark.

"Cross hiding behind non-combatants just soaks my biscuits in hot sauce, but I've got to grin and swallow like my Aunt Suzie made 'em."

"I don't even know what that means," Harpole said.

"Blue picks up on what I put out. I get angry or upset, so does he and he won't be at his best to sniff you out some bombs to defuse," Copper said.

"Assuming we have the right place. Last two targets we found nothing," Harpole said.

"Well you know what they say—third time's the charm. I just think it's funny that Benedict holds back the rest of the troops and lets the three of us take point."

Harpole shrugged. "Defusers are used to working alone. Don't make no sense to risk a hundred lives when you only have to risk one. Or three in this case. We need Blue to find the explosives, me to defuse the detonators and you to look pretty."

Blue did his cross between a laugh and bark again. Twice.

"Don't hate me because I'm the best looking in this bunch." Cooper made a show of looking between the woman and the dog. "Not that it's a big accomplishment in this motley crew."

Blue whimpered like his feelings were hurt. "Come on, you know you're the best-looking dog I know." Cooper bent over and took the lead off the 120-pound dog. "Okay boy, it's up to you. Go find those bombs so Louise here can turn them off and we can get those kids out. If they're here, that is."

Blue barked and nodded again, then proceeded to start sniffing the entrance to the underground tunnel. Although the planet Kilimanjaro was able to support human life, the surface tended to be hostile during much of the year, so the colonists had built most of their settlements underground. The entire planet was littered with tunnels and bunkers, which made the task of finding a planet-full of kidnapped children a tough one.

The 142nd Starborne's ship *Behemoth,* the last known Colossus-class warship, had received no less than seventeen distress calls, each from a different rebel faction. Apparently Cross's governing style involved pitting different factions against each other so they fought among themselves more than they did him. Their forces were divided so sharply that they couldn't put aside their differences long enough organize an attack or rescue.

When the 142nd Starborne arrived in orbit, Cross first tried to negotiate. He had a lot of loyal troops between him and danger and assumed he had plenty of wiggle room. To his surprise Major Hans Benedict offered only one deal—let the children go and live. Or don't and die.

Cross ignored it, perhaps assuming that the man threatening him would never get past all of his soldiers or was bluffing. It might have worked if the local military had either the firepower or the training of the Host. It took less than an hour for the 142nd to take the governor's mansion.

Benedict didn't kill Cross outright. At first, he opted for a flesh wound to give him a chance to rethink taking the deal. The negotiating technique didn't impress Cross and he told Benedict to go screw himself, then did something so old-school that it was ludicrous. He bit down on a poison tooth.

Benedict stuck his own fingers down the man's throat to make him vomit up the poison, but it was too late. Cross was reduced to a drooling idiot who died moments later. Benedict kept his corpse on ice in case they needed DNA, fingerprints, retina scans or the like to defuse a bomb. So far they hadn't.

That left the 142nd Starborne with the Herculean task of searching an entire planet to find the children before their food and water ran out.

Many of the bunkers were built to military specs, which is why the orbital sensors were useless. Even using Harpy dropships had been only minimally effective. Taking advantage of local intelligence, they'd found several bunkers holding thousands of children, but the bean counters' best guess was they had only rescued seventy-two percent of those missing. That left far too many kids unaccounted for.

Blue stopped and froze, pointing his nose at one particular wall panel. The imitating a statue was part of canine corps training as some explosive devices were triggered by movement. Remaining still was a safer way to notify the bomb tech than barking.

Corporal Harpole walked over and whispered, "Good boy, Blue."

Cooper used a hand signal and the dog unfroze and went to his side. Harpole used a multi-tool from her vest to remove the panel, revealing two blocks of industrial grade Z-5 explosive hooked up to a system of wires. Harpole made a gun signal with her hand to let the rest of her team know it was a live bomb. Her multi-spectrum goggles allowed her to see the power flow through the system and other things not visible to the unaided human eye.

Although it was against regulations, Cooper moved closer to watch Harpole at work. He wasn't certified as a bomb technician, but had learned the basics and then some. One never knew when he might be called upon to help. Or worse, finish the job if something happened to Harpole. Both soldiers were so engrossed in the diffusing process that they didn't notice a wall panel at the far end of the corridor slide open and three soldiers wearing planetary colors step out with their weapons drawn—modern scatterguns, perfect for tunnel fighting. On the other paw, Blue did see them. The canine solider leapt up, knocking both humans to the ground an instant before a round would've hit them. It hit Blue instead. His canine body armor deflected the bulk of it, but the angle allowed some of the pellets to penetrate the gaps. The dog collapsed to the floor.

Both human members of the Host returned fire, dropping the soldier who had made the shot on Blue.

"Drop your weapons and surrender," Sergeant Cooper shouted.

"No, you drop your weapons," said one of the planetary soldiers. "We outnumber you."

Both members of the 142nd Starborne could see there were more soldiers behind the opening in the wall.

Corporal Harpole turned her persuader rifle and aimed at the Z-5. "You shoot me and I blow us all back to Earth."

"What are you talking about?"

"Cross lined this place with explosives to keep the rebels from trying to rescue their kids. Anything goes wrong and the whole bunker goes."

"Bullshit."

"She's not bluffing. Use your scopes to look at what was behind that panel," Cooper said. "Even if you drop us, she'll get the shot off, which will trigger a chain reaction that'll bring this place down on all our heads. Or maybe one of you will miss and do it for us."

The soldier looked through his scope and the blood drained from his face. "Oh shit."

"All of you come out of there. Put your safeties on and slide your weapons to me. Then put your hands on your head," Cooper ordered.

The eight planetary soldiers who were still upright obeyed with one exception. A man with the rank of captain who looked easily in his fifties, bent to treat the wounded man.

"You're a medic?" Cooper said.

"Doctor. The governor assigned me here in case anything happened to the children."

"Fine, you can tend to your injured after you work on our wounded," Cooper said.

"Wounded? That's a dog. This is a man."

"What's your name, Doc?"

"Wilmer."

"Well, Dr. Wilmer, that dog is a soldier of the Host and my partner. He is also our only shot to find all the explosives and keep everyone in here alive," he said.

"That's fine, but I'm taking care of Jonesy first."

Cooper stood then walked over and pointed his weapon at the doctor's head. "That man is an enemy combatant who shot first, wounding my partner. We'd be dead if it wasn't for Blue. I have no problem putting a bullet through this man's head if his being injured is distracting you from saving my partner. In fact, I will do just that if you don't get over there and take care of Blue. If the dog doesn't survive, both of you may get a bullet to the brain pan. Understood?"

The doctor's eyes narrowed. Through gritted teeth he growled, "Yes."

As Cooper took off Blue's canine body armor, Harpole positioned herself so she could shoot any of the enemy soldiers if she had to. Once Blue was prepped, Cooper searched the planetary soldiers for weapons and took their helmets and body armor. A few had knives, but otherwise weren't concealing anything.

Cooper bound their wrists and ankles with strappers, variations on the old pull tie, except they were laced with metal. A prisoner needed an acetylene torch to cut through one. It would be easier to cut their hand off, but few people wanted freedom that badly.

Neither Cooper nor Harpole could hide their concern over the condition of their K-9 partner, but they tried, not wanting the doctor to realize he could turn things into another hostage situation.

The doctor reached for his utility belt and was greeted by two rifles clicking.

"The blast gave him multiple wounds. I need my surgical tools to get out the shrapnel."

"Just don't get any dumb ideas," Harpole said.

"Don't worry. I don't want a man's death on my conscience so I'll save the dog."

Cooper leaned in, putting his mouth next to the corporal's ear. "Nice bluff by the way. A bullet would never set off Z-5."

Harpole smiled, knowing full well it would take an electric charge. Unfortunately, that included static discharge. "Thank you. Now if you don't mind, I'm going to get to work if you think you can handle things here?"

Cooper nodded and took out his first aid kit. He went to the wounded planetary soldier and patched up the man so he could hold on long enough for the doctor to tend to him. Wilmer stopped his surgery on the dog long enough to look at Cooper and nod his thanks.

It took the better part of an hour, but the doctor managed to stitch up Blue. When he was done he took out an injector, an automated syringe and placed it against the dog's side.

"Wait," Cooper said, but it was too late. He heard the hiss of the injection. "What did you give him?"

"Painkillers, antibiotics and a sedative," the doctor said.

"We need him to find the rest of the explosives."

"He'll be in too much pain to be much use to you."

"How long will he out?" Copper said.

"A few hours probably. I'm not a vet, but I estimated his weight and adjusted the dose accordingly." The doctor looked at his wounded comrade. "May I now help Jonesy?"

Cooper nodded and sat down next to Blue. With one hand he held his persuader rifle so he could fire on any of his prisoners or the doctor. He put the other hand in front of the dog's nose so he smelt that he was there.

Cooper, Harpole, and their prisoners all twitched at the sudden alarm, followed by the booming of several bunker doors slamming shut.

Harpole moved away from the bomb and put her sidearm along the doctor's temple. "What the hell's going on?"

"Somebody must've breached the children's area. I'm the only one coded genetically to be able to get in and out. Anyone else goes through the doorway—even one of the kids—and this place goes into lockdown."

"You think one of the kids tried to get out?"

"Probably," Wilmer said, but Cooper's gut said he was lying.

"Are there any other soldiers here?"

Some of the men exchanged a glance.

"We are the only men here," Wilmer said.

Cooper looked over at where the Z-5 was. A timer counted down from one hour. "Corporal, I think we may be in trouble."

Harpole rushed to assess the situation, then cursed for quite some time.

"It was set so if anyone tried to bypass security, it would blow everything. The countdown was probably to give the governor enough time to decide if he really wanted it to happen.

Harpole took out her radio.

Cooper grew nervous at the violation of protocol. "Regs say that we're not supposed to use any broadcast device in case explosives are on a detonator that would pick up the signal."

"We're locked in an armored bunker that is going to be lit up with Z-5 in an hour. We don't have a lot to lose here," Harpole said, lifting her radio up to her mouth. "Boom Squad Alpha to Harpy Delta." The corporal repeated the message several times, but no answer came. "Walls are too damn thick to get a signal out. We're on our own here. We really need Blue."

"That's not likely to happen," Cooper said, looking down at the drugged dog. He and Harpole turned to the doctor. "Can you wake him? Or do you know how to override the system to get the kids out?"

"No. I knew Cross was unbalanced, but I didn't know there were explosives. I'm here for one reason—to keep these children safe. My grandkids are among those taken and are here with the rest of the children. I wouldn't do anything to hurt any of them and I'd get them out if I could."

"Corporal, could we use some of the Z-5 to blow a hole?" Cooper asked.

"We could, but the way the bunker's built, the tunnel nearest the blast would be at risk to collapse. And it makes no sense to leave without the children. Where are they, Doctor?"

The doctor wavered, looking at his patient.

"We all have less than an hour to live at this point. Jonesy will die with the rest of us. Do you think it's better to finish surgery on him now or later?" Cooper said.

Dr. Wilmer sighed. "I have most of the internal bleeding stopped. May I have one of the men apply pressure to the wound?"

Cooper nodded and the doctor pointed to one of the soldiers and showed him what to do, but Cooper left his strapper on.

"I'll show you where the children are and maybe together we can figure a way out," Wilmer said.

Cooper turned to the soldiers. "Listen up, gentlemen. You are on the honor system. Right now we are the only chance anybody has getting out of here alive, yourselves and the children included. If we do not stop the timers on the explosives, we all die. Anyone gets up or tries anything, you will be shot. If you're not here when it is time to leave, we will not come looking for you. When we evacuate, you will be left to be buried alive. That is if you survive the blasts. If anyone touches one hair on Private Blue, I will personally put a bullet in his head. If Private Blue is missing or dead when we return, all of you will be left to die. Is everyone clear on the ground rules?"

Everyone nodded in acknowledgment.

"The children's quarters are this way," Dr. Wilmer said and lead them down a series of cement corridors.

Eventually they arrived at what had probably originally been intended to be a hanger or garage. The large area seemed small with the over-abundance of children crammed into the space.

"How many?" Cooper said.

"Over two thousand. We've been running low on food and had to break out the emergency ration bars two days ago. Not very tasty, but one bar has enough nutrients for a day. The system recycles and purifies fluids with minimal loss."

The children appeared terrified by the wailing of the alarm, some of them huddling together in groups. The doctor waved to two girls who smiled and waved back. Cooper assumed they were his grandchildren.

"How do we talk to them?" Cooper said.

"Blue switch. Flip it and speak into the microphone," Wilmer said.

Cooper turned on the speaker system and cleared his throat. "Hello, children. I'm Sergeant Cooper and this is Corporal Harpole. We are with the 142nd Starborne and have come here to take you all home, once we take care of what is making the alarm go off. Please sit tight and we will be back shortly," he said, flipping the switch off. "At least I hoped we will. Doctor, do you have any idea what other areas explosives might be in?"

"None. Why wouldn't there be just the one?"

"Structurally speaking, there needs to be at least one more set of explosives to bring this entire bunker down. Possibly more. In the other bunkers, we found at least three batches. Each of them was shielded from technological detection, which is why we needed Blue."

"So if Blue was back to normal, maybe you'd be able to defuse the bombs and we be able to get the children out," Wilmer said.

"That was the plan, but we figured on having Blue and not having to beat the clock like this," Cooper said. "It doesn't matter, because Blue is no shape to help."

"What if I told you there was a way that he could be?" the doctor said.

"You got a magic wand?" Harpole said.

"The next best thing. We have a splicing chamber."

Harpole let out a whistle and a few colorful expressions. "You're telling me a backwater world like this has a SC?"

"We're not that backwater. The Host has splicer soldiers and set up chambers on different worlds to replenish their ranks. Do you have any in the 142nd Starborne?"

"None. Humans only, no monsters," Cooper said. "Major Benedict is big on that."

"How's a splicer going to help Blue? It's supposed to mix animal DNA with humans to get werewolves and other man-beasts," Harpole said.

"It has a reset button. They can sample unspliced DNA and reboot it," the doctor said.

"Then why isn't it used for dying people and fallen soldiers?" Cooper said.

"Because it's dangerous. Subjects sometimes die. And on humans I've never heard of a case where the subject came through with his or her memories intact."

"Then it's no dang good. Blue went through a lot of training, well over a year. We revert him back to a puppy and he'll have the talent, but not the ability," Cooper said, frowning. "What was Cross doing with it?"

"After the Host returned to Earth, he took control of almost everything they left behind. He announced everything would be safest with him. I believe he was planning on building up his forces with splicers," the doctor said, breaking eye contact. "I have another idea. We can mix your dog's DNA with one of you. You already have the knowledge and as a splicer you'd have the ability to sniff out the explosives."

"And live out the rest of our lives as a splicer freak? You've got to be kidding me. How about we do it to you?" Harpole said.

"First off, because if any of the children get injured I'm the only doctor. Second, I have no idea how to do your jobs. You'd have to train me. You think we can do that in enough time to defuse the bombs?"

"No," Harpole said.

"I'll do it," Cooper said.

"Coop, are you nuts?" Harpole said.

"It's the only choice. We're willing to risk our lives to save these kids. It's part of the job. Why? Because we're soldiers. Nothing's changed. I do this and maybe two thousand kids live. Plus you and Blue. I don't, we all die. Doctor, does this machine have stored DNA?"

"No, the Host took that with them. You'd have to put Blue or at least a tissue sample in the extractor portion of the splicer."

"Doc, will it hurt them?" Harpole said.

"Blue, no. It will only be reading him. The sergeant, well it's very likely. Rewriting DNA is painful."

"Then we are not turning you into a splicer freak. We'll find another way," Harpole said.

"Okay, so long as you can do it in the next thirty seconds, because that's about all the time we can spare. If you have another way out, trust me I'd be happy to do it."

Half a minute worth of ticks counted off. Then Corporal Louise Harpole did a very uncharacteristic thing and authorized a single tear to roll down her face.

"Damn it, Coop. You outrank me. Order me to do it," she said.

"Not a chance. Doc, let's go."

They retrieved Blue and the doctor led them to a sealed room. Inside was the splicing chamber. It was a large metal tube with all sorts of energy emitters attached to it. Legend had it that it was originally designed for teleportation, but there was a fly in the ointment when the first person to try it wasn't the only living thing to go through. It ended messily, but the technology had been improved since. Cooper stripped down and got inside the tube. Anything extra on him could end up reconstituting inside of him. The doctor took a blood sample and put it in small glass tube, then did the same for Blue. Instead of a teleport chamber, there was a scanning one. Harpole placed the still unconscious dog inside so he could be scanned fully. The doctor claimed the sampler could work around the wound and bandage.

"Sergeant Cooper, are you ready?" Wilmer asked.

"Get it done, Doctor," Cooper said.

Harpole leaned into the doctor's ear and whispered, "He dies and you won't make it until the bomb blast."

The doctor nodded and worked the controls like he had done it before. Harpole watched exactly what he did. She was a quick learner. She had to be to survive in her profession.

Cooper's screamed as the chamber filled with energy that lit up the room like the place had been filled with magnesium flares. The power drain dimmed the lights making the glow even more blinding. Then the screams stopped and Cooper was gone.

"Turn it off," Harpole said.

"It is too late. If we turn off now, he won't reform. He'll just be dead. We just have to wait and pray," the doctor said.

Harpole thought it would take longer. From her perspective, it did. However, it was only a matter of minutes before the chamber returned to its inert state and the lights came back on. Harpole ran to the door and pulled it open. She caught her naked partner before he collapsed to the floor. "Coop, are you okay?"

Sergeant Cooper seemed to be taking stock of his own body. Slowly, he tested to see if his legs could still support him.

"I think I am. I feel stronger. My senses are sharper, like a flea on steroids with a telescope and a hearing aide set for eavesdropping."

"You still look like you," Harpole said. "And sound like you. I still don't know what you are talking about. I guess I was expecting you to be more furry."

The corporal had spoken too soon because Sergeant Cooper fell to his knees screaming as the hair on his body grew longer and thicker. The shape of his skull changed to something halfway between human and canine. His face elongated, his teeth grew larger, as did his ears. Cooper's hands twisted into a mix of hand and paw that ended in claws.

"Coop, are you in there?"

"I'm still me," said a voice that was still the sergeant's, yet animal. Cooper tried to pull on his uniform pants. The results were less than satisfactory. Not only had he grown larger and more muscular, but the shape of his legs and joints had changed. He was able to button them, but just barely and only due to the belt and waistband being adjustable.

"Give me the Z-5. I'll take a sniff then I'll start searching the place."

It took him a few moments to get used to his new body. He stumbled a few times and had to close his eyes more than once to get used to the new way the world looked. He didn't lose color vision so much as to have a new vision layer overlap everything. He could hear heartbeats and smell emotions. Once he had the basics sorted out, it didn't take long for Cooper to find the second batch of explosives in the soldiers' living quarters.

Cooper put his earpiece back on, although it didn't fit properly anymore. "This is all that's in this area. I'll search for the next batch and radio you when I find it. Doctor, you're with me."

A search of all the areas except the largest turned up nothing.

Doctor and sergeant stopped in front of the children's quarters and exchanged a look.

"How do we get inside?" Cooper said.

"It's simple. Plug in a code to the door and walk through. Someone already set off the alarms, so there's nothing to stop you."

"You're coming with me. I look pretty scary now and I don't want to frighten the children, so it's your job to keep them calm while I search the place."

The doctor told him the code. Cooper hit the key pad and the door slid open.

"Doctor, you go first and prepare them. I'll be right behind you."

The doctor went through the doorway and pulled a wireless microphone from his pocket. He hit the button on the side and spoke. "Children, we have a man who is a splicer. He needs to search these quarters for something. Then he and his partner will be getting all of us out of here, so give him space and don't worry. Despite his appearance, he is a soldier. He won't hurt you."

As the man-dog came through, Cooper was surprised to see not so much panic as curiosity and wonder. The children had never seen a splicer and were far more intrigued than scared. He stopped short under the gaze of all those young eyes and found himself wanting to growl. Instead he saluted, then got to work. He caught the faint scent of the explosive and followed it to the far end of the chamber where it was stronger. Cooper pulled off a panel and hit the side of his ear set comm. "Partner, I found the third explosive cache at the back of the children's chamber."

"I've got this one deactivated. I'm on my way."

As Harpole rounded the corner to the entrance to the children's chamber, she saw someone disappear around the corridor. "Freeze!"

The shadow kept running in the direction of the splice chamber.

"Sergeant, we have a hostile running loose in the compound. You want that I should pursue?"

"Negative, Corporal. Explosives are our first priority. We'll track him down later. Who knows, I may be able to find him just like a bloodhound."

Cooper told her the entrance code.

"Doctor, who is that? You said there were no more soldiers."

"No I said no more men."

"So it's a woman?"

"No."

"Doctor..."

"That is all I'm going to tell you."

"We will finish this later. For now, please get all the children away from here." Cooper's voice was almost a growl, although there was little hostility in his tone.

"Will moving save them if the Z-5 goes off?"

The dog soldier shook his head. "Detonators can explode too."

The doctor nodded and did as instructed.

By the time Harpole arrived, Cooper already had the wall taken apart.

Harpole got to work testing wires and circuits with her tools and goggles. Several minutes later, she turned and smiled. "All safe."

"But you did it wrong," Cooper said with what could now be easily described as a wolfish grin. Harpole cocked her head to the side. "You know you're not supposed to disarm the final one until the last ten seconds for dramatic effect. We had a good eleven minutes left."

"We defusers don't want more drama than we have to have. Are there any more explosives?"

"None that I can smell," Cooper said.

"Fine, then I'll try to hack open the doors. Plus I can use their comm system to contact Harpy Delta and give them an update. Let them know that the splicer dog solider is a friendly."

Cooper nodded his canine head, then went over to the doctor. "The corporal is trying to get the doors open. However, someone is running around loose. I'm going to go check the prisoners. Doctor, you need to tell me right now, no more games—who else is in the compound?"

The doctor was torn between loyalty to the unit he served and to the people who just saved the life of said unit and over two thousand children, some of them his own family. "Carlos Samsa was here before our group and the children arrived. It seems Cross may have started his own splicer soldier program already. Carlos is one of them and as such is not in my chain of command. He tends to keep to himself. Since the log showed it was someone entering, he must be the one that set off the alarm. He's not the bravest man in the world despite his new advantages."

"Which are what exactly?" Cooper said.

Doctor Wilmer looked down at his feet and answered in a whisper. "Insect."

"What kind?"

"Cockroach. They followed us from Earth and Cross figured it was the best choice for his select forces. There were a Baker's dozen made."

"Made by who?"

The doctor sighed. "Me. It was the price I paid to be in command here. I didn't want to do it, but I had no choice."

"We always have a choice, Doctor. It's just not always a pleasant one."

"Don't judge me. Not all soldiers are good men and I knew some of them might look upon the older girls as women. By being in command, I could protect the children."

"So we're dealing with thirteen roach splicers?" Cooper said, trying to keep panic from coloring his new voice.

"No. One died in the process. Five went mad soon after. Cross sent the others out to crush the rebels. Carlos Samsa stayed behind to guard the splice chamber."

"And you didn't think to mention this to us when we went there? Hoping we would be ambushed?" Cooper said, trying not to focus on the fact that almost half of the splicers lost their minds or wonder if or when it would happen to him.

"No. You are our only hope to survive. Carlos had deserted his post days ago. I assumed we would be safe."

"What about having him loose among the children? How would a bug man think of them?"

Wilmer looked defiantly at the dog soldier. "He knows I would kill him if he harmed any of them."

"And he is afraid of you?"

"No, but he believes me. And the other men do not like what he has become, and they have orders to kill him if he hurts a child."

"Is he rational?" Cooper asked.

"As rational as he was before. Maybe less."

"I want you broadcasting on the speakers, asking Samsa to turn himself in. We won't harm him, only immobilize him like the other planetary soldiers. If he doesn't, we will hound him and hunt him down...."

Dr. Wilmer smirked. "Interesting choice of words." The doctor did as he was asked, but there was no response. Then the power dimmed.

"The same thing happened when you were in the splicing chamber," Harpole said.

"Blue!" Cooper said, already running before he finished shouting his partner's name. He stopped only to punch in the code to get through the door. Harpole followed right behind. Despite his new form, Cooper had not abandoned his weapons. The soldiers used standard procedure to enter the room, one covering the other. Blue was still unconscious and off to the side where they had left him, but the chamber was smoking as if it had just been used.

"Did he use the slice chamber again?" Harpole said.

"We have to assume yes. I don't see him anywhere in the room."

"That's because you didn't look hard enough." The voice came from the ceiling, a good twenty feet high. The 142nd Starborne soldiers lifted their persuaders toward the ceiling and were greeted with a sight that was more insect than human. Samsa opened fire on them with a sidearm. They both returned fire, but Samsa had scurried away.

"I swear I hit him," Harpole said.

"Judging from the smell, you did, but it didn't slow him down."

The splice chamber had cement blocks that went up to the ceiling, except for one section that was open for power conduits, but it left room enough for whatever it was they saw to get into the next section of the bunker.

"We have to go after him," Harpole said.

"But we can't leave Blue. The bug might come back." Cooper took the uniform shirt that was still on the floor where he left it and fastened a makeshift sling for the injured dog, which he slung across his back.

"I'll go up and over, you go around," Cooper said.

"Needed goggles?" Harpole said, putting hers on.

"I think I can see better without them now," Cooper said. With Blue on his back, Cooper scaled the twenty foot wall quicker than he thought possible. His Host training had included scaling buildings and mountains, but he had never been this fast before.

The two soldiers came into the next chamber, one high and the other low, but there was no sign of the bug man. As they stepped inside, Cooper heard a faint click and pushed Harpole back into the corridor, shielding her and Blue as the room exploded.

When the ringing in his ears lessened, Cooper shouted, "Are you okay?"

Harpole nodded.

"Was that Z-5?"

"No. Gas, probably a tank from the kitchen. We need to squish this guy," Harpole said.

The soldiers cautiously moved down the hallway, which circled back around toward the main section of the bunker. They came to a place where the corridor split.

Cooper lifted his canine nose in the air. He sniffed both branches and chose the one on the right.

The soldiers exchanged a look of concern as the corridor led back to the children's chamber. Their worry was well-founded. As they rounded the corner, children were screaming and pouring out of the door of their gilded cage. The soldiers didn't bother with crowd control and instead went back inside.

The dog soldier got down on one knee and gently stopped one of the fleeing children. "What's going on?"

"There's a monster bug and it grabbed two of the kids. I think he's going to eat them," the child said.

"Don't worry. I'll find the bug man and get those kids away from him. Which way did he go?"

The child pointed and both soldiers rushing in that direction. They got to the far end of the children's chamber, where the doctor was trying to reason with the insect splicer, who was holding the one of the doctor's grandchildren on either side of him.

"Let them go and take me instead," Dr. Wilmer said.

"Nope. You might cause trouble. They'll behave if they know what's good for them."

"Carlos, you don't want to do this. Our job is to protect these children, not put them in danger."

"That's your job, Doc. Mine is to protect the splice chamber and you let outsiders in and made one of them into a splicer. Cross will have your head."

"Cross is dead. He lined this place with explosives and you set off the timer when you came in here the first time."

Samsa shrugged. "Figured the Host wouldn't be shooting up the kiddies and I wanted to last long enough to offer them my services. Since I used the chamber as bait in a trap to blow them up, that's probably not going to happen. I just want out of here. And if you try to take me out first, I got shields."

"We're not going to try and take you out," Cooper said, his persuader pointed at the roach man's head. The dog soldier was not sure how well his motor memory carried over to his new body and didn't want to risk a shot.

"Tell that to Jonesy. Survived my little ambush, huh, dog man?"

"Jonesy fired on us first. We were protecting ourselves. Why don't you put down those kids and we can talk about this like civilized men," Cooper said as Harpole moved to flank the insect splicer.

"Have you looked in the mirror lately? Neither one of us is a man any longer. How about you just let me go?"

"Okay," Cooper said.

"What do you mean okay?" Samsa hissed. The two girls the insect soldier held started sobbing, then tried to stop, their eyes darting at the bug man's face, their bodies trembling. It was a valiant, but ultimately doomed effort and they starting crying again.

"I'll let you go if you let the kids go. Easy solution. Everybody wins and nobody gets hurt," Cooper said.

"You mean you'll let me walk right out of the bunker?" the roach man said. His face had been warped by the insect DNA, which made his expressions hard to read, but Cooper's best guess was that it was one of disbelief.

"My mission is to save the kids. You haven't hurt any of them, so I have no reason to stop you. If you were to hurt them, my view on that would change."

The roach man nodded. "Fine. Leave your guns with your partner there and then we'll walk out to the bunker exit. I let the kids go there and I'll leave."

"I can do that." Cooper took off his persuader rifle and his sidearm and handed both of them to his corporal. He tapped his earpiece and used the hand signal for report. Harpole nodded understanding, but her eyes looked at him as if he were crazy.

Cooper tried to hand Blue off.

"Leave the dog where he is. It'll slow you down and make you think twice about doing something stupid because he'll be the first one hurt," Samsa said. "Now how do I know this isn't some sort of trick?"

"Because I give you my word as a member of the 142nd Starborne that I will let you walk out of this bunker, provided you give the children to me unharmed before you leave. That and what other choice do you have?"

The insect solider nodded and Cooper led the way to the exit, holding his hands above his shoulders. He could hear the children's rapid heartbeats and smell their fear and tears. One had even peed. It was disconcerting to say the least. Samsa on the other hand, smelled of some odd amalgam of clean and decay. Cooper could still smell whatever passed for blood in him, but the bullet wounds had already closed over and healed. He failed to understand the desperate logic that convinced Samsa that it was better to live on as a bug than to die as a man. What could Cross have promised him to entice him to give up his humanity?

When they got to the exit, Cooper did a quick count of the tied and bound soldiers. They were all still there, even the one applying pressure to the wound soldier. They looked at Cooper and Samsa with a mix of fear and disgust.

Sergeant Cooper hit the open switch and the bunker door whooshed open, the sunlight almost blinding in comparison to the bunkers low-level lights.

Samsa backed his way up to the door and dropped the children. They stumbled, then ran to Cooper. He knelt and wrapped a furry arm around each of them. "You're okay. You both did very good and were very brave. I'm proud of you. Now go back to Corporal Harpole and she'll take care of you. And sent your grandpa to take care of Jonesy."

Cooper turned to watch the girls run down the corridor and found he had an instinct to race after them, but was able to suppress it with a little difficulty. Unfortunately, during the time his eyes were following the children, Samsa came at him, the roach man throwing the dog soldier against the wall. Copper turned and took the blow on his shoulder rather than hurt Blue. The dog soldier barely got his arms up in time to catch the roach man's two human arms from grabbing Blue, but Samsa also had four smaller stubs growing out of his sides, each one of them with hands and fingers. This wasn't hand-to-hand, but many-hand-to-hand combat.

"I don't trust you to not try and put a bullet in my head. Not that more bullets would hurt me much now, but why take the chance?" Samsa hissed.

The bug man was larger and stronger and pinned the dog soldier. Cooper couldn't get better leverage without risking Blue being crushed.

Cooper's knees started to give. Much more and he'd be on the floor. He growled his frustration and another voice took up the song.

The pressure from the insect hands suddenly lessened as the growling from the vicinity of Cooper's waist got louder. The dog soldier looked down in time to see Blue's jaws snap shut around the roach man's groin. All of Samsa's arms went limp as he crumbled over in pain.

"I guess the splicing didn't get rid of all of the man," Cooper thought wryly, trying to suppress a grin. Blue let go and Cooper very gently set the dog on the floor.

Blue growled at Samsa. Cooper dropped into a defensive position, ready to attack. Samsa looked from one to the other, then chose the better part of valor and scurried out of the bunker and into the sights of about fifty soldiers of the 142nd Starborne.

A voice ordered him to freeze, but the roach man ignored the order. Cooper looked outside as bullets riddled the insect body. It was enough to make Samsa stumble, but not fall. However a grenade launcher reduced him to so much goo, like a giant exploding boot smashing on him from above.

Cooper put the dog down and got on one knee. "Thanks boy, but this could get messy. Safest if you just stay here."

Cooper touched his earpiece. "This is Sergeant Cooper. I assume you got Corporal Harpole's report. My appearance is now a bit unusual, but I'm a friendly. Do not open fire. Repeat—do not opened fire."

"Roger that, Sergeant Cooper."

Dartanian Cooper slowly walked out of the bunker, his hands open and out to his sides. Blue ignored his orders, and protectively limped along beside him. There were fifty armed soldiers, but Cooper was happy to see that not one of them trained their weapons on them. However, he also noted that not many fingers were that far away from the trigger. Cooper sighed because he realized in their place, he would be doing the same thing.

He was a little surprised to see who came out to greet him.

Cooper gave a quick salute. "Major Benedict, sir."

It was unusual for a major to hold command over those with much higher ranks, but the 142nd had adapted to it. Benedict returned the salute. "Sergeant Cooper, the mission was successful?"

"Yes, sir. All the children are safe. With the exception of soldier Samsa there..."

"Samsa? That was really the name of the bug splicer?" Benedict said with a grin. "Was his first name Gregor?"

"It was Carlos, but I'm not sure why that is amusing."

"Not a big fan of 19th century literature, I take it?"

"No, sir. These days I don't get to read much except for explosive and bomb technical manuals."

"Understandable. We've already encounter one of the other bug splicers and we'll have to locate the other five. Finish your status report, Sergeant."

"The planetary forces have a wounded soldier, otherwise no casualties. He needs more medical care. Their doctor was helpful in assisting us. All two thousand children appear to be safe and Corporal Harpole has disarmed all the explosives."

"Excellent work. Harpole's report was very brief, but am I to understand that you willingly spliced yourself together with DNA from Blue?"

"Yes, sir. Blue was wounded protecting Corporal Harpole and myself and was unable to complete the mission. The children's lives were in jeopardy. We had little time to come up with a plan. This is the only way I could see to finish the mission. The planetary governor had booby-trapped the place.

Within an hour, we and all civilians and enemy combatants would've been buried beneath the rubble."

Hans Benedict met Cooper's eyes unflinchingly. "You are aware that there is no known method to reverse a splicing?"

"Yes, sir. I knew that before I did it. I also know your opinion on monster soldiers, sir. If need be, I can retire from active duty."

"Nonsense. It is true, I have issues with some of those the Host has chosen to employ as soldiers, but I see no monster here. Only a hero." Major Benedict stuck out his hand. It took the canine Sergeant Cooper a moment to realize what he was doing and return the handshake. "Excellent, selfless work. Congratulations on a successful mission, Captain Cooper."

"Sir, I'm only a sergeant."

Benedict smiled. "Not anymore. With the fall of Earth, the 142nd needs all the brave and selfless officers we can get and I'm not above jumping a qualified candidate a few ranks. You just proved yourself one of that number." Benedict bent down on one knee and extended his hand to Blue. The dog return the shake, then whimpered at the pain the movement caused him. "Medic, we need a stretcher over here now for Private Blue."

Two medics came over and gently put the dog on a stretcher. Blue lay down.

"It's okay, boy. Rest," Cooper said and Blue fell asleep almost instantly.

Major Benedict placed his hand on top of the dog's head and petted gently. "Good job, soldier," he whispered.

"What's going to happen to Blue, sir?"

"We'll make sure he's patched up as best we can. If he's able, he'll return to active duty with you. If he's not, he shall continue to live with you. A soldier wounded in the line of duty deserves the right to grow old with his family. We owe him that much. And perhaps stud him out to father his own replacements."

Cooper smiled. "I think Blue might must be hoping for retirement just because of that option, sir."

"Wouldn't we all? And I suppose there is no reason he can't do both. Do you feel fit to help with evacuation of the children and the return to their families?"

"Yes sir, but what about my appearance? It might frighten some of the families."

"It might, but we'll let those same people know that you and your partners saved their children. I think that will go a long way toward helping them get over their prejudice. If any of them you any grief, I will talk to them personally. That goes for anyone, planetside or shipside."

Cooper snapped off another salute. "Yes, sir. Thank you, sir."

Benedict again returned the salute. "No, Captain Cooper, thank you."

The major made a mental note to arrange for counseling and monitoring of Captain Cooper. Splicer soldiers were phenomenal in battle, but more than half of them eventually took on the instincts of the animal they shared DNA with and had to be put down, often by way of suicide missions.

Cooper was thinking along similar lines, only with a great deal more worry. The only thought keeping him from panicking was that his spliced DNA came from Blue, a dog willing to die to protect his human partners. A dog that was braver and more loyal than a great many people. Cooper couldn't see how having those parts of Blue inside of him would make him go mad. In fact, it might end up making him a better human.

I GIVE MY HEART TO THE HAWKS

A Devil Dancers Story

Robert E. Waters

Victorio "Tomorrow's Wind" Nantan, captain of the Devil Dancers fighter squadron, watched Blue Bird stroke the tender head feathers of her red-tailed hawk. It was a marvelous young adult, confident and commanding, as it waited anxiously on her arm to be released. His second-in-command cooed lovingly as she unfastened the leather cords that held the bird's sharp claws in place on her arm guard. It flapped its mighty wings in anticipation, letting its white underbelly ruffle in the breeze. Blue Bird cooed again, then pulled the cord away and let the bird go. Victorio shielded his eyes from the rising sun and watched as it rose into the bright sky. It was a beautiful creature, and he loved it. He loved all the squadron's birds and Blue Bird too.

But she would not love him back for what he was about to tell her.

"Isn't she wonderful?" Blue Bird asked, pointing into the sky toward her rising hawk. "She has a strong totem. I can *feel* it."

Victorio nodded and placed his hand on her shoulder. He watched for a while longer as the hawk joined its partner in the sky. He watched as they flew together then locked talons in a death spiral. Down and down they went, and Blue Bird giggled by his side. They were copulating, or trying to at least, she and her male counterpart, barreling through the sky, barely conscious of their surroundings. If they mated, they would be together forever, he knew. Blue Bird knew, as well, and somewhere in her brilliant mind was an image of them fucking, her and Victorio. They had done so many times, but no babies. Not yet at least. Not until this terrible war with the Gulo was over.

"I need to speak to you."

She turned to him, and her smile changed. "What the hell does Admiral Cho want from us now? My birds and I are on R&R until Monday."

"And you will remain so," he said. "But afterward... there is a mission we must conduct."

She waited, her breaths short and constant. She put her weight on her left leg, her arms crossed, her hip jutted out in defiance. She favored her right foot since its reattachment not long ago from the squadron's deadly engagement at Castor V, but he knew her stance was just a feint. If she got angry, she could round on him in an instant, weak foot or no. The hawk totem was strong in her. Too strong sometimes. "What kind of mission?"

"*Celia* has fallen to the Gulo."

Blue Bird shook her head. "Not familiar with it."

"Zeus Sector. Out of our jurisdiction, but strategically important nonetheless. Primarily Europeans, old Spanish, Portuguese families. It has fallen and is now suffering major privations. Cut off from supply and communication. We need it back, and Admiral Cho has decided to strike in three months. Plans are afoot, but he needs reconnaissance beforehand. The Gulo are cagey, intelligent, as you are well aware. They hide their assets well."

The Gulo were a violent, wolverine-like race that had invaded human space about thirty-five stellar years ago. Since then, they had pushed hard in every sector, making it all the way to Mars in one offensive before squadrons like the Devil Dancers and commanders like Admiral Cho turned the tide. Now the invaders were being pushed back in every sector, but it was a hard, slow slog.

Blue Bird huffed, and turned back to watch her hawks. "He wants the Devil Dancers to run recon on the blind, and deep inside hostile territory?"

"No, in fact, he doesn't." Victorio shook his head and cleared his throat, choosing his words carefully. "He wants to borrow our birds."

Blue Bird stiffened, and Victorio braced for an assault. But it did not come. Instead, she turned quietly and stared at him. Her face reddened. "He wants what?"

"Our hawks. Three of them at least. A fighter squadron, even as skilled as ours, would draw too much attention from the Gulo and would most certainly be detected by their sophisticated defensive shield-net. We might be able to gather the data that's required, but in the end, we'd be blown out of the sky. No. The best observers here would be hawks, birds of prey with visual acuity three, four times as sharp as human beings. *Celia* is a human planet, and much of its flora and fauna were transferred there. They have a lot of animal species from Earth, including birds. A few more hawks in the sky won't ruffle Gulo feathers."

It was a bad pun, he knew, and Blue Bird made him pay for it with an angry glare. "We're not talking about dogs here, Vic. Hawks aren't easy to train. You can't just give them orders and expect them to fly over what you want."

Victorio sighed. "That's not exactly how it's going to work, Blue. We will control them remotely from the *Star Chariot.*"

Blue Bird squinted. "How?"

"An ocular booster will be implanted in their corneas," he said, "which will allow them to submit images to a relay buoy stationed within the planet's debris ring. As far as controlling them is concerned, a small neural weave will be placed just inside their craniums, allowing us to emit pulses into their brains which will let us guide their flight over the areas we need reviewed."

Blue Bird shook her head. "I didn't know we had that kind of technology."

"One of the perks of being at war for 35 years."

The Gulo were highly sophisticated warriors. Their ships, troopers, and weapons were on par, and in some cases, superior than human technology. But when it came to subterfuge, espionage, and manipulating technology to enhance those activities, the Gulo seemed oblivious. Everything was a blunt object for them. It was a great strength, but also their greatest weakness.

"I won't allow it," Blue Bird said, holding her arm out over the ledge. "You won't take my birds."

"They aren't your birds. They're the squadron's. It's already been decided."

"Without consulting me? Your second-in-command?"

"I'm doing the best I can for us all, Blue. I'm doing what I can to help the war effort."

"But why our birds?"

"Because I love you more than them!"

He didn't mean to snap. He didn't want to raise his voice at all, especially to her, but the stress of this whole thing, this war, was beginning to weigh heavily upon him. "If we can prove that this technology works," he said, "then we can infiltrate any human world conquered by the Gulo, learn their strengths and weaknesses, and then orchestrate counterattacks more effectively. If our hawks can accomplish this, then other animals could be fitted with these technologies. It could be the turning point we need. And then maybe this goddamned war will finally end. The goal here is to *end* the war."

Blue Bird accepted the hawk again on her arm. She smiled as she cooed and stroked the beast's beautiful white neck. The bird accepted a small piece of meat, swallowed it, then nuzzled its sharp beak against her tender affections. Blue Bird said, "They will die, Victorio."

"No they won't. It's just a recon mission. They'll be in and out quickly. I promise."

Blue Bird shook her head as she placed the hawk in its cage. "You can't promise anything, Victorio. This is war. There are no promises here."

They were silent while the male hawk came down and accepted Blue Bird's arm. She caged him, slipped slices of meat to them both between the bars, then placed the travel cover over them. As they stilled and grew quiet, she picked the cages up, turned and said, "You are my commanding officer. You are Captain Victory. And we are duty-bound to carry out your orders. But understand this, Captain. If these birds die... then there will be no more *us*. That, I *can* promise."

She walked away, and Victorio stared at her as she worked down the hill to the waiting truck. In her wake, he could feel her strong hawk totem and knew that she was telling the truth. If he failed, if these hawks died, then there would be no future for them.

Never.

But they would not fail. He was certain of it. He was Victorio Nantan, Captain Victory, commander of the Devil Dancers, 3ʳᵈ Sol Fighter Wing, the best squadron in the fleet. It was just a simple recon mission.

"Nothing will go wrong, my love," he whispered to himself as she walked away. "I promise."

On the *Star Chariot,* they sat in a triangle of three chairs, Victorio, Blue Bird, and Shines Like the Sun. The rest of the squadron would be monitoring progress from the bridge. They would also be responsible for launching the relay buoy, ensuring its successful implantation in *Celia's* debris ring, and then launching the carrier probe into the atmosphere so that the hawks could be successfully released undetected by Gulo defenses. In some ways, those lucky enough not to actually fly the mission had the hardest tasks. If they failed, the mission would be aborted. Blue Bird would like that,

Victorio knew. But their tasks could not fail. He had forbidden it, firmly, and with passionate direction. If they failed, the war would go on and on and on. It was a warning that got everyone in the squadron focused to their tasks.

"Buoy target identified," a voice cracked over the comm. "Launch imminent."

Victorio nodded but remained silent. It seemed like the right thing to do. There was nothing more to be said anyway. Soon, their minds would be connected to their respective hawks, and speech would be impossible in such a state. Across from him, Blue Bird stared into nothing, unblinking, showing her strength and fear, the feelings that he was certain were also printed on his face. Shines Like the Sun sat at his left, eyes closed, rocking gently back and forth, lips moving slightly, giving up a solemn prayer to Yusn Life-Giver, god of all and the great father of the Apaches. Victorio nodded approval. *Say a prayer for me as well, my friend.*

"Target struck."

A channel opened in Victorio's mind with a piercing ring. It threw him a little, more so than it had in practice, but the sensation went away finally, and now he could detect Blue Bird's and Shines Like the Sun's presence. He was in their minds. Not completely, not in the way that he would soon be in the mind of his hawk, but he knew his squadron mates were there without even having to place eyes upon them. It was a weird sensation, but one that Blue Bird assumed easily. 'It will be even more challenging when you enter the hawk's mind,' she had said during practice. 'It is simple, but focused. You will feel strong, powerful sensations of fear, joy, lust, hunger, flight. Those are the emotions that define the hawk, and you must learn to control them.'

'How can I do that?' he had asked.

She had smiled. 'You must give yourself to the hawk. *Be* the hawk.'

It was not a skill that he had easily mastered, and sitting here now, waiting restlessly for the mission to begin, he wasn't sure if he ever would. He was a *di-yin* shaman, and one that had used his spiritual powers to thwart enemies in the past, but the hawk totem had always escaped him. Perhaps it was because the bird's emotions were simple, clear, straightforward, and Victorio's had always been muddled. *Should I or shouldn't I? Will this work or not? Was it the right thing to do?* Even in practice, when Blue Bird told him to give himself up to the insatiable pangs of the hawk's hunger, he had refused to swoop down and pluck a mouse from a rotting stump. Why? Because it just didn't seem like the right thing to do... tactically. To break formation for such a silly reason as eating a rodent. But that was human logic, and the purpose of giving oneself to the hawk was to experience its sudden and powerful instincts, so that one could learn how to harness them effectively. Blue Bird understood that. Shines like the Sun understood. It had taken Victorio twice as long to figure it out.

"Carrier probe launched."

Victorio mouthed *I love you* to Blue Bird. She did not mouth it back, but she smiled faintly and nodded.

He closed his eyes and his emotions changed. Simple, powerful, he was in the mind of his hawk, the youngest one, but the fastest according to Blue Bird. First was fear, anxiousness for their rapid descent in the carrier. It was just large enough for three birds, and they had been given a mild sedative to keep them from trying to flap their wings and potentially break them. Like a bullet, the carrier would plunge through *Celia's* upper atmosphere until it reached the correct level, then break open like an egg and disperse its cargo.

Victorio worked through a few sub-routines in his mind and finally gained access to the hawk's eyes. Nothing but darkness as they descended, but even darkness was nothing to his new visual power. He could easily discern the other two birds ahead of him in the carrier, tightly packed, but struggling to free themselves. *Patience, Blue Bird,* he said through his mind. *You taught me that.* The hawk in front of him stilled, but a talon reached out and nicked his breast. Victorio chuckled and it came out as a screech, but he followed it up with something more serious.

Remember, target is ten kilometers due east. Five fly-overs, first two tight, last three dispersed. Then make it to the extraction point. Thirty standard minutes.

The carrier dropped, then shook, then cracked into four pieces that drifted away in the thin *Celia* atmosphere. Victorio fell separately for a few seconds before gaining control of his wings, righting himself, and shifting his light body to the East. He could feel the cool, Earth-like air on his breast feathers. It felt good. He felt good. He felt alive, free, wanting to find an air current and drift for hours. He forced the desire from his small mind, shook his head and joined Blue Bird and Shines Like the Sun in I-formation. They would go in twenty feet apart, and then fan out slightly to make detailed pictures of their target.

Victorio spread his wings to let the air currents shift him down beneath a cloud bank. Then he turned on his boosted ocular scanner, and the world came into view.

Celia was rockier than Earth. Almost everywhere, the spikes of jutting grey and black rock appeared, peppered here and there with small patches of foothills covered in bright green and yellow grass. His mind exploded with so many colors and shapes. He almost toppled over. But Blue Bird fell back and nudged him on course. *Keep sharp*, she said, flipping upside down and rolling through the pleasant sky.

This was a human planet that had been terraformed and reshaped for over a hundred years. Between the rocks and throughout the hills were human settlements, many now lying in ruin, soot, and black ash. Victorio's heart sank. Such beauty, such clarity could he find through this wonderful bird's eyes, and yet, the clarity of desolation and the meaning of such was almost too much to bear. And amidst that ruin, Gulo settlements were being constructed, half-fabricated, half-earthen tunnel complexes that cut through the landscape like sharp, angular worms of green and white. And how many humans had died with the first Gulo invasion force? How many were still down there serving as slave labor? Victorio did not know the answers to these questions, but he hoped Blue Bird was looking at it all too.

Their target came into view, a sprawling Gulo naval complex that filled the valley from end to end. It was the largest enemy site Victorio had ever seen outside the vacuum of space, and it seemed that its ship bays were large enough for Destroyer-sized hulls. A marvelous station and once again a testament to Gulo skill in warfare. The Federated Union would never dare to house such massive ships in-gravity. Indeed, *Celia's* gravity well was smaller than Earth's, but the risk of having such large ships near the ground was too great. The Gulo were willing to risk it, however, which meant *Celia* was a prime target. *Break them here and ...*

Fan out, he told the others through his mind, and they did, shifting to the left and right of him, he the anchor in a triangle that mimicked their seating arrangement on the *Star Chariot*. The first flight over would be a test, to gauge any enemy response and to acquire a full measurement of the complex with a passive scanning beam. If the enemy did not pick up on that, then the scouts would engage digital patterning in haste.

Victorio flipped on his passive scanners and flew at top speed over the target, taking full measurement of the central portion of the complex. Blue Bird took scans of the right quadrant, Shines Like the Sun the left. As he scanned, Victorio saw dozens of Gulo lurching around, moving from this location to the next, a worker unit doing construction on a new set of modulated structures, fully kitted with radar dishes and beacon towers. They seemed intent on their work, paying no attention to the few simple birds drifting above them.

Near the perimeter of the complex were laser bunkers and rocket squares. The Gulo preferred a mixture of precision and gross-area protection. Sometimes they even threw in anti-matter munitions, but not here, not on-planet. Those kinds of weapons were used in space, where the dispersal of energy could help keep collateral damage focused on enemy craft. Here, there would be little of that. Through the hawk's eyes, Victorio trained his scanners so that all point defense boxes would be clearly noted and marked.

The first fly-over was successful, so they shifted in the wind and made another run. As directed, Blue Bird and Shines Like the Sun pulled in closer, taking on a raven-style pattern that the Devil Dancers used often in space flight. High and tight, and the hawks were performing well. They were not trying to break formation, nor trying to dive low in pursuit of food, nor were they trying to drift away toward the sun to warm their wings. They were doing well, and Victorio was pleased. Things were going as planned.

On their fourth and final fly over, with roughly forty meters between them, Shines Like the Sun broke formation. He fell like a rock, recovered, and tried to reset in the pattern. He dropped again, struggled to recover again, then fell once more.

What's the problem? Victorio asked. *Keep formation.*

I'm trying, Captain, Shines Like the Sun said, *but there's an errant sub-command in my cranial web, overriding my electric impulses. I can't get control of it. It's overwhelming me.*

Suddenly Blue Bird jerked out of formation as well. Her hawk rolled through the sky. *What's happening,* Victorio called to her.

Same thing, Vic. My bird is not following my commands.

Victorio checked his own cranial web, over-riding the security locks. And there it was, a shadow program, cleverly buried within the million lines of code that had been written by the Union's programmers for this mission. It was a simple command: Drop. Its priority algorithms were superior in the codex hierarchy of the entire program, so no matter what happened, no matter how many exceptions were fed into the code, the "drop" command rose to the surface. The only way to knock it out was to remove the web itself. And that was impossible. The commands were on a timer. Shines Like the Sun's command apparently first; Blue Bird's second; and his third.

What do we do? He asked as Blue Bird struggled to keep her bird from falling.

Save him! She blurted.

And Victorio saw what she was referring to. Shines Like the Sun was falling uncontrollably now, his hawk totally taken over by the intrusive command that had been placed in its web.

Victorio pursued, still in control of his own hawk. He dove and dove, pushing his wings against his body to sheer through the air like a blade. He put his talons out and stretched them wide as he neared Shines Like the Sun's posterior. He reached out and tried to lock his claws around the diving hawk's red tail feathers. He got them, but the weight and force of its fall was too great. The bird's feathers slipped out of his grasp, and it kept falling.

Shines Like the Sun screamed as his link was severed, and his hawk struck the complex and exploded in a blast of feathers, blood, and green gas.

What the hell...?

Where had the gas come from? It spread and Victorio pulled up and soared to safety as the gas cloud continued to expand.

Sabotage, he heard Blue Bird say through his mind. Yes, it had to be. The green gas continued to expand and balloon over the complex, more rapidly than Victorio would have imagined. The only way it could have done that is through the shock of the explosion as the hawk struck the complex.

There were several inert compounds that, when combined with liquids and the catalyst of heat and intense pressure—such as striking a wall— would create a toxin. Yes, it had to be. But how that toxin had been put into the hawks and where... well, he didn't have time for speculation.

Blue Bird was falling out of the sky.

He flew to her, like a rocket, like he had seen his bird do countless times in Chaco Canyon when they were let out for exercise. His mate was in his sights, and he went to her.

Down he flew until he was near enough to wrap his talons around her, press his small body against hers. But the desire was not there, not in her eyes. Only fear, uncertainty. She was crying.

We're going to die, she said. *They are going to die.*

No, he said, holding her tighter, pulling her closer. *What did you tell me when we practiced? How do you control a hawk?*

She didn't respond at first, uncertain perhaps of what he meant. Then she said, *You must be the hawk.*

Yes, and what is one of the hawk's chief emotions?

Fear.

And what does the hawk do when it is afraid?

It flies.
Are you afraid?
Yes.
Then be the hawk... and fly!

He let her go, let her drop from his grasp. No longer did the neural weave in the bird's cranium affect his movement. He found himself ignoring the synaptic impulses of its commands. The 'Drop' command fell silent, inert—like the foul green jelly placed inside him—and he flew.

He saw the world now through hawk's eyes, different than before. Clear, focused, consumed with the desire to fly, to flee, to reach heights where no other bird could find him, in the clouds where only Yusn Life-Giver resided, in the blue haze of a distant mountain range where the mountain spirits would give him further strength. Blue Bird found it too; he could feel her new-found strength. The hawk totem that had escaped her was now back and strong, stronger than ever. And they flew together, ignoring the incessant tickle of the errant command that lay fallow in their minds.

They flew over the sharp spires of the Gulo complex. They spread their wings and let the wind take them away, through cloud bank and light rain, until they found a small patch of trees. Down they went until they found a sturdy branch. Victorio spread his wings to slow his descent. He grabbed the wood and felt it give under his weight, but it did not break. Blue Bird then lighted beside him.

They perched there on the tree, looking at each other, not able to speak, not able to share their thoughts. Only short screeches escaped their long, sharp beaks. But Victorio understood now what he was. He was not human anymore. He was a hawk, he and Blue Bird. They were hawks.

They were happy.

A darkness consumed Victorio, and then he was back on the *Star Chariot*, in his seat, sweat rolling down his face. To his left Shines Like the Sun was slumped over, his face deathly pale. To his right, Blue Bird sat erect, but weak and moaning.

"Report, Captain!"

It was Admiral Cho's voice. Victorio blinked, wiped his face, and saw the admiral before him, flanked by guards.

Victorio flew out of the chair. "You sorry son of a bitch! You nearly got us killed!"

The guards grabbed him before he could lay a finger on the smug little commander, but that didn't temper his rage. "You lied to me. Why?"

"So that you could do what needed to be done."

"You said it was just a recon mission."

Admiral Cho nodded. "And it was… in a sense. But this is best, whether you accept it or not. We do not have the strength to take *Celia* back in force, not without severely damaging their capabilities beforehand." He smiled. "Now, the toxin will spread through their population, and they will be depleted before our attack."

"You failed, Admiral," Victorio said, giving a smile of his own. "You failed. Only Shines' bird impacted. Mine and Blue Bird's flew away."

Admiral Cho gnashed his teeth. His face grew red. "That's a lie."

"It's true. Check the digital. We got away, Admiral. Not enough toxins were released. We got away, and those hawks will live out their days, shitting out your poison like a digested mouse. That's what you are, Admiral. A filthy little mouse."

"Take him away!" Admiral Cho yelled. "Take them all away!"

As they were dragged to the brig, Victorio imagined himself flying, soaring through the air, looking for prey.

Three months later, Victorio Nantan sat under guard on a lip of rock overlooking Chaco Canyon. The cuffs on his wrists dug into his skin, but he didn't care. He watched two hawks play in the bright sunlight, and he imagined himself with them, flying through clouds, looking down on the world. He breathed deeply and closed his eyes.

Someone came up behind him. He could hear feet shuffling along the loose rock and gravel. He couldn't see her, but he knew who she was. He could feel her.

"The tribunal has adjourned," Blue Bird said. "Sentence has been passed."

Victorio did not speak. He waited until she unrolled a piece of paper and read aloud so that the guard might also hear. "In the matter between Victorio "Tomorrow's Wind" Nantan, Captain of the Devil Dancers Fighter Squadron, and Admiral Tsing Lau Cho, commander of Special Fleet Operations for the Federated Union, the charges being Dereliction of Duty and Insubordination by Captain Nantan. For Dereliction of Duty, the tribunal finds Captain Nantan… not guilty. For Insubordination and Attempted Assault Against a Superior Officer, the tribunal finds Captain Nantan… guilty as charged, the sentence of which shall be three months solitary confinement, loss of pay, and reduction of rank to First Lieutenant for six standard months, after which time, all rank, status, and benefits thereof will be reinstated."

"What about the charges against you and our squadron?" Victorio asked.

"All other charges have been dropped."

"And Shines Like the Sun?"

Blue Bird nodded. "He'll be fine. He's recovering from his aneurysm."

Victorio nodded. "Good. Admiral Cho?"

Blue Bird chuckled. "He was... *encouraged* to accept early retirement."

She sat beside him and placed her head on his shoulder. "I'm sorry, Vic."

"Don't be. It could have been worse. And at least the Union realized Cho's deception and dropped the dereliction charge. I'm just sorry that I failed you. I lost the birds."

"Only one," Blue Bird said.

"The other two are stuck on *Celia*."

She nodded. "But they are safe. And they will be together forever." She kissed his cheek. "Just like us."

He looked into her eyes. "Will this war ever end?"

Blue Bird shook her head. "I don't know, Vic. But let's not worry about that right now. Let's just close our eyes, fly, and be at peace."

And they did. Victorio breathed deeply and imagined himself moving powerful wings. He heard the hawk's screech and let it inside him. He lifted up into the clouds and floated on air that gave him breath and courage. And beside Blue Bird, beside his love, he soared.

TOWER FARM
Vonnie Winslow Crist

THE BUZZ OF THE PERIMETER ALARM WOKE CROWE. HE FUMBLED FOR HIS PIStol, then sat up, flung his legs over the side of the bed, rubbed his eyes, and studied the status console. Jax already stood in front of the screens and monitors. She glanced over her shoulder at him and gave a slight wag of her tail.

"What've we got, girl?"

Crowe laid his handgun on the desktop in front of the console, leaned forward, and scanned the displays. Something had disrupted the current that electrified the security fence. Since no sentient, human or otherwise, had tried to enter the tower farm since Jax and he'd been stationed there, Crowe figured it was a nocturnal animal.

Hardly seemed worth starting the rover up to check it out. All they'd find was a fried critter of one sort or another, cooked and ready for the morning scavengers. What was he thinking? The carcass would likely be consumed before the first moon set. Still, he and Jax were duty-bound to identify what had tried to breach the perimeter.

"Duty-bound," he grumbled. His fingers drummed the desktop in frustration. Guarding a tower farm, no matter how vital to planet-wide operations, was a far cry from the battlefields, heli-drops, and rescue missions of the past. Jax and he'd been one of the elite teams called into action when a situation looked dire, but that was before The Explosion.

He pulled on his pants, laced up his boots, slipped on a combat vest, and filled various sheaths and holsters with weapons, including the pistol.

Granted, it was old tech and only good for up close encounters, but he'd slept with the gun ever since a band of deserters murdered his parents and younger sister. Crowe was visiting with his uncle when the attack occurred, otherwise he'd have been killed, too. Afterward, he never went anywhere without a gun, even to bed.

Jax sat by the door to the rover's bay patiently waiting for him to dress her for the night-time outing.

"Probably nothing," he told her as he Velcro-ed on her burn vest.

The Explosion had burned both of them severely, but cosmetic surgery wasn't available for military dogs. Jax had been issued a specially-designed vest that shielded her scarred and nearly hairless right shoulder and side from sunburn and chilly temperatures.

"And we'd better put this on, too. Just in case," Crowe said as he lashed a heavier combat jacket over her burn vest.

Jax barked three times. One of her signals for "Yes."

"Let's go, partner." Crowe couldn't keep the eagerness out of his voice as he unbolted the steel door between the rover's bay and the living compound, pushed open the heavy barrier, and stepped into the bay. He couldn't help but hope they saw some real action as they hadn't since before...The Explosion. Maybe there really were enemy combatants trying to knock out communications, or scrappers, after the copper used to ground the towers. Or something, anything, that would require the skills of an experienced K-9 and her handler to neutralize the threat.

"Not likely," he muttered. "We're has-beens assigned to a babysitting post."

Jax looked at him, tilted her head, and seemed to understand his longing to engage in battle one more time.

The bay was much colder than the living compound, but they wouldn't be staying there long. He punched the unlock code into a panel imbedded in the wall, unplugged the power charger, then manually lowered the door in the belly of the rover. It formed a ramp, which Jax and he walked up. The inside of the cabin rumbled as Crowe turned on the rover and closed the belly ramp. Once everything locked secure, the cab swiveled one hundred and eighty degrees until they faced the outer hatch. Crowe flicked the switch and waited impatiently as the door slowly lifted. Finally, the rover quietly rolled from its subterranean lair.

With all three moons out, a blanket of stars overhead, and the flickering of the towers' aircraft warning lights, Crowe doubted they'd need to turn on the spotlight attached to the rover's roof to determine what had triggered the alarm. Thanks to the rover's electric engine, they traveled the road that circled the tower farm just inside the fence in near silence searching for the culprit. He rolled the window down just a crack until they could hear the wind whoosh across the mountain top and whistle through the towers. Tonight, the direction and speed of the gusts were just right. The wind seemed to sing as it rushed between mono-poles, lattice towers, guyed-towers and their anchor wires, and all the various antennas that sprung from the metal structures like spindly appendages.

A quick scan and we'll be done, he thought as Jax and he surveyed the chain-link.

A low growl stopped Crowe's musing. Jax's ears pricked as her lips drew back exposing her teeth. He followed her gaze and saw a breach in the fence about seventy-five feet ahead. Razor wire lay useless on the ground and the chain-link curled back where it had been cut.

"Jeezus. That was no critter." Crowe stopped the rover, but decided against using the spotlight. If someone had gone to the trouble of winding their way through the vast network of canyons surrounding Devil's Spine, climbing to the high desert plateau below, then scaling six thousand feet of sheer cliffs to reach the tower farm, he assumed they'd still be somewhere on the premises. The quiet approach of the rover might give Jax and him an advantage against whoever had entered the tower farm.

He touched his lips with a forefinger. Jax stopped growling. With the calmness of a seasoned warrior, Crowe picked up his semi-automatic. Antiquated in most battle situations, a semi-automatic fitted with a night-vision scope in the hands of an expert marksman was the weapon of choice on a tower farm where destruction of the towers and their equipment was to be avoided at all costs. A pulse rifle, blaster, or explosive of any sort could not only damage the towers and their antennas, but also blow the satellite dishes scattered amongst the towers to bits.

According to the rover's instrument panel, the temperature on Demon's Spine was thirty-nine degrees. Taking into account the strong gusts, Crowe figured the wind chill was below freezing. He pulled a pair of zee-foil gloves from one of his pockets and slipped them on. Snug as a second skin and thinner than parachute silk, they wouldn't interfere with his ability to fire the rifle, but would prevent his fingers from going numb if he was outside for a prolonged period of time. After making sure no one was nearby, Crowe lowered the rover's access ramp, then he and Jax slipped outside.

Directing Jax with barely discernible nods and gestures, they moved to the nearest tower complex. Built of thick, steel-reinforced concrete, the shelters at the foot of the towers housed a base transmitter station for each tenant. He checked the door. It was still locked. His jaw clenched in grim realization. Whoever broke in wasn't after copper then. Scrappers would have stripped the shelters closest to their entry point, then made a quick get-away.

With a tilt of his head, he sent Jax to the next complex. Making little sound, his dog raced through the scrubby grasses, checked around the far side, then turned her head and nodded the all's clear signal. Crowe followed Jax's path until he stood by her side. He reached out and tested the shelter's door. Again, everything was secure.

They repeated the process two more times with the same results. He knew the importance of the towers' tenants grew as they moved toward the center of the facility. The towers on the outer edges of the farm were used by mining companies, cell phone firms, and other commercial tenants. The highest towers, located in the center of the farm, were utilized by the military, public safety command, defense contractors, and classified entities.

He considered who'd be interested in sabotaging or destroying the base transmitter stations of those tenants. Maybe humans with plans to hold a shelter's worth of transmitters for ransom. Perhaps a radical group with a political agenda wanted publicity. Of course, there was the possibility of non-human sentients, but he wasn't aware of any recent alien attacks in this quadrant.

He was about to send Jax to the next shelter, when she froze in place with her nose pointed in the direction of a tower about a hundred and fifty yards to the west of their location.

Crowe followed her line of sight and spotted a group of bipeds attempting to pry open the tower shelter's metal entrance door. He frowned. Even from this distance, the fluidity of their movements didn't seem human. The over-sized shelter the trespassers had chosen contained the base transmitter stations for two five-hundred foot military guyed-towers and a public safety self-support tower. It was one of the most vital shelters on the farm. Once inside, they could not only disrupt the legal tenants' signals, but alter the programming and use the towers to send their own messages.

His pulse quickened as he realized this was no group of amateurs, they knew what they were doing. With his left hand, Crowe slowly reached up and felt for the emergency button built into his vest which activated a distress signal on the rover. Once he located the device, he pulled off the protective cover and pressed the button. As he'd lowered his hand, he felt himself slip into a calm, clear-headed battle mode. He knew by now the distress signal had reached Fort Destiny. Though they wouldn't arrive for twenty minutes, Special Forces were at this moment being deployed to Demon's Spine.

Until they got there, it was up to Jax and him to protect the tower farm.

Using satellite dishes, towers, and shelters for cover, they crept closer. As they got within Crowe's optimal firing range, he raised his hand slightly. Jax and he stood still as stone and studied the individuals who'd illegally entered the restricted area. Three bipeds whom appeared human were working on the door and nine biped guards carrying some sort of long-barreled weapon formed a semi-circle around them. Three of the guards also looked human. The other six appeared to be four-armed beings with long, oddly shaped fingers.

Crowe pressed his lips together and raised his weapon. Pressing his eye to the scope, he tried to get a better look at them through his scope. Their faces appeared slightly furred and their eyes were huge. The hands clutching the weapons seemed to have suckers on the ends. Whatever they were, he didn't recognize these particular aliens from his training manual. Unless their existence was above his clearance level, they were a new threat. He could imagine how handy those suckers had come in scaling the cliff; who knew what else they were capable of? Sweat broke out on Crowe's brow at the thought, but he also felt the thrill of adrenaline again coursing his veins at the prospect of entering combat once more.

With back-up forces still ten or more minutes away and the bipeds determined to break into a shelter housing high-priority base transmitters stations, there was no choice. Crowe reinforced Jax's stay command, then charged his weapon. As he took aim, one of the human-appearing guards transform into a four-armed alien.

Hell's bells, biomorphs! Crowe's gut clenched as he realized how easily they could blend in with the human settlers. For all he knew, the planet was crawling with them. Were they an alien threat intent on invasion, or worse— were they indigenous, bent on eliminating the human presence on their planet?

Whatever their intent, right now Crowe and Jax were the only obstacle between them and success. Jax stood next to him, ready to follow his commands. She didn't even flinch when he shot the first biomorph. Before the aliens could react, Crowe hit four more. Dead or wounded? It didn't matter so long as they weren't able to return fire.

Screeching in rage, the remaining biomorphs assumed their natural form. All of them turned toward Crowe and Jax, eyes intense with what Crowe could only assume was hatred. He ducked behind cover and fired again as the four guards shot burning projectiles from their weapons at Crowe and Jax. Where the fireballs landed around them, the wind-dried vegetation burst into flames.

Crowe's ears pounded and bile climbed his throat as the radiant heat threw him into a flashback. For a moment, he was back on Perseus Three. *Jax and he left the cave where his unit hunkered down to walk the quarter mile or so back to base camp and get some grub. They'd remained on guard duty, so they were the last to head for chow. Everyone else, dog and soldier alike, had a full belly and were settling in for the night. He could hear their muffled voices and laughter as they waited to drift off to sleep, then a high-pitched whine cut the night air. He and Jax turned around in horror, but there was nothing they could do as the incoming the missile targeted the cave. Their whole squad disappeared in the fireball.*

Crowe had spun away and attempted to escape the blast zone, but the fire roared all around him. Jax, who'd been clear of the fireball, had rushed head-long into it trying to get to his side. Crowe remembered seeing the reflection of the blazing hillside in his dog's eyes before he blacked out. When he'd come to hours later, the medics told him Jax had drug him nearly back to camp before collapsing from the burns she'd sustained in his rescue. She'd lost the tips of her ears and had been severely burned because she came back for him. He owed her his life.

He clenched his teeth and suppressed the urge to retreat as the flames licked closer and the aliens continued to fire. Sensing his elevated level of anxiety, Jax turned her muzzle up and gazed at him. Just like that day on Perseus Three, he saw blazing brush reflected in her eyes. Hating the necessity, he gave her the signal to send her through the flames toward the biomorphs and their fireball guns.

He pointed at the aliens, nodded, then lifted his weapon and began to shoot at the advancing biomorphs. Without hesitation, Jax rushed forward with her jaws slightly open. Expression grim and his heart pounding, Crowe followed. Despite the fire-retardant fabric of his pants, his legs screamed with pain, and higher it felt like a swarm of yellow jackets stung his jaw. Crowe ignored the pain and the terror licking at his insides. He held his weapon steady and shot at the advancing biomorphs. Three of them fell beneath his fire as Jax tackled the fourth.

His dog ripped out the biomorph guard's throat, then looked up for orders. Crowe gave her another nod toward the remaining targets. Jax leapt over the body of the guard and raced toward the remaining bipeds.

The biomorphs gained access to the shelter just as Jax and he neared the reinforced concrete building. A pair of the four-armed aliens remained outside the damaged door while their comrade slipped inside the shelter. The two biomorphs on guard raised their fireball guns and shot at Jax. Unable to dodge away, the war dog collapsed as the fireball engulfed her.

Crowe screamed. Charging forward, he fired a stream of bullets, and kept firing until he was out of ammo and the biomorphs outside the shelter were dead. After bursting through the shelter's door, he attacked the remaining alien with a serrated blade he kept in a sheath on his belt. He stabbed and slashed the last biomorph until its lifeless body slumped to the floor, then glanced around. Alien blood and tissue matter splattered every surface, but other than the door, it appeared the biomorphs had not had time to damage the base transmission station's equipment.

Ignoring the sensation of thousands of fire-ants biting his legs, he kicked aside the biomorph's body, shoved open the door, and ran to Jax. Moaning, he knelt by his dog. Even with the protection offered to her by the combat jacket and burn-vest, she was badly injured. A quick glance told him she'd lose the lower part of her front legs if she even survived the burns. His throat closed on that thought. The legs could be replaced, thanks to modern biomechanics; Jax could not.

She raised her charred head, looked Crowe in the eyes, and tried to wag what was left of her tail.

"Easy, girl," he whispered as he ripped the zee-foil glove from his hand. He wanted to touch her, but had to restrain himself from caressing the side of her face.

As his adrenaline drained away, he felt light-headed from the agony in his legs. Between the pain and the smells of burnt flesh and dead alien, his stomach turned. He clenched his jaw and resisted the urge to retch. Looking down at Jax, he told himself that it was the smoke from the scorched grass making his eyes tear.

Stay conscious, Jax needs you, he reminded himself.

Suddenly, shouts and gunfire brought his focus back to his surroundings. Through the smoky haze he saw soldiers running toward them while other uniformed men and women finished off the still-breathing biomorphs. A third group of soldiers bagged alien bodies and collected the fireball guns.

Crowe was vaguely aware of soldiers stopping beside him, then kneeling as they laid a stretcher down. Their mouths moved, but he was too numb to make out the words. He recognized the cross emblem on one soldier's uniform, and realized she was a medic. And as she readied an IV, Crowe surrendered to the pain and slumped down beside Jax. He fought to remain conscious as the medic grasped his wrist and cleaned a spot on his arm for the IV needle.

"No!" he screamed. "Jax first. Treat my dog first."

"Sir, you're injured. We need to stabilize you and get you back to the base." The medic then looked over at Jax, "To be honest, I don't think the dog's going to make it."

"I'm not leaving without her." Crowe struggled against the soldiers who were trying to restrain him so the medic could stabilize him before he was loaded onto the waiting 'copter for transport.

The lieutenant commanding the unit walked over to see what the commotion was about.

"Please, my dog," Crowe begged. "Please, try to save her."

The officer shook his head. "She doesn't look good, son."

"She saved my life. Helped save this facility. She's served with honor."

The world seemed to stop as he waited for the lieutenant to speak.

The officer knelt down and studied the critically injured Jax. "Do as he asks," he said, a hint of warmth in his gaze.

The medic started to protest, but the officer cut him off, "That is an order. You will treat and transport both soldiers. This war dog deserves a chance."

As the military helicopter flew through the darkness, the last thing Crowe remembered before he passed out from pain and meds, was looking over at the stretcher next to him and seeing Jax gazing back.

THE WAG OF HIS TAIL
C.J. Henderson

**"Money will buy a pretty good dog
but it won't buy the wag of his tail."
—Josh Billings**

"Just relax, Lieutenant," said the officer acting as prompter for the investigation. "Take your time, and tell it in your own words. There's no need to rush."

The man in the chair sat at an odd angle, not so much slumped, as shattered. Not worn, but broken. There was no disrespect meant to his superiors by his physical arrangement. All present understood no disrespect was intended by his inability to sit at attention. Indeed, the dazed, battle-fatigued state in which the officer in charge had been discovered explained all. Those in attendance—they were military men. They knew what combat was all about. But, still—

They needed to know what had happened. How what had apparently transpired on the planet could even be possible. The lieutenant was alive, so *ipso facto* it must have been possible. But, considering the utter unlikelihood of it all, as military men—still—they had to know.

"If there's anything you need, a drink, a shaker, anything—just ask. There's no hurry." The words were honestly relaxed, and to those in attendance, they seemed to be working—the officer was calming down—his eyes responding slightly.

"We have all the time anyone could want."

They had to know.

Despite his awkward posture, and his mostly vacant stare, Lt. Everet Cooper could hear the man standing before him just fine. He understood him as well. Knew what those there before him wanted to know. The problem was in his ability to marshal any response at all.

His mind had been so black, so filled with mad hatred that he now shivered from the thought of it. He had been so angry, destroyed so much—killed so many—

And now he lie crumpled in a heap, as if his very bones had melted along with his heart and soul. The object of all pity allowable in the situation. The board of inquiry waited with understanding patience. The young officer there before them—utterly empty of all human emotion—had seen something, done something, been in the middle of something—something unexplainable—which had, if not snapped, at least bent his mind.

Luckily, it seemed he had not been permanently damaged. The staff physicians had assured those sitting in judgment that the officer could stand up to a fair amount of general questioning. Just as long as those putting forth the queries used a little common sense and did not push the man too hard.

None present intended to do so.

"We just need to know as much as you can tell us of what happened ... back out on Felner."

It had to be understood that as far as the board was concerned, the lieutenant was in no manner of trouble. He and his men had been sent into an impossible situation. It was militarily and politically understood that Felner was nothing more than a tolerably habitable moon circling a gas giant in the Silgorn System, basically a nothing little world tucked away at the armpit end of the Confederation of Planets. Although the satellite had developed all manner of life on its own long before being discovered by anyone that could exploit it, none of the indigenous forms had been even beginning to approach sentience at the time it was registered as another claimed/surveyed/annexed plot of Confederation real estate.

"We're sure you can understand ..."

Those that took up residence there were the usual after-thoughts—those that were typically called upon to follow humankind's great outward push. When the Confederation had deemed Felner suitable for long-range colonization, as always, there were those ready to brave the task. No one needed to be coerced or bribed. People, no matter what shape, size, or method of locomotion, are often willing to risk everything on even a slim chance of getting everything in return. Find enough of them ready to roll those dice, and you had a colony. Something to which, in their "generosity," the Confederation was always willing to lend a hand.

"Whatever happened there …"

The military was only interested in establishing a flexible base in the area—a combination rest stop and staging platform. They needed a spot that could be utilized for whatever purpose might suit the powers-that-be at any moment. Those that would settle around such a presence would need protection.

The same deal was struck all the time.

Those willing to serve as civilian support in exchange for a home and a future got to change their lives. Space would always be filled with both those looking to pursue their dreams, as well as those desperate to escape this or that. And the Confederation used them like chips the same way everyone else in the galaxy did.

"How you managed to survive …"

Felner—its population was one of the lucky ones. Never noticed by any kind of major trouble, it had been home to a quite self-sufficient base for some seventeen years when Cooper and the others had arrived there for a simple change of senior staff. New colonel replacing the old one. New support officers brought in, ones with whom the new head of operations felt comfortable.

"Let alone to …"

Over the two months—Earth Standard Time—it had taken for the transport to haul the replacements to Felner, the men and women under Colonel Matthew Hardy had familiarized themselves with everything they could about the planet, its parent world, and the system in which they both dwelled. The ship had delivered them with proper military precision at the exact prearranged moment.

Catching planets within their solar systems at the optimum moment of trajectoral positioning meant massive savings in both time and energy. The replacements were off-loaded without fanfare. Those they were replacing passed them in the upper atmosphere—one shuttle ferrying upward, one headed down. Before Cooper and the others were on the ground, the ship that had brought them to Felner was already departing orbit.

"Well, don't let me get ahead of things. Please … if you could, Lieutenant … if you could just tell us all you can of your tour on Felner—"

And then, something in the way the prompter pronounced the planet's name, or the manner in which he tilted his head, or some other unknown, unchartable factor registered within young Cooper's brain. Blinking suddenly, the change in his demeanor was noted by all present. Instantly, the prompter went silent, stepping back, out of the way of those who needed to make eye contact with the lieutenant.

Cooper pursed his lips, swallowed hard, then coughed in response. His tongue was dry, his throat raspy. The prompter moved slightly, gently placing a glass of water within the lieutenant's hand. The young man nodded in gratitude, then raised the glass to his mouth and drank. He coughed again as he did so, but managed not to spill more than a few drops.

Recovering, the lieutenant licked his lips, set his glass on the small table before him, and concentrated on forcing his emotions off to the back of his mind. He had to clear his brain. He had to get down to the task of telling those who were not there what he was fairly certain they would not understand.

That no one would ever understand.

"So, this is Felner."

"Sure smells like a place that oughta be called Felner."

Everyone in the small group laughed. The replacement force—comprised mainly of troops from the 609—had been on planet for close to three hours. The colonel had assumed command, handed his authorization over to the old security chief who had stayed behind, and claimed his office. Before entering it, he made his oft-practiced speech assuring everyone not lucky enough to be transferred off the middle-of-nowhere moon that things were not going to change to any great degree. Immediately after, as usual, he told the officers he had brought with him from his old command to go out and listen for signs of what, if anything, might actually need changing.

"So, what first?"

"Listen to Cooper," laughed the taller of his two friends, a blond fellow by the name of Shelby. "Can't wait to get to work."

"Who said 'work?' What, you got dust clogging your ears? I said, 'what first?' It's a phrase very open to interpretation. But, we see how your mind 'works.' What you think of others. Very telling ..."

"I hate you—"

"You hate everyone," chimed in Rainer, a dark, hard man with a voice too high for his frame, "but he's got you."

"Fine," responded Shelby with a snort. "Who cares? Let's just go find out whatever it is they have on this dump that most tastes like beer."

As the marines exited through the front gate of their base, they saw a group of locals herding some sort of hefty quadrupeds from a ground-based transport vehicle into a large pen. The animals seemed dull-witted, but docile—things that were probably prized for both their meat and hair. Scampering around them were several reptilian-like creatures. Long of leg, ear, and snout, spindly of body, the trio of snappish things appeared to be acting as helpers to the humans.

"What the hell are those things?"

"Which ones," asked Cooper. "The fat hairy ones or the little punks dancing around them?"

Before either of his friends could answer, one of the lizards suddenly turned its head and began to study the young lieutenant. Walking away from its duties, the thing ambled slowly, its unblinking eyes scanning Cooper with a somewhat disturbing interest. Taking note of that interest, one of the wranglers called out;

"Careful, soldier. Them grodds can be mean."

Cooper looked down at the oddly jointed animal, and was just about to shout back to the rancher that had warned him when the grodd darted forward. The lieutenant tried to throw up his hands to fend the thing off, but it was deceptively fast, landing on his chest before he could react. While everyone shouted, Cooper's friends reaching for their sidearms, but the lieutenant held up his arm, saying;

"Hold off, hold it."

"Them thing's killers, son," shouted one of the wranglers, running forward with his herding rod held out defensively. Not sensing any threat, however, Cooper answered in a louder voice;

"Well, maybe not this one. Maybe not today."

As the others merely stood and watched, the lieutenant talked in a cautious voice to the creature clutching his chest. The grodd had pierced his flak jacket with its claws, but not his skin. Cooper had no way of knowing if the thing understood humans and their clothing, or if it had just been a happy accident, but he decided to wait and find out.

There was something about the bizarre creature clinging to him that he found interesting. Fascinating. And, he decided, the grodd must have felt the same way. The two stared at each other for quite some time, long enough for more than just the original wranglers to crowd around. Cooper's friends only found the incident amusing. Those residents of Felner present, however, were amazed.

Yes, many had found it possible to form alliances of sorts with the creatures. They were willing to herd, act as guards, or help track game. But always it was done strictly for rewards. When a grodd found a human food it liked, it would work for more. But the colonists had always found such relationships to be tenuous things. None had ever seen one of the surly lizard-things ever act in such a manner.

"Ain't hardly able to believe it," said the wrangler who had first shouted a warning.

"You said it, Springer. It's goddamned unbelievable. You must have a way about you, son."

"Or he's got a cake block tucked away in a pocket somewhere."

Cooper took the crowd's comments as good-natured kidding. Everyone was in a fine mood, and the lieutenant knew the colonel would appreciate his men getting off on a good footing with the locals. Several of those that gathered commented that they thought the event to be a good sign, and left to go back to their lives with smiles on their faces. As the crowd broke up, Cooper shouted out to none in particular;

"Hey, how do you tell the males from the females?"

"Don't know," answered one of the wranglers. "Nobody ain't never wanted to turn one over and find out."

"Well," said the lieutenant, staring into the grodd's eyes, "I'm thinking you remind me a lot of my Susie, from when I was a kid."

"You had a lizard for a pet," asked Rainer.

"No. But they had the same eyes."

"You have a dog with evil lizard eyes that promised to eat your liver when your back was turned?"

"Jezzit, Shelby, what kind of sick damn childhood did you have?" Placing his hands gently under the grodd's sides, Cooper picked the creature up and held it at a point where their noses were only an inch apart. Smiling wide, he told it;

"You're my little Susie, girl. What do you think of that?"

The grodd responded by flicking out its rough tongue and running it over the lieutenant's face. It ran the purple length first up one cheek, then the other, finally ending by running it around his left ear, and then inside it. His friends jeered, reminding him that they had alcohol to track down. In response, Cooper pulled the grodd away from his face, then set it on the ground, pointing in the general direction of town as he commanded;

"All right, Susie girl, go on. Find us beer."

Immediately, the reptilian horror turned and dashed off down the road. As the creature disappeared into the distance, Shelby said;

"Three to one, you never see that ugly thing again."

"I'll take some of that action," answered Cooper, somewhat surprised when Rainer added;

"Me, too. I'll throw twenty large at that."

Shelby sputtered in good-natured protest, but after a moment the three returned to their quest, all of them wondering if, when they finally found what they were looking for, they would find some twenty-eight pounds of fangs and claws and tongue waiting for them patiently. Perhaps even wagging its barbed tail.

And, of course, they did. Susie was sitting off to the side of, not the first bar the town had to offer on the road the marines had taken into town, but the most popular. The trio debated mightily if the grodd might actually have understood the word "beer" from having been around humans for a while, or if it had simply camped out in front of the loudest establishment on the strip. They never came to a conclusion acceptable to all of them, but it had not mattered. Susie was suddenly the camp mascot, and everyone knew it.

Life continued on from that moment for the inhabitants of Felner, new and old, as it had since the world was first discovered. The sector was a calm one. Because of their distance from everything, there were no problems with neighbors. Because some eighty-five percent of Felner had yet to be claimed by anyone for developmental purposes, there was little in the way of internal disputes, either. Colonel Hardy, as planetary governor, filled his days with passing judgment on visas, expansion petitions, and trade agreements. The locals continued to harvest bloker hair and meat, slavin grass, and all the other natural and imported resources of their world.

As for Hardy's marines, they were in the enviable position of being able to enjoy a fairly relaxed way of life. With no hostile forces—external or internal—with which to deal, their duties amounted to little more than those of a rural police force. And, with Susie running along at their heels whenever they were mobilized for any kind of local conflict, all their crisis situations seemed to work themselves out as easily as possible. Word had spread rapidly of the soft-spoken marine and his loyal grodd. Indeed, it seemed Cooper could defuse almost any situation by having Susie roll over or sit up.

"I gotta give it to you, Ev," said Shelby one evening as he exhaled an expansive puff from one of the better local cigars, "that critter of yours is making this one damn easy tour of duty."

"Of course she is," responded Cooper. "And that's Lt. Ev to you, soldier."

Those assembled chuckled. Life on Felner, one and all had to admit, was as good as it got. Light duties, limited conflicts, good food, easy access to the local luxury items, and a populous which simply wanted to get on with carving out fortunes for themselves—it all added up to a quiet life for a professional soldier. And, there was not a biped among them that did not give credit to Susie for a great deal of that comfort. Although few could agree as to why the scaly, oddly staring little beast had bonded with Cooper, there was not a one who was not happy it had happened.

There was just something about the odd pairing—the buttoned-down, bookish lieutenant and his scampering, sharp-fanged companion—that made everyone smile. No one would suggest that the previous command had been plagued with massive tension between the civilian population and the stationed military presence. They had certainly eased the way by running a proper post. But, it had been Cooper and his Susie that had changed Felner from a protectorate into a community.

Indeed, Colonel Hardy had sent several reports back to Confederation Central Command, not only praising his lieutenant, but suggesting that the idea of tactical forces looking for opportunities to repeat his success be studied. As the months rolled by, and the mild Felner seasons changed one to another, it began to seem as if humanity might have finally found a paradise out among the stars. And then, four hundred and seventy-six Felnerian days after the new command staff had arrived, something went wrong.

A trio of incoming ships registered on the system scanners. They were of a design unseen previously, traveling at a speed unprecedented. The Colonel's first hope was, of course, for a peaceful first contact. As the unknown ships began targeting and destroying the communications relays in orbit around various worlds in the system, however, that hope was dashed by bitter reality.

The Confederation's automatic defenses in the system proved utterly useless. Only one of the invading vessels was damaged, and that one only slightly. Unbelievably, the unknown force had completely silenced the system, eliminating all of its communications and shields in only a handful of minutes. The one distress message Hardy had been able to transmit was an old-style, sub-space broadcast—one that would take weeks to reach anyone outside their system.

To the credit of the marines stationed on Felner, they were prepared for the invasion force before it entered the moon's atmosphere. Every one of them was at their post, fully armed and armored, ready for combat. Those in charge of alerting the populous had done so. The streets had been cleared in the three major towns. Every citizen had been beamed full details of what little was known. Those who wanted to hide or flee had been given ample time. Those who wanted to witness what came next were already congregating in the main square of the capitol city when the unknown force's lead ship descended into view.

"Here they come," said Shelby in a cool tone, his weapon trained on the descending vessel. "Four will get you one they're ugly as sin."

"Now, there's a lot of wiggle room in there," countered Rainer. "I mean, you talking a little sin, like a white lie or stealing a loaf of bread when you're hungry? Or do you mean ugly as a big sin, like murder, or when your father and mother did the dance with no pants?"

Cooper smiled. He was not foolish enough to believe that the coming combat would be an easy thing. But, he was glad to see that his fellows were calm and prepared. Radio chatter from across the city let him know that all the counterparts of his own team were in place, ready to defend Felner, if need be, from whatever was landing so close to their position. The lieutenant was aware that there was little chance, given the aggressive entrance the newcomers had made into their sector, that conflict could be avoided. But, first contact protocols were very specific. You waited. You ascertained. You did not panic. You did not shoot first.

"Seems taking out all our defense and communication satellites could be considered shooting first," thought Cooper as he continued to train his weapon on the ship settling in the distance. "But, I don't write the rules. I just ..."

The lieutenant let his thought trail off. Suddenly he was overcome by the realization that he had not seen Susie since the initial alert had sounded. Where was she, he wondered. She was a smart little critter, would understand that something was wrong. Was she frightened? Lost? Looking for him?

Cooper shook his head at the thoughts crowding him at that moment. Susie could take care of herself. His concern made him smile, considering he had no idea where the grodd stayed when she was not with him. Yes, she might trail him and the others every time they left the compound. Yes, she had an amazing ability to penetrate base security, and had shown up where she should not have been a hundred times. But, she was not his pet. He did not own her. There was no water bowl in the mess hall with her name on it.

Still watching the ship coming down in the far field, it struck Cooper that he did not actually know if the grodd actually was a "she." He had never checked—had not wanted to know. He had been content to have the creature in his life, to know that somewhere on the face of his current world there was a bundle of life that considered him important. That cared for him. That was willing to show him if not love, then at least affection.

"What more can you ask out of life?"

And, with that thought, the alien craft landed. Through their helmet comms the various tactical groups were given their instructions. Those surrounding the unknown vehicle tightened their perimeter. An effort would be made at a peaceful meeting. If such was not achieved, the base's main guns would attempt to take out the ship—an outcome not given much of a chance at success considering what the invaders had been able to so easily do to Felner's outer atmosphere defenses. After that, each group leader would attack whatever targets presented themselves using their best judgment.

While Cooper watched through his weapon's enhancement field, what was likely the main door of the invader's ship opened. What came forth were a species the lieutenant had never before imagined, let alone encountered. The three-member protocol team approached the first to disembark, but never got a chance to make their opening remarks. They were slaughtered the instant the alien's weapons could be brought to bear.

After that, the unthinkable creatures began their attack in earnest. That initial conflict lasted less than twenty minutes.

"Then what happened, lieutenant?"

"They wiped us out," answered Cooper, his voice far stronger than when the interview had begun. "Tore through us. We couldn't ... couldn't do anything to stop them."

"Their weapons were that powerful?"

"No. No, sir." The lieutenant took another long sip from his water, then continued.

"When they swept through the system, it was our fault. They caught our people off guard. We didn't have much in the way of off-planet defense to begin with. They targeted the comms first, then cleaned the rest."

"But, if their weapons weren't that powerful—"

"It was their minds, sir. Some kind of mind control. They communicated mentally. With each other. With us. When they attacked, they just sent out wave after wave ... confused us, made us pause ... freeze ... panic." Cooper sat staring forward, silent for a long time. Then, finally blinking, he said;

"They rounded us up, those they didn't kill rolling into town, sent commands out across the planet. The farmers, ranchers, miners ... they all just started coming in on their own. Couldn't help themselves ..."

The board of inquiry's members glanced one to the other. Despite their knowledge that this new, unknown enemy had somehow been routed, still their looks were those of, if not fear, at least trepidation. Taking a calming breath before he spoke, the senior officer prompted Cooper once more, saying;

"So then what happened, Lieutenant?"

"Then, they ... they let us know what was coming. We were their slaves. We would build ... something ... wasn't clear. Something they needed. Entire invasion force was coming. Waiting. These ships had cold jumped into our galaxy. Their job to risk coming out inside a star, black hole, whatever. If they survive, then they find an isolated world ... conquer ... establish beach head—"

Cooper dropped his head, unable to even look in the general direction of his superiors. His breaths came in short, harsh gulps, each one shorter than the one proceeding until finally he began coughing violently. The prompter moved forward quickly, slapping the lieutenant sharply on the back several times, fetching him his water at the same time. Cooper drank gratefully, then went back to his testimony.

"They filled our minds with what they would do next. I think they were looking for trouble-makers. Those that might rebel. We were still too stunned to act. They started executing at random ... one of them turned toward me—"

Cooper's voice lowered in tone. His head lowering toward his chest, tilting, he growled;

"It's thoughts filled my head. Laughed about killing me ... aimed its weapon ... fired. That's when it happened."

"What, son? What happened?"

"Susie. She ... came out of nowhere. Jumped up on my chest ... just like that first day. She ... she took the shot. That thing, that goddamned thing ... it killed her. It killed my Susie."

Tears rolling down his face, the lieutenant told the rest of the story. Of how he had leaped forward without thinking. Of how he had killed the alien with his bare hands, driving his fist so far into the invader's head that he had broken open its skull. After that, the rest had fallen just as quickly. Cooper's blind hatred had scorched the alien's minds, thrown them into utter chaos.

His fellows had followed his lead, the residue of his anger filtered through their minds by the group connection the aliens had imposed on the world. The Felnerians—soldiers and citizens, men and women—had risen up and slaughtered the invaders, Cooper's raging grief something they had never before encountered. Those in the orbiting ships had been just as defenseless against the psychic blast. Overwhelmed, they had lost control, both vessels falling into the atmosphere and burning as they crashed to the planet's surface.

None of the board members commented. The lieutenant's story was too much for them to take in all at once. Telepathy, mind control on a planet-wide scale, Cooper's luck in breaking what for the invaders had become a winning formula. The lieutenant told them how he and the others had been overwhelmed, how the images of system after system falling to the aliens within their own galaxy had numbed them—flooded them with futility. Robbed them of their will to fight.

"And now," mused one of the generals who as of yet had not spoken, "now they're coming here."

"No, sir."

"We understand that you gained us a respite, Lieutenant," said the prompter. "But we have to assume they will send another exploratory team. It is their way—yes?"

"It was their way, sir."

When the board members merely waited, Cooper took several deep breaths, then told them;

"After we beat them, the ones ... the ones that were still alive ... the others herded them together. Asked me ... what we should do."

The lieutenant clasped his hands together, elbows on the table before him. Head shaking, the enormity of his actions finally dawning on him, he said;

"Their mind link, worked both ways. Once we'd beaten them down ... they stayed beaten. We could think to them, read them. They couldn't stop us." Cooper stared at his hands for a moment, then continued.

"I realized ... then ... even while I'd been fighting, killing them ... I'd never put Susie down. I saw, saw what was left of her ... in my hand ... and that's when it started. We found one of them that understood their systems. We tortured it. Made it think on how their transmitter worked—"

As the board members leaned forward, each of them filling with a hope they had not dared allow moments earlier, the lieutenant said;

"The white super giant in sector B-17, we sent the coordinates for its center back to their home. We sent the all clear. Waited for their approach signal then, we sent their last ship to the same spot."

"Why ... what did—"

"When we knew they were opening their end of the worm hole, that's when we sent their ship back, exploded all its weapons. Figured it would set off chain reaction ... explode all their ships, all their weapons—"

Cooper looked up then, a terrible gleam flashing from his eyes.

"All their stars."

Understanding that the lieutenant had neutralized a possibly unstoppable threat, still the board members were stunned by the magnitude of his actions. As later probes would confirm, a dwarf galaxy some 163,000 light years away did flare into nova-brilliances at the same time as the attack on Felner. A billion stars obliterated. Countless solar systems. Trillions upon trillions of sentient beings—simply erased.

All because one man would never again see his faithful companion wag its tail.

BROTHERS

An Alliance Archives Adventure

Danielle Ackley-McPhail

THEY TOLD ME THE DOG'S NAME, BUT DON'T BOTHER TO ASK WHAT IT IS. I ignored them. I'm good at that; retreating deep into the core of my thoughts where they cannot touch me. Where I cannot hear such things as names. You see, they taught me well in Basic. Names mean something. Names make things personal. Personal is important.

I've had enough of names. Life's easier when nothing matters. I turn it off, the way I've been trained. With nothing left to fight, or fight for, I retreat to my fallback position. I fill my world with the faceless, the nameless. I can ignore what doesn't matter. I tell myself that's everything.

Buried deep in my heart, a still, small voice calls me a liar.

Me. I tell it to shut the fuck up.

The soldier sat in the center of the room, back straight, flat eyes staring off into the middle distance, arms folded carefully in his lap so that no portion of his body touched the frame of the power-chair any more than necessary. Other than the occasional tic across the blade of his cheek and breath so shallow it barely expanded his chest, the man did not move. Just outside of kicking range lay a golden retriever, body position projecting non-aggression as its eyes remained locked on the soldier's face. Mirroring the man, the dog scarcely moved, but for anxious little twitches of its brow. Occasionally, a faint whine escaped to jar the silence.

It was impossible to tell from which of them it came.

Two men stood just outside the hospital room, watching its occupants through an observation monitor mounted beside the door. One wore captain's bars on the collar of his lab coat; the other had an eagle tacked to his chest.

"Permission to speak freely, sir?" the doctor asked.

The colonel's brow flattened in a foreboding manner, but he nodded.

"Are you certain about this, sir?"

His superior's forehead dipped lower into an actual frown as he turned sharp eyes on the doctor. "Captain?"

"I'm sorry, sir, but that man hardly seems a viable candidate for a service dog. Sure, he needs one, but I see no sign he has any interest in improving his standard of living. Hell, to be frank, sir, I don't see he cares much about living at all. He won't even sign the release for the basic prosthetic enhancements that would get him out of that chair, let alone the advanced limb regeneration you brought me on for." The doctor braced himself and pushed on despite the colonel's darkening expression. "There's not one damn thing I can do for him without his cooperation. When I think of how many soldiers are still waiting to rebuild their lives...men and women who are desperate for a chance like this..." His voice trailed off and only by extreme effort did he keep from gulping back his unspoken words.

The colonel pivoted and stepped into his personal space. "And if that was you in that chair? Would you want us to give up on you because your head wasn't in the right place yet?"

Shame drained the doctor's cheeks of color. His back straightened and he gave a sharp shake of his head.

"We don't give up on our own, Captain. Is that understood? In my infantry days we shouldered our brother's burden when he struggled to press forward. This is no different. There are two heroes in that room and neither one of them deserves to fall through the cracks because someone else didn't have the patience to give them time to sort themselves out."

"But he won't even acknowledge the dog!" the doctor's frustration overcame his sense of military protocol. "We're wasting everyone's time— sir..."

"If we give up, we've already failed."

In the distance, the sound of mortar rounds and soldiers screaming grows louder. Gunfire shreds the air. My arms jerk, struggling to raise an absent rifle and return fire. What's left of my legs burn with the need to run.

Toward the fighting? Away? Who can say... Neither one is possible. My jaw clenches tight enough I swear I feel the teeth shift in their sockets as my head falls back. The memories of combat claw their way along every nerve until my body shakes with equal violence. If my chest held any breath, it would have machine-gunned out in sobs. Good thing the flashbacks leave me breathless.

A familiar ripple runs up the edge of my jaw, jarring me out of the nightmare. I lay there, stunned, as a gentle, but urgent *woof* whispers across my bonejack, the subvocal communications device the military had embedded in my jaw. I didn't realize the dog and I had anything in common, let alone military-issue hardware. I'm that stunned that I scarcely realize I've sat up. The first I've done so on my own since being dragged in pieces off the front line.

My gaze scans the semi-dark of the room and I scowl as I realize I can't locate the dog. And then I hear it. A low thud rises repeatedly from the floor beside my bed. I drop down to the pillow with a snarl and turn my back to the sound. I tell myself a tail wag in the dark is nothing and bend my will to pushing the memory of the dog's face from my thoughts even as the thudding lulls me to sleep.

The doctor gritted his teeth in frustration as he came onto shift. He had put years into perfecting his skills and each day of this assignment only drove home how those skills were being wasted. He hid his resentment behind a professional expression and approached the nurses' station.

"Good morning, doctor," the day nurse greeted him as she handed him a digital tablet already displaying data from the night before. "We've had some progress. Biometrics indicates a more restful night. Only one nightmare and a couple of minor episodes. The lieutenant even sat up briefly around 2 am...unassisted."

The doctor *humphed* beneath his breath. Progress, or anomaly? He stepped to the monitor outside the lieutenant's door. Skepticism twisted his lips as he stared at the familiar tableau of soldier and dog, nearly indistinguishable from each day before, but for a rhythmic twitch of the man's right hand. It appeared as if he fought a subconscious impulse to reach for a sidearm.

The remote biometric scanners embedded beneath the soldier's skin fed a steady stream of data to the monitor. Based on the elevated adrenaline and cortisol levels, paired with increased activity recorded in the amygdala and hypothalamus, a flashback gripped the patient, the twitch the only outward sign.

A faint frown bowed the doctor's lips. He reached for the monitor controls, ready to administer a fast-acting sedative via the subdermal implants should the lieutenant exhibit violent behavior.

As the doctor's finger hovered over the hotkey, he spied movement on the monitor. Instinct shouted at him to jab the control releasing the sedative, until it registered that the movement came from the dog. Slowly it rose until it sat back on its haunches, eyes still locked on the soldier's face. The dog barked sharply, abrupt, jarring in the silence of the room, even through the speakers. It was a no-nonsense bark, not aggressive, not playful. Stern, the doctor would have to say, if anyone asked, like a good squad leader bringing a soldier in line. The lieutenant jerked and briefly seemed to focus, his eyes tracking with precision on the dog. They stared one another down for several long moments until the soldier scowled. The dog merely looked calmly back, slowly swishing its tail against the tile floor. Then the moment ended. The dog lay down and the soldier went back to staring off into space, his hand no longer twitching toward a holster that wasn't there.

The doctor stepped away, feeling something akin to embarrassment, as if he'd spied on something private. Pensive, he went about his rounds, his inner cynic refusing to put much store in the incident while his inner optimist cheered.

I wake up to the stench of blood, cordite, and piss and I'm damned if I can tell if the smells are real. All I can be certain of is the silky head wedging itself beneath my shaking hand. I yank my fingers into a fist, pulling away, only to have a moist tongue swipe lightly across my knuckles. Jerking myself upright to get further out of reach, I glare into the gloom, my eyes slowly adjusting to the low light of the one remaining monitor as my chest continues to heave in the aftermath of night terrors.

A subtle shift in the texture of the darkness to my nine shows me the dog's position. The edge of the bed completely obscures its body, all except for the head. I can just see the outline of its muzzle resting on the mattress. I growl, primal and deep from my belly, warning it away from my territory. An all-too-human sigh answers my aggression, followed by a soft thud, as the dog lays back down on the floor, nails gently scraping against the tiles as it curls up to sleep.

Something that might be guilt twists in my gut. I shut it off, crushing the blankets in my fist as I hump my ass forward until I drop flat to my back. Pain sends sparks across my vision as rough, institutional-grade cotton strafes across what's left of my legs. I'm glad of it. The pain feeds the anger, killing any other emotion that dares raise its head.

Just as well.

I refuse to feel grateful to a fucking dog.

That's what I tell myself as I pursue sleep with the same grim determination with which I used to approach an enemy line.

"Do you see that?" the colonel greeted him as he came out of his patient's room. The doctor pivoted, expecting some monumental change, some sudden breakthrough between the time he turned to leave and when he walked through the door. His eyes, doubly trained for observation, spied nothing.

"What, sir?"

The colonel's head slowly nodded with satisfaction. "The dog...he's lying closer."

Dumbfounded, the doctor watched his superior stroll away.

I wake in the night to the sound of whimpers and for a humiliating moment I think they are coming from me. Shame sends the bitter taste of bile surging to my throat. Then I hear a sudden thrashing from beside the bed and I know for once the weakness is not mine.

Not for the first time, I curse that I am no longer equipped to kick. Nearly as frustrating is the realization that there is nothing within reach I'm willing to throw, given the impossibility of independent retrieval. I lie there glaring at where I know the ceiling to be. I won't allow myself to feel enough to be angry or annoyed; but, as whines begin to join the thrashing, I carefully rotate onto my belly toward the edge of the bed and smack at the pain-in-the ass dog. My hand comes down on its flank, tangling in long, sweaty strands of hair.

How the hell does a dog manage to feel clammy?

My instinct is to yank, but what I feel beneath that coat startles me. By touch I identify a familiar texture, knots and ropes of intruding scars where smooth muscle should be. The flesh beneath my fingers shudders, involuntary movements that I myself suffer. The dog's jaw snaps at the air, but nowhere near my hand. As he continues to cry, I realize the sounds are again subvocal, transmitting across my bonejack.

I don't want to feel kinship. I don't want to feel a thing. And yet my hand, of its own accord, strokes the damn dog and that fucking voice deep inside of me hums with satisfaction as the thrashing slows, then stops, and no more sounds ripple along my jaw to echo deep in my ear.

For a moment in the dark, I leave my hand resting on the dog's flank to feel the returning warmth, finding peace in fighting off nightmares, even if they aren't my own. Then I flinch as I realize what I'm doing. I shove away from the connection and roll over onto my back. I commence glaring up at the ceiling as I tell myself I am not listening for the sounds of returning nightmares the way I'd been trained to listen for covert activity on patrol.

I have my own demons to battle. The dog is on its own.

An orderly with corporal markings on his collar grabbed the next chart in his assignment slot. He sighed as he saw the patient. Not that it surprised him. New to this posting, he drew the shit assignments and this was the worst one. Time to take the lieutenant to his therapy session.

Man, this one is screwed up, the orderly thought. He had to wonder why they didn't house him in the psych wing to begin with. The routine was already too familiar: wrestle him into the chair and escort him down the hall, leave him for an hour in the head shrinker's office, then back again. And never once did the guy even blink, let alone spill his guts.

It was like that sometimes. The bodies came home, but the spirits remained trapped on the battlefield.

"Time to go for a ride." He started to manhandle the patient into his chair. It was no easy task. Even with bits of him missing, the guy was dense, heavy with muscle not yet gone soft. On top of that, the orderly suspected he purposely went dead weight, making the task harder than it needed to be. The soldier hissed as his left stump smacked into the lowered bed rail, but made no effort to cooperate, his gaze still fixed on nothing, though his facial muscles tensed and a faint hint of satisfaction seemed to gleam deep in his eyes.

The orderly cursed and struggled to pull the soldier closer to the chair. "Come on, man, cut it out and help me here..."

Again—completely unintentional—flesh met metal.

Suddenly, the orderly froze as he felt pointed teeth pierce his scrubs, though not his flesh. He looked down to find the dog's jaws gripping his ankle. A rumbling growl slowly filled the room. Before he could react, the door opened and the doctor hurried in, a second orderly behind him.

"Sergeant, stand down," the doctor ordered. The first orderly looked up, confused, until the jaws gripping his ankle tightened briefly, then released. The dog sat back at attention with a slight snarl curling his muzzle, but made no further sound.

The doctor shifted his gaze toward the bed and continued, this time more sternly. "Lieutenant, get in the chair." As he spoke, the second orderly came around the side of the bed to assist. He wasn't needed.

The soldier set his jaw and jerked away from the orderly's grip. He pivoted on the edge of the bed and yanked the wheelchair around so he could slide over the back into place. His arms went taut with the effort and his movements were the slightest bit awkward, but capable.

Moments later, they were back on schedule and ready to deploy.

They want me to talk. I want them to leave me the fuck alone. What right do they have to know the hell I've been through? A soldier doesn't show weakness. A soldier doesn't hand the enemy a weapon to use against him. I have learned to treat everyone as an enemy. That way it's safer if I'm wrong.

Enemy... Friend... Either way, I won't share my demons with them.

They wheel me away from my cell, down long, featureless beige hallways, and into a butter-yellow room I suspect is meant to lull me. Fat chance. I retreat within myself once more as the psych doc starts his usual chatter. Only distantly do I hear the words he says. Again talking of focal points and mantras, then extolling the virtue of meditation. And finally, the need to purge the darkness...to expose my memories, even if only to myself.... Each time, I stare a hole into his forehead until he gives up. He speaks, as he has before, of the benefits of reconstructive surgery and physical therapy. I briefly surface from the depths to slam him with a glare.

The bastard doesn't even seem to notice. He grips my shoulder and tells me to have a good day.

The psych doc has a death wish, only I'm helpless to deliver. My jaw grinds at the private admission. The orderly is wheeling me out of the door before I can peel back the layers of cold indifference enough to respond.

A faint ticking sounds behind me. It takes me a moment to recognize the dog's nails tapping an irregular rhythm on the floor as he shadows us. If I cared more, I'd order them to take the mutt away. I tell myself it's not important.

That fucking voice calls me a liar.

On third shift, sudden darkness engulfed the hospital wing housing long-term care. For a split second, total silence reigned as the usual symphony of monitors and machines and quietly bustling personnel abruptly halted. The briefest instance of chaos gave way to well-trained responses as the staff secured the floor and checked on each patient.

At the nurses' station, the charge nurse answered the emergency comm as security called in for a sit-rep.

"Total loss of power," she reported. "Emergency generators are non-responsive. The wing has been secured."

"Acknowledged. Engineering is already aware of the malfunction. They are working to restore main power and repair the defective unit. Are any of your patients at risk?"

Sudden yells and screams from one of the rooms interrupted the charge nurse before she could respond.

I watch them die tonight. Everyone. The ones I rescued. The ones I couldn't get to in time. Soldiers I haven't seen since my first tour of duty. Everyone I know. Even the fucking dog. I'm left alone in total darkness. My mind screams at me this is wrong but it's overwhelmed by the sounds of the dying. The cries go on forever and my nose shuts down in defense against the sweet, acrid stench of blood and death and spent ordnance.

There is a sound to my three o'clock; a faint click, followed by the careful steps of soft-shod feet making an effort not to be heard. My combat instincts go on alert, muscles tense and my breathing drops into a steady, ready rhythm. I curse the dark, even as my hindbrain tries to tell me there should be light. A faint glow instead of unending black. More noises come across the intervening distance distracting me from what should and should not be. Without thought, I slowly edge myself up, bracing for attack. The sounds of the line gradually filter through the background. A growl rumbles across my 'jack. I run the blade of my hand over the ground looking for my rifle, a grenade, hell, even a pistol, but I'm left with only my hands. I move to crouch, ready to launch myself at the enemy creeping up.

Something doesn't feel right. My balance is off. I try to compensate, only to fall backward, my head thudding against something hard and metallic. I catch myself before I land on my back again. There is a gasp in the darkness as I shake my head to clear the fog. The intruder hurries forward, no longer making an effort to be silent. My jaw clamps down and my fingers curl into powerful claws. I feel capable of tearing muscle from bone. As the darker patch of shadow moves closer there is a faint glimmer. Low, like the moon's reflection. Or a shielded light.

I bunch my muscles to launch myself at the target. My lips twist in a silent snarl as a battle cry builds in my chest ready to be unleashed. I don't forget that everyone's dead. That I'm alone to face this unknown enemy. One of how many? As I push off I let loose a roar.

Even as a piercing, feminine shriek rises from mere feet away, something comes at me from the opposite side. I fail to counteract the assault as my attacker slams across my chest from low and to my left. I'm thrown back, a heavy weight pinning me to ground much softer than it should be.

First comes a sharp, commanding bark, then warning growls rumble beside my right ear. What seems like a supernova explodes the darkness as a distant *thunk* and *whir* penetrate my haze. The monitor beside what I now realize is my bed flares to life revealing one of the nurses, pale and trembling in the sudden glow. Behind her, several orderlies hurry through the door.

I barely notice as I my eyes lock on the damned dog weighing down my chest.

Slowly, the dog angles its head until its gaze connects with mine. If I look past the fur, it's like looking into the mirror. The ghosts of familiar horrors drift behind its gaze. *His* gaze... He doesn't make another sound. He doesn't have to. My heart stutters as I realize what I've almost done. My hands come up reflexively to wrap around the dog, clutching him to my chest as I accept the truth.

He saved her.

He saved *me*.

I recognize the power of names even as my heart calls him Brother.

My head drops back on the flattened pillow and I struggle to breathe as the woman scrambles from the room, completely forgetting whatever brought her into the devil's den to begin with. I wait for the sound of the orderlies filing out behind her. I wait for what I know I must do, though my instincts scream *No!*

They want me to talk? So I talk, but not to them. I lay there in the darkness with a warm mound now stretched out beside me. Absently, I stroke the dog's gnarled flank and his tail gently thumps the bed. I don't make a sound anyone but the dog can hear. Instead, over the bonejack I whisper the horrors I have seen. Done. Been unable to prevent. I admit my sense of helplessness. My feelings of failure. The pillow is drenched with tears beneath my head as I battle for my life. Pain pours from my heart like blood from a wound. Cleansing. Healing. Purging.

By the time dawn tints the sky I have survived the first engagement of my on-going war.

Christopher M. Hiles

THE SHEPHERDS

Chris Hiles is a nurse and emergency manager specializing in Mass Casualty and Mass Fatality Incidents. He serves in the Civil Air Patrol, the United States Air Force Auxiliary, where he has held the position of Squadron Commander and Wing Health Services Officer. He lives in Baltimore, Maryland, with his wife and puppy.

James Chambers

FATHER OF WAR

James Chambers' tales of horror, crime, fantasy, and science fiction have been published in numerous anthologies and magazines. In 2011 Dark Regions Press published his collection of four Lovecraftian-inspired novellas, *The Engines of Sacrifice*. *Publisher's Weekly* described it as "chillingly evocative." In 2012 and 2013 Dark Quest Books published his zombie novellas, *The Dead Bear Witness* and *Tears of Blood*, the first two volumes in the *Corpse Fauna* novella series, as well as his dark, urban fantasy novella, *Three Chords of Chaos*. Chambers is also the author of the short story collections *Resurrection House*, published in 2009 by Dark Regions Press, and *The Midnight Hour: Saint Lawn Hill and Other Tales* with illustrator Jason Whitley. His stories have appeared in the award-winning *Bad-Ass Faeries* and *Defending the Future* anthology series as well as *Allen K's Inhuman*, *Bare Bone*, *Deep Cuts*, *The Green Hornet Chronicles*, *Hardboiled Cthulhu*, *In an Iron Cage*, *Mermaids 13*, *The Spider: Extreme Prejudice*, *To Hell in a Fast Car*, *Walrus Tales*, and many other anthologies and magazines. He has also written numerous comic books including *Leonard Nimoy's Primortals*, the critically acclaimed "The Revenant" in *Shadow House*, and *The Midnight Hour*. He is a member of the Horror Writers Association, the chairman of its membership committee, and the recipient of the 2012 Richard Laymon Award. His can be found online at www.jameschambersonline.com and https://www.facebook.com/Three-ChordsOfChaos.

Brenda Cooper

FOR THE LOVE
OF METAL DOGS

Brenda Cooper writes science fiction and fantasy novels and short stories. Her most recent novel is *The Diamond Deep*, October 2013, from Pyr. It's book two of a two-book series that started with *The Creative Fire*. She has seven novels out and numerous short stories. Brenda is also a technology professional and a futurist, and publishes non-fiction on the environment and the future from time to time.

See her website at www.brenda-cooper.com.

Brenda lives in the Pacific Northwest in a household with three people, three dogs, more than three computers, and only one TV in it.

Eric V. Hardenbrook

DATA DOGS

Eric V. Hardenbrook freely admits that he creates because it is cheaper and more effective than therapy, or shock treatment. He resides in central Pennsylvania with his wife and daughter, but was born and raised in New England.

Eric served in the U.S. Army in the early 90s. He recently moved from his position as a project manager for an architectural firm to take a position as a software application engineer, working with and teaching the programs used to design and document buildings. He is a fan, author and artist—usually in that order. He has been part of the team running *Watch The Skies* science fiction and fantasy group and publishing the *Watch The Skies* fanzine for the past decade. When not working on a project he enjoys the occasional video game, board games and is an old school role player.

Peter Prellwitz

EGO TRIP

Peter Prellwitz is the IT Director for a precious metals refining company located in Philadelphia. Peter has been writing stories, plays and skits since the fourth grade.

Born in Arizona, Peter has lived in Wisconsin, California, Hawaii, New York, Massachusetts, and Pennsylvania, where he now lives with his wife, Bethlynne, and four of their sons. He is active in his church, and in addition to writing, enjoys history, backpacking, and languages.

Since 2004, Double Dragon Publishing has published nine of Peter's novels, as well as two anthologies, a novella and several short stories, with another half dozen novels scheduled in the next few years. Horizons, his second novel but first published, was chosen by Mike Resnick as the winner the 2003 Draco Award for Best Science Fiction. Peter is a perennial Finalist for the EPPIE Awards for Science Fiction, having garnered five nominations over three years.

Jeff Young

COVERT STRIKE

Jeff Young is a bookseller first and a writer second—although he wouldn't mind a reversal of fortune.

He received a Writers of the Future award for "Written in Light" which appears in the *26th L.Ron Hubbard's Writers of the Future* Anthology. He's been published in: Realms, Neuronet, Trail of Indiscretion, Cemetery Moon, The Realm Beyond, eSteampunk and Carbon14. Jeff has contributed to the anthologies By Any Means, Best Laid Plans, In an Iron Cage: The Magic of Steampunk, Fantastic Futures, The Ministry of Extraordinary Weapons and the upcoming anthology Gaslight and Grimm. Other short stories are available in ebook form online. He is the editor for the Drunken Comic Book Monkey line for Fortress Publishing as well as the anthology TV Gods. He has led the Watch the Skies SF&F Discussion Group of Camp Hill and Harrisburg for thirteen years.

Judi Fleming

WAR DOGS

Judi Fleming works as a training specialist and instructional designer for the federal government in her day job and thus much of her writing is of the non-exciting technical sort. She is a graduate of Seton Hill University Writing Popular Fiction Master's Program.

David Sherman

SO (NOT) LIKE A DOG

David Sherman is the author or co-author of about three dozen books, nearly all of which are about Marines in combat. On his own he wrote about US Marines in Vietnam (the Night Fighters series and three other novels), and the *DemonTech* series about Marines in a fantasy world. With Dan Cragg he wrote the popular *Starfist* series and its spin off series, *Starfist: Force Recon*—all about Marines in the Twenty-fifth Century. By himself, he wrote a non-conventional vampire novel, *The Hunt*; and with Cragg a Star Wars novel, *Jedi Trial*. His books have been translated into Czech, Polish, German, and Japanese.

"So (Not) Like Dogs" is set in the world of his latest military science fiction novel, *Issue in Doubt*. He's had stories in three other anthologies in the Defending the Future anthology series, and in a small handful of other anthologies.

He invites readers to visit his website, novelier.com.

Edward J. McFadden III

FRIENDLY FIRE

Edward J. McFadden III juggles a full-time career as a university administrator and teacher, with his writing aspirations. His first novel, a mysterious-dark-thriller called *The Black Death of Babylon* (Post Mortem Press) is now available. His steampunk fantasy novelette, Starwisps, appeared in the anthology *Fantastic Stories of the Imagination*, and was selected for the Tangent 2012 Recommended Reading list. His novella *Anywhere But Here* was recently published by Padwolf Publishing. He is the author/editor of: *Jigsaw Nation, Deconstructing Tolkien: A Fundamental Analysis of The Lord of the Rings, Time Capsule, The Second Coming, Thoughts of Christmas,* and *The Best of Pirate Writings*. He has had more than 50 short stories published in places like *Tales of the Talisman, Fantastic Futures 13, From Beyond the Grave, Apocalypse 13, Hear Them Roar, CrimeSpree Magazine, Terminal Fright, Cyber-Psycho's AOD, The And,* and *The Arizona Literary Review*. He lives on Long Island with his wife Dawn, their daughter Samantha, and their mutt Oli. See EdwardMcfadden.com for all things Ed.

Tony Ruggiero

THE FORGOTTEN

Tony Ruggiero is best known for his dark fantasy thrillers about vampires being used by the US military. Ground breaking and fast paced, the novels are a characteristic mixture of the vampire lore and the clandestine secrets of the military. The concept led to a series of books: *Operation Immortal Servitude, Operation Save the Innocent, Operation* Face the Fear, and Operation Endgame. His other novels include Alien *Deception, Alien Revelation,Coven* and *The Evil from Above*.

Tony retired from the United States Navy in 2001 after twenty-three years of service. He and his family currently reside in Portsmouth, Virginia. While continuing to write, Tony teaches at Old Dominion University and Saint Leo University. Visit his website at www.tonyruggiero.com.

Bud Sparhawk

TRUE FRIENDS

Bud Sparhawk has published one mass market paperback novel:*Vixen* and two print collections: *Sam Boone: Front to Back* and *Dancing with Dragons*. He has three e-Novels available through Amazon and other channels.

Bud has been a three-time novella finalist for the Nebula award: *Primrose and Thorn*, Magic's Price, and *Clay's Pride*. His work has appeared in *The Year's Best SF #11* and *The Years Best Science Fiction, Fourteenth Annual Collection*.

Bud's short stories have appeared frequently in Analog Fact/Fiction, less so in Asimov's, as well as in four Defending the Future and other anthologies, publications and podcasts. He has put out several collections of these published works in ebook format. An incomplete complete list of works follows.

He resides in Annapolis Maryland with his wife of fifty-four years and sails as frequently as possible on the Chesapeake Bay.

He writes a weekly blog on the pain of writing at:
http://budsparhawk.blogspot.com/

Janine K. Spendlove

THE MARINE BREED

Janine K. Spendlove is a KC-130 pilot in the United States Marine Corps. In the Science Fiction and Fantasy World she is primarily known for her bestselling trilogy, *War of the Seasons*. She has several short stories published in various anthologies alongside such authors as Aaron Allston, Jean Rabe, Michael A. Stackpole, Bryan Young, and Timothy Zahn. She is also the co-founder of GeekGirlsRun, a community for geek girls (and guys) who just want to run, share, have fun, and encourage each other. A graduate of Brigham Young University, Janine loves pugs, enjoys knitting, making costumes, playing Beatles tunes on her guitar, and spending time with her family. She resides with her husband and daughter in Washington, DC. She is currently at work on her next novel. Find out more at JanineSpendlove.com.

Patrick Thomas

STRAY SHOT

Patrick Thomas writes the fantasy humor series *Murphy's Lore*, which includes *Tales From Bulfinche's Pub, Fools' Day, Through The Drinking Glass, Shadow Of The Wolf, Redemption Road, Bartender Of The Gods, Nightcaps* and *Empty Graves* — as well as the *After Hours* spin offs *Fairy With A Gun, Fairy Rides The Lightning, Dead To Rites, Rites of Passage,* and *Lore & Dysorder.* His *Mystic Investigators* paranormal mystery series includes *Bullets & Brimstone, From The Shadows, Once More Upon A Time,* and *Partners In Crime.* He co-edited *New Blood* and *Hear Them Roar* and was an editor for *Fantastic Stories of the Imagination* and *Pirate Writings.* Patrick's syndicated humorous advice column *Dear Cthulhu* includes *Have A Dark Day, Good Advice For Bad People,* and *Cthulhu Knows Best.* A number of his books are part of the props department of the CSI television show and have been spotted on the show. His urban fantasy *Fairy With A Gun* was optioned by Laurence Fishburne's Cinema Gypsy Productions. Drop by www.patthomas.net to learn more or find out about The Patrick Thomas Show mockumentary.

Robert E. Waters

I GIVE MY HEART
TO THE HAWKS

Robert E. Waters is a science fiction and fantasy writer. Since 1994, he has worked in the computer and board gaming industry as technical writer, editor, designer, and producer. A member of the Science Fiction and Fantasy Writers of America, his first professional fiction publication came in 2003 with the story "The Assassin's Retirement Party," *Weird Tales*, Issue #332. Since then he has sold stories to Nth Degree, Nth Zine, Black Library Publishing (Games Workshop), Dark Quest Books, Padwolf Publishing, Mundania Press, Dragon Moon Press, Rogue Blades Entertainment, and the Grantville Gazette (Baen Book's online magazine dedicated to stories set in their *Ring of Fire/1632* alternate history series). Between the years of 1998 – 2006, he also served as an assistant editor to *Weird Tales*, and is a frequent contributor to Tangent Online, a short fiction review site. Robert's most recent project was *Fantastic Futures 13*, an anthology of science fiction and fantasy stories, co-edited with James Stratton and published by Padwolf Publishing. Robert currently lives in Baltimore, Maryland, with his wife Beth, their son Jason, and their cat Buzz. www.roberternestwaters.com.

Vonnie Winslow Crist

TOWER FARM

Vonnie Winslow Crist, MS Professional Writing, Towson University, is author of *The Enchanted Skean* (YA novel), *The Greener Forest,* and *Owl Light* (speculative story collections), *River of Stars* and *Essential Fables* (myth-based poetry), *Leprechaun Cake & Other Tales* (children's), and several sf/f eBooks. A Pushcart Nominee, she's received awards from Maryland State Arts Council, Pen Women, L. Ron Hubbard's Writers of the Future, and elsewhere. Believing the world is full of mystery, miracles, and magic, Vonnie celebrates the power of myth in her writing.

C.J. Henderson

THE WAG OF HIS TAIL

CJ Henderson is the creator of both the *Piers Knight* supernatural investigator series and the *Teddy London* occult detective series among many others. He has written over 70 books and/or novels, hundreds and hundreds of short stories and comics and thousands of non-fiction pieces. He is a master of hardboiled suspense as well as raucous comedy, and is not shy about saying so even when sober. For more on this truly fascinating teller of tales, he encourages all to stop in at www.cjhenderson.com. He promises free short stories and more humiliate.

Danielle Ackley-McPhail

BROTHERS

Award-winning author Danielle Ackley-McPhail has worked both sides of the publishing industry for longer than she cares to admit. Currently, she is a project editor and promotions manager for Dark Quest Books.

Her published works include four urban fantasy novels, *Yesterday's Dreams, Tomorrow's Memories, Today's Promise, The Halfling's Court:* and *The Redcaps' Queen: A Bad-Ass Faerie Tale*. She is also the author of the non-fiction writers guide, *The Literary Handyman* and is the senior editor of the *Bad-Ass Faeries* anthology series, *Dragon's Lure*, and *In An Iron Cage*. Her work is included in numerous other anthologies and collections.

She is a member of the Garden State Speculative Fiction Writers, the New Jersey Authors Network, and Broad Universe, a writer's organization focusing on promoting the works of women authors in the speculative genres.

Danielle lives in New Jersey with husband and fellow writer, Mike McPhail, mother-in-law Teresa, and three extremely spoiled cats.

To learn more about her work, visit www.sidhenadaire.com, or www.badassfaeries.com.

Mike McPhail

EDITOR

Author and graphic artist Mike McPhail, trained as an aeronautical engineer and CADD/CAM draftsman. His day job was as a proofing supervisor for Phoenix Color Corp in New York, where he specialized in cover prep for the Great Publishing Houses of the Lansraad. Nowadays he's the senior artist at McP Digital Graphics, and co-founder of eSpec Books LLC.

As a member of the Military Writers Society of America, he is dedicated to helping his fellow service members (and some deserving civilians) in their efforts to become authors or break into the publishing industry, as well as support organizations that "help those who have answered the call."